James McDonald

Mistrials and Tribulations

Book Two of Home Summonings

Copyright

James McDonald. Mistrials and Tribulations, Book Two of Home Summonings. Paperback Edition.

First Edition, V1.0

ISBN: Cover Art by: Aleksandra Shiga www.gorillaconcept.com

Edited by: A.J. Ash www.mindcandyediting.com

For the wife who is still putting up with my endeavors.

Prologue

NORA KNELT SILENTLY in the dew behind a large oak and stared at the mansion. It had taken nearly six months, but she'd finally pierced the veil which had hidden the estate from her. Night was giving way to a fiery, red ribbon with spikes of yellow and orange arcing across the sky as the sun peeked over the horizon. A few streaks of pale blue sliced through the gray clouds. But night still owned the ground. Nora sprinted at full speed from tree to bush to hedge, and finally stopped at the corner of the house. It was eerily quiet. No birds sang to the sunrise. No insects droned in the late summer. She peeked into the nearby window. The dark room held sparse furniture and was otherwise empty.

Nora caught her breath and realized she had no plan. Ever since her first visit, she'd been obsessed with Miss Tee and the knowledge contained within her estate. *Mother was less than pleased when she found out I'd been given access to the Forrester journals. She'd expected I would come and only be given a little more detailed version of the fairy tales we were taught.* And mother had had no intention of her ever returning to the mansion. But Nora knew she had to. Needed to. She was called to this place for a reason.

She edged her way along the side of the house, ducking under windows as she passed. At the back of the house, a large, domed greenhouse rose from the ground and dominated the center of a hedge maze that covered acres. Nora turned her view along the back of the house. The library jutted out from the main house about the length of a soccer field.

Continuing to duck behind cover and under windows, she stopped when she reached a pair of large glass doors. Miss Tee sat alone, eating a simple breakfast at the head of a large, center table. It looked like it could easily seat fifty people or more. Miss Tee dropped something and leaned down. Nora used the time to sprint past the door and did not stop until she reached her goal.

Several of the floor-to-ceiling windows were open to the morning air. Nora swung the screen aside and climbed into the library. Gently, she clipped the screen closed. The shelves around her were filled with artifacts. She felt drawn to a wooden box about two feet long. She slid the two clasps aside and slowly opened the lid. A long knife in a black leather sheath fit neatly into the red silk lining of the box.

Intense power ran from the knife and grabbed her aura. As she ran her fingers along the hilt, a tingling sensation ran from her fingertips and up her arm, through her body. She watched as her small, delicate fingers grasped the hilt and drew the knife from the case, freeing it from the sheath. She became lost in the swirling patterns of the silver and black ribbons of Damascus steel which ran its length. The edge on both sides was sharp enough to shave a peach. The energy that hummed from the blade excited her.

"That belonged to him."

Nora's heart nearly leapt from her chest. She dropped the knife and spun around, tripping on the blade now buried in the floor up to the hilt. "Miss Tee. I…uh…"

Miss Tee said, "It is lovely to see you again, Nora. The knife. It belonged to Greyson." She leaned over and drew the knife from the floor. She wiped the blade on a cloth before sheathing it and placing it back in the box. "He carried it for quite a while."

NORA STOOD UNEASILY as Miss Tee shuffled behind her desk. She was hunched over, wearing a thin cotton dress. A scarf covered her head. Thin wrinkles barely indicated her age. Letting out a small gasp, she climbed into her chair, taking a few moments for a deep breath.

Nora said, "I should go."

"Nonsense, child." Miss Tee moved a couple of items out of her way. "Please, have a seat. Does your mother know you are here?"

Nora debated lying, but it would be too easily found out. And Miss Tee may have already spoken with her mother anyway. "Um, no, ma'am."

Miss Tee gave a small sniffle. "Just as well. What did you discuss with her after your fist visit?"

Nora swallowed. "I talked to her about some of what I'd read, but she stopped me. She said these were things I shouldn't know. No one should know. And I should forget about them."

"And what do you think?" Miss Tee examined the spine of a nearby book. "Do you want to not know these things? It can be done."

Nora already had an answer, but she wanted it to appear as if she'd given it some thought. "No, I want to know. I need to know. Why is that?"

Miss Tee glanced up and smiled. "Well, child, you are very special. And since you were able to get here without invitation or

6

instruction is quite impressive. But this is still your choice. But know, if you proceed, it is down a path from which you cannot turn." She placed a large, weathered tome on the corner of the desk. Gold leaf script on the front read, "Chronicle of Greyson Forrester Volume II."

Nora resisted the impulse to grab it from the corner of the desk. She was entranced by the scars on the leather bindings. The cover and most of the pages had been repaired where it looked as if something had neatly sliced the book in half.

Miss Tee said, "Or maybe we pursue other studies, and return to this later?"

Nora took the book in her small hands. The weight was much greater than the sum of its mere pages. She flipped through and studied where each page had very subtly been repaired. "I'll take it now. Thank you."

Miss Tee nodded delicately. "Very well."

Nora rose and looked for a nook to nestle in.

"Nora."

Nora faced Miss Tee. "Ma'am?"

Miss Tee said, "Maybe we should keep our conversations just between us. For now."

Nora's heart swelled. Her mother would not approve. A bonus. Keeping secrets was a family tradition. She would start to accumulate some of her own.

Mistrials and Tribulations, Chronicle II of Greyson Forrester

THE RADIO SQUAWKED to life in my ear. "Forrester, are you there?"

"Hi, Raines. Where's Wynn?" I asked.

Agent Beth Raines answered, "Preemptively meeting with the governor in Des Moines, in case you level the town. This place is pretty small."

I looked over into the sidecar of the Indian at my passenger. The furball sat up in his little leather jacket and crash helmet. His tongue flapped in the breeze. "Do you believe her? Lincoln wasn't my fault. That group was playing with a Winter Storm crystal and trying to create a blizzard in July."

Raines answered over the radio. "I can still hear you. Even the dog doesn't buy that story. It looks like you're about twenty minutes out. I'll meet you at the diner when you get here."

I asked, "What diner?"

Raines said, "The only one in town. Like I said, it's a small place."

It had been two months since the teenage princess for the Winter Fae had tried to mesh the human and Fae dimensions and become ruler of the universe. And it had been two months since Drea's soul had been stolen. Since then, I'd scoured every realm I could access looking for Ailbhe and her high priestess, and Sonja, to find Drea's lost essence and stop whatever they were working on for Plan B.

As a part of the hunt, I'd been working with the Longbow Initiative to break up groups of Erebite cultists and raid their collections of artifacts. Tonight would be the sixth in as many weeks. So far, the groups we had encountered were more a danger to themselves than others.

Ktesippe, the personality incorporated into my classic Indian, purred into my headset. "We are almost to town. Do you want to drive?"

"Thanks, K2. Pick a new outfit to take to town." My Indian was coated with a Leviskin membrane which allowed her to take different forms. My skinsuit was made of the same material. She shifted into a late model Harley and sidecar. I changed into what looked like Kevlar-reinforced leather pants and jacket. My armor was actually much better.

The corn fields stood tall as we flew down the highway. Even at these speeds, the wind wasn't enough to temper the mid-day summer sun. Sweat ran in rivers down my back, even after I shifted the Leviskin suit I wore to wick away the moisture and breathe.

It was just shy of three in the afternoon as we entered Pageland's Ferry, Iowa, population 943. The city limits sign listed the Kiwanis, Lions Club, Grange, Elks Club and the Ancient Order of Spelunkers. The AOS was the one we were interested in, as it hid its identity as an organization of cave explorers, but in reality it idealized Erebus as the gatekeeper to the Underworld.

Raines had overplayed the size of the village. It covered about four square blocks in its entirety, all along the one main road. Merv's Diner shared one of the four corners at the center with the Sherriff's office, the courthouse, and the general store. I parked and walked into the small diner with the furball close on my heels, still wearing his little leather jacket.

10

The older waitress with a name-tag of "Dina" tried to stop me as I came in. "You can't bring that in here." She pointed to the furball. The dozen or so patrons looked at us lazily.

I said, "Service dog," and sat down. My mutt hopped in the seat beside me with his tail wagging.

Dina stood at my booth. "What kind of service dog?"

I sighed. Playing nice was so hard to do. "He gives me warnings before I get migraines. See how his tail wags? I have one coming on now." A fifty-dollar bill landed on the table. Dina pocketed it quickly and took my order.

Raines slid in the booth across from me. She was decked out in civilian clothes. Her tight-fitting jeans and white T-shirt drew a lot of attention. "Hi, Grey."

I said, "Hi, Beth. You hungry?"

Raines answered, "Coffee is fine."

I asked, "So, where's the party tonight, and how many guests?"

Raines slid a manilla envelope accros the table. "They meet at the Pageland's Ferry Inn and Convention Center. We guess about fifty, but according to the chatter, there are going to be a couple of special guests. It sounds like some regional officials are coming in for the meeting. My team is parked at one end, just outside town. Hicks has a team at the other end. The party starts promptly at six. Cleanup crews are staged about twenty minutes out, and roll into town at six thirty, so you have a half hour to do your thing."

I asked, "Local LEO's in on the raid?"

Raines shook her head. "The Sheriff is the local president of the AOS, or whatever they call them. Its part of the reason Wynn is with the governor. It is unlikely we can expect any local support."

Joy. If things went as planned, it wouldn't be a problem. Nothing ever went as planned. "Thanks, Raines."

I flipped through the packet and asked a few small questions, to act like I was paying attention. Raines knew better. She drained her coffee and left town in her rental.

The furball finished off my sandwich. I left another fifty on the table and took the furball on a walk through town on a thin leash. It wouldn't matter if he decided to run. I'd figured out there was a huge beast underneath the small and cute furry coat, but he loved the attention from the ladies and little kids.

We walked around and got a feel for the town. The Pageland's Ferry Inn and Convention Center was at the far end of the main drag. It had been a Howard Johnsons in the sixties, based on the design of the small square of rooms and what had been the restaurant on the end, now converted to a large meeting room. A few people milled around outside, waiting for the conclave to begin.

A readied incantation made the furball and myself nearly imperceptible, and we walked past the few people into the open hall. It wasn't that we were actually invisible, but more we were wrapped in an aura so anyone around wouldn't pay us any attention. A head table was set up at the front of the hall, with a banner and a few cheap implements placed in what seemed to be precise positions. A couple of other tables were stationed for specific officers in the Order. No matter what they called themselves, the last five groups seemed to have used the same arrangement of the room. Seating was laid out for about seventy-

12

five people. Still incognito, I stuck a wireless camera in one corner so Raines and her team could observe.

From my seat in the back, I watched as the room filled up over the next half hour. Unconsciously, the people filtering in formed a small barrier around me. About half of them wore Erebite robes of various forms. The other half were in street clothes. I shifted into robes to blend in further, and used a glamour to age my appearance to fifty. Gradually, I shed the energy which caused people to avoid me.

An older teenager bounced in, looking more Los Angeles urban hip-hop than rural Iowa. He wore tattered jeans and a red leather jacket covered in band logos. He had medium dark hair under a baseball hat and cheap sunglasses. As he slumped into the chair next to me, I wondered if his parents were the special guests.

Hip-hop said, "Hi. I haven't seen you around before."

I nodded. "I'm visiting from Kansas City. I heard there was big news, so I drove up."

Hip-hop grinned. "Enjoy your visit to this bustling little burg." I was thankful when he slipped in earbuds, turned on his iPod, and went to his happy place. Unfortunately, it was still next to me as he bounced around in his private mosh pit.

A few minutes after six, the room was overflowing to standing room only. For better position, I offered my chair to an older man standing in the back. The meeting started like any other civic group. Welcome visitors, old meeting minutes, bake sale to raise money for the field trip, upcoming corn festival once school started.

And then the fun began. Opening rites, pledging their souls, asking to be guided through the cleansing fires of Lord Erebus.

Then they consecrated the altar with the sacrifice of a hamster and a few other small animals to a long black snake. Robbie would have been pissed. Thankfully, no one noticed when the furball let out a little growl.

Sheriff Hamilton, the High Potentate of the local Ancient Order of Spelunkers, rose and banged a small rock hammer for a gavel. "I wish to welcome all of our guests tonight. I believe we are all aware of a few incidents involving our Order have come to pass. The High Priestess for the Midwest and her husband have come this evening to tell us of events of late, and of coming plans for our Order. Please welcome them."

The room rose to applause and cheers as a couple wearing purple Erebite robes walked in, their heads bowed reverently as they slowly marched to the front. They turned around and lowered their hoods. You could have knocked me over with a feather.

High Priest Hamilton said, "Let me introduce High Priests Betty and Dick Gibson."

MY MIND REELED at the revelation. I'd only met Betty and Dick briefly in LA. In fact, it was just as a fight broke out in a little café with a group of Fomorians, a couple of starlet Woodland Elves, and a mating pair of geeky werewolves on their honeymoon. I'd introduced myself just long enough to escort them out of the combat zone to the safety of Longbow Initiative forces.

Hip-hop had stood up beside me. He asked, "Are you staying for dinner after the show?"

I said, "I doubt it. Long drive ahead and all."

Hip-hop snickered. "I wouldn't recommend it anyway. I'm not sure who the meatloaf is made of."

Betty walked to the front of the main table. "Brothers, sisters. I'm sure some of you are aware of the retaliation against our Order for our victory in Los Angeles. Dick and I were there watching when the Great Abomination lost the first battle of the New Great War. In fact, I got in the first strike against the Abomination with a chair."

The crowd gasped. My inner voice laughed. Victory? In Los Angeles? And I was a little aggravated I hadn't noticed she'd been the one to hit me with a chair. That slight would be rectified soon enough.

Betty paced in front of the dais. "While we may have taken a setback in not capturing the Abomination, I have spoken with the Most High Priestess of our Lord Erebus, and she assures me our victory is at hand. The Abomination will willingly come and join us to lead the way."

The congregation erupted in a roar.

Then the assemblage fell silent and turned to look at me as I laughed. In my best stage whisper, I said, "Betty, I seem to

15

remember Los Angeles a little differently. I also remember crushing Drake and Bren, and then kicking Sonja back out of LA again."

The gathered Erebites stared agape at me as I walked to the middle of the aisle.

Betty adjusted her horn-rimmed glasses. "My, you seem to have aged, wizard." The last word hissed off of her lips.

I dropped the glamour and shifted back into myself, with heavier body armor. I triggered an energy shield around the building so no one could escape. "I'm here to take all of you into custody. Please line up single file."

Betty smirked as she looked at me across the top of her glasses. "Thank you for presenting your real self. I take it you are going to detain all of us? Alone? By yourself?"

I whistled. "Of course not. I have my little dog, too." The furball appeared at my feet as I dropped the enchantment which had kept him hidden.

The flock erupted in laughter at our expense. I blamed it on the furball since he was fearsomely wagging his tail with anticipation.

Betty smiled broadly and quieted the room. "Look, my brothers and sisters, the Most High Priestess has prophesied correctly. The wizard has come of his own free will to provide his services to her."

A chill fell over the room as four of the crowd stepped out and dropped their robes and glamours to reveal themselves as Dark Elves. They all stood around six feet tall, with light blue skin and long, flowing white hair. One of them wore the broach of a top level mage. I said, "I suggest anyone not wanting to be hurt should step to the rear." Someone tried to tackle me from behind, but bounced off of my personal shield and crashed to the ground. I repaid the effort by using a small energy ball to stun him into submission.

The mage conjured an energy ball of his own. In a thick voice, he said, "Wizard, please come quietly. My master does not desire for you to be injured as we bring you to her service."

I shook my head. I said, "The hard way then." I open the comm. "Raines, are you about ready?"

A static-filled burst came across. "Little busy here…ambush…interdiction intercept…"

The connection died. I said, a little too loudly and maybe with a little too much concern, "Raines. Hicks. Is anyone on?" No answer.

Dick called to me across the room. He stood calmly, as if we were chatting about the weather. "Is your assistance delayed?" He gave me a smug smile.

My patience was growing a little thin. I'd been having more issues with my temper since LA. "Well, Dick, I suspect they're just fashionably late. And you know how cell connections are in some remote areas."

Betty said to the mage, "Let's hurry this along, shall we? We have dinner plans at 8:00."

I easily deflected the first energy ball out through a window, but missed the second. It burst into a glowing net which shrink wrapped me. The furball knocked one of the Dark Elves to the ground and disappeared into the shocked crowd. I strengthened my armor and tried to move. The bindings tightened in a tug of force until I was frozen in place.

17

Betty sauntered to within inches of me and stared me in the face. "I expected more." She turned to walk away. "Put a bow on him and prepare to leave. If we deliver the package quickly enough, we can make the happy hour."

I was held fast as I tried to port out of the restraints. A pair of the Dark Elves worked at each side of me and started some sort of preparations. One of them began adjusting the energy net, and brushed my arm. A transport spell floated from the depths of my mind. I'd never tried it before, but there was no time like the present. Several other conjurings had come to mind during stressful situations in previous months, and they'd all worked, more or less. Lincoln notwithstanding.

When the elf brushed me again, the spell triggered. The elf and I swapped places. The field held itself in place long enough for the elf to know he was doomed. The force which had held me unmoving were scaled for the armor and the protections I had in place, not a cloaked viscous meat bag. The net collapsed and the elf was pureed, splattering everyone within ten feet in blue and black gore.

Betty swore out an incantation. I drew a silver blade and drove it to the hilt through the neck of the Dark Elf who stood guard on the other side. He dropped, thrashing as he struggled to remove the blade before gasping a last breath.

The mage in the corner summoned a fireball and hurled it at my head. Expecting it to be another diversion, I leapt through some shocked local Erebites and used them for cover. I rolled until I found a small amount of protection from the doorway. The last of the Dark Elf warriors charged me with a small, thin sword emanating an ephemeral glow in his hand. I met him with three explosive rounds from my Colt 1911 and an energy ball flinging him backwards. He was dead before he landed.

The mage's fireball splattered against a wall. People panicked and crammed the exits as fire spread throughout the room rapidly. The mage attempted to port out, but was blocked by my shield surrounding the building. People were also stacking up against the shield just outside with nowhere to go.

Betty shouted at the Sheriff. "No. He's ours."

The Sheriff aimed his Glock at me, but the mage set him ablaze and flung him across the room before he could fire.

Betty began spinning up some sort of energy field. It looked like she was trying to force a portal through the shield. I wondered how she could have that ability as the mage threw a handful of small fireballs in my direction. The air was rapidly thickening and oxygen was running thin as the building became thoroughly engulfed in flames.

Betty shouted at me from across the room. "We can all burn, or you can drop the field." The fire in her eyes was equal to the blaze around us. She almost looked excited to be slow roasted.

Through the thick smoke, screams came from outside as everyone in the hall was trapped and crushed against my barrier by the ones still shoving their way out. Betty had raised a shield between the mage and herself from me. Dick was trapped in a corner by falling debris. I took a shot at the mage, but it bounced off the shield.

Betty gave me a maniacal grin. "Decisions, decisions. The clock is ticking."

I could raise a small shield over me and probably survive the fire and debris. Betty's shield might hold as well. But everyone outside would be immolated or suffocate.

"You win, for now." Furious, I dropped the shield.

Dick struggled to get past a flaming beam to reach Betty and the mage, but was knocked to the ground by a flying furball.

Betty sneered. "Sorry, Richard." Betty and the mage vanished through the portal.

I punched Dick, knocking him out, and grabbed the collar of his robe to drag him outside. Flames licked the ceiling as debris rained down. I scratched the furball's head. "Good boy. Let's get out of here."

Raines and Hicks teams had finally shown up, and the interdiction team surrounded the building. They were in the process of detaining and checking out everyone from the building. Raines was visibly tired and aggravated as she came walking towards me. Her tactical suit was dirty and torn in a few spots, but she seemed fine otherwise.

"I didn't burn the building down. They did it. But I did get a consolation prize." Dick woke up and struggled slightly in my grip. I shoved him to the ground and put my foot in the middle of his back.

Raines said, "It was a trap. They ambushed Hicks' team and mine. They didn't expect the interdiction team who was en route. Interdiction was able to dissuade them by force, and we rushed in."

I said, "Yeah, I figured out it was a trap when Dick here came in with Betty and a handful of Dark Elves. Betty escaped with their mage."

Raines sighed. "Take him to holding. We can sort it out later. This is a hell of a mess to fix."

"I'm taking him now. By the way, the mage toasted the Sheriff like a marshmallow. There are three dead Dark Elves inside. Everyone else made it out."

The furball ran up to my side. "Woof."

Backup had arrived with two black tractor-trailer mobile detention facilities. I dragged my key prisoner into the nearest one, and threw him into a cell. "Dick, we're going to give you a lift and accommodation since it looks like you missed your ride."

RICHARD GIBSON COWERED glassy eyed in the small cell and refused to talk. He looked to be slipping into a catatonic state. The cells were built to block and absorb a lot of magical energy, making them nearly escape proof. As a side effect, they were very uncomfortable for people from the Veiled world.

Hicks looked like he'd been through a rougher time than Raines as I met them outside of the trailer. A loud crack drew my attention to the smoldering remains of the convention center as another section of it collapsed. It had been reduced to a husk. The nearby end of the hotel was scorched and soaked in water and flame retardant.

Raines said, "Mostly minor injuries and smoke inhalation. We've detained everyone in the area, especially anyone who was inside the bubble when you dropped it. We are holding about ninety in total. Most of the people we've spoken with are traumatized. They really don't know what's going on. To them, it's a social club with spirit boards."

I said, "So, the same thing we've run into before. A bunch of people playing with forces they don't understand, being led by people planning to use the followers as cannon fodder."

Raines nodded, "Pretty much. Wynn should be here shortly. The governor is not happy."

Hicks asked, "Who was that you dragged in? He looked familiar."

"Do you remember our tourists from the bistro in LA? It looks like they were on point for the Order and we gave them a safe way out."

Hicks shook his head. I knew how he felt. We had all begun to suspect everything and everyone around us.

Raines, Hicks, and I were sitting in the conference room of the Mobile Command Post by the time Girard Wynn, the Director of Operations for the Longbow Initiative, arrived with Captain Ron Seifert of the Iowa State Police. Right behind them was my number one detractor and Longbow's public relations spin queen, Selene LeGasse.

As we settled into the cramped conference room, Senior Director Edward Norwich knocked. "May I join in?" He was of medium height and build, in good shape, but sporting a small paunch. He'd been in the British Army and still kept up his fastidious appearance and rapier wit. I'd only met him a couple of times, and if he was in the field, it meant someone was concerned.

Raines and Hicks provided a status update on the detainees, the ambush, and containing the convention center. We replayed the video from the camera I'd put in the corner, and I provided a high-level recap of the events.

Captain Seifert was visibly shaken at the video, and even more so with the answers we gave to his few questions. I was very certain Seifert was uncomfortable sitting in the same room as me as he watched the Dark Elf explode under the energy net a few times. Despite whatever briefing he'd been given, it was clear none of this fit into his world view.

Wynn agreed to hand over all but a few key detainees to the State Patrol. We would be clearing out by the next afternoon, once all of the prisoners had been handed over.

LeGasse glared at me as she led Captain Seifert out to prepare a public statement concerning the incident, the death of the Sheriff, and the quarantine of the town.

Wynn asked me, "Did you learn anything with this debacle?"

I nodded. "I think a couple of things. One, we are hitting them hard enough they set up a trap. And I think I understand how they masked all of the Fomorians back in LA."

Wynn said, "I'll bite."

I brought up video of the holding cell with Dick Gibson on the monitor. I asked, "Does he look familiar?"

Norwich frowned slightly. "Who is he?"

"From the bistro in LA. There were a couple of tourists wearing convention bling. Hicks led them to cover, and we released them as collateral damage. It looks like he and his wife, Betty, are high up in the Erebite Order. Betty seems to have a fair amount of power, as you can see on the video."

Wynn asked, "That was her?"

I nodded. "I suspect she was Pushing out some sort of massive dampening on the area. Betty has the power. Dick is just along for the ride."

Norwich asked, "Do you think she'll want him back?"

I shrugged. "She didn't seem too concerned about leaving him behind."

Wynn said, "OK, check him out as a Trojan horse, or some sort of trap, then ship him and the others we want to keep to the facility in LA and we can question him there."

Wynn dismissed Raines and Hicks, but held me behind. Norwich patted me on the back, and went to rein in Miss LeGasse.

Once we were alone Wynn asked, "Are you OK? This was another close call. It seems to be becoming a habit."

"I'm fine. I'm tired of being one step behind, but this shows we are catching up. If they try again in Kansas City…"

Wynn shook his head. I saw the message coming. "Kansas City will need to wait."

"But…"

Wynn said, "You need a break. The team needs a break. Besides, Priscilla called me earlier today. She needs you for something in LA."

"Did she have any news?"

Wynn knew what I was hoping for. "She didn't provide any details, and I didn't ask. Go home for a few and let me know what's happening, and I'm going to send the team in for a couple of weeks of rest and training time. Try to take some down time yourself. We need to digest the intelligence of the last few months and work on our next steps. Norwich came out here to check on our progress personally."

I asked, "Is that good or bad?"

Wynn smiled. "He's been very happy with our progress, but is concerned we've pushed too far and too hard. He believes something big is on the horizon, and we need to be ready. Now, get out of here."

I shared his concern. But my feeling was we needed to continue to press, not to back off. And I had my own needs as we raided the Erebites. Being a consultant meant I'd have few restrictions about working on my own, as long as I was willing to run without backup. "Thanks, Gerry. I'll call you in a few days."

The furball followed on my heels as I left the command center, climbed onto the Indian, and lifted him into the sidecar. He stuck his head up for me to slip the helmet on. I clipped him into his harness and slid my own helmet on.

"Hi, K. Can you patch me through to Priscilla?"

Ktesippe, nicknamed Special K, or K2 since this was her second body, purred in my ear. "You already have a message. Would you like me to play it?"

"Go ahead."

Priscilla's face appeared on a small HUD in my helmet. Her long blonde hair was pulled back into a pony tail. Her penetrating gray eyes were softer than normal. "Hello, Greyson. I had a discussion with Agent Wynn, and we both agree you need a change of pace. I've got a favor to ask, one I believe will be enjoyable for you. Come by my home when you get here."

"K, can you please open a line to Kizzy?"

She purred, "One moment."

Kizzy's face appeared in the HUD. A huge grin spread on her face. "What did you break now?"

"I'm coming for a visit. Is the garage bay clear?"

Kizzy laughed. "Of course. I'm shocked you're giving me a warning. How long before you get here?"

I said, "An hour or so. I've got to find a spot to open the portal."

Kizzy said, "See you then."

The HUD went blank. I started K2 and we rode a small way out of town until we reached where Raines' team had been staged and then ambushed. One of the team Suburbans was rolled onto its side, and bullet holes covered the vehicle. The side of the truck in the air was crushed. A bulldozer rested not far away. Blood was splattered over the cab and the ground. Hundreds of evidence markers were scattered to the distance. Raines had downplayed the intensity of the ambush, or maybe it was a matter of scale in comparison to the intense raids of the last couple of weeks. Though she was the newest and youngest of Wynn's team, she was rapidly becoming one of the most capable.

A couple of Longbow agents patrolled the scene, but gave me a wide berth. I got a wave and a nod before they continued on their routines.

I drew a small stone out of my pocket and slid it into a slot on the gas tank. "Go home."

We ported directly into the Long Beach garage. I'd put a permanent portal into a bay for K2, and the other half of the stone was embedded in the floor as a beacon. I was working with Kizzy on establishing other permanent portals for some of the other key vehicles. Iowa to Long Beach in milliseconds. It definitely beat the airlines.

Kizzy waved from across the garage. "Priscilla is waiting for you. I'll give my girl a check while you're gone. I can keep an eye on the furball, if you wish."

"Thanks." I said. "But go easy on the snacks."

Kizzy turned with a dismissive wave. "You really need to give him a name."

I PARKED INSIDE of Priscilla's estate. My loaner from Kizzy was a comfortable ride, and it was a nice break not having the autopilot wanting to take over. The small mansion was perched on an overlook of the Pacific near Long Beach. The opulent, three-story, Mediterranean-style palace was designed more for entertaining than living.

Priscilla was the Mother Superior for the legendary Amazonian Warriors. I was still perplexed as to what kind of being she was. I knew she was ancient, and saw all of her warriors as her daughters. Somehow, I'd lucked out and was the one and only son of the Amazons.

Through Calliope Enterprises, governments, corporations, and executive types used her services when discretion, unique knowledge, or simple deniability was worth the price tag. Even so, Calliope never wanted for business.

Melanippe waved me up from the second floor balcony. The double doors to the large front room were open, showcasing the wide marble staircase leading to the second story.

Priscilla seemed lost in thought as she leaned on the railing and gazed at the moon on the ocean.

"Hi."

Priscilla turned to me with a motherly hug. Her presence, her very aura, could fill a room and awe even those closest to her. Every time she touched me, it drew out a strong sense of arousal and longing. Tonight, her touch also gave me some small measure of peace and solace.

She said, "Hello, Greyson. Thank you for coming."

Priscilla's assistant delivered a martini for Priscilla, and one of Alvin's ambers from the Gin House for me.

Priscilla said, "We have a few items to discuss. First, Anraoi and his makeshift clan are settling into Phoenix Grove quite well. I believe they have moved into an area outside of town and expanded the small Fae community."

Anraoi was the exiled chief of the Woodland Fae, and the former Lord for all of the Summer Lands. He and his queen had been overthrown in a coup, and his queen was believed to have been killed. I'd not told Anraoi I believed his queen may have still been alive and she'd helped me to rescue their daughter, Claire, princess to the People of the Wood and potential heir to the throne of Summer. She'd been placed into hiding with his family's most trusted aides in the mortal world. When their alternate identities were exposed in an effort of rogue Winter forces to merge all the non-Divine realms and to take control of the mortal and much of the immortal world, they took refuge in Phoenix Grove, my home village and a refuge for people of the Veiled world. Thinking about it made me long for home, a place I was no longer welcome.

I said, "That's great to hear. How is Robbie?"

Robbie was an actor, and an aide to the Underhill family, the mortal cover used by Anraoi's people. Through a bizarre series of events, which I believed to have been a setup, he'd become a werehamster. The only one of his kind as far as anyone knew.

Priscilla chuckled. She'd guided his transition to werehamster instead of the intended wererat. "Robbie is fine. He's living in a cabin with the Woodland folks, but I think there are offers for him to move closer to town. From what I hear, he's making friends quickly."

I said, "That's good."

Priscilla said, "And so to the favor. Aindrias has elected to continue with his mortal identity of Evan Underhill, and Underhill

Productions. A few of their actors have been invited to an event in Atlanta and require some assistance, security and the like. Robbie asked for you specifically. Claire will be there as well. It will give you a nice and quiet long weekend, and should help you take your mind off things and relax a little bit."

I asked, "And when is this?"

"A couple of weeks. The beginning of September, I believe."

I said, "OK, sure. Longbow operations are on hiatus for few weeks anyway."

"And to another matter." Priscilla got a more serious look. "As promised, I've looked into the mark you bear."

A few months back, in dealing with the Fae, one of them had brought out an unknown sigil on my chest. I believed it was related to the night I'd lost my family and a lot of others from my village, but had nothing to back it up. Priscilla had promised to use all means at her disposal to identify it.

She took a deep breath. "I am unsure, but some information has come to me the mark may actually be a sigil of the Divine. As no one had found it specifically in any of the texts…"

"But they found something?"

"Be mindful, this is not certain by any means." Her face was solemn.

"Please, Priscilla. Just spit it out."

"Some associates…" I'd never seen her at a loss for words. "Scholars have indicated… they did not say it this way specifically, but it may be… of the Fallen."

The thought settled into my chest. My heart sank. Was I marked as a fallen angel's property? Was that what the events which had me banished from Phoenix Grove were all about?

Priscilla waited patiently as this sank in. "My inquiries made their way to a Jesuit priest. He believes he knows more, but he would not reveal it to me. He'll only discuss it with you in person. He lives a couple of hours north of Atlanta in the mountains. I would suggest you see him. He may hold some of answers you seek." She handed me a card. "But I cannot guarantee your safety."

I said, "Thank you. Even if the answers are ones I don't want, it's better than not knowing."

Priscilla asked me the one question for which I knew she dreaded the answer. "Have you found any leads at all on how to help Drea?"

The body of Priscilla's heir, her blood granddaughter, lay in a special hospital not far away. Her soul, her spirit, had been stolen by a Dark Elf mage. The thief was Anraoi's son, Drake, twisted by the time he'd spent as a hostage to Winter before becoming its agent. Drake lay in the same facility two floors up from her, where I put him. Or at least the pieces left of him. I hadn't been to the facility in the six weeks since the start of the Longbow road show. The mention of Drea's name hit me harder than I'd expected. Even though everything I'd done was in an effort to help her, I'd stayed focused on the prize: making her whole.

"I've got a lead which may help restore her. In an Erebite library in Seattle, I found a text with a picture of a knife similar to the one used in the attack. I kept the book, along with a few other items of interest. The rest of the haul went with Wynn's people. The entire text is dedicated to a small group of similar rare implements."

31

Finding a solution was now the only focus of my life. My own issue had to take a back seat. The blade was supposedly forged from ethereal elements from an unknown source over a lava pit in one of the hell dimensions. The name poorly translated as "The Forge at the Edge of Creation." The crystals used to extract and capture the soul were grown in a particular cave over centuries and millennia to be pure and without defects. Even to me, the story was a little hard to believe.

Priscilla said, "I see."

I said, "I'm still deciphering the text. I've found a few notes on its use, and the ability to restore the soul to a body, but I'm just getting the general gist of it so far. Even the author of the text believed none of the blades had ever been made successfully due to the complexity."

Priscilla said, "Someone found a way. They always do."

I nodded. "Myths and rumors."

Priscilla asked, "Speaking of myths and rumors, have you developed any ideas as to how and why Fae are partnering up with daemons?"

A cool breeze settled in from the ocean. It made me realize how long it had been since I'd decompressed. For barely a moment had I stopped or rested since… well, since Drea fell. "Not a clue. Not yet. When I can answer that…" My statement must have revealed how tired I really was. And I'd done such a good job of hiding it from everyone, most especially myself.

Priscilla said, "I understand. I know you're doing everything in your power." Concern and a hint of pity shone in her eyes. "You must be exhausted. Would you care to spend the night here?"

I shook my head. "I think I'll go to the suite. I could use a little beach time in the morning. And I need to swing by and have lunch at Obi's."

It appeared to appease Priscilla.

A few minutes later, I was back on a freshly tuned K2 after getting another lecture from Kizzy, who had delivered her and the furball. Hard to lie to the mechanic when your motorcycle can and happily does disclose any and every thing you do.

THE VALET ESCORTED Ktesippe to her reserved space in the garage of the Athenian Palace Resort and Spa. As it was one of Priscilla's properties, she'd given me one of the suites on the top floor as my residence in LA. It had been Drea's before I moved in.

Dom, the concierge manager, met me as I opened the glass doors with a key, and offered to care for the furball as required.

I reached out and felt the wards in the room before I entered. The only the energy was from the few hotel staff with access to the suite. As usual, the refrigerator was fully stocked.

I set about opening all of the windows for fresh air and wandered onto the balcony. A strong breeze stirred up the waves which roared from crashing into the shore. A few scattered souls wandered the beach.

I'd managed to put off sleep for several days, and hoped to do so for a little longer. It would be another restless night when I surrendered to the bed. Ever since the dream had started months ago, I hadn't been able to take it to the next step. It was always the same and resumed at the same place and time.

With what Priscilla had told me about my mark, some of my worst fears seemed to be confirmed. I gave up on channel surfing and decided it was time to face the Sandman head on.

A hot shower washed away some of the stress. I placed additional wards around the bedroom and raised a protective field. Exhausted, I closed my eyes.

The double doors of the keep were solidly bolted behind me. The flood of energy that had torn at the door was gone, replaced by a long stone hall. Nervously, I crept past a small pantry, and then a kitchen. At the end of the hall, a set of stone stairs circled high into the tower. Muffled noises floated down from above as I passed the second level. The floor below dropped away as I spiraled upwards to the third floor, and to the fourth.

An ethereal and harmonious woman's voice bickered with a genteel European male from behind a small wooden door in the parapet. The first time I'd opened this door, it had revealed an impossibly large library. A beautiful young woman with long platinum hair in a white robe and an older gentleman in a golden suit had been in the midst of a heated chess match.

Every time they spoke to me, something in their tone made me panic and I slammed the door shut. I couldn't remember what was said, just how it made me feel. Nearly every time I'd gone to sleep since then, I'd been drawn here, had walked through the keep to come and stand in the same place, my hand frozen inches from the handle. Thus, I would spend the rest of the night unmoving, listening to the conversation from the far side.

Tonight was no different as I stared at the black iron handle. The now familiar panic began to bubble up even as I thought about turning it. The woman's voice flowed through as if nothing stood between us. "You have nothing to fear. Please, come in. We have much to discuss and time is running short."

Before my courage could fail again, I grasped the cold handle and turned it, thrusting myself into the room. I was committed to whatever would happen next. It was just a dream. Wasn't it?

The collection was beyond my imagination. Books, scrolls, parchments, stone tablets, and objects I couldn't describe covered shelves farther than I could see. The woman was radiant and beautiful. Long blonde hair streamed down her back, where a pair of translucent wings were barely visible. She wore a modest white cloak and sat at a simple wooden table in a matching chair. She

35

looked at me occasionally while she studied the crystal chess board.

The man examined a wine rack which reached from floor-to-ceiling, selecting bottles and placing them back on the shelf. His shoulder-length, golden blond hair was lightly frosted at the temples and hung down over bronzed skin which stood out against his golden herringbone suit.

"Um, hello?"

The woman rose and glided across the floor to me. "Greetings again, Greyson. I am overjoyed you have finally joined us. My cheerful friend in the corner is Ladon and I am Tsauriel."

Ladon had selected a bottle of red wine and poured himself a glass. He sat down in front of the chess board, sipped the wine, and made a move. The open bottle sat on an intricately carved wooden chest, stood on its side at the end of the table. I was fascinated by the unrecognizable runes on the pair of straps latching it closed.

"Where am I?" I asked.

Ladon spoke up. "Are you really so daft? So foolish?" His voice resonated in the chamber, triggering my flight response. I fought to keep it in check.

Tsauriel said, "Please, Ladon, manners?" Tsauriel led me away from the door to walk down one of the shelved corridors. "Well, Greyson, we are tucked away in a place somewhat like your laboratory. Access is quite restricted, though we seem to have had quite a lot of visitors recently."

I said, "That's not really an answer."

She gave a thin smile. "I suppose not. Let it suffice to say you are safe here."

I said, "So, who are you then?"

"Well, you can consider me something like a guardian angel."

I was nearly blinded when I opened my Sight. I got the impression of a bright light and wings, but had to stop before I could discern any details. When my vision cleared, I lay crumpled on the floor. This was feeling less and less like a dream.

Tsauriel offered a long tapered hand, which I reluctantly grasped. A gentle flow of warmth spread through my body as she helped me to stand. She asked, "Are you satisfied?"

"Not in the least." My head was swimming from the brief visage. "This may be indelicate, but are you a fallen angel?"

Tsauriel gave me a polite smile. "I am definitely not of the Fallen. I may be a little lost, but I am of the Host."

"And what about your friend over there?"

"Ladon? I was here by myself for a very long time. I am unsure how he arrived here, or why, but I can assure you it was not of his volition." She forced a smile. "He does grow on you, eventually, but, no, he's assuredly no angel."

"Another non-answer. Who or what's he?" I dared not try my Sight on him.

Tsauriel said, "I would suggest you ask him yourself. I would, however, permit him have another glass of wine or two first. It makes his charming personality a little more accommodating."

I said, "So, if this place is so secure, how did Fae get in here a couple of months ago? This is the same place, right?"

Tsauriel said, "They did not, or more precisely, she did not steal her way in. I believe when she touched your mind, you retreated here, and she followed. In fact, she never breached the castle. You led her in the outer door, but when she finally tried to get inside, you stopped her at the gates. I believe Ladon and I've secured the gap which allowed her to follow, but you have much work to do to shore up the defenses now that others are aware of this... place."

"And how did I retreat here if I don't know where here is, or that it even existed? And why can't I stop from coming here?" I felt my trepidation giving away to wanting to break something. "And why should I care?"

Tsauriel patted my shoulder. "Excellent questions. But we have more pressing matters. You need to resume working on your skills, since some of the constraints on your abilities have been lifted. Another challenge looms near, and I fear for your safety."

I took a deep breath. My fear was becoming frustration. "Tsauriel, can you provide me anything useful? I'm more confused now than when I got here. What kind of challenge? What skills?"

Tsauriel touched my chest. "May I see the sigil?"

I opened my shirt. "I should be charging for this. Sure."

Tsauriel looked at the mark with a slight look of disdain. "Tsk. Let me fix that." She reached out and gently placed a hand over the mark. It began to glow with a bright white light and warmth radiated through my entire body.

Tsauriel backed away and studied her work. Satisfied, she touched my forehead. "Sleep. We will speak again in a few days."

I AWOKE MIDMORNING. It was the first peaceful sleep I'd enjoyed in longer than I could remember. Even the furball slept in late. The sound of the waves and a few gulls carried in through the open sliding doors.

The view from the mirror reinforced the idea my encounters had been more than just vivid dreams. There had been some subtle changes in the design of the sigil. It was no longer a light red, but had faded into a white scar. It still meant nothing to me, but at least it was less visible.

My curiosity sated for the moment, I slipped on a fresh Leviskin skinsuit and put my standard gear in place. With the merest of thoughts, it could become armor and make any weapon I carried at the ready. Instead, I went with shorts and a *Serenity* T-shirt.

The furball took me for a walk on the beach. Even in the bright sunlight, the events from the night were fresh in my mind. I tried to make myself believe it had all been a dream, but the change in the sigil convinced me otherwise. With the furball stashed in the suite, and after a social lunch at the Gin House with Obi Ramla and Ichabod the Kraken, it was time for a visit to the local medical facility for the supernatural.

Security greeted me at the front door of the nondescript office building. I'd spent enough time here to know Brad before I'd taken off chasing the followers of Erebus. My active status with Calliope confirmed, he slid me the visitor ID which gave me access to all floors, and I slid him a cup of fresh coffee from the small shop across the street. The next stop was on the second floor at the nurses' station. Nancy, the head day nurse, smiled. "Hi, Grey. She's normal and stable. I'm glad to see you come by. It's been a while."

"Thanks, Nancy. A little something for the shift."

Nancy gave me a smile as a box of mixed pastries landed on the desk. She had to be sixty and smoked like a chimney, but took fantastic care of her wards, especially Drea.

Her room was like all of the rest on the sterile hall. Disinfectant masked with a light floral scent stung my eyes and nose. Stark lights and loud chatter filled the halls. Her room droned with the beeping of monitors and the equipment which kept her body going.

It looked like Onyx had spent a lot of time here, judging by the stack of books teetering on the nightstand. I opened my Sight and was comforted to see the thin silver thread running from Drea off into the ether. From a worn leather recliner, I talked about nonsense for a while, kissed her forehead, and made the same promise I always did. To find her and put her back where she belonged.

My final stop was the secure zone on the fourth floor. It was restricted access holding for protecting high-profile patients, or more often, locking away dangerous or criminal entities needing care.

The elevator opened onto a small waiting area walled with large clear resin panes giving an unobstructed view into the ward without granting access. Tougher than hardened steel, the same material was used for all of the doors to the individual cells. Enchantments and sigils embedded in the walls prevented almost any use of magic.

Tony, the afternoon lead for the high security wing, waved me in and buzzed me through.

"How is my favorite inmate doing?" I dropped a baggie holding a couple of donuts with sprinkles on his desk.

"Good to see you," Tony grumbled. "I was worried since you hadn't been by in a while. Drake is healing, too well for my liking. He managed to put a whammy on one of the nurses. He almost got her to cut his jugular, but was stopped just in time."

I nodded. "As much as I'd like to see that, I'll restrain myself. I still need more from him."

Tony waved and answered the phone.

By agreement, the Longbow Initiative had agreed to let Drake recover in the facility. It was owned and controlled by a board of powerful beings, including Priscilla, and was one in a network of facilities around the globe and in other realms. In return, Longbow had stationed a small security team in the building next door.

Drake was a Woodland Elf who had been a Fostered Hostage to Winter during negotiations some years before. The Winter Queen had sent her daughter, Ailbhe, in exchange. When the coup in Summer happened, Ailbhe was hidden away by Anraoi with his daughter, Claire, as a part of the Underhill identities. Even so, Abhile had been able to maintain a hidden relationship with some of the beings of Winter.

Somewhere along the way, Drake had turned, becoming a Dark Elf mage for the rogue forces within Winter, and got engaged to Ailbhe, or Abbie, as she was known in the mortal world. When I busted up their party, Drake stabbed Drea and took her soul with a cursed knife. In the melee, he'd been broken, burned, and had finished going insane while Abhile had fled with an Erebite priestess.

I'd visited him every day until returning to the field. I needed to know where the knife was and how to use it. It was the only reason he was still alive.

41

Beating back my frustration, I entered the cell. Crisp and blackened skin had been replaced by pale blue scars on his face, neck, and remaining arm. For spite, I turned the temperature up to ninety. A true Woodland Elf would love it, but his Winter side, not-so much. I turned down the volume on his only entertainment. Anraoi had gotten some of his native Woodland music cut onto a disc, thinking it could help bring Drake back to his roots and to recover. A little time had revealed the song he especially hated, and I'd it set to play twenty-four hours a day.

Drake's one remaining eye glared at me with venom as he turned to face me. I spun a small chair around to take a seat.

"A visitor. I've a visitor. Is the coward here to deliver on his promise to kill me?" A thin, coughing laugh crept out. His voice was rough and barely a whisper crossed his lips as he spoke. It was very different from the powerful voice he'd once wielded like a sword.

"Nope. I came by to see how you were doing." I flipped the thin blanket and sheet away for a good look.

Drake said, "What do you think of your handiwork?"

When Drake and his merry band of mayhem had attacked the Underhill estate and tried to perform a ritual to raise their dead god, I'd flung Drake into the debris of the ice altar they'd manifested. When Sonja, the Erebite High Priestess, had targeted me with a fireball, I'd deflected it and it had found Drake instead. In the end, both of his legs were reduced to stumps and one arm was vaporized at the shoulder.

His once thin but strong body had shriveled to near skin and bone. A patch covered the gaping hole where his other eye had been before it was lost to the fireball. Thin wisps of translucent hair sprouted where a thick head of luminescent snowy hair had

42

been. His one good arm and torso were securely strapped to the bed. His light blue skin paled in the rising temperature and the little moisture he held beaded on the few spots of unmarred flesh.

"Tell me what I need to know, and I'll see about improving your odds of taking what of you which isn't overcooked out of here in a doggie bag."

Drake sneered and turned away.

"If you want out, all you need to do is tell me about the knife you used, and where it is now." Heat rose in my chest. My need for the information was beating out the desire to take the little remaining life from him at that instant. My Sense told me at least part of the drive came from Drake himself, in a poor attempt to compel me.

Drake muttered with all of the malice he could muster, "I will be free soon enough. Besides, I think it is about time for my icy sponge bath."

With my Sight open and searching, I examined Drake for any other tricks he may have wanted to use. His thin tendril of a connection to Abhile had strengthened, if only slightly. A new but weak connection trailed off to someone nearby. The most logical assumption was that it was tied to the nurse he'd mesmerized to kill him.

Not to be ignored, I walked to the other side of the bed, and loomed over Drake to stare him in his one working eye. It swirled with a blackness capable of sucking in all the evils of Hell. "I'll find her. And I assure you, things can become much more difficult for you."

Drake gave me a malignant smile through thin, cracked lips. His few remaining teeth glistened. "What exactly do you think you can do to me? Take my arm? My remaining eye? Turn on a little heat? I'm even beginning to like the song from the old country. Why don't you have them change it up a little? And when I do get out of here, you will wish you had delivered on your promise. Abomination. Coward."

His feeble attempt at a compulsion on top of my own desires nearly drove me to snap his thin neck. I knew it was what he was trying to goad me into doing. Instead, I reached over and plucked a few of his thin hairs and dropped them into a sterile plastic bag.

"Always a pleasure, Drake. Stay frosty." I turned the volume up as loud as it would go, and turned the heat up a little higher. For Anraoi's sake, maybe there was some hope he could return to his roots. For all I cared, it would be as fertilizer for a *Cerbera Odollam,* but he'd most likely taint the poison of a suicide tree. But not until he gave me what I needed.

I stopped at the front desk on the way out. "Be on guard. I get the feeling our friend may try something again before long. And change up the song."

Tony nodded. "Sure. I'll find a different version of the bird screeches. See you soon?"

"You can bet on it. Thanks Tony."

THE DAEMON ARMORY was a medieval compendium I'd acquired during the raid on a group of Erebites a few weeks earlier. I'd it and a few other references laid out on the desk in my laboratory as I studied the dark blade it referenced as the Anima Arca, or the Soul Coffin. Much of the book was cobbled from folklore, but other pieces were copied from older and much more authoritative sources.

I made notes about the sketches filling pages which were otherwise largely undecipherable. I was able to translate the occasional word or phrase, but more than half of the book was written in code. Grimoires were frequently written in the unique language of a family line or magical tradition, and this line used the symbol of a quill pen. So far, nothing else about the authors had come to light.

I added my latest notes to the walls covered with every fact, rumor, and idea that might be useful. I'd learned the knife was one of several types of implements which used rare and specially grown crystals that held and used different energies, but I hadn't learned enough to translate the details. I'd also partially translated the process for taking a soul, and for instantiating it back into a body, if I could recover the right crystal.

After an hour of being stonewalled by the text, I decided to resume searching for Ailbhe. I worked up a tracking potion using both one of Ailbhe's hairs, left over from the original search months earlier, and Drake's from earlier in the day. Using Drake's location as an anchor, my hope was to could get a lead.

A second batch would let me focus on Drake's new connection. I expected it to be a residual tie to the nurse he'd enchanted, but if I could get a read on how it was done, I might be able to prevent it in the future.

It was well into the night when I ported back to the suite and stepped out of the closet where I'd hidden the portal entrance. Insomnia had given me the time to build a semi-permanent portal to my lab from my bedroom closet, which gave me an emergency back door into the suite. Before I could leave, I had one more errand to follow up on in Los Angeles. I needed to talk to Daire and find out if she really was Anraoi's Queen of Summer, Dáiríne.

There was no traffic as K2 cruised into Santa Monica and the area of the former Fomorian hunting grounds. A Grand Reopening sign hung over the front of the small bistro wrecked in the battle with the Fomorians. We parked in an open space in the front and I checked out the store.

Daire had run an eclectic shop called Bella Donna's, and had helped me in the search for the missing girls. She'd also given me a gift which had come in very useful during the rescue. The shop was across the street, but looked uncharacteristically dark. It had been that way since the street battle, but I'd hoped she would have returned as the other shops reopened.

The skies were starting to lighten with the morning, so I stopped in at The Koffee Klatch. The neighborhood was quiet. No traces were left energetically of the Fomorians who'd used the area as a hunting ground to abduct Fae beings selected for sacrifice. Bare traces of telluric energy hung in the air.

I turned my Sight to Bella Donna's. Energetically, it was as dull as the surrounding shops, but looking through the front door it was clear the shop had been reorganized and looked very commercial. Around midmorning, an older woman opened for business with me close on her heels. I'd been right. All of the old texts were gone, and only commercial books were stacked on the shelves. A few low-grade gemstones and crystals were in the case.

"Um, hi. I'm looking for Daire?"

The woman was small, but friendly. She gave off a pleasant and strong energy, even though she looked to be at least in her seventies. "Hello. I'm not sure who which would be."

I said, "She was working here a couple of months ago? It looks like the shop has changed a little since then. I just got back into town, and she'd helped me with a special request."

The woman shook her head. "You must be thinking of someplace else. I just reopened after the terrible circumstances across the street. We were closed for several months while I was away visiting family. My first granddaughter was just born. I'm the owner and only staff. Is there something I could help you with?"

"Thanks, no. It must be my mistake."

I shook my head and walked out the door. A single red rose lay on the ground.

I SOAKED UP some afternoon sun and caught a few hours of fitful sleep from the balcony of the suite after my failed search for Daire. The furball sat in a chair next to me, enjoying the breeze. The dead-ends were stacking up. I wasn't sure what message Daire's rose calling card was meant to send, but I took it as a good sign.

I tried to open my mind and see if some of the pieces would fit together. The bindings on me had started to loosen and slip away, if only slightly. Memories long withheld from me were coming in fragments and flashes. Sometimes it was triggered by an action, taste, or smell. Most often, they came in dreams during the rare times I slept and wasn't drawn to the keep. More and more, I hoped that, too, was just a dream.

Whatever had happened to me in the circus tent to save my life had had other effects as well. Spells, conjurings, even tricks, like what I'd used to transpose myself with the Winter Elf in Iowa, were coming to me in small spurts. Under stress, I was able to control small amounts of magical energy. So far, all I was really able to do when I was alone was knock something over with an energy ball, but there were a lot of other possibilities. Especially in working with people under some sort of influence or compulsion.

If the Assembly or the Inquisitor found out I was using powers bound from me, it would be held against me at the Inquest, but I was fairly certain judgment had already been rendered. The worst part was every time I stopped to rest or to think, it felt like I wasn't always the one behind the wheel. Something else was taking control at times. So far, it had saved my life, but why? And was it trying to take over entirely? It didn't seem to be Tsauriel or her friend, but how could I be sure?

Not that it really mattered. I'd make the best use of the little time I had left before the Inquest.

I quieted my mind and manifested a small, blue energy ball about the size of a ping pong ball. It drained me rapidly as I tried to focus on it, and within a few seconds, it fizzled out. I got dizzy after trying a few more times, as the bindings took hold.

Vexed by my failure to find a hint of Daire, and by only being able to use the least of my powers, my patience evaporated. I was running out of time, and I had to help Drea if it was the last thing I did.

I left my next steps to the Fates and flipped a coin. Heads, I would resume the search for Ailbhe. Tails, I would check out Drake's new connection.

Tails won.

With a map of the region spread out on the table, I dipped an iron ball bearing in some of the solution, and placed it on the map. It rolled over to the general area of the hospital. After dabbing some of the tracking solution onto a cheap compass, the needle spun and locked onto the same direction. Down in the garage, with a little Will and a few kind words, K2 created a small mount on the handlebars for the compass and locked it into place.

The needle stayed steady and on target as we circled the care facility. The compass verified my target was inside. My skin started to crawl as Brad slipped me a visitor's badge. Something was off.

Klaxons blared and the elevator jerked to a halt midway between the second and third floors. Muted screams and crashes drifted from above. The lights flickered and resumed their steady glare.

A Push of energy blasted the emergency hatch open. I jumped up and pulled myself through the opening. The service ladder carried me up to the fourth floor, where I dangled by the tips of my fingers and toes. From the other side of the door, the screaming intensified. I nearly lost my tenuous hold on the door as something heavy crashed into it, shaking the frame. The emergency release on the door did nothing since the alarm had everything locked down.

I loaded a magazine of explosive rounds into my Colt 1911 and fired into the locking bolt. A small hole exploded and the elevator doors popped open by an inch. I pried the doors wider and crawled into the small holding area. The pulped body of a nurse slumped over against the wall next to the elevator as the doors stuttered aside.

Blood was sprayed across the guard desk and the clear resin doors to both wings stood open. As this was the secure floor, I could assume any patients were extremely dangerous. All of the doors to the secure cells were open. All but one. Drake's door was sealed.

A jarring thud and angry snort drew my attention. A giant beast lumbered out of a room at the end of the hall. The head of an oversized longhorn steer bobbled around on the body of a shaggy giant wearing a basic hospital gown. The Minotaur we had captured at an Erebite ritual weeks earlier over stood eight feet tall. He'd been splayed on an altar for sacrifice when we'd interrupted. Oddly enough, he didn't seem to be appreciative about being rescued.

Tony lay bleeding under the desk. He was pale and in shock, and a large slash gushed blood across his chest. I reached up and hit the emergency lockdown, slamming the room doors shut on the other inmates and dropping the emergency barricades. I drew one of the potions from my bag and poured it into his bleeding wound.

50

On seeing me, the Minotaur charged and crashed into the resin barricade. It cracked, but held. From the look it gave me, I guessed it remembered I was the one who had trapped it, denying it what it seemed to think was its duty to either be sacrificed or make a snack out of the Acolyte who'd revealed the location where the ceremony was being held.

It backed up to build up speed for another try.

I flinched as the beast's second assault on the door knocked the upper and lower tracks of the barricade loose.

The frame gave way on the third impact, and the Minotaur rolled past into the door sealing the other side of the hall. I used the desk for cover and slid Tony to a safer corner. It cracked, but held, as a half-ton of muscle and fur slammed into it. It narrowly missed goring me as its horns bored through my makeshift cover and into the wall.

I grabbed the emergency tranquilizer gun and scrambled to load a dart. It was stuck and weighed down by the desk as it alternated between struggling to get free and using the desk as a Grey-swatter. I rose over the desk and fired the tranquilizer dart into his neck at point-blank range.

The Minotaur snorted with fetid breath and lifted the desk again, ramming it further back into me and the wall. The filing cabinet saved me where it made a small gap. I ducked down and loaded a second dart. The desk rolled away as its horns came free.

The beast staggered back into the wall and readied for another attack. The drugs seemed to be taking effect, but too slowly for me. The second dart found its meaty shoulder mid-charge. It crashed to the ground and struggled to rise. Blazing eyes bore holes into me with fury while its body failed him. While it still flailed about, I shot it in the neck with a third dart. It fell still, other than the rising and falling of its chest with each ragged breath.

I called to the main desk for support. They were having trouble reactivating the elevator or getting in through the stairs, and were preparing to breach. The potion had done its work and Tony was no longer bleeding, but was still pale and sweating. He was gasping in shallow breaths.

I loaded a dart into the gun and crawled through the debris of the desk and barricade to Drake's cell. A small, dark-headed woman dressed as a nurse leaned over him and struggled with his bindings. The emergency release on the door clicked, but it had been secured from inside. The woman spun around to face me. Betty Gibson winked at me as she pulled Drake free.

Her smugness quickly faded into a sneer when the portal she attempted to open fizzled spectacularly.

I yelled through the door. "Betty, give up. The entire building is warded, especially this floor."

Betty ignored me as she pulled Drake's bed away from the wall and stashed him in the corner. She drew her hands back and tried to muster a spell. She stiffened when it collapsed. I was a little in awe as she kept her cool.

I banged on the glass door as she pulled a small shaped charge out of her bag and placed it on the wall between Drake's room and the next. I tried to warn the being wrapped under a blanket in the cell next door, but the figure didn't seem to hear me. After raising a small shield over herself and Drake, the charge detonated and blew a gaping hole through the wall.

My mouth went dry as she pulled a short blade and a larger charge from her bag. I tried futilely to open the door to the room as she entered. The explosion had bent the frame and wedged it closed. The occupant of the cell lay crumpled on the floor.

She placed the second charge on the outer wall.

I yelled and banged on the door. "Betty, where do you think you are going? This is the fourth floor."

She calmly walked back into the other room with Drake. She said, "I would move, if I were you. We don't need you dead...yet."

The second charge ejected the mangled door into the hallway and sent me flying down the hall. Daylight streamed in through the settling dust.

Betty sauntered out of the destroyed cell to loom over me as I lay stunned on the floor. Coldly, she said, "This is for Richard." She flicked her blade and opened a thin gash across my neck and chest. I struggled to lift the tranquilizer gun as she took a bandage, swiped it in the blood, and put the sample into a small sterile bag. She then poured a vial of faintly sweet-smelling liquid on me. "And this gift is from your future queen."

She chuckled as she kicked me in the head, and the world went dark.

BRIGHT LIGHTS BLINDED me as efficient hands made their way around my body. I must have tried to thrash about in self-defense, because a few voices cried out and more hands grabbed and held me fast. As my vision cleared, I realized I was on a gurney being examined and bandaged. Seeing I was awake, Nurse Nancy sat me up and checked me over. They thought I might have a mild concussion, but nothing too serious. My head throbbed and my temper flared.

Special Agent Girard Wynn stepped out of the elevator. "Greyson, this doesn't look like the vacation I ordered you to take."

"It's not quite meeting my expectations, either. I was in the elevator when the alarms went off." He could at least believe I was on my way to see Drea.

Wynn said, "I'll assume fortuitous timing. How banged up are you this time?"

I said, "I'm fine. I'm pissed. That crazy witch has my blood."

"I saw the video." Wynn had some idea of what could be done with the life essence of another person. "Can you do anything about it?"

I drank down the one unbroken healing potion I still carried. "Possibly. That's not the immediate problem. If they went to this much trouble for Drake in his condition, what do they want? It doesn't make sense to take on this much risk."

Wynn said, "That thought had crossed my mind as well."

The cool wall soothed some of the pain in my head as the adrenalin rush wore off. I was getting woozy. "How big is the mess?"

Wynn pursed his lips. "The guard is in surgery. He lost a lot of blood, but it looks like you may have given him a fighting chance. We found the empty vial. The nurse they coerced did not fare so well. We found her body, or what was left of it, next to the elevator. The Minotaur is rather furious and a little hung over. I'm assuming you're the one who brought him down?"

I nodded.

Wynn said, "Interesting thing about the breakout. The patient killed in the room they used to blow the hole to the outside? He was a Fianna warrior who was among the hostages in the Fomorian camp. She took his hand and his ear. Does it mean anything to you?"

I shook my head. "Why was he here?"

"The Dagda asked to keep him here while he recovered, for his safety. He was going home at the end of the week." Wynn was reading from a file in his hand. It looked like a list of everyone on the floor.

I strained to clear my head. The Fianna mostly stayed in the old Celtic realms, and occasionally strayed into the Summer Lands of the Fae. "It was a clean-up job. He was caught spying on the Fomorians, and was lined up as a sacrifice. A trophy? Maybe more."

Wynn said, "I hate to say it, but at least it's their problem."

I said, "It depends on what they are trying to do."

"I'll notify the Dagda. You need to get out of here. Go to Atlanta. And try not to blow anything else up." Wynn pointed me to the repaired elevator.

No need to wonder how he knew about me going to the East Coast. Wynn and Priscilla maintained a tenuous but open relationship. At least, it appeared that way in regards to me. "Any sign of them?"

"No. Video shows her opening a portal outside, a couple of feet away from the building. She carried Drake and jumped into it." He placed a firm hand on my shoulder. "I'll call as soon as I know something."

Dismissed, I stopped by to visit Drea on the way out. Onyx sat cross-legged in a chair, reading to her. She'd gone with a pink stripe down the left side of her now platinum-blonde hair.

A large bouquet of flowers sat on the nightstand. "Hi, Onyx."

I got a wide smile until she saw the bandages. "Aren't you supposed to be taking it easy?"

"Just visiting," I said. "Drake is gone."

Onyx nodded slowly. "I heard."

I wondered if Wynn had paid her a visit as well. "Nice flowers."

Onyx said, "They are. Where'd you get them?'

"It wasn't me." I took the card from the flowers. A small note read, "She's in the good care of the Order. You can make sure she stays that way."

"Betty." A nurse gave me a strange look as I threw the flowers in the trash outside. This was the reminder they could get to her at any time. They didn't need her body; they already had her essence. And they would happily use her to threaten me.

Onyx looked puzzled. "Problem?"

I shook my head. "No more than we already had. Just a reminder."

Onyx nodded in understanding. "I hear we get to party in Atlanta."

I said, "You're going?"

She smiled. "I'm going to be Claire's assistant. Priscilla thinks I need to get away, too."

"Joy."

THE SUN DIPPED below the horizon while a gentle breeze blew across the balcony. I'd flipped the card Priscilla had given me back and forth in my fingers to the point the telephone number was a smudge. I closed my eyes and listened to the ocean.

My head was still fuzzy, but a couple of noxious potions had taken care of the worst of my injuries. I was a little stiff, but mostly, my pride was hurt. And my best lead was gone.

I took a deep breath and before I could talk myself out of it, punched the number into my mobile. The line clicked open after the third ring.

An old deep voice answered. "Si'."

"Hi, this is Greyson Forrester. I was…"

The voice slowly croaked back map coordinates and told me to be there in twenty-four hours. The line went dead before I could ask a question. What door I'd opened?

I quickly wrote down the information on the card. The coordinates were a remote point in the Smoky Mountains. I wouldn't be able to port all the way there, but I could get into the neighborhood.

I used the circle in the closet to get into my lab and packed. When I was a young kid, we had travelled to a lot of national parks, and I'd collected rocks from all sorts of places for their magical properties. I found a piece from a trip to Judaculla Rock indigenous to the area I wanted to go to.

After a few hours of sleep, I loaded up Ktesippe with my bags and put the furball in his sidecar for a ride up the coast. I found a suitably quiet spot and drew a circle around us. I dropped the small rock onto the sigil on the gas tank. I uttered, "Road Trip" and the world around us warped until we appeared in a corn field.

Ktesippe's GPS in the HUD put us outside of Athens, Georgia, a couple of hundred miles away from the target. It was further than I'd planned, but close enough. By late in the afternoon, we'd wound our way through the mountains of northern Georgia and crossed into Tennessee, not far from the North Carolina border. K2 continued to navigate until we left the main road.

Ktesippe stopped and grumbled as we cut onto an old clay logging trail. A lone set of fresh tracks sliced through the overgrowth into the thick woods. After a short debate, she gave me control, and we started the slow trek up the bumpy road until we found a small Jeep parked in an open area. A long-unused campsite had a lone figure sitting at a picnic table.

It was too cool and damp to be this late in the summer. The musty scent of decaying leaves had been invigorated by a short shower. The low gray skies looked like they would offer more chances for rainfall before the day was out.

I released the furball from his harness and helmet before checking to make sure my Colt 1911 was at the ready. Tufts of white hair crawled from under a wide-brimmed, khaki bucket hat. It took a minute to register it was Father Mike O'Brien rising to face me in old jeans and his black shirt. No collar in sight. His old S&W revolver was strapped to his hip.

"I could have come by the mission a whole lot easier." Father Mike was an old friend with a parish just outside of Las Vegas.

He was over sixty, and had a small paunch, but was in good shape otherwise. He smiled and shook my hand. In his mild brogue, he said, "I'm just here to be a guide, advisor, and moral support. The one you're here to see is my mentor."

I said, "I take it this is more than an academic visit."

Fr. Mike said, "Very much. The man you are to see has had little direct human contact in a long time. He's an eremitic monk. I was his most recent student, and I still come out a few times a year to check on him. Word of your mark was enough for him to send me a message, and for me to fly out on a red eye."

"Thanks for coming. Where are we going? A cave in the side of the mountain?"

Fr. Mike laughed. "You know how these things go. It's not far, but an incomprehensible distance. At least to me. I see you have a new friend as well."

The furball snorted.

I said, "Yeah, the furball and I seem to both be mutts in common. Let's go find your hermit."

Fr. Mike opened the back of the Jeep and handed me a pack. He loaded a similar one onto his back. "We need to carry him some supplies." Fr. Mike led us up a small path for a couple of miles through the wilderness to the base of a cliff.

I said, "Are we climbing up?"

Fr. Mike reached out and touched a rock and said a small blessing. The side of the cliff shimmered slightly and a stone staircase appeared in the rock. Fr. Mike pulled out a couple of flashlights, handing one of them to me. "No, we're going through."

After we entered the staircase, it shimmered again, and the tunnel closed itself off.

I said, "Nice trick."

Fr. Mike walked on.

The tunnel was cool and damp. A thin layer of slime coated the walls and floor, and we slipped a few times along the way. Small pools formed where slow drops came from the rock above. I lost track of time. We made steady progress until rushing water echoed ahead. The tunnel opened onto a medium-sized cavern, and the trail continued into a waterfall, which then fed a small underground stream that disappeared into a fissure.

Fr. Mike said, "Are you ready for an old-fashioned baptizing?"

Like many living streams, the water was icy cold but energizing as I followed Fr. Mike and carried the furball through the falls. The other side continued into a small sandy valley where the air was warm and dry. The cagey codger had taken us through a rift.

Scattered scrub brush dominated the landscape as we hiked two miles along a stony path. Fr. Mike stopped, dropped his pack to the ground at the foot of a small mesa, and reached into a small niche. The gentle ring of a bell wafted from above.

A hooded figure peeked over the edge to get a look.

Fr. Mike yelled up, "Salve Ephrayim!"

The hooded figure disappeared behind the cliff face and a basket swung out into the air a moment later. Loud clicks and squeals of a winch provided an accompaniment to its slow descent. "I'll go up first, then you should send the bags. I'll call when he's ready for you." The basket looked even smaller and more rickety after I helped him climb inside. He hung onto the rope as he was slowly lifted the sixty or so feet to the edge. We repeated the process with the supplies.

Whispers of conversation floated from above. Seeing the basket was not on its way down, I found a seat on a rock and waited for my turn. The furball wandered around but stayed close by me. Chirping and droning sounds picked up from the surrounding hillside as time dragged on.

Dusk settled in and the basket finally dropped over the edge. The clanking of the winch sounded more hurried this time. Fr. Mike yelled down, "Hurry." His voice carried some sense of urgency. I grabbed the furball and climbed in before the basket fully hit the ground.

A low growl rumbled from the furball in my arms, followed by a moaning cry from the surrounding hills. The clicking sounds from above became more frantic. The wail rose and fell like the death rattles of the desert around me. I knew no creatures which could make such a sound. My pulse raced when shrieks and howls came from all around me. The furball squirmed in my arms as I fought to not drop him, and I clipped his harness to my tactical vest.

The gondola sluggishly climbed as the racing darkness consumed the valley. Tall, indistinct shadows paced and edged closer at the boundary of the receding sunlight, predators waiting to be released from their cage.

I fought to keep my breathing steady when the last direct rays of the sun dipped behind the horizon. We were barely twenty feet off the ground. I knew it wouldn't be enough.

A dozen glowing, red eyes leered hungrily at me. Gray skin stretched taut over long bones. One of them flashed a set of sharp talons and sprang into the air.

The furball's eyes flashed blue and he released a low growl.

I raised a shield around the basket and drew my 1911.

Flames flew from a claw as it was repulsed by my protections. I grabbed the rope and fought being spilled out as the basket was swung like a giant piñata. On the next pass, a flash of claws was repelled in a fit of angry sparks. We barely climbed out of their reach as the third attack was rewarded with a slice of the basket.

I dropped one of Melanippe's new-and-improved Holy Hand Grenades out of my pocket. The explosion of holy water, holy oil, and a dash of herbs and minerals burst just after it passed the remnants of my shield. The wraith-like creatures scattered at breakneck speed with flames erupting where the blessed brew had landed. Deafening shrieks and cries reverberated and took my breath away. The few remaining untouched retreated to a safe distance, but were still within sight. The howling died off to a mournful and ravenous cry.

A tingling sensation passed over me as we went through to the protective barrier of consecrated ground. I dove from the gondola when the basket reached the top of the cliff and breathed a sigh of relief as I knelt in the dirt. Fr. Mike nodded and offered me his help to stand.

An old, small man in a tattered monks robe stood slightly hunched at the winch. He pulled the cowl back and stood as straight as he could. He had only a little more meat on him than the creatures which had nearly taken us. Powerful brown eyes and a grim smile cut through his long wild hair and beard.

Fr. Mike said, "Greyson, I am very happy to introduce Brother Ephrayim."

"WHAT THE HELL?" I found a corner and tried to control the trembling in my voice. We had gone a short distance to a crumbling stone building surrounded by an untamed garden and a morass of tall scrub. Wispy smoke trailed from the chimney that rose above the terra cotta roof. Inside was simple but cozy, and reminded me of my lab in many ways.

Books and scrolls buried shelves from top to bottom and were stacked around the room. A few pages of parchment covered in notes lay next to several open texts on a small desk.

A deep, raspy voice with a thick accent crawled out of Brother Ephrayim. "Not Hell. You have passed to the Land of the Dead."

"What in hell were those things?"

"Soul Reavers. They are the remnants of people who lost or sold their souls. They try to steal the souls of the redeemable to satiate their misery."

As infuriated as I was, I figured at least for the night, I wasn't going anywhere. The furball was in an almost equally foul mood curled up next to me. I suspected some of it was for not letting him into the fray.

In broken English, Brother Ephrayim said, "Please, be comfortable. I have few visitors. At least, visitors that don't desire to take my soul." He'd a small, hacking laugh. "Thank you for the bountiful gifts." He started rifling through the packs we'd brought and stacking the goods on the almost bare shelves.

Fr. Mike began preparing soup in a cast iron Dutch oven dangling over the fire in a small hearth.

"Interesting place, Padre."

Fr. Mike laughed nervously and eyed his teacher. No matter how old you get, there's always someone who can make you feel and act like a neophyte. "Yes. I usually visit about once a year. As you can tell, it's a dangerous trip. Only a few of us students are left to come and visit. I studied here for almost thirty years with Brother Ephraim."

I shook my head in disbelief. "Wait…you aren't that old."

Fr. Mike stared into the simmering pot. "When *you* are the one hopping through dimensions like the White Rabbit, *you* expect everyone else to accept it as normal. We have our ways, too. Time runs very differently here. A year in here might be a week out there. Or it could be a century. For me, I physically aged as if I was still outside, and only about six months had passed. But I acquired the lessons of many lifetimes. And gained knowledge which should've been lost with long-gone worlds."

Brother Ephrayim held out a hand. "Please rise. May I see the mark on you?"

I removed my shirt and modeled like a show pony.

Brother Ephrayim said to Fr. Mike, "Does not look like the picture. Has changed?" He reached out with long, bony fingers to probe the white scar. "I know this now. I remember." A thin smile crossed his lips.

Fr. Mike looked at the white scar. "When did it change?"

I said, "Recently. I suspect I was only shown part of it as a distraction."

Brother Ephrayim shouted excitedly, "Yes. Yes. This is it. It is back. The angel has returned."

He shoved a crumbling book into Fr. Mike's face.

Fr. Mike said, "It doesn't make sense. I thought you said it was a myth."

Brother Ephrayim said, "I had believed so. A specter angels and demons alike used to scare their own." A vexing grin crossed his face.

"Would anyone care to clue me in?"

Brother Ephrayim's eyes shone with ebullience and a hint of madness. "The lost angel. When the Light-Bringer's rebellion was forced outside the gates, a census was taken of the angels that remained with God, and those who fell. One angel was out of the sight of God. They were the Caecus, the Invisible One. You bear the mark of the Divine Key."

How crazed, if not clinically insane, was he? I supposed if I lived on the outskirts of the Land of the Dead, trying to cater to the souls of the damned and spending my quiet time reading forbidden texts, I'd be a little mad as well. Who was I kidding? Fr. Mike was right. When one lives in rabbit holes, one should not flood the neighbor's tunnels. "How is it even possible?"

Fr. Mike said, "Even God's house can have cracks in the floorboards. Some mystics believe our universe was created out of His curiosity. We are a grand experiment, and there are indications this is not the first or only one. Have you heard of the doctrine 'as above, so below'?"

"I'll bite. The magical arts are based in part on the principle. Our abilities are based on our control of our Will and our energies."

The priest nodded. "Not only do the actions of God above influence us, but the idea is free will has an influence on the Divine realms, and ultimately, on God as well. We believe in some way, God's growth through our experience has also broken Him."

"Who is we?"

Fr. Mike shifted uncomfortably. "A small group, mostly esoteric scholars who have also taken up the holy life. And they are all much more studied than I."

The only solace for my head throbbing was pain meant I was still alive. The adrenalin rush from earlier had passed and I was crashing hard. I stopped pacing and found a seat in the corner. "Mike, how does this angel thing fit in?"

Brother Ephrayim answered me. "The Caecus is said to bring salvation, damnation, and death in its return. It will be the end of the age. End of mortal time."

I WANDERED INTO the twilight which passed for night and randomly followed one of the trails until it ended at a cliff overlooking a large grassy plain. Dozens of small cities glowed against the skyline into the distance. Some stood bright and beckoning. Others were dim, like dying fireflies. The horizon fell into a space so dark, it seemed to swallow the night.

I sat, kicked my feet over the edge, and contemplated the realm around me. A warm glow bobbed and floated through the plains, cutting a path through the shadows undulated and swam through the tall grass. As it neared the mesa, the light jerked and rolled across the ground to illuminate a small, robed figure.

He scurried forward to retrieve what I could now see was a lantern. Something knocked the light out of his reach, and my chest clenched at his panicked shriek as the shadows dragged him into the darkness. I deliberated jumping the hundred feet to the ground to help, but he was gone.

I didn't sense Fr. Mike's approach until he sat beside me and stared into the distance.

A small group carrying similar lamps recovered the lost one laying on the ground. Shadows stalked just outside of the dim light. "What's all of this?"

Fr. Mike said, "When I first came to study with Brother Ephrayim, I used to sit in this same spot. It took a long time for me to come to terms with this view. It is beautiful and terrible at the same time." A small, red fire blossomed among the shadows. "Another soul lost."

"Mike, why am I here?"

He let out a sorrowful laugh. "That…is the oldest question in the universe."

"No, why did you drag me out here?" A gentle voice in my head tempted me to join the other lost souls on the plains.

Fr. Mike said, "Brother Ephrayim has tasked us to watch for the signs and portents of the next Armageddon."

Dread filled my being. "The next Armageddon? "

Fr. Mike shook his head. "We have had many great devastations. Someday, it will be the last one. The coming one may be it."

Was I losing my mind? What had Mike involved me in? "Who is this lunatic you have for a mentor?"

The old priest wrung his hands. "Ephrayim was a scholar at Qumran. Their Armageddon was the Roman siege after the Jewish revolt. He drew the lot to be the Last Man, the one to take his own life and be condemned for all eternity. A lone Roman soldier entered the compound when Ephrayim stood alone, surrounded by the dead of his entire community. He'd just slit the throat of his brother. They'd slain themselves to prevent becoming slaves to Rome or tortured by their soldiers.

"Ephrayim charged the soldier, hoping to be slain himself. Instead, the soldier calmed him and convinced him to sit and talk. He and the soldier sat on the outer wall as they watched the Roman army build a ramp up to the outer gate. The soldier showed him a mark, and said there was another option. Ephrayim could continue to cater to the souls of the fallen of his community. He agreed, and wound up with the fortress and settlement being restored to life here. In those days, it was this island of stone surrounded by a small valley.

"His people grew those fields below, and had peace. Over time, other souls called for help. Ephrayim sanctified this rock as a beacon to call to anyone seeking redemption. Towns grew in the distance, and the people rejoiced. The land lived in the light in those days."

Another red flash burst in the distance. "So, what happened?"

Fr. Mike pointed to a large canyon which divided the land. "The Asphodel Meadows are to the west over there. Sheol is across the river to the south. This land was carved out to become what we call Purgatory. This is not the first or only dimension of Limbo, or land for the lost souls, but it was one created to give hope. In recent times, it seems to have been overwhelmed."

A small, blue light flickered. Fr. Mike had a small smile. "Did you see that? A soul was lifted." Several more sparks of angry yellow and reds flashed in the distance.

I said, "So, one soul in a thousand is saved today?"

Fr. Mike said, "Destruction is easy and comes in waves. Salvation comes one at a time." He rose and patted my shoulder before slowly walking back up the path.

The gentle tug invited me to walk the field, but its invitation carried an ominous feel. I was unsure if the sensation was real, or something the creatures below used as bait. I decided to not find out and returned to the house.

"HERE IT IS." Brother Ephrayim excitedly waved a page from a crumbling text. "See here. The sign of the angel has appeared through history. He instructed Noah as how to build the Ark. He led Alexander the Great and the elephants through the pass. He was with Octavian at Actium. And his sign preceded the Black Death. Hundreds of references, going back to Eden." His face took on a more retrospective look. "Our meeting at Qumran."

"Let me guess: this angel was the serpent in the garden?" I hadn't come here for fairy tales.

Brother Ephrayim looked contemplative. "Not as far as I am aware. That was Samael. No, the influence of our unknown angel appears in times of great trials and tribulations."

It was hard for me to believe a lot of the stories they'd spread in front of me, but common themes were throughout. Some of the carriers of the mark were famous names at incidents, and usually, it signaled disaster, but there were a miracles, too. One thing was clear, however. It rarely worked out well for the poor bastard or anyone in his vicinity.

Fr. Mike said, "We wanted you to come to know what had happened in the past. This is the first chance we've had to really meet with the bearer of the mark. Do you know what it means? Have you been given a message? Do you know what you are here to do?"

I closed my eyes and rubbed my temples. They knew even less than I did. For them, it was a historical and academic exercise as much as a way to help me. I couldn't mention Tsauriel or my dreams of the keep, even if I knew what it meant. Maybe I'd lost my hold on reality, and this was my nightmare. Or I was dead, and it was time for me to join the monsters on the plains.

"Look, I came here for answers. You gave me some, but I don't think I know anything helpful. The mark on me was uncovered by the Fae originally, and it just finished becoming what it is. How do I know it won't change again? Maybe it's not even real."

Brother Ephrayim sat, stone-faced. "Your role in the future is set. We shall be here to help you stick to your path when your destiny becomes clear."

His message was very clear. His intent was to make sure I worked towards his agenda.

It was also clear he was collapsing under the weight of being the caretaker of Purgatory for so many eons.

Most of what I'd looked at in the book had had a variation of a quill pen sketched into each page. The style varied, but the overall symbol was the same. "What's this?"

Fr. Mike said, "A long-dead mystery, the Monadics. They curated many of the great libraries in history. Alexandria, Egypt, Nambia, Rome. Why?"

"I've seen something similar a couple of times. Do you know anything about something called the Anima Arca, or a knife with the ability to steal souls?"

Brother Ephrayim leaned forward. Something dark and distant shone behind his eyes. "You have seen such a knife?"

The hair on my neck and arms snapped to attention. I'd hit a nerve. "It was black, about eighteen inches long, and had a crystal in the handle. It was used on a close…friend."

Brother Ephrayim shuddered. "Either the Forge of Tartarus works again or the Armory of Abaddon has been opened."

"How many of these things are there?" I asked.

Brother Ephrayim said, "Very rare. Only a few were ever thought made. It and some other dark objects were created and locked away until the time of the Final War." He picked up a book from a stack close to him. "Is this it?" He showed me a detailed sketch.

"Very close. I've only seen it once, at a glance." I studied a sigil on the side of the blade. "I don't remember this. Could another be made?"

Brother Ephrayim asked, "Where did you see this?"

"I was in a battle with followers of Erebus, but it was wielded by a Dark Fae." I paced in the small room. "I stopped him in the fight, but others escaped, and the knife was gone."

Fr. Mike lamented, "If the fallen have recruited the Fae, then war is coming. They are making the final play."

"No." Brother Ephrayim was gleeful. "War is here."

THE TWILIGHT BROKE over the valley leading back to the land of the living, and home. Brother Ephrayim grasped Fr. Mike in some sort of brotherly hold, and they talked in hushed whispers. I just held out hope the damaged gondola could survive long enough to get us on the ground in one piece.

A distraught wail came from nearby. A small figure with a lantern was corralled by the Reavers and was swinging the lantern to force them away. The darting shadows circled and steered the figure, trying to drive them away from the approaching daylight into the darkness.

I couldn't stand by any longer, as if something was pushing me to the edge. I drew my Colt 1911 and took aim at one of the shadows. My shot with blessed rounds was rewarded with a screech.

Brother Ephrayim shook his head and said, "You cannot help them."

"Maybe you can't." Nothing happened when I attempted to port to the ground. One word screamed in my head. *Jump!*

I beat back my fluttering heart and cast my thoughts aside. I ran to the edge and leapt before reason could take hold.

Fr. Mike screamed from behind me. "No!"

The ground rushed up at me for a brief second, but a golden glow surrounded me, slowing my fall, and I glided to the ground. On the way down, my skinsuit shifted to body armor and my silver dagger flew into my right hand. On landing, a fireball took form and levitated about five feet over my head. Where was this power coming from?

The pack backed away as I ran to the figure, now cowering on the ground. A large claw swiped at me, but I removed it mid-arc

74

with a swipe of my blade and poured more energy into the fireball. The Reavers backed away to the very edge of the flaming orb's warming glow. The severed member dissolved into the ground.

I extended my hand and helped up a small girl of nine or ten dressed in a dirt-covered white robe. She cradled the small lantern in her delicate hands. A pale, blue-white orb floated in a wooden box with panes of thin glass. The small, iron loop acting as a handle was broken on one side.

The dawn was retaking the valley, but I was running out of energy too fast to maintain the fireball. The shadows darted and tested me with feigned attacks. The girl was terrified and frozen to the spot. I swept her up in my arm and ran, keeping our only defense just overhead. A hundred yards later, we were finally bathed in the first rays of sunlight. The shadows melted back into the darkness with a last, mournful wail.

The small girl looked up into the sunlight, smiled, and said, "Thank you." The small, blue orb floated out of the lantern and over her head, bathing her in a golden light. Slowly, she faded out of existence, and the blue orb flashed.

THE VALLEY WARMED as the shadows retreated to wherever they went in the daytime. I was drained and happy for the break as Fr. Mike rode down with the furball in his hands.

My hound got to me first as the priest extracted himself from the creaking basket. "That was foolish. And when did you learn the trick with the flying?"

"I don't know. I was called, no...*compelled* to help the girl. What did you see?"

Fr. Mike shook his head. "All we saw was a bright, golden ball glide to the ground."

It was the second time it had happened, and still no one could tell me what it was.

Having recovered, Fr. Mike said, "You saved a soul today." He smiled.

"One at a time. Isn't that what you said?"

Fr. Mike nodded. "How many of the lost did you kill in the process?"

Quite proudly, I said, "None. One might have gotten too close and be missing a hand. "

Fr. Mike waved to Brother Ephrayim. "Let's start back. Darkness falls quite early here these days."

The return trip was quiet. We exited through the same cave and walked into the setting sun in the world of the living. Fr. Mike's watch synchronized with the atomic clock. "Well, we have been gone a whole thirty-eight minutes. We had best hurry before it gets dark."

Fr. Mike guided us down the mountain on K2. We stopped at a small town diner for a late dinner. Mike wasn't one to miss a meal, and he knew the place well.

The furball curled up at my side in the booth. Fr. Mike sat across from me. Other than the cook and waitress, the place was empty.

An insistent snout nudged me for attention. "Mike, what was the trip really about? I'm guessing it was more about studying me than me learning anything."

Fr. Mike nodded. "Brother Ephrayim needed to see you. He's spent the last two millennia in our time working out what happened to him. I'd hoped you could help each other. He told you what we know."

"Come on, Mike, you're holding something back."

Fr. Mike stalled. The internal dilemma showed on his face. "It was also a test. Actually, three. First, the damned found something in you they wanted."

Fr. Mike had just confirmed a suspicion. "You hung me out there as bait."

A flash of regret crossed his face. "Just so you know, they wanted you quite badly. You're a very strong soul. Second, you were able to enter the consecrated ground and showed discernment for the situation. And third, you risked yourself for the good. Self-sacrifice. And you get bonus points for not slaying the damned." Fr. Mike fidgeted with the straw in his drink. "If you were really controlled by the fallen, you would never have been able to set foot in the fortress. Likely, the damned would have made you their new ruler. Regardless, you would have never been able to set foot here again, or that was the plan."

I struggled to keep my ire under control. "I'd have been just another lost soul? Cast into the darkness?"

Fr. Mike closed his eyes and breathed deeply. "No, definitely not just another lost soul. His worry was that you were fully possessed by a fallen angel or full-blown demon. Had it been the case, either you would have reigned as the supreme predator on the plains, or been sucked straight to Hell to join your brethren." He opened his eyes. "If it makes any difference, I always had faith in you."

IT DRIZZLED RAIN while I set up the small tent and placed wards around the camp. It was a couple of days before I needed to be in Atlanta, so I'd found a secluded spot in the Oconee National Forest. With K2 securely hidden, I drew a circle and created a portal to my laboratory. The camp was mainly to dissuade people from stumbling into my circle. I needed to be away from everyone and everything for a few days. I was still furious about the trip to the Underworld.

The furball joined me in the circle. "Open Sesame."

We stepped out into the lab. My small companion curled up in the corner as I dumped some food and water into a couple of bowls. My old leather recliner beckoned and I was asleep in moments.

Tsauriel sat across from Ladon at the table. Both stared intently at a chess game in progress. Ladon sipped red wine from a gold-rimmed, crystal glass.

Ladon exclaimed, "Duplicitous strumpet,"   "Now, Ladon, it is but a game. Would you care to set the board again?" Tsauriel returned pieces to their starting positions.

Ladon sneered. "Not now. Besides, your pet is here. Please ask it not to soil the floors." He drew a cigar from his jacket pocket. "I'm going out for a constitutional."

Tsauriel ignored Ladon as he stomped out of the Library. "Hello, Greyson."

"Is he always so cheerful?"

Tsauriel said, "I've found him to have a gruff manner, but deep down he's a very intelligent and well-intentioned curmudgeon."

I sensed a new gravity on my presence. *"I'm back. Why? What is it you want from me?"*

Tsauriel looked over with a knowing smile. *"Yes, you have returned. Did you learn anything from your trip to the Underworld?"*

"It's all going to Hell." Did she know everything I do?

Tsauriel nodded gently. *"Purgatory is a symptom. It was opened as a land of redemption, a path for lost souls to find their way home. Now, as you say, it is quite literally going to Hell. More accurately, it has become an easy spot to capture more innocent souls, but it may become a region of Netherworld completely, unless it can be saved. It's is a problem for another day."*

"So, what's today's problem then?"

Tsauriel motioned me to the recently vacated wooden chair. If she sensed the derision in my tone, she ignored it. *"I believe you may have some questions. It may be time for you to have some answers."*

The chessboard drew my attention. The crystalline pieces sparkled with great energy. *"So, where or what…is this place?"*

Tsauriel said, *"That's a somewhat difficult answer. For ease of description, this is a manifestation of your being. This is the inner space so many teachings try to reach, but so few are able."*

I said, *"And this place? Why does it look like this? What's all of this…stuff?"*

Tsauriel shrugged. *"Only you can answer why you have manifested this specific place. It has remained as such for many of your lifetimes, and has held this appearance since the last time you were able to reach... here. The books and items around you are, ultimately, you. Each shelf holds the books of your life. Your deeds and those things important to you. Every item of importance is here as well. In essence, this is the compilation of your incarnations of being."*

"And you were able to see and hear our discussions when I was... over there?"

"Yes."

"Are you... do you see and know everything I do?"

"Mostly, yes. There are times hidden from me, but a very few."

I said, "And are you who they say you are? This...Caecus?"

Tsauriel shook her head. "Gnostics are always a fascinating lot. They divine so many truths, and then transform it within the human psyche. The demented hermit has some essence of truth, closer than most. Of course, He's taken residence on an island floating on the edge of Purgatory. That name has no meaning for me, but it may have for them."

"And who or what are you then?" I was getting a headache from the double talk.

Ladon spoke as he walked in the door. "If you can get it out of her, you are doing better than I have in all my time confined in this slice of Dante's Paradise."

"And you, what's your story? How did you get here?"

Tsauriel answered for him. "We have not yet solved that puzzle."

Ladon sniffed and began rifling through the wine rack. "Have you drawn the simpleton a picture?"

Tsauriel spoke softly, but strongly. "We have not yet discussed the matter at hand. Maybe you could be more contributory and less... you."

Ladon ignored Tsauriel and turned to me as he selected a bottle of wine. "You really need to go out and try some wines so I can add them to the collection. In any case, we have decided it is time you resume your training from your youth. You will find the bindings on your abilities are loosening and you will need to practice to recover your skills."

Tsauriel gave Ladon a withering look before turning to me. "With your visit to the Hermit, you have become aware of the coming confrontation. You must be prepared."

I waved my hands. "Whoa. I'm out. In all likelihood, I'm about to get a quick trip back to the hermit, either at the hands of Erebites or by the Inquest. I'm already a dead man. My only reason to fight is lying in a hospital room. I'll find her, or die trying in the time I have remaining."

Tsauriel bowed her head. "You are free to make that choice."

Ladon snorted. "What the pretentious angel is trying to say is you have the free will to decline. Others have the free will to include you in their own designs. The angel believes you need to be trained in preparation for what is to come. I believe you need to be trained as I don't know what will happen to me if you die, but until then, I am looking for a way out of this oubliette. And I am quite bored with nothing but a chess board and the same old wine collection. Thus, my free will dictates your training begins now."

82

I yelled, "What? Screw—"

An unseen hand ripped me from the chair and effortlessly tossed me through the open window. A string of fireballs followed me like buckshot to a clay pigeon.

A shield formed around me and I braced for impact with the ground. Instinctively, I did something which sent me into a glide, slowing my fall.

Ladon dove from the window with a rapier in hand. A wicked grin spread across his face as long, translucent, golden wings sprung from his back. He dove for the ground, and pulled back just in time to land solidly. "This will be entertaining." Daggers of flame shot from his hands at me.

I swore as I strengthened my shield and angled it to deflect the rushing, flaming missiles. I shoved my energy field and crashed into Ladon, knocking him off-balance.

Ladon righted himself and straightened his coat. "Interesting approach. Let's see how you handle this."

I braced as Ladon pulled together a swirling mass of energy.

I AWOKE SHAKING and sweating profusely. My clothes, and even the chair, were soaked in my sweat. I hoped that's all it was. The furball jumped into my lap and snorted.

It took a few moments to shake off the events from the long night. Ladon attacking, me raising a shield, and getting thrown to the ground. There were a few variants, including being tossed into midair, and tumbling end-over-end. After I managed to land one good shot, Ladon stepped up his attacks. Now awake, dead tired, and physically aching, I needed to figure out how things worked over there. In there. In me. Whatever.

My PDA said I'd been out for more than a day. It explained why the furball had made a mess, and all of the food and water was gone. My muscles screamed in protest when I stretched. If it was all in my head, how could it feel like I had put in a solid day of exercise and combat training? Or, in my case, being the training dummy.

It took three hours to clean up the lab, restock supplies, and prepare a few needed items. Another hour to beat back the impulse to hide. The mutt I had temporarily disowned jumped in the circle and we ported back to the campsite.

The dense forest was in twilight even though it was early afternoon. Every ward and protection had been tripped and destroyed. The tent was in tatters. Paw prints of all sizes had beaten the ground into submission. I had a good bet as to what had destroyed the camp. The furball sniffed in the air and gave one loud bark. Once he had my attention, he bared his teeth with a low growl.

With the 1911 in hand, I scouted around, but nothing tripped my Senses. I gathered the remains of the tent and camping gear and piled it in the fire circle. The contents of a vial flared to life and reduced the pile to ash.

I could Sense and hear movement around us. We were being stalked, and it seemed we were surrounded. I'd waited too long to escape without a fight. The Leviskin stiffened into body armor and we slowly made our way to where K2 was hidden.

She started griping immediately as the helmet slipped over my head.

"K, not now."

Ktesippe said, "We have company."

"I know."

Moving quickly and deliberately, I stashed the satchel and hound in the sidecar and pulled out the Saiga 12 shotgun and a mix of magazines.

The first shadow showed its face from behind a tree. I'd guessed right. It was no longer a mastiff. The hungry red eyes of a hellhound focused on me. I locked my gaze as I loaded a magazine of alternating silver-plated slugs and silver-dust buckshot.

Another couple of slightly smaller hellhounds moved into the gloom behind the first one. I Sensed others closing in from all sides. The furball growled and pulled at the tether to get free and join the action.

An invisible signal instructed the hounds to attack from all sides. I raised an energy bubble around K2 in an attempt to shield us all.

In seconds, the magazine had been emptied into the first wave of hounds.

One knocked me off-balance as it bounced off of the shield from my left. It left a thin trail of sparks as it banged its head against the weakening shield. Two rounds from the 1911 dropped the beast at my feet.

A fresh magazine and the first round was chambered in the shotgun as the standoff resumed. At least a dozen hounds circled us within easy reach. More stood back in the tree line. One finally broke ranks and charged. My slug caught it in the shoulder as it launched for an attack.

Before it could land, several of the circling hellhounds grabbed onto the wounded hound and pulled it apart before disappearing into the woods. Other hounds left to get some of the spoils as well, dragging off the carcasses of the first four hounds. They spun into a blood frenzy like I'd never seen before.

I pulled out three of the new-and-improved Holy Hand Grenades and tossed them in the air. A Push of Will burst them in a mist glazing everything within sight. The nearby hounds that got doused began to smoke and howl, but none of them backed off, even as small open flames charred their flesh.

More hounds darted in from the woods and pounded against the shield like sharks testing a dive cage. The drain was making me dizzy. Five more hounds were down when I ejected the second empty magazine. It was sickly fascinating to watch their pack feed on their own dead and wounded, and roll around and bathe in the gore.

The pack was distracted. It was our chance. I stowed the shotgun back in place and K2 roared to life as I climbed on. The sound drew the attention of one of the hounds. I removed its head with a quickly aimed shot from the 1911, but the body collapsed my shield.

I hung on with one hand as K2 spun around and sped onto the logging road. We narrowly missed spinning off the rutted track as another hound rammed the back tire. "K, a little help, please."

The Leviskin raised into a thick Kevlar cage around the outside of the Indian turning K2 into an armored vehicle. The trail improved when it merged into a packed-clay road.

We were gaining speed and losing the pack when the alpha lumbered onto the road. My old friend Scar had grown to the size of a small moose.

He stood fast and barely moved when chunks of his meaty flesh blew off as I emptied the 1911 into his left flank with explosive rounds. But it did nudge him to make a small opening. The Kevlar cage scraped between Scar and a pine tree.

Ktesippe barely kept control, but righted us and doubled our speed. I glimpsed Scar gulp down two of his pack as they ran past him in pursuit of us. I pulled out two thermite grenades, courtesy of Longbow, from the side storage compartment.

I pulled the pin on the first one and dropped it behind us. About half of the pack was clear when it exploded. Several hounds kept running as they burned alive. The pack was gaining ground.

I pulled the pin on the second grenade and held it as long as I dared before I dropped it.

The Leviskin armor was scorched by the detonation, but it stopped most of the remaining pack. Three raced through or around the explosion, and though on fire, they refused to let their prey go free.

A lucky shot caught the lead hound in the head. The other two stopped their chase and tore into the fallen and barbecued member of their pack.

I fought the urge to stop and vomit as the stench of roasted hellhound baked into everything. Ktesippe absorbed the cage and drove while I tried to recover and get control of myself as we cruised down Highway 76 to Atlanta.

THE LAST THREADS of the sun were falling while we fought downtown Atlanta traffic to reach the hotel. DragonCon was not going to start for a couple more days. I planned on getting one good night of sleep before the rest of the party showed up. I slipped the furball from his little leather jacket into a vest labeled, "Service Dog." I Pushed myself from a beaten leather suit into something more respectable to check in.

The lobby was decked out with signs for the convention. I got the keys for the block of rooms reserved for Underhill Productions taking up half of the top floor. I took a room on the end with a view across the walkway giving me a full line of sight.

Vaporizing my clothes was cleansing, but a hot shower could only strip away so much of the last few days. Something was happening, and I needed guidance from the one person I wasn't in the mood for. Fr. Mike answered after a few rings, and I filled him in on the last few hours, skipping over my soul-searching visit with Tsauriel and Ladon.

"Hellhounds unaffected by holy water or holy oil? I've never heard of such a thing."

"They smoked like always, but they powered through it. They also were eating their own wounded and dead in the middle of the fight. It was a blood frenzy."

Fr. Mike muttered something in Latin. "I don't know, son. I've never heard of the like. It sounds like they are a pack of full-blood demonic dogs from the depths of the Pit."

"Scar has gone up a couple of sizes, too," I said. "He was larger than a buffalo."

Fr. Mike took a deep breath. "Well, that tends to correspond with an increasing turmoil in Purgatory. Darkness is

89

strengthening across the realms. Any idea how they are tracking you so closely?"

"No, I've been wondering about it myself. I've tried everything I can think of to mask myself, but it's not working." Could Mike be involved somehow? He'd supplied me with all of the blessed materials. I pushed the idea aside. If I couldn't trust him, I was screwed anyway. "Any updates on the knife?"

Fr. Mike said, "Nothing concrete. One of our Order is researching what he can. It's possible the knife is not an original dagger, but a copy used by some sects in death rituals."

"Thanks, Padre."

I could sense the hesitation in his voice as he spoke. We both knew it would take time to bridge the trust that had been breached. "Be wary. If darkness really is putting on the hard press, all of us are in danger."

I TRIED MEDITATING to clear my head, but the voices in my mind wouldn't shut up. The furball curled up next to me on the couch as I tried to watch Underhill Productions' latest made-for-cable flick, *Revenge of the Rodents*, on the hotel closed circuit. Robbie played the part of the rebel leader of a rodent army fighting against their rattlesnake overlords. He shifted into his werehamster form and strapped on a few pieces of foam armor. When Robbie's character climbed onto a giant CGI hawk to fly into battle, I figured out I could not physically ingest enough psychoactive compounds to have the film make sense. It convinced me to go out instead of having room service and myself as bad company.

With a quick thought, the Leviskin suit shifted into comfortable attire for the hot and humid, late summer, Georgia evening. I Sensed a presence on the other side of the door before I heard the knock. Agent Beth Raines greeted me with a mischievous grin.

She knew me too well, and I didn't even try to mask my mood. "Why are you here?" I said.

Raines batted her eyes in her best faux flirt. Her long, sandy hair was pulled back into a ponytail. She too had opted for comfort, in jeans and a tight-fitting T-shirt. I suspected the small shoulder bag concealed her firearm, and any other toys she might need if things went to hell. "Nice to see you, too. I'm on vacation, just like you, so I'm here to embrace my inner geek. And play assistant to Sesha Aislinn."

"Who? Never mind. I'm going to grab a bite."

Raines looped her arm in mine. "Fantastic. I'm starved."

So much for a quiet evening.

Historical Underground Atlanta was a short walk away. Raines was looking at a map of the restaurants in the area, but I'd spotted my destination. The Gin Sluice was hidden in an unlit alcove behind an old oak door. Even among the initiated, few would recognize all of the protections carved into the intricately carved granite facade.

Lights flickered on after we closed the outer door behind us. The inner door was old oak reinforced with cold iron. I knocked and flashed a Ramla chit to the eyes peeking from behind the slit.

The door creaked open and a couple of tentacles shot out. I smiled and said, "You must be Phil, Ichabod's cousin."

We received a deep grunt instead of a pat-down. "I'll be looking for some sushi next time." A less than gentle shove guided me through the door. I guessed Ichabod had given his cousin a lot of info when he'd said I was coming.

Meaty aromas mixed with the scents of a dozen species. The inside had kept the original mahogany bar and oak floors from when it had first opened as a prohibition bar in the 1920s. Dim, stained-glass hanging lamps cast their warming glow on the packed crowd. High wooden booths with green leather seats lined one wall. The tables were packed with customers, who talked noisily and ignored the musical duo on the corner stage.

Aquil Ramla, Obi's younger cousin, cleared a space and greeted us as we shuffled to the bar. Young was a relative term among the Djinn. Aquil was shorter and a little rounder than Obi, but had the same dark hair and strong features. "Greyson, my friend. You should have called ahead. Come on in, it is good to see you." He led us to a private booth in the corner. "And you must be Agent Raines. You are lovelier than Obi   described."

Raines flushed and said, "Thanks. Please, call me Beth." I snickered as Aquil kissed Raines' extended hand. She kicked me under the table.

Raines whispered to me, "Maybe you can take lessons."

I said, "Obi and Fifi are starting to acclimate to each other. He hasn't run off in months."

A stout arrived for me, along with an apple martini for Raines.

Aquil said, "I believe those are your normal orders. Obi shipped me a couple of cases of their special brew, but you will need to try ours while you are here. I am happy to hear Fifi is settling in. The damn cats are a growing plague in my home."

"I'll thank Obi next time I'm back. And quit trying to kill the cats. You know it's why they multiply." I couldn't help but laugh at the running competition between the cousins. "Aquil, your hospitality, as always, is impeccable."

His eyes beamed with pride as he nodded. "On to business. The preparations for the party Sunday night are underway, as requested. We will open the room by the back entrance. Are you still expecting around two hundred or so?"

I said, "Give or take. Maybe more."

Raines leaned forward and raised an eyebrow. "What party?"

"The Underhill Productions invitation-only reception." I nodded to Aquil. "Can we see the room?"

"Absolutely." Our host led us through a corridor past the office and through a reinforced steel door.

Raines gasped as we entered the impeccably refinished ballroom. It could easily seat five hundred and leave plenty of space for the dance floor. A long, intricately carved mahogany bar ran the length of the back wall. Around thirty ten-person tables were placed around the room.

Decorative material, plus what I Sensed was a bit of the ethereal, was staged to build a summer-themed alien world with a lot of Fae influence. Live plants and blooming flowers were interwoven with strategically placed Underhill Productions movie posters and cutouts. The dance floor was surrounded by Jacob's Ladders and Tesla coils.

Raines felt the foliage. "What's the theme?"

"'Flappers and Zappers.' Science fiction and fantasy with a 1920s motif. Art deco."

Aquil said, "Now watch." He snapped his fingers, and the lights dimmed slowly. An earthy scent laced with jasmine filled the room. Haunting but beautiful music flowed from all around. Small lights twinkled among the flowers, and tiny fairies danced amid the decorations. The energy in the room began to rise.

He snapped his fingers and the lights came on. The effect disappeared immediately. He said to the air, "Thank you." Grasping my arm, he said, "We will be ready. Final preparations are underway, but that is the show they will get in the third act."

Heat filled me as my face flushed. "Real Fae? What kind of deal did you make? You know how fickle they are. I don't need guests being, well, you know how they can be." I pictured guests being charmed and turned into playthings. Or worse.

Aquil said, "I'm giving them the location for free for their convention, and they get to use the décor." His smile told me there was more to the deal, but I wasn't going to ask. "I can assure you, they will be on their best behavior."

"How reassuring." Best behavior was a relative term.

Raines' mouth hung open as she wandered around the hall. But judging by the way she walked, she was also doing a security analysis of the location.

I whispered to Aquil, "Any problems?"

The Djinn gently placed his hand on my shoulder. "Dark days approach, my friend. But your celebration will be secure here. Your wards have been tested, but you may wish to check them yourself. There are whispers on the wind, however. We will have our people watching the area, but you know as well as I, nothing is impervious if someone has sufficient resources and will."

I'd installed the wards a year earlier as a favor. A quick check wouldn't hurt. "Anything specific with the threat? Is it a mass attack?"

Aquil shook his head. "I do not believe so. The rumors indicate covert action. Very targeted."

"Claire?"

He sighed. "Possibly. It would make sense. This will be her first excursion outside Phoenix Grove." He paused. Concern flashed behind his eyes. "Have you considered they may be coming for you?"

I laughed. "Always. No, there's a lot easier ways to get me."

Raines beamed from the other end of the hall. "This place is amazing. It was a speakeasy, right?"

He waved back. "You are correct, Miss Raines. I am overjoyed you appreciate my humble establishment. Shall we sample the menu?"

I snorted. "Humble?"

WE WADDLED BACK to the hotel after being stuffed by Aquil's hospitality. Wispy clouds of steam drifted low over the pavement from the shower that had passed through and turned the night into a sauna. Occasional flashes and low rumbles from the storm were in the distance. Within a block, we were both soaked in humidity and sweat.

Raines said, "The food was incredible and your friend's place is fantastic."

"You'll want to run an extra marathon tomorrow to burn it off."

Raines nodded in agreement. "So, that's Obi's cousin? How many of them are there? And do they all own clubs?"

"Yeah, they have a friendly rivalry, but I understand they're quite close. I've met a number of the family and been to six of their clubs scattered around. Apparently, my family has some history with theirs. We've done a few favors for each other." In the time I'd known her, she'd never seemed so excited and even a little giddy. It was a bit creepy. "Raines, how did you get roped into this?"

She punched my arm. "I told you to call me Beth. I'm on vacation and embracing my not-so-inner geek. Mr. Underhill asked if I could help out, and it doesn't hurt to have a federal agent around when *you*'re in a crowd."

I feigned a hurt grin. "Whatever do you mean? I'm here to help out a few friends. So, does this mean you are officially off duty?"

Raines responded with a plastic smile. "Let's just say I'm here for some well-earned play time, but Wynn isn't hitting me for any PTO."

"So, who is Sesha Aislinn?"

Raines spun around in the middle of the sidewalk. "Do you pay no attention to the living world? She's only one of the hottest up-and-coming actresses in their early twenties." Raines pulled up a picture on her iPhone.

"Oh." I flashed back to sitting in the café before everything went to hell. "She's one of the fairies from the fight. Drea was starstruck."

Raines nodded slowly as if I'd been hit in the head too many times. "Very good. Yeah, she and the other fairy, Brianna Coterie, are doing a full feature for Underwood Productions. Mel is going to be Brianna's assistant."

One big happy family. Amazons, Fae, and wizards, oh my. The likelihood of something catastrophic grew every moment. My hope was the fallout didn't exceed Priscilla's impressive credit card limit. "Drea said something about them hating each other?"

Raines shook her head. "All part of Hollywood drama. There'll be a lot of posturing during the day, but the two are old friends."

Among the Fae, it could mean a lot. And I suspected they were both much older than their advertised ages. At least a few hundred years' worth. "You have fun with that. Robbie will be enough to contend with."

The weight of the last few weeks had taken their toll. My body ached and my head was swimming. The next few days were going to be busy, and being surrounded by throngs of people would be an assault on my senses. Raines hinted she was looking to start her vacation off with some clubbing, but I was tapped out, even if I'd been in the mood. She didn't know anything about the last few days, other than Drake's escape. I needed to keep it that way.

Raines escorted me to my door. "See you bright and early. You're taking me sightseeing."

I forced a smile. "Can't wait. Do you want the smelly mutt for tonight?"

Raines' eyes glistened. "Sure. You really need to give him a name."

The furball wagged his tail and greeted Raines with a happy sneeze. I gave her the leash and the two of them disappeared into the elevator for a walk. On the road, she'd frequently taken him with her. If something happened to me, she might give him a good home. *When* something happened.

I happily passed out moments after falling into bed.

The stars twinkled overhead. A warm hand brushed mine, and the beautiful green eyes of Brighid Sinclair gazed into mine. The night was warm, and a gentle breeze was not enough to dispel the heat between us. Her alabaster skin glowed under the moonlight. Her long, curly, red hair was splayed on the blanket in the grass.

Her light and melodious voice sang to me. "Will you ask him? Tomorrow?"

I looked away and smiled shyly. "Ask him who and what?"

Brighid rolled her eyes playfully. "Will you ask my father tomorrow? We will both turn of age within months. Don't you still wish to wed me?" There was no doubt in her voice.

I kissed her lightly on the lips. "Of course I do. And we both know what he'll say. Again."

Brighid sat up and patted me on the face. "Persistence, beloved. It is how we girls get what we want."

I kissed her again. "Endurance. That's how we boys get what we want."

Brighid kissed me again. "Really? Endurance? Well, then, let's see how much endurance you have." Brighid kissed me tightly and my arousal flared.

I flushed. She jumped up and ran. "See if you can catch me."

I pulled what dignity I had together and chased her into the forest.

She teased me with glimpses through the woods as she dashed between trees. I Sensed others around us just in time to trip over Cedric and one of the Lahti sisters. Not the one I thought he was dating.

I jumped to my feet and resumed the chase. I grinned and said, "Sorry."

Brighid fell to the ground in a clearing of wildflowers, sending fireflies dancing. Too late, I realized it was a setup. She was surrounded by a large blanket and a picnic to match. She snapped her fingers and candles flared into life.

She stifled her delicate laugh. "So much for endurance. Maybe you need a snack for a little energy."

My face flushed. "You have always been a fast woman."

Her face flushed in the candlelight and her eyes bore into mine. "Only for you."

I pulled her to me and we locked in a fumbling, excited kiss. Her gentle gasp became a panicked scream as large, rough hands grabbed me from behind and jerked us apart. Large shadows held me and threw a bag over my head.

Brighid screamed my name. I called to her and felt a solid hit across my jaw.

A cold stone floor chilled my naked body. Smoke and sweat burned my lungs. A few scraping noises rattled around me, like a chair moving. Thrashing around, I struggled to free myself. A hand snatched the bag from my head.

Ladon's face was inches from mine. He said, "That's new, even for you. Get dressed. I wondered what your delay was getting here." He flicked a thin blade and parted the ropes binding me.

Adrenalin kicked in as I climbed to my unsteady feet and visualized heavy armor in preparation for an attack. I wanted to kill the gremlins beating drums in my head. "Where am I?"

Ladon looked as if I'd asked him for deep-fried white wine. "I thought the insufferable cherubim made it clear."

"Just checking. Speaking of Tsauriel, where is she?"

Ladon threw his hands in the air. "Off on some fool's errand. I was thankful for the quiet. Now that you're here, we can resume your training. The last session was abysmal. Today, I think we'll work on hand-to-hand."

The armor slowed my reaction and my arm only partially deflected the spin kick aimed at my head. Could I be knocked out here? The thought barely had time to take form as I reflexively threw up a shield and caught Ladon as he tried to stomp on my head.

I caught his foot and twisted, pushing him back. It barely gave me enough time to jump up.

Ladon fell into a defensive stance and I dropped my shoulder and charged. I caught him low in the stomach. Momentum carried us both into the hall and tumbling down the circular stairs.

Ladon flew to his feet and removed his coat with a grin. He folded and placed it over the rail of the stair. I lay panting on the floor.

He offered me a hand. "Okay, the warm-up is done. Let's move outside where you have somewhere softer to do a pratfall." He tossed a short blade at my feet. "You'll need this."

The armor was providing no protection, and each time I fell, it was a fight to get to my feet.

Ladon grinned and said, "You look as if you're a turtle stranded on its back."

Not willing to admit he was right, a thought shifted me into reinforced and padded Kevlar. "You're a bastard."

Ladon sniffed. "You do not yet know the meaning of that, nor the lengths to which we shall go. My intent is to keep your body alive for as long as possible, and for me to get a mild workout."

"Happy to be of service." A tired grunt escaped my lips.

I flipped the blade over in my hand and lunged.

VACATION BE DAMNED. My couple of days slated for recovery were shot. Ladon had conscripted me into two more intensive sparring sessions. I imagined he was preparing for his tenure as a torture trainer in Hell. In between, Raines had dragged me around for a full day of sightseeing and a night out partying. I'd rather have spent a week playing tag with werewolves.

Now it was down to business. Most of the Underhill Productions crew had arrived and been corralled into their rooms. The booths were ready for business to start. They'd kicked off the Con with a party in the hospitality suite, but I'd hit my limit.

The attendees were starting to pile in so I sat in the lobby to get a feel for the crowd. I Sensed a few real practitioners come through, but I figured that was to be expected. Nothing was putting me on edge.

The street outside was a different matter. Anywhere Peachtree crossed Peachtree to become Peachtree parallel to Peachtree had to trigger some alternate dimensions. I sat in a faint haze as I closed my eyes and let the energy wash over me to sift through the flood. Between the surges of happy con-goers, a few thin, predatory tendrils lurked, tasting, touching, feeding a little here and there on the effervescence of life. A crowd this big would always present easy opportunity for bottom feeders. I had a sense something darker and with more intent was building.

The vibration of my phone dragged me out of my fugue state. A glimpse at the caller ID told me it was more good news. "Hi, Wynn."

He uncharacteristically stammered, "Sorry to disturb you on your time away. Do you have a minute?"

There was no way this was good news. "Sure."

Wynn said, "This is completely confidential. No one else should be read in unless absolutely necessary. Especially Raines."

"Understood."

A tone and a slight hiss indicated the line was now encrypted. "We have a report about a small group of Erebite acolytes are en route. They may even be there by now. It could be a coincidence, but intelligence indicates Betty Gibson is with them. The report is unconfirmed, but members from Chicago flew to Kansas City a few days ago. A dozen high-level members in total are unaccounted for, and a known associate of a member rented a small bus to Atlanta as a part of a football package."

A cold fist gripped my heart. "Any reason I shouldn't fill Raines in?"

Wynn took a deep breath. "She may be compromised. Her, and anyone else detained in the Winter camp."

"Including Onyx and Claire."

"Yes." Wynn coughed. "We have a temporary OPS Center not far from you. Three teams are on standby and a few observers are on point, floating around the entire convention area."

I unclenched my jaw. "I'll keep an eye open. Thanks, Wynn."

"Save me a reservation for the party Sunday."

"Sure. Period costumes are required."

Wynn grunted. "I'll be there. Check the desk at your hotel for a package."

"Flowers, champagne, and chocolates? You shouldn't have."

Wynn grunted. A tone indicated the line had been closed.

Rivers of sweat poured down my neck. I wouldn't admit it was from more than the sweltering heat as I stormed my way back to the hotel.

I retrieved a duffel bag from the hotel desk and carried it to my room. A small note lay on top.

Forrester,

This comm unit is tied into the command center and is not on the standard channels. Safety glasses are included for your protection.

Wynn

The bag was packed with surveillance gear. Several hours of effort later, cameras were mounted throughout the venue, with a special focus on our floor, the elevators, and the hospitality suite. A pair of lightly tinted glasses allowed me to monitor the cameras remotely from anywhere in range. To the casual observer, they were just glasses.

As the sun would rise soon, I went to bed.

THE SUN BLAZONED through the open curtains. Mercifully, I'd mercifully slept uninterrupted for a couple of hours. No Tsauriel. No Ladon. No training. No dreams.

The morning was busy. The different stars from Underhill Productions had already done a Q&A panel on their up-and-coming studio. A small film of theirs had become a sleeper hit and sprung them into the mainstream. Sesha Aislinn sat on one end of the stage and Brianna Coterie on the other. Raines, Onyx, and I stood backstage and laughed as they cut a few well-timed looks and a few well-placed snips at each other. Robbie played up his role as referee in the middle. It was impressive how far he'd come in such a short period of time.

By the end of day one, Robbie had signed more autographs and turned down more proposals than he'd had in his entire life. I was quickly becoming an expert in politely dissuading the inexpert offers of phone numbers and room keys from star-struck fans. The only threat of the day was an enthusiastic agent who tried to have Robbie sign an autograph with an enchanted pen. A quick reversal spell I had at the ready sent the collector home with a hangover and a dozen broken attempts to poach talent.

Raines and I sat in a lounge during a break overlooking the main floor of the hotel where we could watch the flow of traffic. Taps ran into the main security system across all of the local hotels and participating locations. A pack of teenage werewolves dressed like Jedi rode up the escalators and a pair of witches enchanted drunk guys for free drinks at the bar. So far, everyone was behaving. Between snapping pics of the few potential threats and celebrities we saw, she filled me in on the day. Onyx had found a new boyfriend. Melanippe had been inspired by seeing a steampunk troop for some new toys for the armory.

As events wrapped up for the day, we herded our wards to the relative safety of the private party in the hospitality suite. So far, no signs of our acolyte friends or other major threats. The occasional touch from something dark drew my attention, but nothing yet of consequence. I was numb from the overload of people and energy, and was nodding off.

I was in the hall on the way to my room when my phone rang.

The silvery voice drew me alive. "It's Sesha. Care to take a walk?"

I closed my eyes and leaned against the door to my room. Why me? "Look, I…"

Fae nectar dripped in one word. "Please?"

My heart skipped a beat.

"I'm going, either way."

Damn.

I hesitated, and then knocked lightly on the door. My exhaustion fled when she greeted me in tight black leather pants with a matching corset and thigh-high boots. She'd strapped on a holster and prop gun. A little bit of a glamour had enhanced her natural beauty and attraction, and did nothing to hide her identity.

Wordlessly, she kissed me on the cheek and looped her arm in mine. As we rode down in the elevator, she whispered in my ear. "Thank you."

I fidgeted every time we had our pictures taken, which was much more frequently than I was comfortable with. Most people just wanted to have their picture taken with her and I was happy to oblige and get out of the way. A small glamour obscured my appearance, but then again, she was the focus.

Tremors worked their way up my legs to my torso and arms. "Time to go."

"It's still early." Her eyes locked onto mine and the corners of her mouth dipped slightly. "Maybe you're right."

The public area was packed when the doors opened. A small amount of life flowed back into me when she caught me with another deeper, and very public, kiss.

Shockingly, no one else got on to ride with us. She wrapped her arms around mine, and leaned against me as we rode up watching the view through the glass front.

I was numb and tingling as she led me to her room. I opened her door, and was rewarded again with another peck on the cheek. "Thanks, Grey. That was fun. See you in the morning."

Wasn't it already morning? I shook my head. Mel leaned against the rail, standing watch. She cut me a sideways glance as I stumbled to my room.

I collapsed on the bed, thankful for the few hours of quiet before it started all over again. But wasn't it worth getting only a few hours of sleep to be arm candy for a starlet?

Despite exhaustion, sleep was elusive. A nagging feeling tugged at the edges of my consciousness, and I really wasn't up for an all-night workout.

"Greyson, Greyson, my first and only." I opened my eyes to gaze into Brighid's.

"Brighid?"

She laughed. "Who else would it be?" She ran her hand through my hair. "I've missed you so."

The thick grass undulated beneath the blanket. Cicadas buzzed in the night. It took me a moment to realize it was the night we'd been taken. But Brighid was older. We were no longer love-struck teenagers. She'd grown to become a ravishing woman.

She kissed me lightly.

The kiss felt more real than training with Ladon. More real than Sesha's moments before. My mouth went dry. "But it can't be. You're dead." I pushed away and sat up.

Brighid pursed her lips, then laughed gently and kissed me again. "My love, haven't you figured out there is much more out there? And no, I'm not dead. We can be together. Very soon."

"I don't understand."

Brighid stroked my hair and said, "You will." Lightening jumped through every cell of my body with her touch. Her love and my desire melted to the core of our being. I took Brighid's face in my hand and leaned in to kiss her.

Brighid grimaced in pain and drew back. "No. No. What are you...?"

A powerful blast of air blew me high into the air. Jarring pain spread through my body as I crashed into the stone floor. Tsauriel glared as she towered over me.

I slapped the floor. "What the hell was that?"

Tsauriel crossed her arms. "I was about to ask you the same thing. I sensed another... presence. I Pushed it out."

Ladon rolled a cigar between his fingers. "It is getting a little full at the inn, unless you have found a way for one of us to check out."

"You had no right."

Tsauriel chided me. "I have not only the right, but the duty. Tell me what happened."

"It was Brighid. She's alive. She came to me."

The angel leaned over and tilted her head. "What?"

"Brighid...."

She pointed to the door. "Go. I must contemplate the meaning of this."

"Wait. You...."

A nest of angry hornets buzzed from the alarm clock. Sunlight streamed through the open curtains. My stomach turned with a hangover of immense proportions, even though I hadn't been drinking. A quick glance at my phone showed a half dozen minor alerts, and I was late.

I downed a couple of concoctions from my pack. In the shower, I rested my head on the wall and let the hot water wash over me until the urge to puke passed. Whatever energy which had latched onto me washed away and I was myself again

I stared at the bed and thought about climbing in when another alert buzzed on my phone. After some deliberation, I decided I might as well try to fit in. The skinsuit shifted into jeans and a Browncoat T-shirt.

When I went to move the essentials from the worn Leviskin, I found a small, hard knot at the bottom of one of the

110

pockets. I fell to the bed as a delicate chain unrolled and dangled a small, silver, Celtic Trinity knot on the end. It was the necklace she'd worn most of her life. A tuft of long, curly, red hair was carefully woven through the pendant.

"Brighid.

NOISY CROWDS FILLED the halls on Saturday morning. More autographs. Another panel. Interviews. Autographs. Having learned from the day before, I knocked down potions every few hours to keep up my energy. A regular flow of energy vampires navigated the crowds and gorged on the crowds. Even without them, the mass of happy people having fun was a flood of unknown energies which all needed to be assessed, just in case.

I'd have almost rather faced a horde of angry hellhounds naked in an arena than one more hormonal girl in fairy wings trying to escort Robbie to her private wonderland.

As day two came to a close, Mel and Raines escorted our wards to a private party. I wanted to get away from everyone and take a break for a while. I told myself it wasn't to find Brighid, but the lie fell short.

A whistle escaped my lips when I ran into Onyx as she left her room. The wonders of the Leviskin had let her Push herself into a stunning little Wonder Woman outfit. She was off to see her boy toy, and I was curious to meet him.

The opportunity evaporated on the way down in the elevator. Wynn paged me to meet at a bar a block away. An almost even mix of people in costume and regulars packed the place to capacity. I found him staring into a pint in a back corner booth.

He jerked alert when I slipped into the booth. Before he could speak, I raised a small wall so anyone looking at us would see and hear nothing but babble from the surrounding bar. And it helped dampen the noise so we could talk privately.

"Hi, Gerry. Have you found something?"

Wynn slid me a drink and a flash memory card, which I slipped into my phone. Images of fifteen people flipped by. "Those

112

were taken today around the convention. We haven't seen Betty, but believe she's here as well. There may be more we haven't yet identified."

"Any idea why? Or more specifically, who?"

Wynn said, "We can't be sure. Our analysts believe they want Claire, or you, or possibly both. But since we started monitoring them, they appear to be searching for someone else."

I looked around when a small shiver ran up my spine. Something about the energy in the bar had gone through a subtle change. "Any more ideas on Raines or Onyx? Claire? Is one of them really compromised?"

Wynn must have picked up on something, too. He did a quick scan of the crowd. "Keep your eyes open." Wynn slipped an envelope across the table as he slid out of the booth. "Stay in touch."

A single picture from Autograph Alley was in the envelope. Raines and Onyx were talking in the background. Claire was smiling and having her picture taken with one of the acolytes identified by Wynn. Everything looked normal, as if it were just another fan, not a known follower of Erebus.

I drummed my fingers on the glass and stared at the picture, looking for any sort of meaning, when something jumped out. A large shock of red hair in the background. It was blurry, but it looked a lot like Brighid. Could she really be here? Who was she following?

I sipped on my pint and contemplated my next move. My phone vibrated with a text that the party was over, and the flock was on the move back to the hotel. I responded I would meet them shortly.

I snapped my fingers and vaporized the picture, downing the last of my drink.

I was sliding out of the booth when a languid, dreamlike wave washed over me. No one else seemed to notice the distorted world as I drunkenly fell back against the bench. Brighid materialized into view.

She reached out and touched my hand and pulled me back into reality. She was dressed simply in tight-fitting jeans and a T-shirt. Her long, red hair was braided down her back. "Hello, my love."

I fell slack and stammered.

She flashed a warm smile, one I'd longed for. One I never expected to see again. "It's me. I'm really here, but we don't have long."

"Why now? Here? Is it…really you?"

She gently stroked my hand, like she'd done when we were kids. I was tempted to take her away and hide from the universe. Her simple touch made me invincible.

She said, "Because I finally found you. The Cult of Erebus, they led me to you. But now they know I'm here as well. They will take us both, and that can't happen again. We must go. Now."

"I can't. Not yet."

Tears built in her eyes and her voice was wobbly. "Have you taken…another?"

My breath fought to escape. "It's complicated. I have people I need to protect here, and I need something from the cult to help someone I care about. I think they have the key. Why do they want you?"

Brighid shook her head. "We have to go. They're coming here. I can feel them. They want us all. All of us who survived the night you...." Tears streamed down her face. "Come with me. Please."

I squeezed her hand. Her touch and her scent were drawing me to her will, just as it had always done. I trembled as I pushed myself to my feet. "Two more nights. I hope to have my answer by then, and even if I don't, I'll have done what I promised to do here. The people in my care will be home safe. Stay with me until then."

She swallowed and pursed her lips. "Two nights. I'll remain for two more nights. If I can. If not, I'll come for you on my way out." The veil shimmered and I felt the lightest of kisses on my forehead. She was gone.

The bar was nearly empty. A stream of texts appeared on my phone. According to the clock, over an hour had passed in what seemed like minutes.

I sat back down in the booth and lay my head down. Her scent still filled the booth.

Had she really been here?

Was I losing my mind?

How had she entered my dreams?

Were they dreams at all?

My phone vibrated again with a code signaling Raines was about to call in the cavalry. I responded with an all clear, and that I was on my way.

"WHERE WERE YOU?" Raines slammed the hotel room door behind us. "Where have you been? You sent a message you were coming, and then your transponder dropped off for over an hour. I was about to call in help when it just reappeared."

"It's OK. I went up the street for a break. A talent I know came into the place and you know how it goes. Magic can make things go screwy when it mixes with the real world. I lost track of time." I hated lying to her, but there was nothing good for her in the truth.

"It's not OK. That's not how a team works," she snapped.

"You're right. I'm sorry."

She bit her nail. "You had me worried." She flopped into the chair. "You two are very close, I take it?"

"It's complicated."

"Like some French filmmaker's plot?"

"What?"

She stared at the nail she'd chipped. "Her perfume. You seem to be wearing a lot of it."

My phone vibrated. "We're being paged."

She lifted herself out of the chair and sighed. "We're not done. But I'm glad you're OK."

Raines put on a smile and shoved me into the hallway where the party had spilled over. Melanippe plowed her way through the crowd with a scowl. "You are unhurt?"

Fantastic. A tag team. "I'm fine. No big—"

She stared down at me and stated very matter-of-factly, "Disappear like that again, and it will not be the case."

"May I cut in?" Brianna wore a coy smile as she slid in between us and grabbed my arm. Saved by the Tinkerbell.

"Wow." Raines stepped back to check out her costume.

She lifted my chin from the skin-tight and filigreed, shamrock green leotard to bat her enchanting eyes at me. "About time you got here. I need a big, strong man to take me around, or the mean agent won't let me out to play. Do you know where I can find one?"

"Um, yeah. Wow." Nearly any male on the planet and half the women would have melted at the offer. The only thing saving me was the shock of just having been face-to-face with my long-lost love, but the blood flow was rapidly leaving my brain. I grabbed the rail to steady myself.

"Splendid." Honey dripped from her rubied lips. "I'll be right back."

I shook my head. What had I just agreed to do?

A quick trip through the mezzanine, a few pictures. Just like last night. Either that, or stay here with a pissed off Raines and Mel. If I was going to take a beating eventually anyway, I might as well have a little fun.

The Fae returned with a quiver of foam arrows slung over her shoulder and a small bow. She winked and tipped her Nottingham hat as she took my hand and pulled me away.

Mel glared and Raines cut me with a sharp smile. "You can tell me all about it later, Casanova," she said.

117

I shivered as Brianna's lithe fingers ran down my back in the elevator. The doors opened and she gave me a small kiss on the neck and whispered in my ear. "My hero."

She took my hand and swayed her way through the packed throngs to the large open bar. With a glance, a small crowd of people happily cleared out a few seats, and within moments she began to hold court as a crowd of fans gathered around. She fed off of the attention as much as it was sucking me dry.

She pulled me close and whispered, "Time for a couple of drinks?"

Keeping one eye on Brianna, I used the other to navigate a path to the bar. By the time I returned, her adoring swarm had tripled in size, but she made a show of calling me to her side. Warmth climbed my arm like ivy as she took my hand and her drink. For my delivery boy services, I was rewarded when she pulled me in tight for another delicate kiss.

It drew cat calls from the fans, and more than a few jealous looks.

I leaned on the planter behind her while she resumed playing host. Within a half hour, the crowd had grown so much, I couldn't keep track any longer. Time to go while we could still control the situation.

She acknowledged my signal, and finished up whatever story she was telling before taking my hand. This time, I took the lead and cut a direct path to the elevators. She selected a full one and clung to me tightly for the short ride.

The party around our suites had overflowed and taken over the entire floor. Brianna held my hand lightly as I led her to her room. She batted her eyes as I opened her door. "A lovely evening. We'll have to do it again."

I smiled and gave her a peck on the cheek. "Any time."

Raines' mood had lightened, and I suspected the drink in her hand had helped. She was leaning over the railing and watching the revelry below. She didn't look at me as I slid in next to her. "Next time, you and Onyx take care of the fairy princesses. I'm supposed to be on Robbie duty," I said.

Raines snorted a laugh. "You really are clueless. Anyway, you just missed Onyx and her boy toy. They left to go to the late night bands."

"What's he like?"

"Cute. Real cute. OK, he's smoking hot. Tall, blond, and sharp. Internet millionaire, maybe? If she hadn't snagged him, I'd be tempted to try." She flushed a little at the thought. A few of her emotions grabbed at me as they floated by.

"Have you run a background check on him? Anything unusual?"

Raines arched her eyebrow. "A threat to her clothes, maybe. She's a big girl. Besides, you have your own girl issues."

I shook my head. "You have no idea."

Raines patted me on the back. "Apparently, you don't, either."

"What?" She waved her hand in the air behind her and wandered off to flirt with some actor. The floor was full of them.

"WE MUST SPEAK." Melanippe was uncommonly rigid as she touched my shoulder.

"Sure. Let's go to my room. I was about to change anyway."

Something in the air urged me to look for Brighid. I felt her nearby, watching. Time for fun with magic. The large number of cosplayers meant I could more easily disguise myself, but keep weapons close at hand.

Even through whatever had her ire up, Mel beamed as I spread her handiwork on the bed. I slipped the various blades into their sheaths in the skinsuit. "You wanted to talk?"

She clenched her fists. "I need to understand."

"What is it, Mel?"

"You profess your devotions to my sister, who lays unmoving. And yet, you are here, courting Fae? How can you..." Thin cracks formed in her stony gaze.

"Mel, please sit." She trembled when I touched her arm. "I'm not courting the Fae. And I want nothing more than to be at Drea's side. And I'm doing everything I can to help her. I just wish I knew where to look next."

A small oasis pooled in her eyes. "You're not abandoning her?"

What did you do with a teary Amazon? One wrong word and she could rip my arm off and beat me with it. But if she was worried about the Fae, she sure as hell couldn't find out about Brighid. "No. I won't give up. I'll find a solution or die trying." It was an oath she would hold me to, without a doubt.

120

Her stare cut through to my very soul. She mustered a cheerless smile and nodded.

"Help me into this." A few accents, plus a glamour with Leviskin, made costuming insanely easy. My new visage cracked a real smile. The ridges on my forehead created an unbeatable disguise. Plus, the lift in my boots brought me to her eye level.

"What is this being called again? I've never faced this type of warrior."

The Bat'leth she'd crafted for me sang as I spun it around in my hands. "Klingon. It's where this comes from."

A shiver ran up my spine at the glint in her eyes. "I must meet more of them."

"I'll pull the series out for you when we get home."

"One question, though. If you have not begun courting the Fae, why did you accept their offers to become their consort?"

I shook my head. "I was just acting as their security."

Her brow furrowed. "No. They have both publicly declared their intentions on you. And you have accepted. It was a loose interpretation, but you have done the ritual."

What had this little vacation dragged me into?

"QAPLA' MERE, HUMAN." I flashed a toothy grin at Raines.

She burst out laughing. "You've been waiting your entire life to do this, haven't you?"

Mel looked quite proud of her work as she showed me off.

"I'm going to do a little recon." A thought wrapped Leviskin guards around the blades.

The fun lasted about five minutes before I realized I'd screwed up. The costume was too good. I couldn't get two steps without being tackled for pictures. It would have been a great way to meet women, but that hadn't been a problem recently.

A few adjustments later and I'd struck a balance. I took advantage of hiding in plain sight and making a spectacle of myself to draw the attention, making it easier to check out the surroundings.

After chasing off a changeling with an affinity for shiny objects, I ran into a person of interest. More specifically, I stepped on one. A pair of Erebite acolytes were wandering around in costumes as inconspicuous as mine: Erebite robes and plastic elf ears.

I thought I'd been busted, but he swore and hit me with a minor hex which would have sent anyone else into anaphylactic shock. I feigned a collapse and the rats scurried away. Fairy wings poked me in the eye as someone helped me up.

I cast a veil around myself and the attention drifted away as thoughts of me faded from people's minds and memories. I changed the glamour and Leviskin into plain clothes and picked up the cultists' trail. They seemed to be on the hunt for someone.

I followed a chain of people who had been put under subtle but sloppy enchantments. The cultists were drifting from group to group, putting people in trances to ask a few questions before moving on. I caught a girl who was still deep in a fugue state, mumbling, "Flappers and Zappers..."

They were targeting the party.

DARKNESS VEILED ME as I followed the cultists. They made a beeline up the road for eight blocks until they paused in front of an empty office building. Not entirely empty. A stark glow sprang to life on the fourth floor.

I blended myself into an alley as the pair looked around. A door swung open and they quickly disappeared into the darkness inside. I watched for a few moments until silhouettes appeared in the one lit room.

I focused my Sight onto the building. Swirling darkness surrounded the building with wards, but they were mostly alarms. Nothing appeared to be immediately dangerous, but I wouldn't be sneaking in, either.

The building next door shared a narrow alleyway, and was completely cold and lifeless. Staying close to the wall and edging along, careful to not trigger the wards, I stumbled on an escape ladder going to the roof. All I needed was to be four feet taller to reach it.

I took a deep breath and felt the Leviskin reconfigure into my standard tactical kit. A quick check confirmed all of my weapons were readily accessible. If only I had my pack.

Options? How many could they have inside? I ran my fingers through my hair and hit…an option. The Bat'leth.

The long blade hooked the release on the ladder and rattled loudly as it crashed to the ground. Time to move.

I scrambled up to the fire escape landing and quickly retracted the ladder before climbing two rungs at a time to the roof. A flashlight swept the alley as my leg flew over the edge.

As this building was a full story taller, I had a good view to scan the roof access of the Erebite hideout. I was in luck: they'd been lazy or in a hurry. No wards above the first few floors.

The guard ran his light over the fire escape and made a final sweep of the alley before shaking his head as he walked off.

Was I ready for this? Should I wait on Wynn for backup first? Screw it. I took a running jump and tripped on the sticky tar roof as I tucked into a lopsided roll of a landing. I shook off the road rash from the graceless arrival and investigated the roof access. The door lock clicked open and presented little resistance.

The ladder ended in a dark maintenance closet, but my Sight gave me a clear path straight down. Creeping past the floor of empty offices, the stairwell echoed every soft footfall. The steel door groaned as I cracked it for a look. No one came from the single light at the other end of the hall to investigate. I blocked the door partway open so it wouldn't slam shut.

Kneeling in an alcove, I eavesdropped on the heated conversation inside. The voice berating a couple of poor souls was definitely Betty's. "Idiots. You only needed to find out where a party is being held. I don't care about invitations. We will make our own entrance."

A deep male voice trembled, "It's close by. We only need to follow—"

A loud slap echoed. "Have you ever heard of preparations? Go back, and don't return until you have something useful."

I opened my Sight and Sense as much as I dared. The three people in the office were the only ones on this floor, with three others on the lower floors and a guard at the front door. Only the barest of wards were static in the background. They didn't plan on

125

being here for long. I triggered a beacon for Wynn on the private channel.

A kick flung the door open into the face of the pair I'd followed. "If you wanted an invitation, all you needed to do was ask. I'd even have prepared a VIP lounge just for your crew. How about a nice iron cage motif?" I leveled the 1911 at Betty's center mass.

Betty's nostrils flared as her scowl cut deep lines in her face. "Morons. They sent me morons, not minions." She crossed her arms across the front of a tightly tailored suit which clung to her figure. Her raven hair was tied back into a bun, and rimless glasses made her look like an owl. "Hello, Forrester. Are you here to switch sides? I'm hiring. In fact, I'm about to have at least two openings. I'll even throw in your girlfriend for a signing bonus and you can put her back to work."

The two acolytes froze. The Sight revealed wraiths driving the meat suits.

"I appreciate the consideration, but I don't think I can fill all the vacancies you're about to have. I propose a hostile takeover. Unless, of course, you're ready to surrender? I'll even see about getting side-by-side cells for you and Dick."

"As you wish." She signed something out in the air. "We need him alive."

Minion Number One was tall, thin, and flashing a sadistic grin as he drew out a roughly hewn blade. Sweat was beading on his friend's brow as he tested the charged baton in his hand.

The building shook and glass shattered as the blast from a breaching charge rippled up from the ground floor. The wards did their job and wailed out a useless alarm.

Betty barked something out and a portal opened. "Bring him now. We must be leaving."

I took aim at lucky Minion Number One. "Stop right there."

He ducked down and charged. My first shot deafened the room and creased his robe, but otherwise only managed to shatter a window. The second shot exploded a light and an acoustic tile as his shoulder dug under my arm and spun the weapon away. He lifted me off the ground and over his shoulder.

The world around me slowed. We were mere steps from going into the unknown through the portal. Betty grabbed a briefcase from the desk. Gunfire echoed from floors below. Sigils swam before my eyes and unlocked an incantation for energy balls.

The palms of my hands glowed as power flooded into them. A shimmering silver ball formed and flew through his back, sending the both of us crashing to the floor.

Lucky Minion Number Two's eyes dilated and he backed away.

"Hurry up," Betty screamed and pulled her puppet's strings with another flourish of her hand.

The acolyte snarled something and charged. Mid-stride, he met with another of the silver energy balls into his chest. The ball surged through his body and dragged a shadow from his back. A last flash took the demon and the ball into the ether. The driverless body crashed onto the floor next to me.

Betty threw the briefcase through the portal and swore.

I climbed out from under Minion Number One and retrieved my weapon. "Playtime's over."

"Yes, it is." Betty shouted something unintelligible. An energy net sizzled and sparked as it formed over me. Another pair of acolytes ran through the door. A bull of a man grabbed the net and started dragging me to the portal.

"Nope." I'd done a little research since the last time she'd pulled this and had charged a pair of blades with etheric juice. A couple of slashes and the net faded with angry sparks. Without his yoke, the bull tripped forward and fell through the portal.

Betty motioned. "Bring him at all costs."

I flipped one of the blades at the priestess. She easily deflected it, and disappeared as she stepped into the portal. "Morons."

The remaining acolyte closed the distance in three long strides. Her zombie hunter costume flashed out from under her robe as she drew a black blade and squatted into a fighting stance. The voice of a demonic cheerleader squeaked out, "She said alive, not undamaged." A cruel grin spread across her face.

My hands flashed red and the silver ball sizzled as she narrowly ducked it. She stood up, grinning. I parried a strike she tried with the blade. She countered, and I landed on my back as she swept my legs.

I raised my hands to catch the blow as she reared back to drive the blade into me.

We both learned something new about the silver energy balls at the same time. Once it had a target, they were hard to avoid.

The silver ball emerged from her chest and dragged the dark force with it. The shadow left a thin gash on my arm as it flew overhead. The ball sucked the shadow in and disappeared as it flew into the wall.

The empty shell of the acolyte collapsed to the floor.

Two more acolytes glared at me from the door. They straightened up, sheathed their knives, and walked headlong into the portal.

"See you soon, conjurer." Betty's voice echoed as the portal disappeared into itself.

"IS IT CLEAR? I looked up to see one of Wynn's men peek through the door.

"Hi, Hume. You guys are late to the party. I think there's one more in the building."

Hume offered a hand to pull me up from the floor. He smiled a wicked grin and said, "There is."

His granite fist flashed in my face as he pulled me into him.

Reflexes kicked in and the Leviskin wrapped a tactical helmet and face-mask around me in time to absorb most of the blow. I released a Push of energy hurling Hume into the wall and me halfway across the room.

The former soldier drew out one of his black blades and scowled. "You should've come along the easy way."

The Sight revealed the wraith within Hume. A thin tendril ran off into the distance to his puppet master, reminding me of Drea. I needed one of them to examine.

The zombie-hunting cheerleader would have been easier.

The leather handle of a ceramic blade was comforting as it slid into my hand. It was loaded with a paralytic and sedative combination I hoped would work.

Hume flicked his blade between his hands and feigned attacks. I couldn't know how much of his training or knowledge was available to the demon, but it looked like all of it. He leaned in and his blade left a thin trail across my chest armor. He was toying with me, but even the demon would know it wouldn't be long before help arrived.

He raised the knife high and started a slow downward arc.

If I hadn't practiced it with Raines, I'd have never seen the real attack coming.

His foot slipped between my legs and I jumped to avoid the sweep. As my foot hit the ground, I drove forward and collided chest to chest with the much larger soldier.

His black blade bounced off of the armor on my back as his powerful swing knocked me further into him.

I turned and my armor absorbed most of the blow I felt, more than saw, coming. It was still enough to knock me to my knees.

"If we leave now, I can still deliver you and have time to go hunting." His fist flew forward.

I drove my blade into his leg and was rewarded with a sharp cry. "Little bastard." He kicked me away.

I staggered to my feet and stared at Hume.

He ripped my blade out of his thigh and tossed it into the wall as he fought to stand.

One step. His breathing was ragged and heavy.

I moved back.

He fumbled for his sidearm and dropped it to the floor as it cleared his holster. His hands were shaking uncontrollably as the body failed the trapped wraith. Rivers of sweat poured down his face.

He gritted his teeth and tried to lift his foot, but the paralytic took firm hold. His body seized and teetered. His wrath was locked up in his frozen face.

"Ha! I don't think you're going to be snacking on anyone tonight." His eyes became saucers as his body gave one final spasm. Slowly, he listed forward and met the ground face first.

"ARRarammmm."

"What?" I knelt and rolled him onto his back.

The creature in Hume heaved as it breathed and tried to spit at me, but its shell wasn't moving.

I patted the side of his face. "You're a nasty one, aren't you? So, what are you?" Wynn's men signaled the floor below was clear over the comm.

The door at the end of the hall creaked.

"It's Forrester in here. The floor is clear." I stretched my Sight for an intensive look at Hume.

The wraith looked like a bigger version of the etheric parasites tagging along onto people for emotional snacks, but most of those were about as self-aware as tapeworms. This thing snarled and snapped back at me, but appeared locked into Hume's body. It thrashed around, looking for a way to get to me. If Hume recovered, it was going to hurt.

I turned the Sight to the others lying motionless on the floor. They looked almost like Drea, except the tendrils of their life essence were stronger, but still lackluster, almost faded.

Wynn and two tactical teams came in through the door with weapons drawn.

I nodded to Wynn. "I think we have a problem."

Wynn knelt next to Hume. "He's been missing for about a week." Even Wynn could see his missing man wasn't in the driver's seat. "What's happened to him?"

"I'm not entirely sure. It's not like a normal possession." Was there such a thing? "I cleared out the entities that had control of these others. I left this one in residence to study and figure it out. Keep him sedated and on a paralytic. It seems to keep the little fiend in check and unable to find a new host."

Wynn swallowed. "You cleared them out? As in exorcised them?"

"Something like that. It's not like something else was overriding the owner; they just aren't home. But they do appear to be alive. It was like they could play at being fully human, and may have the host's memories."

"So they could be any one of us."

"I don't know if they could pull it off to someone who knew the person intimately, but to the casual observer, I'd say yes."

One of Wynn's team tapped him on the shoulder. "Not much here, sir. It looks like a temporary base of operations. There are no active leases in the building. I think they just squatted on a nearby vacant location."

"OK, let's pack them up and get out of here before someone notices." I winced when he patted me on the shoulder where Hume slipped in a blow. "You had best get back to the party before you're missed. I'll let you know when and where we have them secured."

I took a deep breath and winced again. "Betty was here. She had them trying to get details on the gala tomorrow night."

Wynn shook his head. "This keeps getting better and better. We'll bring in extra people. I know there is no point in trying to cancel the party."

"Nope. Not without a lot of questions. Got your costume yet?"

GAS LAMPS FLICKERED with a warm glow throughout the back room of the Gin Sluice. Electric light only supplemented to cover in the gaps. You could slide a drink from one end of the bar to the other with a tap on the highly polished wood. The band was setting up in the corner. A classic matte background for a photographer was next to the entrance.

The setup far surpassed my expectations. The guests would pass through a dimly lit tunnel protected by security in zoot suits carrying Thompson's guns. An invitation only got you as far as the door. To get past the bouncers, werewolves in tuxes, you had to know the pass phrase, "I'm here to see the blind griffin." No one needed to know they were real lycanthropes who owed me a favor. The real security, Phil the Kraken and his tentacles, were in deep shadow, and most guests would assume he was an effect.

Posters and props from Underhill Productions films were staged in classic frames and cases. Press materials were readily available.

No costume, no entry. To support my small role, I was dressed out in a white tux and tails as the classic mad scientist but genteel host. Until you accidentally discovered one of my lab experiments gone wrong.

I was part of the show.

Aquil beamed. "What do you think?" He knew he'd gone above and beyond and was proud of it. So was I.

"Amazing. We aren't *actually* in the 1920s, are we?" You never knew what kind of tricks a jinn could use.

He gave an immodest shrug. "I might have pulled a little of the essence of the time forward."

My favorite tinkering angel, Melvin, was favoring the guise of Dr. Jekyll at the moment, but seemed to enjoy Mr. Hyde more. He said, "Grey, buddy. It's ready. You are going to love this. It's going to blow the crowd away."

A shudder went up my spine. "You don't mean literally, right? This is just entertainment. You remember that."

Melvin rolled his eyes. "No, dude, this is going to be great. And totally safe. Nothing like the dragons."

The last trick Melvin did for me was to open a temporary hell-mouth in the Winter lands. "Can I see it?"

Melvin strutted across to the middle of the floor. "Abso-freakin-loutely."

I motioned for everyone to clear out, just in case.

Melvin scratched his head. "Okay, Grey, you're going to be up there on the balcony in the mad scientist outfit. You're going to do your spiel, and say—" Melvin jumped into a big Broadway spread with jazz hands, "IT'S ALIVE."

Tesla coils arced and sang high overhead. Electrical pulses climbed the rails of Jacob's Ladders hanging in midair. Spectral scenes from early black and white films flashed on the walls with aged snippets of films from Underhill Productions. *Metropolis*, *Nosferatu* and *Frankenstein* played next to Underhill Productions' *Crystal Caverns of Atlantis* and the evening's premiere of *Fae, Fab, and Furious*.

Melvin tap-danced across the floor and swept his arms to point to the stage. "And then you port down here and announce the band. What do you think? Awesome, right?"

A small part of me was shocked when we didn't transport to 1920, bring the rubber aliens to life, or just electrocute the room. Or unfold the universe. "Melvin, this is perfect. How are we going to hide the porting?"

Melvin waved to a black-curtained box next to the bandstand. He showed me a switch inside which would cause it to burst open in a puff of white smoke.

Memories of his tinkering came to mind. "Don't mess with it. It's perfect." And it didn't look like anyone would be killed. Or turned into pod people.

Melvin said, "Great. I'll reset everything."

Aquil nudged me and stifled a laugh. "I am surprised we are still alive as well."

"See you in a few hours."

Aquil said, "Hurry back. We're set for five hundred. That's the last number I got from Onyx."

I yelled on the way out the door, "Melvin, no tinkering. None at all."

The grumbling meant I'd interrupted something.

TIME TO DRESS. Wynn's report from the night before didn't tell me anything new. Hume was buttoned up and had fallen into a catatonic state. From what they'd found, the cultists had only been there a few hours. A day at most.

I was jittery. My heart raced as I looked at the report. The cultists knew more about what we were doing than we knew about what they were planning. But we knew they were coming.

Wynn had brought in more people as security, but we were spread pretty thin. If they couldn't get in, they might try whatever it was they were planning while people were in transit. I just had to trust in the game plan. Be ready for anything.

The Leviskin made getting dressed pretty easy. I was losing the battle with the two arms of a bow tie when three short knocks came from door. Onyx the flapper trotted in, wearing a short black dress and a jeweled black band in her hair, now blonde with red streaks. A delicate, silver rune necklace shone through the black feather boa and drew my eyes to her ample cleavage.

She pulled me down to her to fix my tie. She gave me a sisterly kiss on the cheek and said, "Drea is going to be pissed she missed this when she wakes up."

The rune hummed slightly when I touched it. She'd already charged it with her energy. "A gift from the boy toy?"

She grinned. "No, Beth and I each got one from one of the vendors."

"Nice to know you two are having fun. Do I get to meet the new boyfriend tonight, finally?" I inspected the top hat which would complete my look.

Onyx said, "If you stick around long enough."

"And how did we get to five hundred attendees?"

Onyx patted me on the arm. "Ask Claire."

Raines sashayed into the room. Her slinky white dress clung tightly to curves I'd never noticed before. A slit ran up the side that looked like it went to her neck. She spun around for inspection. The back dropped *very* low. I struggled to figure out where she'd strapped her weapon. A white feather boa hung low on her shoulders.

She grinned slyly. "Close your mouth, Forrester. You're drooling."

Onyx grabbed my arm and threw a leg around me. "Take my picture with this sexy beast." Both women cackled as I turned bright red.

Raines grabbed a series of pictures and offered the camera to Onyx. "My turn."

EXCITED CHATTER ECHOED down the dimly lit tunnel. Guests were escorted down a wide red carpet running the length of the seedy tunnel from the outside and ended at the back door to the Gin Sluice. Enchanted lanterns meant to look like gaslamps flickered warm light against the old walls. This part of the underground had never been redeveloped and helped to mask the various businesses catering to the Veiled peoples. For the night, the veil over the ornate entrance to the Gin Sluice had been lifted.

Security dressed in period costume directed invited traffic to the underground tunnels, and gently ushered away those without invitations. So far, the biggest problems were a few counterfeit invitations and would-be party crashers. Give or take a hundred people and a dozen paparazzi, there was a small parade route at the entrance to the tunnel.

Nothing looked out of place as I spot-checked the crowd through my Sight. A couple of Underhill Productions' assistants handed out cards for free movie downloads and a few t-shirts to the crowd. Evan Underhill, Aindrias' alter ego, would be thrilled at the buzz for the studio.

Wynn greeted me at the main entrance. He was decked out like Dick Tracy from the early comic strip days, in a canary yellow suit and hat to match. Apparently, Mel had built him a fully functional wristwatch phone to match to specs. "We have details all the way from the hotel to here, most of them undercover. We have a tactical team on each block and two in the venue. Other than the obvious security inside and out, no one should be the wiser."

"It sounds tight. I've scanned the block for any potential ambushes. Wards are all over the building and the tunnel outside. If they're here, they aren't using anything with power." Even as I said it, my Senses told me to be on guard. "I can't help but feel they are close, though."

Wynn said, "They would be foolish to hit this place. Even normally, this place is a fortress."

"Huh." I poked the special agent in his tin badge. "You came just to see what the place looked like. You know, you could have just asked."

He looked away. "Guilty. I did want to get a peek inside. When I was stationed here for a while, the Gin Sluice was legendary. And very much off limits, so no, I couldn't just ask. I don't live in this world. I, my team, we're in this world, but not of it. We work here. And we try to keep everyone on both sides of the fence safe. You live here. This is your world. I like you. More importantly, I trust you, Greyson. But there are a lot of people who *do not* trust you, or anyone from this side of the Veil. Everyone has agreed it needs to remain hidden from the world at large."

My heart leapt into my throat. I'd let myself become too comfortable. "Thanks, Gerry. For the reminder." I couldn't admit aloud that I didn't live in either world. "Enjoy the party, and I'm happy you could get a look around. I need to check the rest of the preparations."

Wynn and I glided through the checkpoint at the entrance, around the early crowd waiting their turn to get inside. My private security gave a little nod and a toothy grin. Wynn recognized the werewolves as real and stiffened. I guided him through the line before too many questions could be raised. I'd pay for it later, no doubt.

Inside, the band was already playing some background standards, hors d'oeuvres were disappearing, and the drinks were flowing. The rules on the costumes were quite loose, but most of the attendees were at least true to the spirit. Aquil thrived in his element as the not-so-modest host and personally greeted everyone. In his usual subtle style, he was wearing flowing robes and a jeweled turban, and pouring shots from his magic lantern in his own personal interpretation as Aladdin.

An hour later, the room was filled to near capacity and the last few guests were allowed in before closing the doors. Melvin signaled it was time for the show to begin.

Ominous music played as I climbed up into the balcony to start my performance. I'd made a last minute change to my costume and added a pencil thin mustache to the white tux and tails. A spotlight came to bear on me and the orchestra hit a crescendo. My old friend, mentor, and stage magician, Henri Clouse, channeled through me as I made an overly dramatic bow and tipped my white top hat to an expectant, packed house.

All of the stars from Underhill Productions were lined up on a stage beside the band. Onyx, Raines, Melanippe and a few support staff stood nearby. Onyx was talking to a medium-sized guy with dark hair, but I couldn't tell much else in the crowd. I assumed he was the boyfriend.

The band cut off my background music. My heart pounded. I was nervous and excited. I was used to staying to the shadows. For once, I was in the limelight.

In my imagination, Henri put his hand on my shoulder like he'd done so many times before. My voice resonated through the entire hall as I projected Vincent Price.   "Welcome, all, to the evening gala. I am your humble host, Doctor Will B. Demented. Our generous benefactor, Evan Underhill, passes on condolences for not being here personally, but has a few words for us."

The wall next to me crackled to life. Aindrias used his Evan persona in a live broadcast to greet the crowd and tell them to enjoy the evening. The projection faded out on his grin. "Now, Doctor, you may begin the experiment."

The spotlight lit me up again. "All together now, can we do it?" The first Tesla coil shot a bolt across the room. Cheers thundered. Melvin had tinkered with it. I hoped enough guardian angels had crashed the party. Only a few had requested invitations.

I threw my arms in the air and tossed a small fireball. "It's ALIVE!"

TESLA COILS FIRED and the music modulated through classic sci-fi themes, rolling into the theme music for the night's premiere. Lightening climbed and disappeared up Jacob's Ladders. Scenes from *Fae, Fab, and Furious* lit up the walls. A writhing mass of costumed bodies filled the floor.

Even from here, Claire and everyone on the stage was beaming. I readied to port down there.

The black curtains which framed the entrance billowed and an icy wind chilled the room.

Melvin, what did you do? This wasn't part of the script.

Two werewolves burst from the curtained darkness and flew through midair to land on the dance floor. It definitely wasn't part of the show. The crowd screamed with excitement, not knowing any better.

Five figures in black breached the entrance in a show of arms. The lead figure summoned a charge of energy and unleashed it at me. The balcony was charred in a blinding flash singing me as I ported away. The crowd roared without missing a beat as they danced. I felt for my 1911 as I made my grand entrance onto the stage from the secluded spot.

Betty Gibson sauntered up to the stage, flashing claws and dragging a long barbed tail from her skin-tight black leather bodysuit. Four acolytes in simple black robes held stations around her. The Sight confirmed three of the acolytes were possessed shells. Ole Sparky at her side was a Dark Elf mage.

Betty sauntered up the short stairs onto the other end of the stage. Did they give Erebite priestesses lessons in overacting for stage and theater?

My earbud erupted in short bursts from the security teams.

Parading to mid-stage, Betty exclaimed, "Doctor Demented, I believe I have an experiment which may interest you." A round of hoots rose from the audience. I motioned for Raines to stay in place. No one else on stage seemed to have noticed the change in script. Onyx and Claire watched as raptly as everyone else.

My mouth went dry and I strained to speak in a stage whisper. "And what should I call you, she devil?"

Betty grinned, "I am the Scorpion Queen." She turned and whispered, "I had such short notice. I know it was a 1950s B noir, but it's still a classic."

Claire paled as she realized this wasn't part of the plan. I nodded for her to stay put, though her eyes were already looking for somewhere to run.

It struck me as insanity that this woman had the ability to destroy us all with the snap of a finger, and almost no one knew. "So, Scorpion Queen, to what do we owe the honor?"

Betty played to the audience. "A trade."

"How nice. You brought more revenants for my lab?" The zombies in the crowd cheered.

From the end of the claw on her finger, she dangled a long, curly lock of red hair. "I would prefer if you did not force any more of my assistants to relocate to new corporeal shells. They are so hard to come by. Of course, it looks like quite a few here could be made available." More cheers from the oblivious crowd.

I nodded. "A trade it is." I had to get Betty and the rest out the door. After that, I had to hope Wynn could get the situation under control. If I could get them outside, it would be easier for the teams to bring them down unnoticed. We had made preparations to lock down the tunnel. And then Betty would tell me what she'd done to Brighid.

Betty offered her hand to me and passed me off to her guard. My skin crawled, but I took it anyway. The sooner she was outside, the better.

A roar of applause followed us through the heavy oak doors to the underground. We were greeted with an unexpectedly damp, cold blast of air. And utter silence.

The lights, red carpet, and security detail had been replaced by garbage and debris. A few oil lamps and burning trash cans cast a hellish glow. Urine and worse cast a heavy cloud.

Betty tossed a trio of fireballs into the air for light, sending the few denizens scurrying away into the darkness.

She crossed her arms and scorned me. "Now, as to our negotiations, our non-negotiable offer is thus. You surrender unconditionally. We take a little trip. I allow you live, and to become the consort of my queen." Six more of her possessed disciples emerged from the shadows.

"Well, that doesn't sound quite like a fair trade." Where was Wynn? The security teams? It was definitely the underground. What was happening? I stared into the Abyss. I was completely alone. "Where have you brought me?"

"Poor Greyson, always two steps behind. I wish I could understand my queen's faith in you." A thin chuckle came through the priestess' smirk. "I've already lived up to my end of the deal. I left your room full of people alone. No one was hurt, and none knows how close they came to joining my ranks, or oblivion. As to where, that's the back door to the Gin Sluice. The important question is when. I'm not sure of the exact date, but Aquil is hosting his grand opening party inside."

Well, bite me. My suspicions were confirmed. "It looks like I'm at your disposal. Why don't you get me up to speed? Isn't that what your queen would want? Our queen?"

Betty motioned to the shadows. A pair of acolytes emerged with Brighid restrained between them. A third pulled her head back and held a black knife at her throat. Even in the dim light, her eyes called for help she knew I couldn't give. I might have been able to take a few of them out, but not before they could kill her.

I stretched my Senses. Eleven acolytes, including two Dark Elves, plus Betty. A veil was cast over Brighid, so I couldn't cast any protections or enchantments.

The priestess closed the distance between us until I could feel her breath on my face. "Let me sweeten the pot. We release your girlfriend and you come with us willingly. Once we get what we need from you, you will be free. Of course, you may decide to stay with the winning team."

"What is it you want from me?" My hope for an opening to rescue Brighid was fading faster than my control of my temper.

Betty snickered. "I wish I knew. If it were up to me, I would smear your insides on the walls and leave you to die. What my queen desires from you? Ask her yourself. Are you ready to go?"

Even knowing world history, I knew there were worse things than being stuck in the twenties with Brighid. And if this lunatic could find a way around in time, so could I. "I sure am."

I swept my leg under Betty and flung three of the silver balls at the acolytes holding Brighid. Betty landed and rolled away.

Two of the three silver balls found a target. The one with the blade slumped to the ground with one of the acolytes standing at her side. Brighid punched the other acolyte, struggled free, and ran towards me. Silver balls flew from my hands as quickly as targets appeared.

Betty was deadpan as she drew a black blade. She lazily flung a fireball lightly scorching me as it brushed past. I turned to duck and was suddenly face-to-face with her. I blocked her swing with one arm and shoved her away with the other.

An acolyte grabbed me from behind and pinned my arms.

I stomped his foot and was rewarded with the sharp crack of breaking bone. The body slumped from the shock, and I completed the job with another of the silver balls.

"Take him." Betty backed away and waved to her remaining drones.

A chain of silver balls flew from my outstretched hands.

We faced each other with arms outstretched. Power built in her hands. The debate behind her eyes was whether or not to kill me. Or at least try.

"Enough, Betty."

She cocked her head. "It certainly is." She turned and motioned at Brighid.

Fire left her hands.

I wrapped myself around Brighid and drove us both to the ground.

The fireball threw embers as it splattered on the back wall.

Betty began the incantation which would craft an energy net.

I rolled off Brighid and tossed an energy ball back at her. It solidly connected with her mid-chest. The pair of mages withdrew into the darkness before she hit the ground. Soulless acolyte bodies lay scattered around.

Brighid stared blankly at the injured sorceress.

Betty struggled to sit up, rasping as she breathed. She spat out, "This changes nothing."

I pulled Brighid to me. "Are you OK? Are you hurt?"

Brighid kissed me hurriedly and pulled away. "I'm sorry."

My vision narrowed and blurred. My side blossomed in fire.

Brigid tried to hold me up, but jerked away from me when the Leviskin reflexively closed the wound and wrapped around the blade and hilt, stopping it from being drawn out.

Betty let out a raspy cackle as I slowly folded to the floor.

Brighid held me and gently eased me against the wall. Short gasps were all I could pull in. I slid to the side as my life slowly slipped away. Acid burned in my veins as my essence was drawn into the knife. My blood pooled on the floor around me. "Why?" My limbs refused to move.

Brighid knelt next to me and kissed my forehead. "Because you love…her."

Brighid shoved me over, twisting and struggling to draw the knife from my side. The skinsuit had completely enveloped the knife, holding it in place. I heard myself scream as she moved it around, trying to pull it out.

A sliver of light spilled across Brighid's face. Her eyes were saucers. She scrambled to back away from me as the glow spilled into the alleyway from the door behind me.

Betty struggled to lift her arm and aim a small handgun. "Go away. This is not your concern."

The voice behind me was strong, but flat. "You have made it my concern."

MY SIDE THROBBED where the knife extended from my ribcage. The pain was the only thing convincing me I was still alive. Lucky me.

The lamp in the corner was dimmed by a shirt draped over the shade. A soft bed and pillows cradled me.

"Loosen the bonds around the knife. Let me inspect the wound."

The Leviskin holding my blade and the surrounding shirt fell away. The cool air felt good on my skin. "How'd I get here?"

"Not now." He began a humming chant. Warmth and life flowed through me as he focused his hands over my injuries.

He grasped the handle. A not unpleasant shock rippled through me. I felt nothing as he slipped the blade from my side. The worst of the pain and pressure in my chest and side subsided. Slowly, my strength and focus returned.

The low chanting stopped.

The figure helped me to sit up in the bed. I expected a large bloody gash, but instead, my side was a mass of black and bruises. A thin red mark was underneath the dried blood as he wiped it away.

My vision was blurry, but clearing. The shadow studied the knife in his hand. I managed to wheeze out, "Put the knife down. Beside me." I thought my voice was commanding, at least as much as it could be in my current condition.

He chuckled, but placed the knife beside me, with the handle near my hand. It was the black blade I'd been seeking. The crystal in the handle was clear. "Who are you?"

151

He removed the shirt covering the lamp and took a chair at the end of the bed. We were in my hotel room. "Call me Eric."

He slowly came into focus. My strength was returning. "I remember you from Pageland's Ferry. I thought you were one of the cult members." At least I now had a name for Hip-hop: Eric.

A shy, thin smile crossed his face. "A member, no. Call me an interested party. I was there, same as you, to see what the big deal was about. Who knew you'd be the main event?"

Eric tossed my satchel beside me on the bed. I popped a couple of the healing potions. "So, what are you doing here, and why did you help me?"

Eric sat back in the chair and gave me a better look. I didn't have the strength to open my Sight, so I had to go with what was readily visible. There was a small smear of my blood on his white shirt under the expensive black tux and tails. He folded his hands in his lap. "It seemed to be the thing to do. I followed you through the door. It was easy enough to keep the portal open and pull you back through. It seemed a better idea to port you back here than to try to save you in the middle of the party." He looked at the blade. "I must say, I haven't seen one like that in a long time."

I held up the knife. "What can you tell me about this? Obviously, you know something."

Eric stood. "This should help you." He placed a manila envelope in the dresser drawer. "We will soon see each other again. Your people will be here shortly, and there will be fewer questions for us both if I am not here."

"Wait." He gave a half wave behind him and the door clicked closed.

I hid the knife in the bedside drawer and struggled to get up. Less than a minute later, Wynn led a tactical team through the room door. They quickly cleared the room. Wynn sat on the bed next to me and looked at my side. "What in hell hit you?"

WYNN'S MEDIC INSPECTED my injuries. Rebecca had plenty of experience patching me up. She worked quickly and efficiently, without her usual quips. The bruises were angry, but fading fast.

Wynn was debriefing me when shouting erupted in the hallway. I felt a little pity for whoever had briefly slowed up Raines, Mel, and Onyx from bursting in. Robbie and other voices shouted in the hall. They stopped when they saw the bruises.

It took all of my remaining energy to speak. "Somehow Betty created a portal. She wanted to trade me in exchange for not soul sucking everyone in the building. I wasn't sure if she could do it or not, but I wasn't going to take any chances. I figured the best bet was to get her outside. I didn't know where we were going wasn't going to have backup."

Raines said, "What was the deal with the red hair?"

Damn. "She made me think she had a hostage. She didn't. It was a trick to get me outside."

Rebecca said, "Okay, let's get you to the hospital."

I shook my head. "I'll be fine. There's nothing they can do about this anyway. If I was going to die, I would have already. I'll be healed in a few hours."

The bruises faded even more after I knocked back two additional healing elixirs.

Rebecca threw her bag on the bed and scowled. "I still think you need to check in for an overnight."

I shook my head. "I'm safer here. Besides, you should see the other guys."

154

Rebecca wrapped my ribs and made me walk around the room. After making sure I wasn't urinating blood, she relented.

Wynn ushered everyone out of the room and shut the door. He sat in the chair recently vacated by Eric and put his head in his hands. "What didn't you tell me? The red hair. You followed it straight into a trap without a question. Whose is it? What are you holding back?"

I sighed. "Someone I used to be very close to. I thought she was being held against her will. Instead, it looks like she's swapped sides. I let her in too close, and she used the blade on me. I won't make that mistake again."

Wynn nodded. "And how did you get back here?"

"A little trick for emergencies."

He rubbed his neck and closed his glazed eyes. "And Betty?"

My turn to shake my head. "I'm not sure. I hit her pretty hard, and she was hurt worse than me. I booted ten shadows out of the human shells, but I don't think the bodies are somewhere we can recover. If I had to guess, they have them again by now. If not, they're all long dead."

My concerned friend turned back into a hardened agent. "We *will* talk tomorrow. Get some rest."

I stumbled out of bed and opened the door to an anxious gathering in the hall. Most of the physical pain was gone, but a deep chill had settled into my soul.

Onyx gave me a gentle hug. "You look like you need a drink."

After the night I'd had, I couldn't agree more. "So, how was the party?"

Raines said, "Not over yet, if you're up to it. It's almost time for closing ceremonies."

I grabbed a fresh skinsuit, and within a few minutes we were in the back bar at the Gin Sluice. The party raged on in the ballroom. Aquil slid a stout to me. "You look a little worse for wear. It has a little pick-me-up in it that'll help."

The drink quickly disappeared, and whatever was in it made me all warm and fuzzy. I Pushed myself back into the white tux and tails to be dragged onstage for the big finale.

Someone had opened the doors and it was packed wall-to-wall.

Sesha Aislinn and Brianna Coterie each took an arm and helped me back onto the stage. Sesha sashayed out in a skimpy, white, angel costume with wide, feathered wings and a golden halo. Brianna showcased a black skirt and corset with latex wings and little, red horns. I didn't know how much they'd been told, but they gave a good seductive pose while they helped to hold up my body on stage.

I got a surprise when each of them grabbed me and gave me a heart-stopping kiss. A mix of gasps, cat calls, and applause came from the crowd.

"And thank you all for coming tonight."

SUNLIGHT ASSAULTED ME through the open curtains. Raines slept in the chair at the end of my bed. My head throbbed almost as bad as my side. I fell out of the bed when I tried to grab the last two bottles of elixir off the nightstand. I downed the one I'd managed to knock over and waited for the world to stop spinning.

Onyx knocked and entered the room, rolling in a couple of breakfast trays. "Morning, lover boy." She looked like she'd eaten the Cheshire Cat.

I pushed myself back onto the bed and came face-to-face with the Lifestyle section of the *Atlanta Journal*. "Scenes from the Con" plastered across the front page. The center picture was from the night before. Sesha and Brianna each with their lips on my cheeks from the closing of the party. It was captioned "Geek love unites warring starlets."

I lay back down, groaned, and prayed for a quick death. The picture motivated the gremlin to redouble its efforts with the sledgehammer in my head, and his twin had a pickaxe in my side.

Raines flashed copies of different celebrity gossip sites on her tablet. My picture was in most of them, between shots of the Fae. "The identity of their shared companion is not yet known, but he appears responsible for creating detente between the famously disputing divas," she read from another site. "Hey, this one says your performance at the party, while brief, was a compelling piece, predicting a great future as an actor. Especially if you stick to being an extra."

Onyx said, "Good news, though. None of the pictures are good enough quality to show who you are, and you changed your appearance enough to stay anonymous."

Raines threw the tablet on the bed. "It looks like you have a great excuse to stay in bed and recover."

"Don't you two have somewhere to be? Get out."

Onyx giggled. "Most everyone left this morning, but yeah, there's a few things to be done."

"Someone has to pick up your slack." Raines ducked the pillow I threw.

As soon as I was certain I was alone, I took the manila envelope and knife from their hiding spots and ported to my lab.

Examination of the knife was revealing. It wasn't the same blade used on Drea, but it was close. My Sight showed my residual energy, and a unique power signature. It had a singular use: to draw in life essence.

I set the knife aside on a shelf and opened the envelope. The pages from an old, crumbling text inside detailed a list of thirteen of these knives. Each had a unique sigil. I couldn't read the code, but I could match some of the pictures to the Anima Arca text.

My time was running out. I loaded up on a stock of healing potions and liberally applied slime which would aid healing up as well.

I ported back into the hotel and was snacking in the hospitality suite when Raines appeared with Sesha and Briana in tow. They slipped in on both sides of me on the couch and each kissed a cheek. Sesha rubbed my side. "How is it feeling this morning?"

I gasped and tried not to show how painful it was. "Well, doc, it hurts when someone pokes me."

158

"In that case, what I had in mind will have to wait."

Rebecca stood in the doorway with her arms crossed, a copy of the paper with our picture on the front drooping from her hand like an accusation. "All you hussies, out. You, too, Beth."

I raised my hands in surrender. "We can go down to my room."

She slammed the door behind us and waved the picture in my face. "This is not what I meant when I said rest. I should've forced you to go in for an overnight."

"Rebecca."

"I don't want to hear it." She pulled a couple of devices from her bag. "Lose the shirt and the excuses. I don't know why I keep putting you back together."

I stripped and she snapped a couple of pictures of my side. "I don't see anything broken, and it looks like it's healing pretty quickly. What's the goop?"

"Don't ask. It's an old family recipe."

I winced as she poked me in the side harder than she needed to. What the hell was it with being poked in an injury? "Next time I tell you to lay low, do it. What kind of weapon was used?"

"Similar to what they used on Drea, except it didn't slice through tissue. I think they were trying to turn me into one of their pod people."

Rebecca shook her head. "You were lucky to get out intact, from the looks of your bioelectric field." She showed me the screen on the back of the camera. Mel's new tech on loan to

Longbow showed my shredded aura. "It looks like whatever they did sucked most of your life force through a straw and then spit it back out."

"Funny. It felt more like I was run through a smoothie blender."

Rebecca smirked. "From the looks of it, the bimbos in there thought you were tasty."

"Hey," I protested.

"You'll live. I'm out of here. We're leaving for a recon op in the next couple of hours. I'll check with you in a week to see about clearing you for duty. Until then, lie low and get some rest."

ONYX LOOKED INTO the nearly empty hospitality suite. "You busy?"

I was taking advantage of the couch and table to spread out the pictures of the dark blades in the hopes they would talk to me. So far, no luck. "Come on in." I quickly stacked and hid the pictures.

I bit my tongue when she brought her new boy toy through the door. I scrambled to my feet. She was grinning ear to ear. "I finally got you two in the same place at the same time. Grey, this is Eric."

His broad smile hid any hint of our meeting the night before. He extended a strong hand. "Eric Buci. Nice to meet you. I've heard a lot about you in the last few days."

How much and what had she told him? His grip was firm, but gentle. "Good to meet you, too. She hasn't told me much about you. Are you going to be around for a while?"

He squeezed Onyx's hand. "I've got business in Jacksonville for a few days, and then I'm going back home to Pasadena. I'm hopeful this one will acknowledge me when she gets back to Los Angeles."

Onyx gazed up at him with a flirty smile. "You never know. I may get a better offer."

"Let me know how it goes. I'm up for a little competition."

Bedlam made its way up the hall and crashed the almost tender moment with Robbie in the lead. He picked me up in a bear hug, nearly sending me into shock. "We're leaving. I wish you'd come to Phoenix Grove to visit. You'd love the studio."

161

The Grove. Home. At least, it used to be. The next time I visited would be in a few months for the Inquest. "I'd like to, Robbie, but I'd like to breathe more."

He put me down as gently as he could. "Oh, sorry."

Briana whispered in my ear. "I can kiss it and make it better."

Sesha nudged her aside. "Me first."

Fifteen minutes later, after a hurried but excited sendoff, Raines and I sat, exhausted, staring at each other in silence. Everyone else was gone, having left for the airport.

Wynn walked in and leaned against the wall. "So, Raines, are you up for a trip, or are you still on vacation?"

Sensing it was time for business, I used my Sight to give them a quick inspection. Both Wynn and Raines were still themselves. "She's clear. So are you, by the way."

Raines shook her head. "What are you talking about?"

I glanced at Wynn to let him decide how much to share. I leaned back on the couch. Using the Sight had taken the last of my energy.

The lead agent crossed his arms and locked onto Raines. "We lost Hume. The Erebites have gained some ability to..." He pursed his lips.

"Possess people. They have obtained an ability to strip people out of their bodies and insert a walk-in. Like what they did to Drea, and then use their bodies," I said.

Raines' face turned to granite. "Where are we going?"

162

"Neptune Beach. Plane leaves for Jacksonville in two hours."

I sat up. "What's happening down there?"

Wynn shook his head. "It is a scouting trip. Reconnaissance only. You aren't cleared, so park it for a few more days. Rebecca says at least a week."

"Gerry."

He lightly slapped my bruised ribcage and sent me to my knees. "Are you really going to try and tell me you're ready?"

DEAFENING SILENCE ECHOED through the halls after days of the nonstop assault on my senses. Phantom noises and sensations kept me on edge. I'd taken a dive from a mosh pit only to splash down in a sensory deprivation tank.

Wynn had been right. I wasn't any good to anyone in my current shape. I wasn't sure a week would be enough to really recover. I'd spend one more night in a comfortable bed, check out in the morning, and hole up in the lab for a few days of research. It would help to go off the grid.

But first, I needed to go close out a really large tab.

It was hard to believe the difference from the night before. The tunnel was empty of all of the décor, and maybe a little cleaner than it had been. The back door to the Gin Sluice was open and crews had only made a dent in the refuse. Aquil masterfully orchestrated the teams cleaning up the mess and preparing for the next round of festivities.

"Greyson, my friend." He gingerly placed his hands on my shoulders and locked onto my eyes. "You are well this evening?"

"Better than last night. Not that it wasn't a great event and all." I looked up at the large scorch mark where the balcony had been. Betty's opening shot must have missed me by milliseconds. "Sorry about that."

Aquil waved his hand dismissively. "It is I who must apologize. You risked yourself to get them out of here." He handed me a house ale. "I still cannot understand how they did it."

"I don't, either. My wards were stacked on top of your standing protections, but they said we ported back to your opening night. It looked like the timing fit."

A small, blue flame burned at the back of his eyes as they glazed over. "I can tap into the energy of great celebrations from previous days to help set the mood. Maybe they found a way in using these energies, at a time before the protections were in place." He shook his head and returned to the present. "I cannot imagine how it might work."

I shrugged. "Me, either. You might want to look into the vulnerability. In any case, it was a great party. Thanks for opening up your place."

"Mr. Underhill sent his appreciation as well and has already more than generously taken care of the bill. My many thanks to you for the business. And your show will enhance our reputation. Several inquiries for future events have already come in from those in attendance." He broke into a wry grin. "I have a little gift for you."

"Really, Aquil, there's no need," I protested.

A large object lay in his office, wrapped in delicate rice paper. "Open it."

The paper fell away to show a picture from the night before. Every celebrity and personality who had attended the party was on the stage. I was in the center. Nearly fifty people in all, and every one of them had autographed themselves. "I only missed your signature."

"How did you pull that off?"

Aquil laughed. "Photoshop. We caught you from earlier, and did a group shot not long after the…interruption. We ran off the print in the back. While everyone was here, we got them to sign the pictures. I have one for myself as well, of course."

I signed my image in both copies, and he handed me mine. He then pulled out another picture of not only the celebs, but my friends as well. Even Wynn was in the shot. "This is wonderful, Aquil."

A tear formed in his eye. "Come, let's eat.

TIME TO PACK. From the hotel, I ported back to the lab with all of my gear. I locked my shiny new pictures into a shielded locker. Not that I didn't trust Aquil, but there was a lot of energy tied up in it. I could hang it up once all of it dissipated. I unpacked all but the essentials, and restocked my pack. No need to carry a bunch of stuff, when it could be stored in an extra dimension.

With everything in place, I returned to the hotel for a last night of sleep. I'd cleared the room and was ready to leave first thing in the morning. With my mind and body spent, sleep forced itself on me.

I jerked awake when a weight shifted the bed. The room had melted away and the bed rested in the middle of a starlit field. My heart raced. I crashed to the grassy ground, scrambling for safety. "Get the hell away from me."

Brighid rose from the bed and knelt by me on the ground. Her eyes were wide and pleading as she stared at my wounds. Her hands glowed ethereally as she gently traced her fingers over the bruises. "What happened? How badly are you hurt?"

I locked my gaze onto hers. "You happened to me."

Her face contorted in shock, she blurted out, "What do you mean?"

"You stabbed me yesterday with an Anima Arca blade, and tried to rip my soul from my body. Well, yesterday plus or minus a century."

Her face went slack. "I couldn't have done this. I love you too much. And in my deepest depths, I can't imagine my being able to do this to anyone."

I looked for any signs of deception behind her tortured eyes and found none. I'd woken up enough to realize I wasn't in a

167

dream. Not exactly. It wasn't exactly like being in the keep, either. The world around us was fading away. I leaned in and took her face in my hands. Her skin was warm. "How are you here? Where is here?" Her face. She looked like she had when we were teenagers. She was still young and soft. Not the person I'd been with hours earlier.

Tears streamed down her face. "I don't know, but I don't wish to leave you."

"Where are you? I'll come to you."

She shook her head. "I'm...I'm at home. In the Grove. Grandfather's house."

After what had happened, this made even less sense. I couldn't go to the Grove. Could I? If she was alive, what did it mean for the Trial? Why hadn't anyone told me? "OK, I'm coming. It will take a little time, but I'm coming."

Brighid kissed me on my forehead. She looked away, as if she was listening to someone unseen. She nodded, and looked sadly at me. "I have to leave."

"Why?"

Brighid said, "She says I need to leave, so you can heal. And so you don't get into any more trouble." She faded from view. Her voice echoed as she faded away.   "Come back to me."

I said to the air, "I'm coming."

"Which would be a foolish thing to do," Tsauriel said snidely from behind me.

The ruins of the library in the keep took form around me. I sat on top of a pile of debris. Not a shelf within sight was standing.

Books, scrolls, and anything which had been on the shelves lay on the floor. Ladon's wine rack had broken and the chess set was scattered on the floor. A breeze floated scraps in lazy circles through the large crack running up the side of the tower.

I smiled at Tsauriel. "House party, and I wasn't invited?"

Tsauriel scowled in return. "You seem to have upended everything. When you treat your body as a carnival instead of a temple, it means little to me or this place. But I will not tolerate you placing your true being in such jeopardy."

Exhaustion won out over my desire to argue. "Next time, I'll give you advance warning when someone is trying to vacuum out my soul. Maybe open the windows and clear out some of the dust in here?"

Tsauriel waved her hands in a fit of rage and flung me onto a crumbling pile of tomes. "You find this amusing? This isn't just about your short, pathetic existence in this form."

Less than gracefully, I managed to get up from the pile of debris. I mocked Tsauriel's accent. "No, I don't find it amusing." I crossed my arms. "I'm pretty much pissed off. You haven't told me anything of use, and you're the one along for the ride. Either help me or leave me alone. Even when Ladon is beating me half to death, I'm getting something out of it."

Tsauriel narrowed her eyes. "You think I've given you nothing? I've given you more than any mortal should ever know of the Divine."

I screamed and threw a broken clay vase at the wall. "The Sphinx speaks in fewer riddles. Talking to you is like playing Russian Roulette with the last guy finding out the gun wasn't

169

loaded. There isn't a mess, nothing gets done, and everyone is scared and relieved as hell when it's over."

Ladon began a slow clap as he leaned in the door frame. "Bravo. Finally a little drama." He sauntered into the room and placed an arm over my shoulder. "There is a spine in there after all."

Tsauriel turned her glare to Ladon and aimed a finger at his face. "You are tied to him just as much as I am. Maybe more." She fled the room in a fit and stormed down the stairs, a wave of furious energy in her wake.

Ladon chuckled as the door fell off of its hinges as she passed. He found an intact bottle of wine among the debris. He shook out and filled two glasses, and then handed me one. "A toast to your progress."

The red wine was strong and smoky. A couple of pieces of parchment floated on top. "What next?"

He flicked a toe at the debris of a shattered trunk, and stood a chair back up to take a seat. "Well, I expect this will take an eternity to straighten out, assuming you don't get us blown into oblivion. I'm actually quite impressed you survived the encounter with the blades."

I sipped the wine. "Luck, I think."

He folded his hands in his lap. "Luck can carry you only so far. And yes, it probably played a role. But wrapping the Leviskin around the dagger to hold it in place was inspired."

I shrugged. "Reflexes, I suppose."

A mischievous smile crossed his face. "I'll accept credit and your thanks for that. I'd say I'm in too good of a mood to continue to straighten up this mess. What do you say we spar with foils today?"

Ladon really was in a good mood. After a short period of sparring, he looked me over. "Greyson, you're still moving quite slowly and stiffly. Your physical injuries shouldn't affect you so here. I suggest you go and rest."

I wasn't going to argue with that.

THE SUN SHONE brightly through open curtains. The furball was curled up next to me soundly asleep. I scratched his head without opening my eyes. I stretched, hoping to go back to sleep. The alarm hadn't gone off.

A small, high voice whispered in my ear. "Psst. Hey, buddy. Time to wake up." I ignored it, hoping it was noise from the hall or another room. No such luck. A small poke in my cheek finished dragging me back to reality. "Hey, Mack. Wake up. I gots other places to be."

I cracked one eye. A pixie sat on top of the alarm clock on the nightstand. He was maybe a foot tall, with pale, golden skin. He wore a little postal uniform: a pair of brown shorts, a short-sleeved button up shirt, and a small cap reading "FaeMail." His name-tag called him "Tuck."

His name rhymed with the first curse which came to mind. "So, that's how it works?" No one I knew had ever seen a FaeMail delivered.

The little figure squeaked out in a thick accent, "Hey, buddy, I need ya to sign heah."

"Do you have a pen?"

He jumped to the bed and grabbed my thumb. A mouthful of razor-sharp needle teeth flashed and gently nicked my thumb, using my blood to stamp the receipt in one quick motion. "You been summoned by the Assembly. Good luck."

"Whoa. To be there when?"

The little fiend threw the scroll at me. "Now." A portal opened, sucking the furball and me into a dark room. The cold stone floor cut through my thin running shorts. The only light came from a faint glow tracing engravings on the walls and floor. I

172

couldn't be positive, but I had a pretty good bet where I was. I stretched my hand out until it hit the wall of an energy field which returned a slight shock.

I flipped a small fireball into the pitch black air for light. The inner chambers of the Coetum Artium surrounded me in thick stone 150 feet below the City Hall in Phoenix Grove. Thirteen concentric circles radiated out from my seat on the floor. Each circle admitted or prohibited specific energies and entities. I was trapped in the center of the dartboard of all magic, waiting for the first charge to be thrown.

MY MIND RACED to figure out why I was here so soon. I had a few more months before this was supposed to happen. Had they found something to clear me? Had they found something so damning that nothing I said or did would ever matter? Had Brighid done something?

Either way, I was trapped in the innermost chambers of the Assembly of Arts in Phoenix Grove. This group ruled and governed over any human with significant abilities, and was responsible for all treaties and agreements with other races. The Assembly of Phoenix Grove was also responsible for everyone in the Sanctuary.

A whispering wind blew through the chamber. Five barely perceptible figures stood away from the outer edge of the circle in the darkness, at the five cardinal points of the pentagram. Black robes confirmed this was a capital trial.

A deep voice boomed from the dark. "Greyson Merrick Forrester, you stand accused of offenses resulting in the death and injury of multiple parties, use of forbidden arts and practices, willful disclosure of the existence of the place of sanctuary of the refugees of the Veiled peoples, wanton public display of talents and abilities risking the health and welfare of all of the Veiled peoples, deliberate violation of the terms of your release, and various lesser charges. How do you plead?"

I trembled as the voice dragged me back to my youth. Nervousness welled up through me and threatened to spew forth in a very physical way. It could only be Reginald Maxwell Sinclair the Fourth, Mayor and Governor for Phoenix Grove. The High Counselor and wizard who put the Ass in Assembly.

Brighid's grandfather.

I managed to bolster a small amount of bravado as I got to my feet in the small space the field allowed me. "I wish to have a full reading of the charges."

A snort flew from the figure on my left.

Sinclair ignored my request. "How do you plead? Throw your guilt on the mercy of the court and you may pass to your final Trial quickly and painlessly."

I couldn't stop the furious chortle that erupted as an answer. I stood my ground and began to summon any power available to me. If I was going to be summarily executed, I'd go fighting. "I will not plead at all to any charges you refuse to read. I request my counsel."

Sinclair pounded the dais. "I'll take your statement as you are pleading not guilty. Trial will commence as soon as the Inquisitor arrives. We will recess until then."

"Where's my counsel? I want to speak to my grandfather." My voice echoed off of the unfeeling stone walls. The chamber had emptied. Falling to the floor, the furball jumped into my lap. "I told you following me was a bad idea."

A small snort came in reply.

I dissipated the fireball to save energy, and we sat in the dark.

HOURS CRAWLED PAST with nothing more than our breathing to disturb the silence. My best guess was that it was early evening when a faint shuffling echoed from several directions. Small constellations glowed dimly on the ceiling. Even with my Senses opened wide, nothing from past the barriers was open to me.

Taking it as a signal the proceedings were to begin, I rose and tried to look indignant. Or at least the best impersonation I could muster only wearing a pair of running shorts and with a sleeping dog at my feet.

The time in the dark had let me ready myself for the judgment I'd known was coming for years. My only reason to continue the fight was to save Drea, if I could. If they would only give me back the few months I still had left, I'd trade it for a sure sentence.

The five black-robed figures slipped back into their positions at the points of the star. A blinding light shone from above and filled the innermost ring where I was held.

Sinclair got on his pompous soapbox. "This Camera Stellata resumes in the hearing of Greyson Merrick Forrester as to the events pursuant to his personal involvement and actions stemming from the events of the 'Working of Salween,' and the subsequent breaches and violations of the agreed terms of release."

The Camera Stellata. They were going to try me under the rules of the old-fashioned Star Chamber. They were lined up to bury me, but still appear as if they had a farce of a legal proceeding. "I demand my counsel."

I struggled to breathe as a strong force came from an unseen hand. It drove me to one knee. I didn't have to see his face

176

to know he was gloating from behind his hood. "You shall speak only if spoken to, and when a response is demanded."

A soft but commanding voice called from behind me. Glancing over my shoulder, the tall and lean figure speaking wore the garnet robe of the Inquisitor. "The boy has requested counsel, to which he's afforded the right. Governor Sinclair, I am certain you of all members would not prohibit his legal rights."

Sinclair threw his hood back. Even in dim light, I could tell time had not been kind in the years since I'd last seen him. He still stood tall, broad, and strong, but I knew he had to be well over the century mark. His cropped white hairline had receded a little more and the crags in his face had etched a little deeper. He snapped at the Inquisitor. "The identity of the judges is intended to be anonymous. What do you mean by the affront?"

Pompous ass.

The voice snipped from under the red hood. "Reginald, I don't believe there is need for pretense. And no point in trying to hide the man behind the voice. My question stands." He leaned slightly forward and indifferently pointed to Sinclair. "Do *you* intend to deny him counsel?"

Sinclair stiffened at the accusation. "He's already been found guilty. The only question before this court is whether he should face the final Trial or if he's just to be put to justice."

The Inquisitor stifled a sad laugh. "If you have made your determination, then what's the harm in providing him his right? My advocate is available to provide him counsel."

"Have it your way. We will reconvene in two hours. See your advocate to the boy." The old man glanced at his watch. "A few more hours will make no difference."

Sinclair and the other four disappeared into the darkness. The Inquisitor faded into the shadows, but returned within moments, accompanied by a figure in a gray cloak.

The Inquisitor knelt at the outermost ring. A few details emerged from the shadows under his hood. Dark eyes hid in sunken recesses. His aquiline nose and thin mouth made him appear hawkish. Vestiges of a French accent carried in his speech. "I provide my advocate's services to you. Good luck."

He stood and turned to the advocate. "Tell our friend we're even." He disappeared into the darkness.

The figure in the gray cloak passed through the outer barriers to stop just outside of the one restraining me. He passed a couple of bottles of water and a bag with sandwiches through the barrier. He even had a small cup for the furball to have a drink.

"Who are you?"

The figure in gray raised the hood. Nicomedes stared back with a grim look. "When you dig a hole, you stop when it becomes a grave, not a tunnel to the Underworld."

"Nicky! What are you doing here?" A small surge of hope crawled from my toes.

His scowl deepened. "Can you please not refer to me by the pejorative? I'm here to see if there are any options which don't end with you being fed to a grue. Or worse."

"Who knows I'm here, and what's going on?"

Nicomedes shook his head. "No one. I was paged but an hour ago, and I'd to rush to chambers. If this doesn't go well, no one will ever know. A war cannot start over this, not even for you."

TIME RACED BY as Nicomedes rapid-fired questions at me and as quickly was snapping instructions after my responses. As if a silent alarm was tripped, Nicomedes stopped and stood. "I wish we had more time." He raised his hood and took a place outside of the circle.

Sinclair and the other four black robes phased into view. The Inquisitor took a place to the right of Sinclair. Nicomedes held the position on his left.

Sinclair nodded to the Inquisitor. "Are you satisfied? He's had counsel."

The Inquisitor simply responded, "Please proceed."

Nicomedes said, "Governor, we request a reading of the charges."

Sinclair nodded to one of the judges. "I've had them detailed for you. Feel free to read at your leisure." The judge handed a thick scroll to Nicomedes.

Sinclair rambled on about the importance of maintaining the Veil, the protection of the Veiled peoples, and how one may unknowingly risk it all. Nicomedes was speeding through the scroll quickly, but steadily.

Sinclair pointed to me. "This one of the Veiled peoples has been cursed. This curse led to the death of his family, and all of us here have lost due to that night. We gave him reprieve and an opportunity for redemption, and to clear his soul of this curse. Instead, he exposes us to powers which challenge our way of life and threaten to reveal us to the world. He bears the mark of a fallen one on his chest. What other question can there be? What other choice do we have?"

He was trying to finish the railroad job and lay all of it at my feet. I had to at least try the truth, or what I knew of it. "It has all been the Cult of Erebus, in a partnership with Winter Fae."

Sinclair drew back his hood to reveal a cruel smile. "We are aware of your fable. You revived an all but dead cult as the bogeyman, and then tried to say they are working with the Veiled peoples. A naive and impossible fable. Perhaps the big, bad werehamster will come and save you." He slammed his hand on the dais. "No, boy, you stirred up some fools who had a small amount of talent, and then exposed us to the outside world to destroy them, all in the name of your freedom. How many would you sacrifice? How many more innocents must die for you?"

Blood warmed the hands of my clenched fists. Power jumped back and forth between them, begging to be unleashed. "Is Brighid part of the conspiracy, too? Or did you send her to try to kill me a few days ago?"

Sinclair snarled. Sparks flew from my hands as the unseen force slammed me to the floor. "You are never to speak her name again."

He looked away from me to everyone in the room. "See? His lies finally betray themselves. We all know what remains of my granddaughter is up in the town."

He pointed a long finger at my face. "It is time for your judgment. I sentence you to be returned to the demons from whence you came."

The other four in black robes voted in assent.

The Inquisitor stepped in. "Counselor Sinclair, are you certain of your decision? You know my opinion—"

"You are here to observe and validate our proceedings. Do you feel there is some evidence to overturn our decision?" Sinclair snapped at the Inquisitor.

The Inquisitor raised his hands. "I full well believe in the execution of the guilty. I believe Mr. Forrester is a candidate for the Trial, and should be given a chance to prove himself, one way or another. If *he* so chooses."

Waves of energy came from Sinclair as he visibly seethed at the challenge.

A simple gesture came from underneath the Inquisitor's cloak, dissipating the charge.

Sinclair backed up ever so slightly, a battle of wills being fought invisibly. His nostrils flared, and he gave a subtle nod. "Fine. Advocate, you may offer him the choice. We will reconvene as soon as you are ready. Don't take long."

Nicomedes stood with his head bowed until the room cleared. He slowly made his way to just outside of the barrier and lifted away the hood. "I'm sorry, Greyson. You were close to a truth, I believe, but needed more time. I think Sinclair knew that, and he used the last few months as an excuse to expedite this mockery."

I took a deep breath. "So, what's this 'Trial'?"

Nicomedes folded himself into a cross-legged position across from me. "I cannot answer that, not exactly. I've attended only nine of these, but am aware of hundreds over the centuries. Many societies have had their own incarnation of the ritual. The outcome is nearly always one of two results: the person is either returned as less than human, in a state reflecting their true despicable being, and they are mercifully executed, or they are not returned at all. I am aware of only one person who returned intact, but they, too, were changed."

"And who is the one who came back?"

Nicomedes sat contemplatively. "The details are for another time, but let us say the individual was charged with various offenses and not given a choice about the Trial. He was gone for a little over two days. He reappeared dirty and bruised, but otherwise unhurt. But those who knew him well spoke of a distinct change. He was not exactly himself any more. I've never learned any details of the experience I could share with you."

I said, "And Plan B?"

Nicomedes smiled. "You cannot fight your way out of here. I am doubtful you could port out of here, even if you could get out of the protected circle. If you were to escape, it would not be for long. No, the best I can do is to make certain death is quick and painless."

"What would you do?"

Nicomedes looked at me ruefully. "I cannot make this decision for you. We have not always been in agreement, but I've never known you to lay down before a challenge, either."

"I ask two things. No matter what happens, help Drea. My research has led to knives known as the Anima Arca. Find the knife and the crystal, and she can be restored to her body. And can you take the furball? There are a couple of our friends who could give him a good home."

Nicomedes rose and nodded slowly. "I'll make every effort to help her, if you are unable. But as for your familiar, you two shall have to travel together. Good luck." He raised his hood and resumed his position. After a few moments, the rest of the group returned.

The Inquisitor asked, "Have you made a choice?"

I nodded. "I'll undergo your Trial. Give me your best shot."

Though his face was in shadow under the red hood, approval resonated in the Inquisitor's voice. Maybe it was anticipation for a greater torture. Maybe it was because he thought it gave me some chance. Either way, it was better than a quick death. "Prepare him for the ritual. Advocate, will you remain to assist your charge?"

Nicomedes nodded.

Sinclair's hood was drawn back. He scowled, deprived of his gratification. "Make sure to save some of whatever is left when he gets shipped back. Assuming anything is left."

"ARE YOU PREPARED?" This cry came from the darkness. The shift through the portal from one chamber to another had been nearly imperceptible.

"Whatever. Let's get started."

Blinding light shone down from nowhere to illuminate a stone staircase a few feet away. A voice crawled up the stairs. "Are you prepared?"

"Yes." Whatever that meant.

"Please make your descent." A subtle energy nudged me from behind. As the pressure increased, it threatened to funnel us down the hole.

"You ready, furball?"

It seemed I was the last one ready to begin my potentially final journey as he took the lead and trotted down the stone staircase. Not hearing any great disturbance, and being pressured by the invisible force, I followed the passageway. As soon as I safely passed the top of the stairs, stones flew into place and sealed the entrance.

After what seemed like a thousand steps through a luminescent, greenish haze barely bright enough to see a few feet in any direction, I stumbled when the staircase ended and my feet found a solid stone landing. The air was thick and warm and droplets gathered on the surrounding stones like an audience in an arena waiting for a play to start. Fifty feet in the dark distance, bright light shone in through a vaulted doorway. My only path was down the lone hallway towards the light as the stones had formed a ceiling where the staircase had been.

The furball seemed a little less inclined to lead the way now, and followed on my heels into the chamber.

184

The sole light shone over another staircase leading into a deep, clear pool. It looked like a lock awaiting a giant skeleton key. Twelve figures surrounded the edges of the pool in robes of various colors.

Three were readily identifiable.

The Inquisitor stood at one side to the entrance of the pool in his garnet robes. Nicomedes stood ready on the other.

My path was blocked by a large claymore held in a trembling hand. It was not the weight of the sword, but a glaring desire for a quicker end that made Sinclair's hand shake. His voice was strong. "What do you seek?"

"To see you tossed on your pompous ass." A skilled swing brought the hilt of the claymore directly into my solar plexus, and me to my knees.

The Inquisitor's voice telepathically drilled into my head to repeat exactly as instructed.

Doubled over and still struggling to breathe, I managed to blurt out, "I seek the truth and the verdict of the Trial."

Sinclair raised the sword and allowed me to pass. I heard him whisper, "Give the word, and I'll run you through now and save you the trouble."

I held my temper in check and was stopped a second time by the Inquisitor.   Loudly, he cried, "Are *you* prepared for your journey?"

Again, the voice in my head provided my response. "I am."

The Inquisitor asked, "And you do this of your own will?"

I tried to speak, but the Inquisitor's voice echoed in my head as he placed his hand on my shoulder. "You don't have to do this. Sinclair will happily send you on the final journey quickly."

I gently shook my head and whispered, "Screw him." I pushed myself to stand upright and defiantly said, "I do this of my own will."

The thin smile crept from under the shadow of the hood. "The choice has been made. May God have mercy on your soul."

Nicomedes stopped me at the edge of the pool. He cried to the surrounding audience, "Will any spare him this adversity?"

Silence echoed loudly from the walls.

Nicomedes pressed four golden coins into my hand. "One for the trip over, and one for the trip back. Two for each of you."

I whispered in return, "What do I do?"

Nicomedes kept his voice low, though every syllable clung to the air. "Enter the mikveh. The waters will do the rest. Bon voyage, and good luck."

The Inquisitor called to the surrounding audience. "This soul has been found willful and deserving of the Trial. Should he be returned to us, none shall ever challenge him again concerning his worth in these matters. Should he perish or be found wanting, may God have mercy on him, for we have not." He turned to face me. "The accused shall enter the pool."

The furball pulled in close to my chest in my arms. I whispered to him, "I told you to find a better home." A small sneeze was all that came in reply.

More than just the cold jolted me as my foot entered the waters. It was as if my very life force was being pulled from me. I knew I'd crossed into the world between life and death. Limbo. And it was a lot less pleasant this time.

I lost my focus as a commotion rose behind me. "No, Reginald!"

I turned to see who had shouted, but was stopped by a cold burning slicing across my shoulder. My last image as I toppled into the welcoming waters was Sinclair's blade dripping a thin trail of my blood and a look of horror on Delacroix's face. A strong undertow ripped me away from the material world.

Spirits swam around me and beckoned me into the deep. Strong, cold hands pulled me into a tempest of darkness. It took every ounce of strength and focus not to open my arms and lose the furball, and myself. By focusing on him, I drowned out the cries and calls of whatever damned spirits surrounded me. I nearly gave myself over when small claws dug into my bare flesh.

The water under me churned and the claws released me. Something large swept through the waters and devoured several of the creatures around me. The rest disappeared in a panicked shriek. We were floating alone.

The waters around me stilled, though an occasional brush from something in the darkness sent chills and revulsion though my spine. Dark thoughts crept in as I stifled my building need for air. Small bubbles floated away. Voices murmured on the edge of my slipping consciousness, begging me to let go to join them and welcome my reward. I wanted to give in. I deserved whatever was coming to me.

They say drowning isn't a bad way to die. My body began to spasm. My vision narrowed and I felt myself blacking out. My body would soon leave me no choice. One large inhalation of....

COOL AIR OVERWHELMED me as I broke the surface near a rocky shore. The furball was firmly clutched in my arms. We spluttered for air, and I used one arm to paddle until I found footing on the slimy bottom. Something urged me to exit the waters as quickly as possible. The furball thudded to the ground and we collapsed on a rocky shore as pale hands beckoned from the waters to return to them. I quickly crawled back to be out of reach of whatever pitied beings were still there.

It felt like I was standing over my body, watching myself collapse on the shore. My body convulsed and expelled the water I'd inhaled on the trip to the surface. The nicks and cuts from the trip sealed up now that I was out of the water. The gash from the claymore stung, but looked worse than it was. I leaned over and touched the wound, and was instantly cold and racked with pain.

I needed to move. The cool ground sucked at the little heat I had left in my shivering body. I picked myself up and studied my surroundings.

The rocky beach ended in the water a hundred feet or so to my left, and a short pier stretched out fifty feet or so to my right. A solid wall stretched for as far as I could see behind me, up into a gray mist for a sky. Oil lanterns set at the shoreline glowed coldly every hundred feet. Torches lined the pier.

My clothes had been shredded in the trip, but the coins still clinked safely in my pocket. Payment for the ferryman. I'd come up in the river Styx.

Gentle waves broke on the rotting pier. It groaned and rocked with each step. When was the last time some poor fool had made this trip?

Despite corrosion, the small bell rang soundly when I pulled the decaying rope. Oars creaked and slapped at the water

189

somewhere in the mist. A small light attached to the bow of a longboat broke through the gloom 300 feet from shore.

I nearly leapt into the water when a hand tapped me. A high, childlike voice spoke. "Follow me, if you really want to meet your destiny."

The small girl I'd rescued in Purgatory stood behind me, dressed in a white tunic and carrying a small lantern blazing with light. She extended a small hand which I took into mine.

The ferry turned away, disappearing into the mist. With a final look back, I stepped from the pier.

The girl hummed as she skipped up the rocky shoreline. Gradually, the beach became more smooth and sandy.

"What's your name?"

She cocked her head as she replied, "Why does it matter?"

"I'm, uh…making conversation?"

She replied with a cheery smile at my discomfort. "Call me Gabby, then."

"Hi, Gabby, I'm—"

Gabby cut me off. "Yes, I know who you are. It's why I'm here."

"Why are you here?"

"To guide you."

"Where… where are we going?" The wall and shoreline rapidly fell away and melted into a llano. We followed the center path when others broke off in several directions.

"Where you are supposed to be." She raised her eyebrow and looked as if it were the only possible answer.

We followed the line of torches for what seemed like hours as Gabby gleefully skipped along and hummed a nonsensical tune. Finally, we intersected with several other paths into a sort of hub. After seeming to study an invisible signpost, she picked a wandering path which ended at a small grotto carved into a solid wall. A mosaic of pottery sherds covered in runes covered the archway.

Gabby said, "This will do." She turned me towards her and pulled me down to her eye level. "Thank you for helping me. I hope this finds you well, and returns the favor in kind."

Was everyone on this side of the Veil stripped of their minds? Did they lose them immediately, or was it stripped away over time? "What do I do now?"

She released my hand and touched the wall at the back of the center of the arch. The rock face shifted into a shimmering mirror. "Just step through."

"Where does it lead?" A distorted reflection of myself stared back. "And are you coming with us?"

"No, my task has ended. May fortune follow you in your journey." With strength I would have thought impossible, she gave me a small tap launching the furball and me into the portal.

WE WERE TWISTED and dumped out unceremoniously into a sea of grass at twilight. The trip through the portal had cost me my remaining shoe. Our escort was nowhere in sight. The grass was nearly head high and swayed like kelp on the seabed. The furball sniffed around and gave me an unhappy look.

"Pick a direction."

We wandered up to the top of a tall hill. From there, I knew where we were.

Purgatory.

Brother Ephrayim's mesa was a small silhouette in the far distance. One of the cities of light looked fairly close, but in the opposite direction. I had no desire to take on the Reavers while hungry, nearly naked, and exhausted.

Something paced us for the first few hours as we hiked through the plains, but it felt like curiosity, not a hunt. At least not yet. An occasional crack of thunder rolled across the plains from the north. What kind of storms might the boiling skies dump on the plains?

I collapsed into a puddle when we safely reached the outer wall of the city as night fell. It was not so much a wall as a barrier of soothing, healing light.

The furball nudged me to get up. A few hundred feet in, the light dimmed and a small city took shape. Busy but calm streets cut through a bustling open air market and ran into blocks of two- and three-story, adobe-style apartments.

The tattered remnants of my clothes stood out against in the local garb of simple robes or tunics. Animated merchants and customers were in the process of cheerfully haggling.

"Toto, we're definitely not in Kansas any more. Or LA, for that matter."

I took the small snort to mean he wasn't real fond of being called Toto.

An older-looking gentleman pulled himself away from the platform of a short watchtower and came to greet us. He was short and a little plump with a head of wispy, gray hair. He looked like he was probably ninety. Or nine hundred ninety.

He smiled broadly and said, "Hi. I'm Walter Schuler. Welcome to our little town of Megiddo."

He shot out a strong, stubby hand.

"Hi, I'm Grey, and this is the furball."

Walter scratched his head. "We don't see too many of those around here. Usually they go straight up, or straight down." His laugh was friendly and genuine. "It must be his association with you."

"You don't know the half of it. I told him following me was a bad idea."

The old man said, "I'm sort of the welcoming committee. I was a Sprawl Mart greeter and got taken out in a tragic accident involving incoming buggies from the parking lot, some cheerleaders doing a fundraiser for the high school, and a poorly timed slushy fight. But I enjoyed the job so I became the defacto greeter here a while back. You seem new to town. Looking for a place to burn off a few of those sinful deeds? I feel sure we can find you room." He looked me over. "And some clothes, if nothing else."

193

"Thanks, Walter. I think I'm just passing through, but I'll let you know if that changes."

He shrugged. "Feel free to come on in, and let me know if you change your mind. Either way, I'd suggest you stay until dawn to keep away from the critters in the shadows out there. They hunt for fresh and purer souls. You'd be the catch of the day."

"Thanks for the help, Walter. I'll check in, if I'm leaving or staying."

He responded with a friendly wave.

The small, stone-paved streets reached inwards from the market. We passed artisans working on their talents, and others in small groups in conversation. But I saw no clue as to why we were here. What was I supposed to do?

Our new friend Walter found us sitting next to a fountain in a small plaza. He'd gotten off duty and was on his way home. After a short chat, he invited us to stay with him for the night. He guided us through a maze of side streets and winding, tightly bound complexes leading me to believe Dr. Seuss was the city planner.

We entered a three-story complex nearly identical to the others in the city. Walter opened the door to a three-room apartment with a small bedroom, kitchen, and den.

"It's humble, but it's home."

"How do things work around here?"

Walter shrugged. "Souls come, souls go. We try to work out and exorcise our sins. I like to cook, so I've a kitchen. None of us need to eat, but it's habit. And it gives me pleasure, as you can tell." He patted his little round belly. "People work, meditate, pray.

Sometimes they find their way to the next level, whatever it may be."

"And you?"

"I haven't been here too long. So far, I'm here alone, but I hope my wife, Matilda, will find me eventually. But she was an angel to put up with an old codger like me. She might find a better deal."

"That's why you're working the gate."

"Guilty. At least in part. It's rewarding, too. Reminds me a little of life on the other side."

"And what about the people in the fields with the lamps?"

"You know about that already." Walter nodded, a little more sadly. "Some feel called to carry the light out into the darkness to try to give them hope. But some of the creatures out there are... well, I don't know what to call them. It's like they're the opposite of us. I can't say alive, or dead, or undead. They are the spirits of the lost, I guess. It seems there are a lot more of them coming here these days than not."

"Does it work?"

He hung his head. "Sometimes. We see a few called up and freed for whatever's next." He tapped his foot nervously. "Can I ask you something? I mean here, personal questions are part of our healing. But...."

I couldn't imagine what would make the greeter so uneasy. "Ask away."

"You aren't dead, are you? You're still living?"

What did it mean if I was? And was I still alive? "It's kind of hard to explain. I'm not entirely sure myself, but no, I don't think the mutt and I are dead yet on the other side, if that's what you mean."

Walter nodded knowingly. "You walked in through the light. Good enough for me. But if you still have time on the other side, you had better find a way to take it."

"So, does this happen often? The living come for a sightseeing tour?"

Walter snorted. "Nah. I mean, every once in a while we get someone for a moment. If they died on the other side and get revived, they go back. But you're different. You have a job to do here. Something holding you here, if I had to guess."

"Any idea what the job is, or could be?"

Walter rubbed his forehead, deep in thought. "Well, if you're here, it's for a reason. And the only reason anyone ever comes here is either to let go of something they did, or to learn something they were too dense to get on the other side. I'd guess the first one."

"I don't know. I can be pretty dense sometimes."

Walter chuckled. "Aren't we all?"

THE NIGHT FLOWED by like a lazy river as Walter and I talked as if we were old friends. He cooked, and I ate voraciously. As the glow of morning rose, he led me to the outer gates. Something he'd said stuck in my mind. I had to figure out what I needed to do on this side. Was this the Trial? Had the girl led me away from what was to have been my destiny, my fate? Had I already failed?

I couldn't burden my host with those kinds of questions, and I doubted he would have any more of an idea than what he'd already told me. Walter suggested I go to the larger city of Damascus and consult with some of the scholars there. He assured me the furball and I could easily make it before dark.

The road was much wider and better travelled than the path I'd come in on. Foot traffic thinned to a trickle by mid-day on the road as the city retreated in the distance. The ever-present mesa of Qumran loomed in the distance. I could almost feel Brother Ephrayim as he watched over his flock of the dead.

Slivers of gold cut through the pink and red clouds dominating the calmer skies. It was bright enough to keep the shadows in the caves lining the hills. Thunder rolled and sent shock waves through the grasslands.

"How did you get here?"

I jumped and spun around at the familiar voice, but not to the sight I expected. The angel stood a little over 12 feet tall, and his folded wings gave him another foot or two. He glowed brightly as he shrank to his normal size. I suspected it was so he could fit into his more comfortable shorts and Hawaiian shirt.

"Hi, Melvin."

The frenetic angel ran over and threw his arms around me, stepped back, and repeated this a few more times.

"Dude, I've been... You're a hard one to find. You're not supposed to be here."

Melvin was making even less sense than usual. "Slow down. And it's great to see you."

"I've been trying to search for you for weeks, man. I only found you when you stepped out of the city, and I didn't even find you then. I found him." Melvin pointed at the furball who had curled up into a tiny ball. "How'd you wind up here?"

"The Trial. I was..."

Melvin materialized a large wooden trunk covered in runes, and dumped it over spilling a pile of scrolls. After reading each one, he tossed them into a new pile on the ground. It only took a few seconds before he shouted, "Impossible! None of the prophecies saw this. You aren't supposed to be *here*. You shouldn't be dead yet."

"Melvin, I'm not... wait, I'm dead?"

"How else would you be here?" Melvin pulled out a headset which had lenses flying in every direction. Rapidly, he changed them until he found a combination he liked. "Well, that's not possible either."

"Melvin..."

He began to glow again and transformed into the huge angelic form. "We're getting you out of here. Grab the mutt."

I picked up the pooch, and Melvin placed one hand on my shoulder. He began to sing in a voice at the edge of my hearing, and the world around us brightened for a moment before returning to normal. Without warning, his huge wings enclosed us, and the pure white light blinded me. An unseen choir broke out in etheric song. When the wings unfurled, he dropped me in the dusty road.

"Melvin, do you want to explain…"

Melvin shrank back down to his normal human facade. He placed his hands on my shoulders, his face serious. "I can't get you out."

"What?"

"Whoever." Melvin dug in his bag and pulled out the headset again. "Whatever did this, they put a lot of power behind it. I can't break it. I'm not even sure what *it* is."

"Can you at least tell me what I'm supposed to do?"

Melvin shrugged. "These prophesies are useless." He shot a small bolt, incinerating the pile of scrolls. "The worst case scenario was that you were supposed to cross the river Styx and…well, anyway, your odds there were pretty low, but you had a reasonable shot. Here? What's coming here is beyond even me."

He paced in the road. I'd never seen him this nervous. It couldn't be good for me. "What aren't you telling me?"

"Dude, all I can tell you is this place disappears. Falls totally off the map of the universe. And none of the prophesies even give us a clue about how, or why. It's impressive really." Melvin could always appreciate destruction. "This wasn't the Trial. We had a plan…"

""Who's we? Got anything that might help?"

The pile of items on the ground around the angel grew as he rifled through his bag. "I don't have much." Melvin found a package and smiled before tossing it to me.

It was one of my Leviskin kits, including a pair of shoes. Things were looking up.

While I discarded the remains of my clothes and dressed in the skinsuit, Melvin tossed a ball of oilcloth on the ground.

"It might help, but I don't know. I don't have much else for you."

"Thanks, Melvin." The oilcloth held a small collection of silver knives. From the power coming off of them, they were all blessed. In a few minutes, they each found a home on my person. "Any ideas on how I survive the Trial? Get out of here?"

Melvin shrugged. "Put on your big boy panties. I think this is going to be a ride."

DAMASCUS QUICKLY GREW on the horizon. We passed through the outer barrier as afternoon shadows grew longer. This was much more of a bustling metropolis than Megiddo, and magnitudes larger. Overall, the buildings were much the same two- and three-story adobe apartments, but the souls here appeared younger overall.

The light had a brighter and warmer quality that was hard to describe. The energy of the city grew as what passed for night settled in. A large crowd surrounded a hundred children in ultra-bright white tunics. None of them looked to be even in their teens. One by one, they walked to a well and a small globe of white light filled the lamp in their hands with a bright orb.

Voices sang out from around the circle, and they continued to sing as the group moved as one into the darkness. Gradually, the kids scattered in different directions until they were spread through the fields.

I was fascinated and horrified to watch as, one by one, there was a flash and a light disappeared. A few were blue-white, but more often, they were an angry red. It seemed like hours, but the crowd waited until the last light disappeared and its light blue flash dissipated.

I fell to the ground, wondering what I'd just seen. A small tug on my arm drew my attention. A boy of nine or ten smiled at me expectantly. "May I pet your dog?"

"Sure."

The two of them played for a few minutes, and the boy took my hand again. "Please, come with me, Greyson."

I asked, "Who are you?"

As an answer, the boy trotted through the crowd. "Keep up."

My longer legs helped me to pace him easily as he scampered through the crowd. I almost lost him when he darted into a building, but the furball stayed on his trail. The boy opened the door to a small apartment. Twelve pounds of fury jumped up next to the boy on a small bed looking for attention. He pointed to an adult-sized chair and said, "Have a seat."

The wooden chair was welcoming after the day-long trek. "Who are you? And how do you know who I am?"

The boy laughed in a familiar way. "Don't you recognize me?" He transformed into an older form. My father from when I was a teenager.

I jumped up and threw my arms around him. "Dad?" He returned the gesture and wrapped his long arms around me.

He stepped back and spun around. "Robert H. Forrester, at your service. I guess I've been gone longer than I thought. You have grown to be a good man, at least as much as I have been able to watch."

I shrugged. "Well, I'm here. Is mom around too?"

He looked away and shook his head. "I haven't seen her on this side. Others yes, but not her. I haven't sensed anything from her since I arrived here." He swallowed. "She has passed from your side?"

I struggled with what to say. With what I'd seen on the outside, it was possible she'd been swept away by the Soul Reavers. Or worse. "I don't really know. I still don't know what happened when we were all taken, or during the rescue. From what I know, some were saved, but a lot of the people there were killed or vanished. Both the ones who took us and our people. I lost everyone, except Josiah."

The figure of my father shrunk again into a child. Tears welled in his eyes and his body began to shake. I sat next to him on the small bed and put my arm around his shoulders. "Why don't you tell me about this place?"

HOURS ROLLED BY as we caught up, but I was having a hard time calling a ten-year-old kid "Dad." He seemed a little uncomfortable about it too. Everyone called him Bobby, so why should I be any different?

His small apartment was a lot like Walter's, but more sparse. There wasn't much in the way of personal items in the place, which seemed to be consistent with the few houses I'd visited in Purgatory. The theme of life here seemed to be basic and simple, but comfortable.

Bobby decided it was easier to show me than to try and explain about existence here. A little before sunrise, we climbed a circular staircase to the top of a stone spire. It emptied onto an observation platform reaching out several hundred feet above the city. A few dozen people were scattered about, sitting on wooden benches or standing around the railing.

We selected an open bench and looked out over the horizon. More pockets of light from other cities dotted across the landscape. I managed to pick out Megiddo in the distance. The mesa of Qumran loomed impossibly large as the sun rose into the boiling red and yellow sky.

Offhandedly, I wondered what the mad monk was doing on his hill.

"There are millions of souls here. Most shed the essence from their mortal lives when they come to Damascus, and are in their final preparations. That doesn't mean we aren't keeping an eye on our loved ones still on the other side."

"How does it work?"

Bobby shrugged. "I'm not entirely sure what you can perceive, since you are still a mortal being, but it's pretty limited.

204

For us, we can see and feel what we focus on, whether it is a memory of ours, or just checking on our old home. By focusing on our lives, we can understand what we did, and why. Both the good and bad. Once we accept our actions, we are able to unburden ourselves. It's not the actions we take, but the intent and results we have to live with. Only here are we able to truly know how our actions affect others."

I said, "Consequences."

He nodded vigorously. "We don't lose or forget anything, but we are able to accept and integrate it within ourselves. As we shed our burdens, our appearance gets younger to reflect our core selves. Ultimately, we strive to regain our innocence. We are born in sterile bodies into a sterile environment. Everything we do leaves a mark on our bodies, and our souls. Those scars must be healed for us to move on."

The burdens of my decisions as of late weighed heavily on me. How I could heal myself if I couldn't rescue Drea? I couldn't let it go. And I could only imagine the memories locked and hidden away from me. "Would I be able to experience it now? While I'm here and alive?"

I saw hints of my father in the way he leaned back on the bench, apparently deep in thought. "I'm not sure how it would work for you. I can't tell you how it works for me. But there is something we can try."

Bobby jumped up and ran down the staircase. Did he run everywhere?

We entered a labyrinth of crumbling walls and streets at the center of the city. Long runs folded onto switchbacks. We were able to cut through the occasional breach to shorten the distance.

The innermost wall was thick and ancient, covered in a thick coat of dead vines. Power radiated from a tall archway.

"The old city. Come on." He pushed through the gateway.

It was like walking through honey. Heavy and sweet, but every step was slow. I tripped and spilled onto the street when the resistance gave way. The eerie resonance of Gregorian chanting flowed like a river in the air.

We stopped outside of one of the many small compounds inside the wall. Bobby rapped on a wooden door with a cast iron knocker. An old, hunched figure in dirty brown robes opened the door and waved us through. He guided us on a path through a rose garden labyrinth to the front door of a stone chapel.

A withered man with a distended stomach in the tattered rags of a robe slowly hobbled towards us with a gnarled cane clutched in his hand. "Welcome. I am Abbot Wallace."

Bobby prodded me on. What could this old man do for me in this shape? "Abbot, my apologies for the disturbance."

"All are welcome here. We exist to serve." The abbot led us to a modest garden next to the church and seated himself on the grass. Bobby and I sat across from him.

"I'm not sure where to start. Is there a way for someone not yet dead to open themselves, and see the history of their lives? Bobby says that souls here can see and know the truth of their actions."

"If you aren't dead, why are you here?"

"I'm working on getting back to the other side, but I need information. I need to know what happened on one particular night."

206

The abbot's smile showed the few yellow and black teeth still in his head. "I can see deep into you, son. I see the mark of the Trial. You are a sorcerer."

I nodded. Bobby's eyes grew wide, but he didn't make a sound.

"Yes, I am a practitioner. I don't know how or why I'm here. But I am on trial for a night I don't remember, and from which my memories have been locked away."

The abbot's stale breath reeked as he leaned towards me. "I am not here to judge. My brothers and I, we are all sin eaters who weren't cleansed in death. We bear the burdens of more lifetimes than were ours, or we can ever purge. We are doomed to be here until the end of all days. We can see the stains on a soul, like tar dripping from a torch. But for you, I can only see the surface. Your soul is hidden from me. Maybe it is because you have not been entirely freed from the mortal coil. Maybe it is something else."

"Can you help me or not?" A few other wretched figures edged closer to the conversation.

The abbot shifted positions and put weight on his staff. "If you can help me up, then we can give it a try."

I pulled the abbot to his feet with little effort. Slowly, he shuffled into the chapel.

"Abbot, what do you normally do around here?"

The old man took a deep breath as he struggled up the few short steps. He turned to me and said, "Our little Order keeps working to help troubled souls free themselves of their burdens. Let's see what we can do for you."

We took a seat on one of a handful of distressed wooden pews lining both sides of the aisle. It looked like it could hold twenty, at most. We passed a stone altar and moved into a small apse with a baptismal font in the floor. A glowing orb sat in the bottom of the pool.

Another monk knelt next to a middle-aged man. They spoke in reverent, hushed tones. I wasn't sure what to expect as we watched the proceedings.

Apprehensively, the man stepped into the waters and immersed himself. The light grew into a blue-white intensity until it ended in a bright flash.

A few minutes later, the man crawled out of the font onto the floor nearby. The monk began a chant as the soaked figure convulsed and coughed up foam. The convulsions became violent as the man flopped around on the floor. Instead of running to help, the monk backed away.

"What's happening? Why isn't he…?"

The seizure stopped and the body froze in an awkward, contorted position, his face locked in a silent scream.

The abbot bowed his head. "There was too little left in him."

The body darkened and collapsed until it became a large puddle of a black, oily substance. The monk began the pitiable process of mopping up the remains.

"What's that?"

The monk threw the towel and the mass into a large wooden bucket. "These waters can draw out the accumulated weight from your soul. Sins, if you wish to think of it that way, but it's not the most accurate description. Every decision we make adds to who we are. Both the mortal coil and the immortal soul. Some of what's added gives us strength, and the ability to go forward and help those around us. I think of the other as burdens, the negativity weighing us down. It creates a barrier around our soul, until nothing good can get in or out. These waters can wash some of it away, and it comes out as the black oil." The abbot watched the monk carry the bucket away. "Sometimes, it is all that is left."

The abbot rose and stood next to the waters. "The waters may be able to help you, if you wish to try. I am unaware if a living soul has attempted this, though."

Was this the Trial? The reason I'd been sent to Purgatory? If not, I hoped it might reveal something to me. "I'll give it a shot."

"Are you certain?" The abbot gazed into the glowing waters. "This is not without its risks."

I stared into the bottom of the pool. The waters cast a calming invitation. I hoped it was a good sign and not a siren calling me to the rocks. "I hear black goo is the new look for the season."

The abbot nodded and placed his hand on my back and said, "When you are ready, step into the waters."

The abbot began a nearly imperceptible chant. Moisture dripped from the walls. The welcoming glow from the shimmering waters brightened.

I couldn't be sure what scared me more. The ritual would help me get answers or it wouldn't give them up to me. Becoming a bubbling tar pit came in a distant third. Somehow, I doubted I'd know if it happened.

I gently placed one foot in the font. The water was cool and sent a pleasant shiver through my body. Step by step, I went in until I was waist deep. I took a last deep breath and stepped forward.

There was nothing but the glowing orb and me.

TIME LOST MEANING.

Brighid plunged a knife into my side.

Drake ripped the dark blade from Drea's back, and she started to fall.

I slashed a Fomorian warrior's arm off and shot another.

A werewolf crashed into me, knocking me to the ground, and then ripped open a soldier's chest next to me.

Drea, trying to coach a much younger version of myself on how to use a knife.

A cell. No, a cage. Being strapped down. Chanting. Power building in me.

A hooded face. Who are you?

A crash at the door.

A scream.

My mother reached out and touched my face. I couldn't move. Her eyes. What was in her eyes? "It will be OK. Just breathe. We're getting you out of here."

A bright flash.

I rose rapidly to the edge of the font. Cold stone met me. I struggled to crawl out of the pool and onto the floor.

I curled up in a fetal position.

In the distance, I head the abbot. "Stay here. We must wait."

A fire burned in my lungs. Something bubbled in my stomach and fought to escape.

Urgently and violently, I expelled the black ooze and water which had filled me.

Aftershocks touched all of my senses, but nothing I could grasp or hold onto. Sights, sounds, and smells teased my memories. They swam near, but floated away as I reached for them.

Finally, I was just overwhelmed and drained. I was cold and soaked, and lay on the floor shivering.

I must have passed out. I jerked awake at the abbot's voice and gentle touch. "Did you find what you were seeking?" He handed me a cup.

I leaned against the wall. Cool water soothed me as it ran down my throat in sips. "Nothing… nothing I can make sense of."

The abbot nodded with understanding. "It looks like the waters drew out a great weight from you." He took a towel and began mopping up the black mess, which had begun to congeal.

"So, what next?"

The abbot shook his head. "It is for you to decide. We have done what we can. Removing the blockages and guilt should allow the memories and experience to come back to you in a way you can process, but it may take some time. The memories will return, once you are ready to deal with them. Be prepared. You may also find this will open other… insights."

The abbot rose easily and offered me a powerful hand to help me stand.

I said, "You seem a little spryer."

The abbot smiled. "We gain a little strength from helping those in need, but mostly, it lets us know who is deserving if we show our weakness."

"Sneaky bastard."

The abbot laughed. "I lived in a small village in England a long time ago. We were very poor, and I was from a family of thieves. Soldiers of the king raided our village and killed everyone they suspected of having been involved in stealing from the wealthy who travelled a nearby road. My entire family was slain, as were all but a few old and sick, who were left as a message. I was a youth and lay dying. A local monk rescued me and took me to his home. In exchange for saving my life, he raised me to become one of his Order. He was from a line of sin eaters, and was the last in his family. He passed the ability to me, and I took on all of the burdens of his line when he died, along with countless others. When the king lay dying, I was brought in to take on his many sins. Instead of slicing the bread, I drove my knife into his heart to send him to Hell with his sins intact. The guards ran me through on the spot, before I could pass on the ability and all of the accumulated weight of countless lifetimes. So I consider the title an honor. And I continue my work here."

The abbot picked up the bucket and shuffled out the door. "Come along."

"Thank you. For everything. What will you do with that?" I pointed to the bucket.

"Tonight, my brothers and I will dip our bread into it and consume your burdens, to add them to our own. It is our way." The abbot pointed me to the back exit and vanished through a side door.

WHERE WAS I? Bobby sat on the corner of his small bed, staring at me. I barely remembered him half-dragging me through the streets back to his apartment. Wisps of dreams and nightmares disappeared from the fringes of my consciousness as I returned to reality. Whatever it meant. "How long have I been asleep?"

"Time is a little different here, but a few days. I tried to wake you a couple of times, but Abbot Wallace said you could be out for a while, and would rouse when you were ready."

It felt more like I'd been run over by a steamroller driven by a hellhound. A loud crack of thunder was followed a few seconds later by an earthquake that nearly threw me from the bed. "What just happened?"

"The Call." It dawned on me that Bobby was dressed in a thin, white tunic.

"What's this? The Call?"

Bobby shifted back into the form of my father as I remembered him, not many years older than I was. "I'd hoped we would have more time together, but tonight is another mission to the wilderness. It's time for me to take my turn as an emissary, and to try to beat back the approaching darkness."

I shivered. "You can't. I've seen what's out there. You'll... I still have questions. I can't lose you again like this."

He put his arms around me. "Sometimes, you don't get to choose. You just have to be ready when you are called upon. I failed you once. We all did. Now I have a chance to help many others. Come with me. See us off."

I nodded, not sure what to say. I tried to justify it in my head, but couldn't. I even considered trying to restrain him, but I was quickly learning karma is a cold-hearted creature. "You never failed me."

Bobby shifted, again a small boy in a white tunic. Slowly, he shook his head and smiled. He picked up a papyrus scroll held by a thin, linen ribbon. "Let's go."

The furball stayed on Bobby's heels as we funneled through the busy streets. Mardi Gras was a small parade in comparison to this atmosphere of celebration, just with less clothes and more alcohol. Banners and streamers surrounded a large amphitheater on the edge of the wilderness. Bobby stopped me and said, "You can watch from up there. I must join the rest of the emissaries." He leaned over and scratched the hound's head. "You take care of him." I wasn't sure which one of us Bobby was speaking to as he vanished into the crowd.

We moved to get a better view from the tiers of seats in the amphitheater, although no one was sitting yet. I opened my Sight to look around. An uncountable number of souls stood around and watched, even though I hadn't been able to perceive them. I also got a better sense that everything was a reality built by the perceptions of the souls gathered here rather than a real place. Most of the buildings took on an ethereal look and feel.

A young girl walked onto the platform, carrying one of the wooden lantern frames. "Greetings to all of my fellow emissaries and guests. We have prepared ourselves and rejoice today as we go forth to carry the light into the darkness." Cheers rose from all around the arena. A quick count gave me over four hundred emissaries gathered below. "We have welcomed our brethren from the cities of Cadasa and Danos, which have fallen in recent weeks. Though the darkness now approaches our gates, we shall remain a beacon of the light and a safe haven for any who choose to seek it, and turn the darkness back to from whence it came."

215

The young girl placed her scroll into the wooden lantern and held it to the pillar in front of her. The scroll burst into a small sphere of pure, white light. A joyous hymn erupted around us while, one by one, all of the emissaries gathered in the crowd below followed suit and took the etheric energy into the lanterns.

A rough hand with a gentle touch landed on my shoulder. Abbot Wallace stood at my side and stared at the proceedings below.

"What's happening?"

The abbot hung his head. "The darkness gains strength every day. It has managed to do what we thought impossible. First, the brilliant days and starry nights became cloudy. Distant thunder began to roll over the hills. The skies of fire took hold, and we fell into perpetual twilight. Some time ago, the thunder was followed by the great shaking of the ground and air. Now, a cloud of darkness has consumed two of the cities of light. Many of the souls in those two cities escaped, but not all. And now, it is a matter of time for us. The beasts in the field take more souls every day before they reach the safety of the cities. These emissaries will carry light into the darkness, to try to turn as many lost souls to the light as they can and delay the conquering darkness."

I grabbed the abbot by the shoulders and turned him to face me. "You're sending them out to die? They are going to try and fight what I've seen out there with a light bulb? I've seen what happens."

The abbot refused to look me in the eye. He said, "You know, do you? Can you tell me, then? We are all dead already. I can't tell you what the next step is from here. But yes, they are sacrificing themselves so others can be saved. The light is all we have. If we can save a few in the process…"

The singing increased in intensity while two large gates at the back of the amphitheater creaked open.

"Whose idea was this?"

"The caretaker." The sin eater pointed to the mesa of Qumran in the distance.

Children poured out of the gates into the fields.

"Brother Ephrayim? He's behind this?" Was it possible the crazed monk was responsible? At a bare minimum, he was guilty of omission, if not commission.

The abbot looked up with a hopeful, dazed smile. "You know of him?" Didn't these innocent souls know that it was a myth that lemmings ran off the cliff? Bastard. I wondered for a brief moment if Fr. Mike knew. The last few emissaries lined up to parade into the wilds. If no one was willing to come down from the precipice to help these well-intentioned kids from paving the road to hell, I'd do what I could. Even if it was the last thing I did alive.

A tornado-like, howling cry rolled in as the doors began to close.

I looked at the furball. "Are you up for this?"

He dove with a snort over the rail into the floor below and followed Bobby's trail.

Abbot Wallace grabbed my shoulder. "You can't join them. You haven't been prepared!"

I slapped his hand away and jumped the twenty feet to the arena. I brushed through the doors as they closed and found myself in the fields without a plan.

A few hundred souls stopped and stared at me as the rest wandered into the fields, armed only with a small sphere of light each.

Bobby approached, his face furrowed in a quizzical frown. "Why did you come? You don't even have the light with you."

I shook my head. "I brought my own." From the recesses of my mind, an incantation long forgotten formed in my mind. My hands warmed, and I drew a series of sigils in the air. A ring of white fire circled around the few hundred souls who stood nearby. "Which way are we going?"

Bobby said, "We all choose our own path, but most of us have agreed to go to the coming darkness, to turn it from the city."

"Hello, I'm Emily." The small girl from the stage tugged on my sleeve. She seemed even younger and smaller as I loomed over her. "What are you doing? We must carry out our charge. "

Hundreds of beatific faces stared at me. I couldn't decide if it was *Land of the Lost* or *Children of the Corn*. Either way, I knew I wasn't going to change their minds. I doubted it was possible. "Emily, let me escort you to the darkness, where you can do the most good." If nothing else, I could get a look at what they faced, and try to come up with a plan on the way.

The answer seemed to suit the defacto leader. She gave me an innocent smile. "Very well, and thank you."

THE FIRE DRAINED me, but each time it weakened, some of the children would come by to touch me gently and restore some measure of my strength.

The deeper into the fields we walked, the darker the surroundings became, until even Damascus was a tiny glow in the distance. Shadows readily bumped against the ring of light, testing it like a shark does a cage. Occasionally, one of the children wandered into the distance as if entranced by a siren's call, or they were snatched away by a shadow if they strayed too near the edge.

I couldn't focus on it, but the darkness in the distance began to take form. For the first time, I realized it was more than just the shadows in the field. It was more of a shimmering blackness, nothingness taken form.

But there was something more. I'd only heard it once before, but it was a sound I would never, could never forget. No matter how much I tried.

My heartbeat roared in my ears to try to drown it out. The hungry wail sent the nightmares and shadows which had hunted us fleeing. I'd been the one to unleash it before, and the one to shove it back in its box. It was the roar of a demon horde.

EXPRESSIONLESS EYES STARED at me as I turned the ring overhead into a solid barrier and corralled the flock. I grabbed Bobby and Emily. "We must turn back. You can't fight this. We can tell the others what's coming, and find a way to prepare."

Emily took my hand as I struggled to keep enough energy in the light barrier around us. "We are not afraid of the darkness. This is why we are here."

"It's not just darkness," I stammered as I tried to find a way to describe what we faced. "It's the absence of everything. It's a void. Nothingness is out there, if we're lucky." I wasn't sure I could even begin to explain how a hell-mouth had opened here, if it's what it really was.

Bobby gave me a gentle smile. "We know. The only way to heal the Abyss is to fill it. And we will fill it with the light."

I nearly lost the barrier as I fell to the ground. Did the souls understand what they were coming to face? That they marched to oblivion? What could I say or do which would stop them? Should I stop them? Should I try?

The next thought should have terrified me, but left me oddly calm. What if my Trial was to lead them into the darkness? Into oblivion? Was that why I'd come? To give them a chance to fill the Abyss?

As if reading my mind, Emily touched me again. "This is not your task. You weren't prepared for this, and have done more than anyone would have ever asked of you. You have given us safe passage to help us few save everyone. You must turn back now, so we can proceed."

In the moment, I understood. And hated myself for it. They were completely at peace with their mission and the consequences, no matter how much I wasn't. I couldn't change their fate.

Bobby shifted once more into my father and hugged me. "Be safe, my son. You must turn back now. This is not your destiny."

Tears streamed down my face as each of the children touched me. They prepared to march as one to the Abyss, not so far in the distance. I started to open the barrier around us, but was jarred by a force which threatened to force me back to my knees. If the earlier hits had been sharks, this was a school of hungry megaladons.

A shrill roar erupted just outside of our meager protection. Another collision did bring me to my knees and weakened the light barrier. A momentary gap opened and several emissaries were swept away, their Calling at an abrupt end. Fear edged into the eyes around me, and those closest reached in to lay their hands on me, energizing me.

The ring of light flared with renewed life and fire, forcing the attackers into a temporary retreat.

I took a deep breath and studied the melee around us. The wretched shadows of the Reavers were mixing with glistening bodies which had the leering, burning embers of the full-blown daemon. Unquenchable hunger was drawing them all in to the buffet.

It was a standoff. The horrors outside couldn't get to us as long as the barrier was up. But we weren't going anywhere. They just had to wait until I ran out of energy. Even with support from the emissaries, I doubted I could hold through the long night. And the shadows and daemons were satisfied to feed on each other until then.

Emily took my hand and pulled me down to face her haunted eyes. "Thank you for trying. We are ready now. You may still be able to return to one of the cities."

"No, we aren't done yet." Her faith strengthened me, even if but for a moment. "We've come this far. Just give me a few minutes."

Bobby placed his hand on my shoulder. "Greyson. Son. It's time."

A basketball-sized glowing orb flowed in through the storm. A hole opened in the huddled group to let it settle a few feet in front of me. It took a human form with wings. Could it be angelic help?

The light faded, and the angelic wings unfolded from around the being, spreading wide, then folding behind his back. The barrier dimmed when I lost focus at the sight. I drew in every ounce of energy I could from the spellbound emissaries.

Their hope was quickly dashed when they saw the mangled and scarred form of Drake. Or what was left of him.

He flourished a bow. "Ta-da. What do you think of the new me? I mean, you did have a lot to do with it."

The angelic wings were attached to what was left of his crushed and burned torso. His missing arm had been replaced by a bronze angelic arm wearing a golden bracer. His torso perched on the thick, scaly, reptilian legs of a small dragon.

His one eye burned with malevolent desire for me. A contemptuous smile crossed his face. "I'm here to make you an offer." A thin, barbed tail whipped out through the chest of one of the children and flicked him into the ravenous horde.

I ground my teeth as rage seethed from every fiber of my body. The barrier dimmed again as I struggled with my desire to use the few seconds I'd have to wrench Drake's stolen body apart, piece by piece. "Go to hell, Drake. No deal."

His barbed tail whipped through another of the children. He held her terrified face inches from mine, before tossing her into the frenzy outside of the barrier. "They have already made their choice. They are where they are supposed to be. What about you? You see how it's going here. This realm is already lost. And soon it will spread to all of them. She made you an offer once before. As much as I don't like it, she extends the offer again. Become her consort. Lead her armies."

My companion growled loudly at my feet. "He's not real fond of the offer and we're a package deal."

Drake shook his scarred head. "I told her you wouldn't go for it. Even if I offered you back your precious Drea."

"Her name should not cross your lips, unless it's the last thing you say in contriteness." I flicked a silver dagger at Drake's heart.

The sigil of the armies of Jehovah on his bracer flashed and a golden shield sprang to life. It easily deflected the blade into the storm, which unleashed a loud wail of fury and anger. The assault buffeted against my shield with renewed vigor.

Apparently, they weren't fond of the blessed silver.

Drake smiled. "Oops. I think I might have riled the troops a little. As you can see, I'm now all things to all peoples. Mortal. Divine. There might even be a speck of the Fae I once was in there

223

somewhere. There is a little piece of all of them in me. I am the newest god."

Drake grabbed another of the children, a small boy, and held him just out of reach of the horde, tormenting me and them. "This is your last chance. Drop the field, and I will let you walk away." He hungrily licked his lips. "Otherwise, we will shred all of your little dolls one by one, and when I get to you, well, I'll grant you immortality so I can torture you for all eternity."

I closed my eyes. What could I do? I couldn't keep the barrier and engage Drake. If I dropped the barrier, would they shred him along with us? Worship him? Could they even hurt him? Could I, even?

A stream of incantations flooded through my mind. I couldn't hold onto all of it, but in that fraction of a moment, it was enough to give me peace. And an idea. "Go to hell, Drake."

The chimera's one eye flashed with malevolent glee. "I'll keep a chamber ready for you."

He wrapped the stolen wings around himself and was sucked out into the storm.

"See you soon, you crazy bastard."

I looked down to the mutt. His back was arched, and fangs bared, ready to leap into action. "I told you it was a bad idea to follow me."

"Woof."

Vacant eyes plead to me for direction. Many cried out, fearing they had failed. Others had long before accepted their end. But none of their gazes held any doubt for their mission.

Bobby touched me. "This is why we're here. Let us carry the light to them. We may still be able to do some good."

The invocation finished taking form in my mind. I'd never seen anything like it. It shouldn't have existed at all, much less in mortal grimoires.

I called to all of the remaining children. "Hold your lights high and everyone touch each other."

On cue, all of the children used one hand to raise the simple wooden lanterns and the other to touch someone near them. Near the end, Bobby and Emily each held on to me. The white spheres of light in the lanterns glowed brightly, then dimmed as I drew the barrier of light in as close as I could and filled the gap with the same light energy. Slowly, deliberately, the light wall rose and grew until it was high overhead.

My entire body hummed with energy. Unable to hold any more, I slammed the entire field of light into the ground around us in the blinding flash, ground zero of a nuclear blast.

I fell, my ears ringing. The ground was baked hard beneath me. My vision cleared as I sat up.

All of the emissaries lay on the ground around me. Small flashes and a chorus of shrieks rang out as the blast rolled in all directions around us.

DIMMED LANTERNS LAY on the ground near their owners as the tsunami of light dissipated far in the distance. The great dark cloud of the Abyss had shrunk, or at least fallen back. Children struggled to their feet all around me. I managed to stand up, with some help. A few lanterns had been shattered and the balls of light lay on the ground. Within a few moments, the lights gradually recharged and glowed as if they were new.

A small circle of stars was visible overhead where a hole had been blown through the boiling clouds. Golden twilight was breaking on the horizon. Hundreds of people lay unconscious on the ground beyond the edges of where the light barrier had been. They were thin, dirty, and tattered. An educated guess told me they'd been the souls of the recently possessed, picked off when they arrived and not yet fully through the change to become Reavers themselves.

One by one, the bodies on the ground began to stir as the children touched them, awakening them from a nightmare. As the children wandered away into the rising dawn, white orbs in their hands, the souls of the exorcised appeared dazed as they ambled towards me.

Excited shouts came from a few of the children as they moved further into the wilderness. Raging howls rose and drowned them out. I bolted towards the sound, unsure what I'd do when I got there. I was spent, and I didn't think the emissaries had much left for me to tap.

A dozen of the children stood in a semi-circle, safely away from a couple of figures huddled on the ground. A wing unfolded and shook off a coating of ash. Drake's arm found the bloody stump of something's leg, and used it as a cane to prop himself up. The left side of his body was charred. The angelic arm and shield had only protected the less corrupted parts of himself.

Something stirred in a pile of black ash, and a figure unfolded from the ground. It wore medieval-looking black plate armor, trimmed in runes of woven ribbons of gold and silver.

I reached for power I didn't have. A blessed blade would have to do. "Get back." I motioned to the gathering crowd. Were they in such a hurry to meet oblivion?

The dark knight ripped its helmet off and flung it at me in a fury. I deflected it away to the ground. Brighid Sinclair spat back at me, "A little warning would have been nice before you pulled out your dirty parlor trick." A thin trickle of blood ran down her lip, but she looked unharmed otherwise.

Tortured shrieks and whimpers rose and fell behind the pair. Dozens of partially vaporized demons, Reavers, and other creatures flopped on the ground where they'd been shielded by Drake. The ones still able howled in anguish.

The three of us locked gazes, waiting for the next move. None of us looked like we were ready to continue to dance into the night.

My first love reassuringly patted Drake's shoulder. "You've done well to protect us both. Your queen is pleased and will be thankful when we are both returned."

More children and a few of the freed souls staggered in our direction.

She slowly approached me until she was close enough we could kiss. "No matter my feelings for you, this is becoming tiresome. Soon you will either come to our side, or you will suffer the consequences."

I glared back. "I think you need to look around. Both of you. We just kicked your army's ass. Surrender. I don't have the energy to fight this out right now and neither do you."

Drake shook with fury as he began a rant. "This was but a scouting party, and you barely survived it." He summoned a fireball and floated it above his charred hand. "Shall we settle this now?"

I couldn't guess how much my light show had taken out of him, but he'd enough left to summon a fireball. I couldn't have manifested a flame out of a zippo if I'd wanted to. What would happen if I died in Purgatory? Was it an express route? Would I just cease to exist?

I drew a second blessed blade into my hand. "If that's the way you want it."

Brighid stepped halfway back in front of Drake. "Boys, we'll need to do this another time."

I swallowed. My heart broke when she turned to face me. "See you soon, love."

She placed a hand on Drake and barked out a short incantation. They vanished into shadow.

I EXHALED DEEPLY in relief and frustration and collapsed to the ground. Most of the emissaries wandered further into the fields since the show was over. The crowd of newly freed souls was growing rapidly, looking for any sense of direction. An ash-covered furball trotted over and lay next to me.

Bobby knelt next to the dog, ruffling his fur. He hugged me. "I've to go now. I'm proud of you."

"What?" Adrenalin drove me to my feet. "We did what you came out here for. We spread the light. Saved some souls. Presto, change-o, ta-da. Let's get you home and let everyone know."

He shook his head. "You still don't understand. You saved these souls. The darkness is still out there, and my mission hasn't changed."

"And what about them?" I waved at all of the souls gathered around.

Emily hugged me around my waist. "Lead them to one of the cities. They will follow you. Give them a little light." Her touch sent a shock through me. "Take care, Greyson."

I was frozen as the child form of my father and Emily walked in the direction of the Abyss, their orbs in lanterns leading the way. I watched until they disappeared into the fields.

The first rays of warming daylight broke over the horizon. The hole I'd made in the clouds was filling in, but the skies seemed a little less angry. I picked the nearest light on the horizon in the opposite direction of the Abyss. I summoned a small fireball and floated it high overhead. "OK, everyone follow me."

The rays of the morning light revitalized the reawakened souls. Gentle murmuring built among the crowd. Mostly, there were confused questions. I think they were following the moving crowd and the glowing fireball more than me.

Megiddo took shape on the horizon by midmorning. Even though the dazed crowd moved slowly, it was steady, and we had plenty of time to get to the city before nightfall.

I'd never be able to watch a zombie movie again.

We were hitting a good pace when a woman squealed and threw her arms around me.

Her breathy voice sent shudders through me. "How many times will you save me?"

THE BEAMING FACE of Ms. Katie Ashe Clouse stared at me expectantly.

"Hi, Ms. Clouse. Fancy meeting you here." What fresh hell was this?

She was rail-thin, dirty, and disheveled in the remnants of the same red dress she'd worn for her funeral. Sadly enough, she was more coherent than the last time I'd spoken with her. Then again, she'd been rolling around in a pile of possessed cash.

"I think we know each other well enough for you to call me Katie." She looked away with an embarrassed smile. "I'm sorry for the things I said, and did, the last time we were together."

I nodded. "It wasn't you, not really," I lied. The illusion she'd been tangled up in only had the ability to bring out the worst of what was already there. "I suspect you'll be making a lot of amends here."

She looked down with a resigned nod. "Is this... Hell?"

I shook my head. "No, at least, not yet. Welcome to Purgatory."

Her mouth hung open with an unspoken question. She took a deep breath and found her resolve to forge onward. "Have you seen my Henri?"

Henri was her husband, a friend of the family, and my personal mentor. His spirit had been watching over Katie until she crossed over. I was worried for him, but which would have to wait. "No, but haven't been here long myself. I'm sure he's around somewhere."

"So, what happened to you? How did such a handsome body get killed?" She smiled with a touch of mirth as she poked my chest.

I laughed. "I'm not dead yet. It's a long story."

"We seem to have time." She looped her arm through mine.

As we made the trek to Megiddo, I gave the abbreviated version on how I'd wound up on this side of the Veil. In return, she told me what little she remembered. I soon understood what Henri had seen in her. When she was her real self, she was warm, intelligent, and caring. The daylight helped cure the confusion and other effects of possession by the horde.

It became clear she didn't remember much of the last years of her life while under their influence of martinis and Pandora's Box. It was probably a good thing. Her last clear memory was at the funeral, when she and Henri had made the trip across the Veil together.

Joyous cries rose and an uncountable number came out to greet us as we reached the gates of the ancient city. Most appeared to be friends and family rushing to greet the approaching souls.

Walter Schuler met us at the gates with a giant smile.

Katie threw her arms around the old man. "Henri! You're safe."

Walter wrapped his arms around her and shifted into the Henri I remembered. "Katydid!"

I was too exhausted to be anything but happy for them both. "What's up with the Walter gig?"

232

The old magician laughed. "Walter Schuler was a name I used to travel under. I can't believe you fell for the bit. I thought I taught you better than that."

"Being killed by a shopping cart during a slushy fight between cheerleaders is not even close to the strangest story I've heard this week. In any case, I feel sure you and Matilda will be very happy."

Katie looked puzzled, but Henri could explain it to her. I wasn't going to even try.

"I'll see you both around."

Henri tackled me in a bear hug. "I knew if anyone could find her, it would be you." He pulled a scroll out of his pocket. His voice took on a darker tone. "This was left for you."

I accepted it and put it in one of my pockets. "Take care of each other."

I left the happily reunited couple and found a small overlook with a view of Brother Ephrayim's mesa. It was late in the afternoon and the skies were noticeably calmer. The red skies overhead looked to be on simmer and not boil.

The Abyss had retreated, but since I now knew what to look for, I could definitely feel its touch. The light show from last night wasn't enough to save Purgatory, but it had bought the souls trapped here some time.

Seeing how mysterious scrolls hadn't been carrying a lot of good news lately, I held it my hands and stared at it. The furball wandered around the overlook and waited for night to fall. I closed my eyes and listened to the singing as they prepared another group of emissaries to go into the darkness.

I felt some hope for them as the singing faded and the group streamed out and spread across the plain.

I Sensed a presence, and opened my Sight to take a look around. None of the nearby spirits were paying me any attention. The scroll vibrated in my hands. A subtle hint.

A black ball bounded over when I whistled and jumped into my lap.

If the children could chase oblivion, so could I. I unrolled the scroll.

I ignored most of the thee's, thus' and thou's, and went straight to the message.

Findings have been rendered. Your presence is hereby requested in chambers.

Grand Inquisitor

Francis   *Delacroix*

I said in the general direction where I felt the presence, "I'm ready."

THE UNDERWORLD FADED around us and reformed as a dimly lit chamber. I held the furball tight in my arms, and waited for the next hit. It was utterly quiet in the pitch black dark. I knew it wasn't the main chambers because there was no telling feel of magical energy. It was like there was nothing at all.

I was blinded when a sharp circle of light snapped into existence around us. I gradually adapted, but even so, I still couldn't see the presence who had brought me here.

A click from a small lamp brought a dim light a few feet away. A figure sat cross-legged in a folding chair, sipping a glass of wine and reading a cheap novel. He was short and thin, but well-tanned. His dark hair was frosted with gray at the temples. He wore a pair of worn jeans and boots with a long-sleeved, red shirt.

He spoke without looking up from the book. "Hello, Greyson. Do you know who I am?" His accent contained hints of many countries and languages, but a French flourish was the strongest.

"By the sound of your voice, you're the Inquisitor. Delacroix."

He deliberately closed the book and set it in the middle of the chair. He came to within an arm's reach. His blue eyes were piercing and cut straight through me. "I am Francis Delacroix, Grand Inquisitor, Marshall of the Accords of Nicaea, etc." He put disdainful emphasis on the titles. He rubbed his face in thought and said, "You have been a source of many perturbations for me. Did you know that?"

"Sorry. But no, I have no idea what you're talking about." I swept my Sense around me for any sort of trap. "I'm certain you are going to enlighten me."

An exasperated glare fixed on his face. He waved a long, thin finger at me. "You have been an extreme pain in my arse since before you were born. You dribbled magic all around like most children draw on walls with crayon. I still haven't cleansed all of your enchantments out of my favorite chair." He shook his head with a small laugh.

"Do I know you?" Memories tugged at the doors holding them buried and revealed themselves in a few quick visions.

Delacroix paced in thought. "You have a choice to make. First, you may elect to take a go-to-Heaven-free card, with no death and none of the other messy middle ground. Or I've been given the opportunity to make you a rare offer. You are driven to help people. You are being offered wings of your own. Think of it as a ground-floor opportunity to get in as a guardian angel." He clasped his hands behind his pointed head.

"Sorry. I appreciate the generous offer, but I'll need to decline. I beat your test. Send me home. I've got work to do."

"I did not provide that option."

"Are you saying I can't go back?"

The Inquisitor leaned forward and raised his voice. "I'm saying..." He paused and looked towards where the presence resonated.

He turned back to me and sighed deeply. "It would not be an advisable course of action. Consider the bigger picture, as they say. The effect you could have on so many lives."

"I am." I took a deep breath. "I'm considering the effect I've already had. The consequences. Is it something I can fix because you give me wings?"

Delacroix paused, and shook his head. "No. You would not be able to interfere now." He laid his hand delicately on my shoulder, as if he was afraid I'd shatter. "In the dark times coming, you may be able to help everyone you care about. And so many more."

Up next on *This is Your Afterlife*: Door number 1 - onwards to eternal happiness. Door number 2 - an eternity of public service. What's the mystery prize behind Door number 3? Live or die?

"You'll have to give me more than that. And why me? Why offer me such a choice?" The Inquisitor was definitely holding something back. "And why should I trust you?"

Delacroix said, "Reginald Sinclair. He plans to take your head, regardless. I don't believe he expects you to return at all, to be honest about it, but he would be very pleased to have you beg him to end your misery. In this state, I am unsure what he'll do, but I can assure you, even if you are allowed to walk out of the chamber, he wishes you dead, and will do everything in his power to make it so."

A stifled laugh escaped me. "Why? Can you at least tell me why they all want me dead? What is it I am really supposed to have done? I was just as much a victim of that night as anyone."

"I suppose you deserve something." Delacroix squared himself. "You wreaked havoc on a lot of people. There is a lot of speculation about the ones you maimed and killed and even what else you may have done to the ones for which they don't have a body to bury because it vanished. I don't think it was your intent, or your desire. I don't even believe it was your fault, but you are the mechanism through which it happened. You are not responsible, but you carry the blame."

My frustration built into a scream. "Then who is responsible? Who? Someone took us. Someone created the situation where this could happen. Who?"

The slightest crack opened in Delacroix's demeanor, and he gave me a look of empathy, of pity. "I don't know, and apparently, neither does anyone else. I conducted one of the many investigations. Even the acolytes captured in the aftermath were unaware. Their leader was one of the ones vaporized in the blast, and the rest were just following his lead, but based on what we did find out, they seemed to be hired help, not much more. We were never even able to confirm who let them in or how they got past the protections of the Grove. The only real evidence was the fact the rites were held on your family's property, and you were at the center of the blast."

I sank to the floor. "I want your files. I want to see everything."

Delacroix said, "I don't believe I can. Nor is it advisable. The case is open, and you are still an involved party. Sinclair has all of the information, and I don't see him granting you access. I still doubt he and his court will let you leave the chamber alive, no matter my findings. Take the offer. Either of them. Once you re-enter the chamber, it is out of my hands."

"Send me back. I'll handle Sinclair. I'll do whatever I need to do."

Delacroix hung his head and nodded as he spoke slowly and deliberately as if to give me another chance to reconsider. "I will make the preparations. The governor and the others are already on their way. If you change your mind, simply remain on this side of the portal when it opens. If you are who and what I suspect, I did not believe you would take the offer. Even so, I wish you would reconsider."

"I wish I could. I can't, not if Drea's going to have a chance."

He nodded. "I understand. She and her kind are not in my purview, but I do sympathize."

I grabbed the Inquisitor's arm as he turned to leave. "I deserve to know. Why give me the chance at the wings?"

He stared past me, and nodded. "You're an unknown quantity going into dark times, and one in high demand. I can't be sure what is wanted from you, but the Host had hoped to secure you for their side."

I couldn't be sure if that was all he knew, or if just all he was allowed to tell me. "Thanks."

The Inquisitor moved to a newly opened portal. As he passed the spot where I Sensed the presence, he whispered, "I told you he wouldn't go for it."

THE PRESENCE DISSIPATED not long after Delacroix disappeared. A search of the room proved it to be relatively small and empty. It extended only a short ways into the darkness before colliding with rough stone walls. I didn't even have to look to feel the power of the wards and sigils coating the walls, floor, and ceiling.

A short time passed when the light in the center of the room dimmed. A staircase formed and solidified where the light now dimly guided the way. Shouting echoed from above as the furball and I ascended.

Sinclair said, "He's been gone more than a month. I'll be astounded if there is enough left to execute. I may be tempted to just let him rot."

Another voice said, "If he's passed the test..."

Sinclair responded "Impossible. The only question is..."

All conversation ceased immediately as I stepped from the stairs through a portal depositing me into the center ring. "Your only question is what? How you can try to kill me next? If that was your best shot, I suggest you retire to the old politician's home."

A couple of gasps came from the cloaked members of the court. Nicomedes stifled a laugh.

Sinclair took half a step back, but righted himself. The sneer on his face was gratifying. But he didn't miss a heartbeat. "No matter. If the devil doesn't want you, we will send you in pieces. The sentence is death."

Nicomedes yelled an objection.

Delacroix spoke from across the room. He again wore his robes of office. "I take it, you are challenging him to a duel." He muttered an incantation, and I fell off-balance to the floor.

Sinclair raged, "What do you think you're doing?"

Delacroix waved and dropped all of the restraining fields, except the last one. I could walk out of the circle, but nothing could attack me as long as I was inside. "He's survived the Trial, in quite good shape, as you see. I feel certain you remember the laws. If you feel the accused has somehow cheated, or escaped judgment, you have the right to challenge him. If such is the case, he has the right to defend himself."

Delacroix tossed the bag of my gear into the ring next to me. "Or do you now challenge the law through the Inquisitor?"

Spells and incantations teased at the edges of my consciousness. The bindings on me began to crumble. "I'm game." Energy coalesced in my hands.

A gravelly voice I'd painfully missed for the last seven years bellowed in a thick highland accent from across the room. "Reginald, you cowardly bastard!"

For the only time I'd seen in my life, Reginald Sinclair flinched. Two of the robed judges disappeared into the darkness. "Turn my grandson loose from your kangaroo court now." Josiah MacGregor walked into the light of the ring.

More shadows materialized behind Sinclair.

Priscilla's voice was cold. "Reginald, I suggest you do as Josiah asked. He's in an especially ornery mood."

Sinclair turned and yelled at Priscilla. "You have no standing here! Who gave you access to these chambers?"

A tremor ran through the floor from the strike of a staff. The Dagda stood behind my grandfather. "I did, and as I do have standing in this court, would you mind giving me an explanation?"

Delacroix leaned against a nearby pillar. "Are these proceedings over, or do you wish to initiate the duel?"

Reginald Sinclair found himself standing alone as his two remaining judges, including his Sheriff, slunk back into shadow. "This town is my responsibility. I'll see justice as I see fit. This boy is a threat to all of us. And all of you." He pointed to everyone in the room.

Delacroix removed his hood. He spoke softly, but his voice echoed through the chamber. "Reginald, you asked me to come. I came. You asked me to oversee the hearing. I did. You asked for the boy to undergo the Trial. He persevered. You asked me to make the outcome legitimate. I am trying to do so. You now have a choice. Free the boy, and remove all doubts and bindings, or invoke your right to a duel. My only duty now is to discern if you are fit for your office, or if something has incapacitated you or your judgment. Assuming you survive against the boy."

The political survivor in the High Counselor reined in his anger. He seemed to carefully weigh his options before speaking. "Very well. You all get what you've asked for. Remember this day when you come to me, begging to put this mad dog down." The room was bathed in silence as he backed away and disappeared into shadow.

Everyone, including me, let out a collective sigh of relief. Delacroix dropped the remaining field around me. He shook my hand and whispered in my ear, "We will need to discuss how and when to restore your full power and knowledge. I fear releasing it all at once would be catastrophic. Until then."

Josiah snorted. "Senile old fool." He walked over to me and wrapped me in a bear hug, lifting me high off the floor. The crags in his face had been carved deeper with time, and he'd grown a little more rotund, but he was able to lift my six foot frame with ease. "Welcome back." He announced to everyone gathered, "My house in an hour."

WAS IT OVER? I rode the euphoric high as the chamber emptied, until Josiah and I were the only two remaining.

The old skill of shadow-walking came back to me as I followed Josiah into a dark corner at the back of the room and we were dumped out into a dark space. Shadow-walking was the only way to move into some locations in and around Phoenix Grove and many other places. It was a way of travelling without portals, but you had to either be able to visualize the destination, or have something of the location such as a piece of the building or a crystal harmonized to the location. And you needed a dark spot on both sides.

Josiah activated the main defenses of the room by flipping on the light switch. Bright lights blazed from all angles, filling every crevice of the space. Sigils of protection and travel glowed on the walls, floor, and ceiling. He opened the door. The hallway was lined with thousands of tiny boxes holding stones, crystals, and knick-knacks, each labeled with a name, date, and some other shorthand notes. He placed a crystal back into a slot near the door.

Josiah closed the door to the room and warded it. He then opened a door at the other end of the hall and led me into the back room of the Librarium Occultus or the "Hidden Library." Josiah had inherited responsibility from his father, and his line had responsibility for its rare contents going back generations. I'd played among the stacks and artifacts as a kid, but had never dug into the history.

We moved upstairs to where he kept a small apartment for the days when he couldn't or wouldn't go home, or for the occasional guest. He closed the door behind us and raised a ward with the wave of his hand. He grabbed me in a tight hug and said, "I thought I'd lost you, son. It's good to see you."

I slowed down long enough to look Josiah over. A little shorter than me with long salt-and-pepper hair, his craggy face was full, but showed the scars of a hard life. His firm grasp proved underneath the weight he'd put on was still a body of solid muscle. A pair of daggers were strapped behind his back, covered by the bib of old overalls.

"I wasn't sure I was going to make it myself for a while. How'd you know I was there?"

I'd forgotten how much I'd missed his gruff chortle.

"Same way I kept up with you as a runt. When you and your parents moved here, I set up charms to follow you wherever you went. I can follow you outside of the Grove, too, just not as closely or easily. I've never been far away in all your travels. I was sent out of town during the first round of Reginald's hustle. I was too late getting back to stop them before they shipped you off, but I made sure I'd be ready when you came back."

I found a seat in an old leather recliner. Its twin sat in my lab a dimension away. My hound found his spot in my lap. "What's next? A public Trial? How much time have I lost to get ready?"

Josiah sat in his oversized leather chair and kicked his feet onto the ottoman. "It's early October, but the Trial is over. I'll get with Delacroix, but Sinclair made his play and lost. You underwent the Trial, and did something very few expected: you came back. I have to admit, you had me worried when a few weeks passed. But it's over now, and you're free. Because it wasn't public, there are some around won't be happy, and believe it was a back-door deal, but we can make sure word spreads. Sinclair's obvious misery will help, but the first thing we need to do is get you cleaned up, and get to your welcome home party."

Those words hit me harder than I'd expected. Home and free. I hadn't prepared myself for the possibility of being found not guilty and released. Surviving the Trial gave me more than freedom. It gave me my life back. "Free?" It would take time to process the idea.

My grandfather nodded. "Yep. Now, go get cleaned up. You have a lot of friends to thank for their help. Some strange bedfellows, though. You will have to tell me what happened to have Priscilla and the Dagda in the same room and agreeing with each other. Those two have snipped at each other for at least a thousand years, when they weren't starting outright wars with each other."

I thought about what my grandfather had said while I showered. It was obvious Josiah knew a lot more about the people I'd been surrounded by than I did. I also tried to contemplate the idea of being free. No matter what, freedom was an illusion. Getting Sinclair and his sword of judgment off my neck felt good, but it certainly didn't mean I was safe. Ailbhe, Drake, Sonja, the Gibsons, Winter Fae, angels, demons, and Scar were all on my trail. And once things quieted down, I was sure Brighid's grandfather would try something.

The clean Leviskin suit felt good, but I felt naked until my knives and basics were slipped back into their homes. I Pushed it to become a kilt and light black sweater.

I studied myself in the mirror. I'd almost forgotten what I looked like. A little over six feet and thin, but muscled. Specks of white now glistened in my black hair. The last remnants of a light tan gave color to my otherwise fair skin. The dark circles under my eyes ran deep, but for the first time in a very long time, I saw myself and a spark was lit behind my ever-changing hazel eyes.

JOSIAH WAS IMPATIENT as he yelled up the stairs at my cousin, his protégée. "Come on, Mari! Let's go. We've got things to do."

She trotted down the staircase and dropped a stack of leather-bound first editions when she saw me.

"Hi, cuz."

It was clear she didn't know to expect me. Had my grandfather held back because he didn't know what would happen? Had he not expected me to survive?

She leapt over the dropped books and wrapped her lanky arms around me in a clumsy tackle.

"Reunion's over." Josiah opened the door. "People are waiting."

Mari refused to let go of me, as if I might disappear again. "Why don't we port to the house?"

"Nope." The old man waved us through the door. "The people of this town need to know he's home. No time like the present."

Touches of fall chilled the air as we took the long way home. The three of us meandered through the town square. It hadn't changed much in the time I'd been gone, or most of the century before.

The courthouse and town offices were on the north end of the square. The small, wooden church and garden were to the south. Keeley's Diner and the butcher were to the east. The general store took up the entire west block. At the center of the copse of old trees in the square, the cold iron statue of a phoenix clutching the town spire in its right talon stood guard over the town.

247

A few people peeked from behind drawn curtains as we passed the large, old houses which stretched for a couple of blocks in each direction out of town. Josiah's farm was about a mile out. The house and barn glowed with the essence of magical fires. Soft music and loud voices filled the rolling hills which bridged the gap from town.

A few people tried unsuccessfully to stay out of sight at the edges of the fence around the farm. I was the biggest news since Underhill Productions had rolled into town.

I remembered most of the locals who came to the impromptu gathering and was greeted warmly by everyone inside the barn. It was old family friends, mostly. Priscilla stood with Onyx and Kizzy. Melanippe helped the Dag run the bar. Phoenix Grove's latest residents and refugees from the Summer Fae looked like they'd melded in with the town pretty well. All told, about sixty had come out. Not bad on short notice.

Nicomedes and Dorian guided me to the side. "Thanks for what you did for me, Nicomedes," I said.

"No time for platitudes now." Dorian pulled me back to reality. "There's going to be a lot of questions. Sinclair has clout and is making waves among his supporters. As is evident by the attendance, you have a lot of support in this town, but there's still a lot of ill will." So much for the warm welcome home.

Nicomedes said, "I've done some digging as well. Inquisitor Delacroix could only tell me so much, but he's always believed there was much more to the story, and potentially, the event was just the start. In less than a month, it will be the seven year anniversary. You know how those numbers tend to go. If there is an echo of the past, it may become a crescendo."

248

I rubbed my eyes and needed to sit down. "What's the bad news?"

Dorian scowled. "Keep your eyes open. I wouldn't put it past Sinclair or some of the others to take a shot. For now, I suspect they are wary and will give you some berth. But they will be watching."

I nodded.

Priscilla floated into the circle. The tight green leather outfit had garnered her some attention, no doubt. "Back from the dead. Again." She hugged me. "I suspect you boys are talking about the rumors?"

"Rumors?"

Nicomedes scowled. "We'd not gotten that far. We thought we might let it lie until morning."

I threw my hands in the air. "You may as well tell me."

A mischievous smile grew slowly on her face. "Well, the first story is you have become a necromancer. I suspect the old fool Sinclair started that one. The other one is Nicomedes here pulled a fast one and hid you out to make it look as if you had prevailed through the Trial and miraculously returned."

I shook my head. I tried to talk about what I'd seen, but it was near impossible. The thought doubled me over with a searing pain through my body.

Dorian said, "You won't be able to talk about it. It's part of the whole experience. The Trial is for you and you alone, and it's locked away inside of you for eternity."

I was screwed. How did you disprove a negative? I wouldn't be able to talk about what was happening in Purgatory, or what was headed our way.

I tried to make an offhanded comment about the darkness and the next thing I knew, I lay on the ground. Priscilla had me in her arms, and had apparently caught me when I fell.

Nicomedes stared into my eyes. "The more you try, the worse it'll get."

My head cleared some, but I wasn't in the mood to be around anyone. "I need some air."

MY THOUGHTS WANDERED with the meandering path beaten through the woods. I'd spent a lot of hours here as a kid, and the forest had always helped me center my thoughts.

Too late, I sensed someone in front of me. I was knocked off my feet by a blast of energy. I tried to stand, but was stuck fast.

I focused on the glowing crystal on the end of a long staff directed at me. Whoever held it was readying a charge for another blast.

Sorrow permeated the voice of the woman behind the staff. "I should kill you now, for both our sakes." If not for the message, the tone sent me back to my childhood. "Can you give me a reason not to do so? Are you the monster I hear you to be?" It was Rhea Sinclair, Brighid's mother.

I was ten years old again. I'd spent as much time in their home as my own. Rhea was a powerful seer, sensitive, and clairvoyant.

"Take a look for yourself." The simplest touch from her would let her find anything she wanted, and restrained like this, I couldn't do much to stop her. At least not without hurting her and doing a lot of damage. "I never could hide anything from you anyway."

Rhea drove her staff into the ground. Stress had taken its toll over the years. She was a wraith of her former self. Her long red hair, now streaked with white, was tied tightly behind her in a ponytail. Fire and desperation burned in her deeply sunken eyes. "No, you couldn't. Nor can you now."

She grabbed the sides of my face and gazed into my eyes. Memories streamed by in a torrent. Some of them, she would stop and study for a moment, but most she let flow by on fast forward.

She focused in on the night Brighid and I were taken, and then sped forward to a glimpse I'd had of her as she was led past my cage. She tried to look deeper into the night of the incident, but it was only fragments.

She sped through most of my last seven years until she came across my memory of sitting with Brighid not so long ago. She replayed her stabbing me over and over, making me relive the pain. I was helpless and betrayed, again and again. She tried to latch on to the memory of her from Purgatory. We were locked together as fire burned through both of us. I couldn't take it any longer. I had to drive her back, force her out. Obliterate the source of the pain.

My heart and my concern for Brighid and her mother overwhelmed me and kept me from killing us both.

Brighid's mother sank to the ground, sobbing. She cried, "It can't be. It can't. It's a lie."

With her concentration broken, I easily shattered the spell which held me frozen. I was dizzy and nauseated from the pain of her accessing my memories of the Trial, but I knew I needed to be ready for another attack.

She curled up on the ground and sobbed. When I moved, she shrank back "You... you can't, shouldn't be able to do that."

"I'm not going to fight with you, or anyone else, if I can help it." I offered my hand to help her up.

She trembled as she took my hand and accepted my help pulling her to her feet. I thought she would run, but instead she loosely fell against me and continued to sob.

We stood together as statues for a long time, unmoving and silent. Finally, she looked up at me. "How is this possible? Brighid is…broken. She's in the house, even now. It can't have been her."

"I want to see her. I need to see her."

She nodded slowly. "She wants to see you, too. She's been crazed since feeling you come back to town. We'll have to hurry. I came to seek you out to see if what Reginald had said was true. He's telling the town you faked your disappearance for the Trial, and your friends then rushed a verdict. I've seen the truth, or enough of it, but he won't care. He's trying to pull together his few trusted friends to run you out town and hunt you down later. I can let you see her for a few minutes, but only if you leave immediately after. You need to run. And never return."

"I'm done running. If he forces it, we will have to duel. I don't want to, but I will, if I'm forced to defend myself."

Torch lights and muffled voices approached on the path from town. Rhea pulled us off the trail and veiled us both. Reginald Sinclair led a small group towards the farm.

I struggled as Rhea pulled me the other direction towards town. "We have to stop them. We can't let them cause trouble at the farm."

Rhea shook her head. "No. Josiah can take care of himself, and you have enough friends there if he can't. If they can't take you quickly, they'll make a scene until you appear. Even Reginald wouldn't dare challenge Josiah. It is the best chance to get you into the house."

I was torn, but she was right. I needed to see Brighid. We ran up the path and through the back gate into the house.

I set foot inside, and a pandemonium of screaming and thuds came from the back of the house.

She grabbed my arm before I could rush in. "I... I don't know how to prepare you for this."

THE CACOPHANY CEASED when I touched the handle to the bedroom. It made knocking a bit redundant, but I did it anyway. It seemed like the thing to do.

Slowly, I cracked the door and peeked in. The room was dim. The only light came from the lamp laying on its side in the corner.

I eased myself into the room. It was a wreck. The bed and frame were flipped over. The contents of the bookshelves littered the floor. A rocking chair gently rocked unoccupied in the corner next to the lamp. Otherwise, the room appeared empty. My Senses told me otherwise.

The room was cold, but wasn't what triggered my hair to stand on end. Brighid's voice whispered in my ear, "Close the door."

I shuddered and broke out in a cold sweat. I wanted to crawl out of my skin. My Senses screamed at me to run.

Instead, I closed the door. As it clicked shut, sigils flashed with a neon glow for the briefest moment. They covered every inch of the room, from floor-to-ceiling. "Where are you, Brighid?"

As the sigils dimmed, Brighid's form took shape. She materialized, looking like the teen girl I remembered and loved. She let out a gasp and a shriek and charged towards me. Instead of a tackling hug, she passed through me.

The ephemeral presence circled around me, her legs becoming just a little less visible. She looked disoriented as she twirled around the room in a frenzy. "I forget sometimes."

I mustered together the ability to whisper, "Hi, Brighid." My heart slammed against my chest in an effort to escape.

She floated and circled around me. "You look... older." Deep furrows ran across her brow.

"It's been a while."

Brighid floated to the rocking chair and began to moan. "I'm dead. I'm really dead."

Those words rocked me to my core. If her spirit was here, who was in control of her body? Had she been possessed for all these years?

I opened my Sight and studied the specter. The sigils around the room resolved into clear view. Someone else understood something I'd only suspected. This room was meant to hold her spirit together, and apparently allow her to become at least partly physical. Threads of life energy streamed from her to a sigil on the wall. It seemed to keep her connected to reality. Did it also connect her to her body?

"Brighid, I'm still here for you. Like I promised."

Shouting came from outside. I strained to tell what was being said. Rhea screamed, "Leave them be!"

I reached for the door. "I'll be right back."

Brighid flew across the room. "No, stay here." She blocked the door.

Reginald Sinclair pounded on the door. "Come out here, boy. Now. I won't let you do any more damage."

I whispered, "Brighid, it's OK. It will be OK."

"No." Her eyes were wide. "Please, don't. Just leave. For me."

I nodded, and looked around for an escape route. The sigils around the room were locked down to help Brighid keep her form. I opened the closet and found it was nice, dark, and relatively unprotected.

I watched through a thin crack of the closet doors. Outside the room, the elder Sinclair uttered something and the sigils flashed. Brighid disappeared as the door flew open.

I took a handful of mud from my leg, focused on it, and shadow-walked back into the forest.

I half-ran back to the farm, expecting a hunting party with torches and pitchforks to appear at any time. I made it back to the farm without running into anyone else.

The barn was empty except for Josiah, Priscilla, and Dorian, who sat around a table, looking solemn. The mood didn't improve when I sat down.

Josiah said, "Did he catch you?"

I said, "Who?"

Josiah slammed his fist to the table. "Don't play dumb with me. Reginald came by with a few of his people, making a fuss. He got a call, and they all tore out of here like they were on fire."

"Rhea took me to the house. I got to see Brighid, but only for a moment. He didn't see me, but I'm pretty sure he knows I was there."

Josiah said, "Interesting."

I knew his accusatory look. After glaring at me for long enough to make his point, his face softened and he let out a loud,

"Humph." I knew it meant he would be asking about details later, but he pretty well knew what happened.

Dorian said, "While you have been gallivanting about, the situation has degraded rapidly. The missions in Florida led us back to the hub in the Midwest. An operation in Kansas City did not go well. Wynn was injured and there were significant casualties. He's trying to pull the team together and regroup. Hayden's Longbow team disappeared two days ago. His unit was investigating some ruins found outside of Las Vegas. It seems the Erebites have been busy. At Wynn's request, Nicomedes and I are going with Priscilla to check out something in Miami. We're leaving in the morning."

I said, "I need a couple of hours in the library, and then I can meet you there."

Dorian shook his head. "We've already discussed it. As far as Longbow is concerned, you are MIA. There have been other incidents among the Veiled peoples around the world. Many are going to ground, or to other realms. It may be time for us to do the same. Something is coming. You need to disappear while we investigate."

"I'm done running, from Sinclair and from the cult. I don't know much, but I know something bad is near. I've seen it." A jolt of pain surged through me. I took my grandfather's hand and spoke to him. "But Dorian's right. It may be time to prepare the Grove."

Josiah said, "This is a Sanctuary, one of the best protected places for the Veiled peoples. We need to be a refuge if something really is coming. It's why we exist."

Priscilla said, "It is best for you to stay in hiding. We may need a trick up our sleeve. Someone in reserve, as it were."

Their stolid looks told me they were still holding out on something. "What aren't telling me?"

Furtive glances shot around the table.

Priscilla closed her eyes. "Your disappearance was too well-timed with the other events of late. There are concerns as to whose side you are actually on. Some believe you were eliminated to give someone the advantage. Others believe you fled. LeGasse wants you for questioning about your absence and the events in Kansas City. We believe it wise for you to keep a low profile, for now."

I went numb. "I understand. I have some research to do here anyway." I started scrambling for a plan. "What next?"

Dorian said, "We can fix this, but it will take time. Wynn still wants to believe in you. But you have ruffled more than a few feathers. And the timing of your disappearance... was inconvenient."

"Do you doubt me?"

"No." The look in his eyes told me something different. "We must leave shortly."

I nodded.

I pulled Priscilla aside when everyone rose to leave the table. "How is Drea?"

Fear crept into her eyes. "Her body is slipping. I don't know how much longer it can hold out. They are watching the hospital. You will not be able to go there for now."

She turned to leave, but then turned back to me and whispered, "Be smart about this. She would not want to lose you, even to save herself."

Josiah put his arm around me. "Come on, let's get you in a bed."

I shook my head. "I've got somewhere safe I can go." It was a phrase my mother had used in times when she went to the lab. I hoped he remembered. "They'll know I'm gone, and it'll be safer for everyone."

Josiah gave a slight snarl. "Just remember: this is your home and it's here when you're ready. Do what you think you need to do."

"I need to spend a little time in the stacks. Hopefully, they're in a mood to give me what I need." Finding information among the old texts could be a challenge.

Josiah agreed. I could tell he wasn't happy about me not staying at the house, but I'd stirred up a lot around town just by showing up. "Mari can help you, if you need it," he said.

After everyone had left, I used a bit of leftover lemon juice to draw the circle on the floor behind a couple of bales of hay. I finished the sigil and grabbed the mutt.

"Laboraorium."

THE LAB WELCOMED me with silence and a thin layer of dust. I fixed a bowl of water and some food for the furball, and checked everything out. As usual, all of the wards were in place, and the lab was undisturbed.

As I hadn't slept in a couple of months, I dragged out the old cot I kept in the corner and wrapped up in a couple of blankets. The pup was passed out before I was.

A strong finger tapped on my forehead.

Ladon said, "Look who decided to show up."

I refused to open my eyes. A cold stone floor had replaced the cot. "I'm not getting up. I haven't had any sleep in over a month. Catch me tomorrow."

"Tsk, tsk." A cork popped, undoubtedly from a bottle of wine. "Oh, lad, if only I could. I'd send the both of us out of here. The preening swan has been in a tizzy since you dropped off the map."

I sat up on the floor. "Really? Is one night of sleep too much to ask?"

Ladon waved a bottle of wine in my direction. "And a decent Semillon appears to be out of my grasp as well. Alas. It appears neither of us get what we want."

The library around me was mostly back in order. Books and intact objects adorned the righted shelves. A makeshift restoration area was set up further towards the back, where various items were in repair. Stacks of loose pages and scroll fragments were being reassembled. Another corner held a pile of debris apparently too damaged to even evaluate.

"She's been a taskmaster through the countless hours of curating this mess. I'd say another couple of decades and we may have all of the pieces back together."

A gust of wind blew through the hall, sending scraps of paper flying.

Ladon sipped at the glass of wine and sneered, "The walking feather duster has arrived. Huzzah." He began placing the scraps back into place. "You know, Tsauriel, flapping your wings sends these flying as well."

Tsauriel crossed her arms and stood in front of me. She tapped her foot impatiently, shaking slightly before speaking. "And where have you been hiding? All I could Sense was you were playing around in the Underworld. It is no place for the living. And we have work to do. The Trial is—"

"Over. Where do you think I've been? They sent me for the Trial. I've been in—" A searing pain shot through me and hit my last nerve.

I clenched my fists and shook uncontrollably. "Really?" I yelled at no one in particular. "I can't even verbalize it here? Son of a bitch!" I grabbed a partially reconstructed vase and threw it at Tsauriel. "And you! I can't even get one night of sleep, uninterrupted by whatever game you want to play. I'm out. Let me out of here. We're done."

Tsauriel hung limply. "You have survived the Trial? And returned?" She pulled two chairs out from the table, offering me one. She sat in the other, facing me.

Ladon quipped, "What about me?"

She snapped back, "Get your own chair."

262

I refused to sit. "Go to hell. I'm done."

Tsauriel gave me a frustrated but sympathetic look. "Please, sit. Depending on what you have to say, we may all be through." She stretched out a hand without looking at Ladon. "And give me a glass of whatever swill you have there."

Ladon placed a glass of white wine in front of me, and said to Tsauriel with a snide tone, "Get your own."

I grabbed the glass of wine and downed it in one shot. It was blatantly obvious the odd couple were taking up permanent residence in my soul, whatever that was. My experiences in Purgatory had raised more questions than I would answer in a lifetime. I laughed to myself. "How many angels can dance on the head of a pin?"

Tsauriel stared at me blankly. "What?"

Ladon let out a small laugh. "It's worse than you thought. They made him a student of pop philosophy." He placed an unopened bottle of wine on the table. "With such spirit, in vino veritas."

"It is supposedly an unknowable question. Give me one complete truth, and I'll sit down. Otherwise, we're done here, no matter the cost."

Tsauriel walked two aisles over and selected a book. She returned to the table and opened it. "Read this. You will not be able to remember or comprehend it, but it will give you the answer you seek, when you need it."

I was unable to decipher the angelic script in the book, but a couple of images became quite clear. One of which was Tsauriel hiding away, and the other was a flash of her being released into darkness. The Abyss.

263

I slowly sank into the seat. "History?"

She shifted uncomfortably. "And prophecy." Tsauriel flipped the book to the last few pages. The flash came through showing Tsauriel walking through a door into a devastated wasteland beyond.

I asked, "So, the Abyss. You encountered it in the War of the Fall."

Anger and fear flashed behind her eyes. "Do not pretend to know what happened in the War of the Fall. But yes, I've encountered it before. It is, in part, what drove me to hide in the Well of Souls."

"How was it defeated?"

Tsauriel looked at me like an elder would a toddler holding the trigger to a nuclear weapon. "The Abyss. It just is, or more precisely, it is not. It is the blackness which existed before there was light. It is neither good nor evil. It is the matter of creation and destruction. Its presence means the physical realms are unraveling. It is not something to be defeated or beaten back. It is defined by absolute zero. Absence. Nothingness. Everything."

I sat in stunned silence. I'd assumed it was some form of conjuring or storm of etheric forms.

Tsauriel said, "I feel its residue on you. It is how I know you encountered it. Where?"

Pressure began to build, and shooting pains stabbed through my body, but I managed to blurt out "Pur—" before I passed out.

I awoke to Ladon propping me up on the floor and holding a glass of wine to my lips. "Wake up, lad."

Tsauriel was lost deep in her own thoughts. "I take it you encountered it during the Trial. I suppose it makes sense, in a way. Certainly not what I was led to expect. I am assuming you were drawn to Purgatory. The easiest place to break through would be one of the realms of spirit."

I drug myself back into the chair. Tsauriel placed a small fetish made of bone and angel feathers around my neck. "This should help alleviate the stress of talking about your Trial."

Gradually, the pain and pressure subsided. When my mind had cleared, I was drawn to a cylinder on one of the shelves. I unrolled it on the table to find a map of Purgatory and its place in the Underworld. The central areas were loosely mapped to the ancient cities of the Middle East. An odd mark was near the city marked Casada.   "What's this?" A number of similar marks were scattered around the map in other areas.

Tsauriel studied it briefly, and then pulled out another map. "Those were construction pathways from Tartarus. But they were closed off once Purgatory was completed."

My head started to hurt, this time because I was trying to remember mythology. "Tartarus? What does it have to do with anything? And each of these marks, it's a path to a different realm?"

Tsauriel gave a small nod. It was about as much positive feedback as I would ever get. "Tartarus was one of the early underworlds, a prison for the natural gods, demigods, and even some of the Divine who became too tied to the physical world. Tartarus also holds some of the original energy of creation. It was tapped when Purgatory was created, and a few of its inhabitants were used as labor in its construction. Once Purgatory was complete, the denizens of Tartarus were returned, and the pathway closed."

265

I was diving into thoughts I was certain no mortal was meant to contemplate. I sensed Tsauriel was revealing secrets not meant for gods or mortals. I pushed her. "So how do you create these realms? Are they not all part of creation?"

Tsauriel looked at Ladon. It appeared it was an answer he didn't want to be part of. I was pretty sure I didn't, either. She waited for Ladon to walk out of earshot before speaking. "Something only comes when a pocket in the nothing gets filled."

"What does it mean?" I rubbed my head, and knew I was losing to more than exhaustion. I was way out of my depth. "So, how can we do it and can it fix a broken realm?"

Tsauriel stood. "You are tired, and I've said too much. We will see each other again soon."

I fought to stay as I was being propelled out. "Tsauriel, can it be done?"

She turned away from me. Her head drooped, and her translucent wings fell to her sides. She whispered, "I cannot answer for sure. The angelic were brought into a world of light. But there are forbidden texts. It may even be rumors or lies. They speak of a being who can exist in the nothingness, a being who can create in the nothingness. If the Abyss truly has entered our space, then all may be lost. This is all I know. Now go. We will see each other soon enough."

I STRETCHED OUT and sat up on the side of the cot. I was hungry, thirsty, and exhausted. My dreams had been frantic once Tsauriel had let me go. I guess I'd had a lot to process.

I grabbed the Anima Arca blade, wrapped it in a piece of warded oilcloth, and threw it in a small pack along with my usual supplies. With the still-sleeping mutt in my arms, I stepped into the permanent circle, muttered a few words, and we ported into the barn.

A warm midafternoon sun shook the rest of the cobwebs out of my head on the way to the back door of Josiah's house. He'd left a note on the table.

Mari is at the library, taking care of business. I had a couple of errands to run. I'll be back tonight. Stay low and out of trouble.   We'll   talk   later.

I wasn't going to look for trouble, but I wasn't cowering, either. The furball followed me on the trek to town and to the *Librarium Occultus*, the repository of arcane and hidden knowledge. From the outside, it looked like a three-story Victorian mansion befitting Norman Bates' summer home. A wraparound porch surrounded the entire house.

Once I passed through the front double doors, I could Sense its sentience as if the building were alive.

The ground floor was the gift shop and public front. It was full, wall-to-wall, of bookshelves with texts for sale. Most of them were current titles of fiction, nonfiction, and arcana. Each room covered a couple of different genres. In the back corner was a public portal room, which allowed practitioners from around the world and other realms to visit.

A dozen or so people wandered about, or were in line to check out. Mari's influence was evident on the day-to-day operations. The door to the portal room was painted like Dr. Who's police box. How did the house feel about it? I wondered.

Mari was delivering books to the reading rooms on the second floor. The bookshelves here were loaded with common reference materials, and were the main focus of the library. Each room had a couple of chairs, allowing the patrons to use them as comfortable reading rooms.

She motioned for me to come in. Delacroix sat cross-legged in a high-backed leather chair. The table next to him was stacked with books.

The Inquisitor said, "Nice to see you. I was hunting for you earlier, but it seems you found a safe refuge for the night. Probably a wise choice." He nodded towards the rocking chair on the other side of the table. "Have a seat."

"Thanks, but I actually have a lot to do and not a lot of time. Can we do this later?"

Delacroix shook his head. "I really must insist you take a seat. I shan't take but a few moments of your time."

I handed Mari a list. "Can you see what you can find on these?"

She reviewed it and smirked. "Why don't you ask where the Holy Grail is, while you're at it? It'll take me a little while for your wish list. Enjoy your chat." She raised a privacy field around the room as she left. All of the rooms were equipped with built-in protection controlled by a light switch.

I slid into the seat and faced the Inquisitor. "I'm sorry if I was rude. I do appreciate what you did for me during the Trial."

Delacroix nodded. "I did nothing more than my job. I have some history with your family, as I do with the Sinclair's. Not only did you survive the test, you have persevered. Unfortunately, it doesn't seem to be the end of it, as it should have been."

"What next then? Another Trial? Something more public this time?"

"I'm unsure. He may still pursue the duel, if he can make it to his advantage. The law is clear, and you have returned from a personal Trial intact. Reginald still wants your head. He blames you for what happened to Brighid, and to his son, her father. There are others around town who still look for someone to hold accountable."

I leaned forward far enough to make him shift in his seat. "Do you know what happened that night? I don't. I don't even know what I was accused of, not really. I know people I loved and cared about were killed. And whatever happened to Brighid."

Delacroix studied me in silence. I felt a chill as he used some technique to stare into my soul. I remembered the stories about Delacroix, the Grand Inquisitor. He had some Divine ability to see the true selves of others. What might he find in me?

Finally, he spoke in his odd accent, a thick mixture of European influences. His presence was commanding, even more so when he whispered, as he leaned forward and did now. "You will need to find out for yourself. I've been able to garner quite a few facts and even more rumors. You must not share what I am about to tell you. None of it."

I paused, and then nodded.

He leaned in close. "The Forrester family had an estate on the outskirts of Phoenix Grove in its prior location. As you know, the Grove was established by a few families to be a refuge for practitioners, talents, and what are now known as the Veiled peoples, to hide them both from man and other Veiled peoples, with whom they were at war. Before the Grove was here, it was most recently hidden in the mountains of what's now West Virginia. In the late 1700s, during the American Revolt, the British employed talents of their own, as well as some undesirable creatures of the Veiled peoples as mercenaries. The Grove was moved, but the estate was left behind."

Only the town elders knew how it worked, but I'd heard enough around to have an idea. As kids, we were all taught the Grove existed close to the material world, but not in the same physical realm. We lived on the same plane, and shared the space. The essence of the Grove could move to different locations if it was at risk. But I didn't really know how. Josiah was an elder then, but wouldn't break his oath and give me details.

"Since the estate was created as a part of the Grove, it should have only been accessible through the Grove. During the attack which forced the relocation, your family estate was the point of the breach. It happens. No veil is ever perfect, and strangers occasionally wander into town here by accident. No matter what happened, the estate was sealed off and left behind. Later on, your ancestors went back to assess the damage and seal the breach.

When you and the others were taken, we followed the trail. A portal to your old family estate had been opened. A scouting party, including your parents, pulled together to follow the trail. Josiah, Reginald, and others gathered together a larger group to assist in the rescue. I was along in the second group. The trail led past your family house to a stone circle within a larger temple building. When we arrived, you were chained to a makeshift stone altar. There was a large blast imprint and everything within about thirty feet was vaporized. It had even toppled a few of the stones and blown out part of a wall.

We found a few bodies of some children from the Grove, and some from other communities. We found some more still chained up in cages inside of the house. The only survivors from the scouting party were involved in a firefight on the other side of the house. They'd run into some people claiming to be acolytes of the Cult of Erebus. They were using some half-breed Fomorians as mercenaries. Most of them escaped or were killed. We managed to capture two of the acolytes for interrogation, but all they seemed to know was they were trying to resurrect their old god."

"Erebus."

Delacroix nodded. "It was apparent at the time. I, however, have had reason to doubt the story. We recovered a few of their implements." He handed me a folder with handwritten notes, including a detailed sketch of an Anima Arca found among the items. "Because of the evidence, some of the townspeople were led to believe you were, and are, the re-embodiment Erebus. It is possible the cultists believe it as well."

Wonderful. If word had reached Wynn, or others outside, they might have the same opinion. The problem was, I couldn't refute it. Not even to myself. "So, what do you think now?"

Delacroix gave me a knowing smile. "I am certain you are not one of the lords of the Underworld. I see the doubt in your eyes. Rest assured, you are not Erebus. I cannot, however, tell you what role you do play. I have my own suspicions, but I'll keep them to myself. For now."

I didn't feel any better about it. Besides, why should I trust him? Was this a trap to give me the rope to hang myself with? Was it to give Sinclair another reason to hunt me down? He'd admitted he was holding information back. What else was he hiding?

The Inquisitor leaned back in the chair. "Now to more pressing matters. Your abilities. You are still bound, even though the restrictions have been loosened. I fear if I release the bindings all at once, it will drive you mad, and you will become the villain Sinclair seeks."

"I've already been able to do a few things. Things I don't remember, or never knew."

"This is one of the ways people such as yourself - talents, practitioners, wizards, whatever you wish to call yourselves - have survived." I noticed a special emphasis and venom when he said, "wizards." "Your abilities were bound as you entered your teens, when your abilities naturally started to develop. From what I understand, abilities come through a combination of training and study, along with some inherent skills. Sometimes, these abilities, even specific conjuring, are retained and passed along in what you would call 'genetic memory.' Sometimes, people never develop any of their talents, only to have a powerful witch emerge out of nowhere generations later."

"What does this mean for me?"

Delacroix shrugged. "You come from a confluence of multiple powerful family lines. We have already seen power come from you not usually seen until practitioners reach the century mark, or more. And that's with your abilities bound. If you agree, what I suggest is a gradual release of the binding. We can structure it in such a way, if you need something, it can come forth, but you may still find sometimes you are prohibited from using the skills. No matter what, there are always consequences."

Had someone told me I'd be sitting across from the Inquisitor discussing my power, I'd have bet my life I would either be on the rack or broken on the wheel as a part of my confession. My own abilities had started to scare me, but at the same time, they were mine. A sudden flash of ire coursed through me. I beat back the urge to wrench the key to my bindings from out of Delacroix. I saw the incantation to pull the information from his mind. I could Push him and force him to release me.

A cool breeze washed away my delirium. I stared at my hands and watched the energy dissipate. What was happening to me? The idea of what I'd contemplated, however briefly, terrified me. What else was in there trying to escape? Should I let him bind me completely? Should I find a way to remove the abilities?

Delacroix nodded. The entire scene had taken microseconds, but he seemed to have understood it. "Your type of power, it changes you. Part of you feels cheated and wants it all back. You have control and balance for now, but some day, the balance will give way. It will tilt one way or another. My approach will temper it."

"And what if... I want it all gone. Stripped away."

He froze for a microsecond. "It could be done. Probably. It would make it easier for you to hide, for some time. But eventually you'll be found. And unable to defend yourself. If it is really what you desire, you were already given easier options earlier."

I nodded in understanding. "I'll go with your plan. For now."

Delacroix gave a slim smile. "Excellent. Drink this when you are ready." He handed me a small ampule of a thick, amber liquid, and two small pills. "Those will help with the hangover."

"Thanks. Sounds like a fun trip."

He also handed me a calling card covered in gold filigree. "You can reach me through this at any time. If you need counsel, I am available." Delacroix flipped the switch and dropped the privacy field. "Good luck with your research. You may keep the file, but it's for your eyes only. Keep it safe. Destroy it if you must."

I FOUND MARI in the basement among the stacks. Only a handful of people knew they existed, much less were able to get this far. She and I'd played down here as kids, engrossed in writings long forgotten when the pyramids were built, in languages long-dead. One of the marvels of the Library was its ability to help readers translate and understand the works in its care.

She always argued the place was a giant enchantment. I still thought it to be in some way conscious, living. And today, it was being ornery.

Mari was a little shorter than me. I couldn't understand how she could look so soft, as she was stronger than an ox, and fit otherwise from carrying stacks of texts up and down, all day, every day. Her only break was an hour a day of sparring.

Dust was flying as she nonchalantly slammed heavy texts. She was swearing at the library in a one-sided argument.

"What have you managed to find?"

She cut me with a look across the top of her wire-rimmed glasses. I was certain she only wore them to have more of an academic air. "Just wonderful." *The Tome of Metlecrafte and Darke Artes* flew at me. This version looked to have been revised around 1200 A.D. I said, "I need the original. This one had too much cut out."

My cousin forced a smile and shoved my list into my hands. "Maybe you'll have better luck today. Besides, most of these are in the restricted texts." She narrowed her eyes as her grin grew mischievous. "Besides, *she* wants to give you a personal welcome home. Good luck."

I chased around the stacks, looking for anything which would get me something on the Anima Arca or the Abyss. After an hour of chasing tomes only to watch them move and vanish before I could get to them, I knew I wasn't going to have a choice. I finally gave up when a book vanished from my hands.

Mari chuckled from behind the sales desk as I stormed out the front door and over to Kukka's Greenhouse. Vivi and Sylvia, the twin sisters who owned the shop, were indirectly bickering when I walked in.

Vivi was the town herbalist and could grow anything. Sylvia was almost as good with the plants, but her specialty was healing. My grandfather had tried to date both of them when they were all young, but they still looked like they were thirty. They were both tall, thin, and had flawless porcelain skin. The only way they'd aged at all was the platinum white in their hair taking over the blonde.

Even so, I could never tell them apart, and neither could anyone else. I got a little nervous when I walked in and they both got a little wide eyed, until they moved to embrace me. One of them said, "Well, I heard the rumor, but I wouldn't believe it until he came to see us."

The other said, "And here he is, in the flesh."

In unison, they said, "Look who's all grown up."

The banter made me ache for simpler times. They'd taught me how to flirt when I was growing up. I was still really bad at it, but they'd always made it fun.

They finally spoke enough for me to figure out who was who. Vivi asked, "And are you here for a social call, or do we need to do a little business?"

With a smile, I said, "Oh, some of both."

276

Vivi returned the smile. "Who's the lucky girl?"

"Seshat."

They both looked at me with pity and a little bit of mercy. "Oh. My. Hold on."

Vivi returned with a bundle of lilies. "Good luck. Come by and let us know she turned you loose.

"MARI'S PRINCESS WAVE matched her Mona Lisa smile as I passed her on the way downstairs. I returned a less friendly hand gesture.

At the back end of the stacks was a small elevator. I braced myself for the start of the ride, and relaxed once I felt the gentle wave wash over me as I passed through the portal. It was a good sign. If she wasn't going to see me, I'd have landed on the ground floor of an empty cave. Or maybe not so empty.

An ibis stalked by and a hot breeze welcomed me as the door opened to an Egyptian-looking palace on the Nile. It was an illusion, but a good one. I guessed she was feeling homesick. It also hid all of the oldest and most important texts.

Seshat was the sexy librarian to end them all. She changed her appearance and the setting for each of her rare visitors. I sometimes wondered if she was not the consciousness behind the library, though Josiah had told me otherwise.

She draped herself across a thinly padded divan. Her bronze flesh was barely covered by a linen tunic and her braided, raven hair was pulled back. Josiah always referred to her as a man-eater. I wondered how literal it was. More than a few people had been known to disappear down here. But today, she looked almost cheerful.

"Hi, Seshat. Lovely to see you as always." I bowed slightly as I handed her the lilies.

She plunged her face into the flowers. "My favorites. You have always been so thoughtful."

She motioned to an oversized pillow on the floor. "Come, sit. It's been so long since I've seen you. Tell me everything." This

278

was the real and very dangerous part of Seshat. Her main commodity was knowledge, and she knew how to use it.

I sat cross-legged on the pillow, facing her. "You know how it is. I've been off to see the world."

She flashed an all-knowing grin. "I hear off to see the Underworld as well. How are things down there?"

I shrugged. "Rumors of my travels may be somewhat exaggerated." As always, word travelled fast, and it all flowed through here at some point. She knew something. What would the cost be? Any tidbit of knowledge I traded could wind up anywhere, for the right price.

"Come now." I'd snuck down here so many times, and gotten in trouble for every trip. I'd always been open with her before, but then again, I didn't know much in those days. Today, she was carefully observing me and devouring every detail, weighing it against whatever else she'd heard. "I've missed our chats, and I am quite pleased to see you have returned. You have grown much since we last were together. Surely you have some little tale for me?"

The hook was baited. The information I wanted was going to be costly and Seshat only took a few forms of payment. "It's been a long time. I expect you know all about why I had to leave for a while?"

Her black eyes were pools of anticipation. "I may have heard a few stories, seen a few of the records. It sounded like quite a trying affair. You wish to fill in the missing pieces? Or are you looking for my help to do so?"

I smiled in return. "Maybe some other time. I'm still working on that particular puzzle. But if you're interested, I can tell you of my ongoing travels." The line was in the water. Seshat loved nothing more than salacious stories.

She was rapt in her attention, while expertly trying to appear relaxed and uncaring. "If you wish, I would love to hear what you would share with me. May I capture them for posterity?" The floater bobbed on the water as she took a taste.

I nodded. "It seems my fate has been intertwined across the Veiled realms." Seshat loved the flowery language. I told her a story about being asked to find a couple of kidnapped girls who turned out to be Fae. She wrinkled her nose with a slight look of derision at their mention, but excitement won out behind her eyes. I wound my way around Fomorian mercenaries and I may have exaggerated some of the action. I even pulled out a few pictures from the scenes. "It appears the Cult of Erebus is involved deeply, and may be behind it all."

The goddess of knowledge stiffened. Her poise reminded me of a cobra readying to strike. "You have proof of this?" The hook was set and she was on the run.

I pulled out a few of the pages with sketches of the Anima Arca. I pointed to one of the blades. "This one was used on Drea." I flipped the page. "And this is the one they tried to use on me."

Seshat sat calmly, her jaw slightly slack, her eyes burning with desire. "I did not believe the rumors to be true. More importantly, I did not want them to be true. Their death cult has no respect for the soul. And if they have these weapons, they may have others which are far more dangerous. Where were the lost notes?"

I hesitated. I realized I hadn't thought far enough ahead in the discussion. "I found them. They'd been in a cultist collection. They were retrieved after a raid." Not entirely a lie. I'd taken and hidden items from Erebite libraries and I created the memory where it had happened. She couldn't be allowed to know the real source, especially while I wasn't entirely sure myself. I wasn't ready to point out I didn't know who Onyx's powerful new boyfriend was. Not yet.

Seshat closed her eyes but for a moment, and a book appeared in her hands. It was very old and had a leather-bound cover. She opened the book and the pages merged back into the text. "Thank you for returning these."

It hadn't been part of the plan, but at least I had copies. "You're most welcome. Now, what can you tell me about them?"

Seshat shook her head and the book vanished. "This is not something with which you should trouble yourself."

Her eyes snapped to my hands. I realized I was charging them with power. I shook them and dissipated the energy. "It's a little late for that. They have already tried to use one on me, and they've taken the spirit from one who means a great deal to me. And she's not the only one. I need to know. How does it work, and how can it be reversed?"

Seshat closed her eyes and posed with her hands over her head. "Very well. One moment." The room changed from a temple overlooking the Nile to a dark, rocky tunnel. Red and amber glowing lights came from several directions. The heat was uncomfortable, bordering on dangerous. Loud shouting and the clang of metal on metal filled the air. She rose and offered me my hand. As I stood, all of the furnishings disappeared. "Come with me."

We didn't move as the view shifted and a large cave opened around us. The blackness of the Abyss made up most of the far wall. Shadows shimmered in obsidian-like glass, lit from the fires of several furnaces smelting ore. A gigantic blacksmith hammered on a small black blade. In the hands of the giant, it looked like a small toy. Of the half dozen or so beings working in the blacksmith's shop, they all were large, sweaty, black with grime and ash, and muscular. Each had a singular red eye glowing like furnaces as they toiled.

"Welcome to the Forge of Tartarus."

HAMMER BLOWS RANG and echoed off the walls. My heart skipped a beat with every resonating strike.

Seshat squeezed my hand to snap me out of my state of shock. "This is where the Anima Arca and many other dark devices were made before most gods were born. This is a memory of when they were forged."

I said, "The Abyss."

Seshat let out a small gasp of excitement. "Ah, so you have seen it."

I'd had a momentary slip. The shock had been too much. "Yes." I waited for the reprisal which didn't come.

Her hands grasped my face and turned me towards her. She had a grim but caring look on her face. She said, "This is very important. Did it look *exactly* like *this?*" She pointed to the darkness of the back wall.

I took a deep breath, and then exhaled. "As best I could tell, yes. But it was at a great distance. It was also growing."

"Where? How long ago?"

Lightening touched every nerve in my body. Ice floes formed in my mind. I barely comprehended I'd fallen to the ground, or her hands rubbing my temples and trying to probe further.

She jolted back when she touched a memory we both wish she hadn't. "The Trial, then."

I doubled over as feeling returned to my limbs. I began vomiting uncontrollably. As the waves faded, I nodded. "Please don't ask those types of questions again."

Seshat nodded and her touch took away the worst of the symptoms. She shuddered, and the scene around us faded briefly as she took the affliction into herself.

The scene around us solidified as the effects subsided. She said, "This was the Forge of Tartarus, after it was closed off to but very few. The beings there are cyclops blacksmiths who had worked for Hephaestus. He used this shop to help build many of the lower realms for the dead, and in some cases, the not-so dead. After Tartarus was sealed off, some of the residents began to dig, to expand their world. As they expanded their tunnels, they hit pockets of the Abyss. In those places, much like lava boiling into water, it becomes something like a living obsidian. Worked in a certain way, it became a material which some in the Underworld believed could be used to escape Tartarus and reclaim the middle worlds."

The work tables were covered in scattered implements in various states of completion. Several of the Anima Arca blades were in the process of being forged. There were also swords, shields, armor, and a variety of weapons I didn't have the ability to imagine. "What happened?"

Seshat shed a lone tear. "I don't know. The story has it someone found a way into Tartarus and made a deal. The inhabitants of Tartarus would bide their time, and the weapons were hidden away for safe keeping." I wasn't sure if her sorrows were because there was something she didn't know, or if she had an idea about what her ignorance meant.

The scene shifted to another cave. It was very hot and humid. Small, translucent creatures scampered around, working on crystals growing from the ceiling. It was very dim, lighted only by small, glowing pockets in the walls. She said, "The farm where the holding crystals are grown. I do not know where this is. Getting

284

this information was…costly." The scene appeared to be very short and looped every few seconds.

She waved her hand and we returned to a warm summer afternoon on the Nile. Seshat spread herself across the divan again, looking drained and happy to be soaking up energy from an imagined midafternoon sun. I sat back down on the pillow myself, trying to Will the remnants of the headache and nausea away.

Her eyes drooped. "I think you have much more to tell me." She looked hungry. Was she going to try to make me her next meal?

"Yes, but not this trip. I need to complete the story." I hoped it would get me out, with the promise of my return. And she knew I'd have to come back.

"Very well." She lay her head against the pillowed rail and closed her eyes. "I need to rest anyway. I get so few visitors any more. This was quite draining, but a welcome diversion."

I hoped her exhaustion would make her a little more giving. "How can I reverse the effect of the blade?"

"The information I have on the Anima Arca blades, as well as the other items you saw in the vision, is limited. You may know more than I. But yes, the blades have the ability to restore souls which have been taken."

"Do you know how?"

Seshat said, "I'll see what I can do, but you know my price."

I couldn't decide who had come out on the better end of the deal from my trip. "One more thing." I pulled out a sketch of the sigil from Brighid's wall, the one to which her life force was connected. "Do you know what this is?"

Seshat looked puzzled for a moment, and then a lazy smile of understanding crossed her face. "I give this one to you for free, though I've no idea how you would have ever seen it. It's the reverse of a sigil for one of the storage crystals. It tells you the soul held inside is a practitioner of the magical arts. Did you see this when they tried to use the knife on you?"

"Thanks, Seshat. I'll see you soon." I climbed into the elevator before she could ask any more questions.

I WAS RELIEVED when the elevator dumped me into the closet outside of the stacks. Mari had a large smirk on her face. "I'd have thought you'd be a little more mussed after taking a trip down. Then again, you weren't gone too long."

"Get your mind out of the gutter. This trip was all business."

"Really. Well, I guess you aren't interested in the gift she sent along." She held up a box wrapped in linen paper and tied with a red bow.

I snatched the box with a grunt and carried it to the reading room in the back. The room looked just like I remembered. A few reading lamps cast angular shadows everywhere. It was just big enough for a four-person table and chairs and for stacks of crumbling texts overflowing from the room outside. The chipped black chalkboard on the back wall had a few obscure notes in Josiah's handwriting, and notes from a few other hands. It looked like they'd been working on my defense strategy.

I placed the box on the table and took a seat on the side facing the open door. I couldn't feel totally safe, even here. Time slipped by as I stared at the gift.

I was startled when Mari spoke from the doorway. I had no idea how long she'd been standing there. "Are you going to open it or what? I want to see what's in there." She leaned against the door frame trying to look bored, but the little kid was bouncing behind her eyes.

She'd spent her entire life here, protected. Against my better judgment, I invited her in. "Close the door and secure the room."

She jumped in the chair beside me and stared at the box. "What do you think she sent you? Were you a good boy?" She gave me her goofy smile and tried to be coy.

Gently, I pulled on the red ribbon. The parchment wrapping fell away to reveal an old wooden box covered in hieroglyphics.

She gently pushed back from the table. "Then again, this is yours. I think it should be private."

I glared at her. "Are you in or out? I can't read this, but you can." What had her so spooked?

She swallowed, reached into a drawer, and pulled out a pair of thick-rimmed glasses. She put them on and handed me a second pair. "These will help. They have an enchantment built-in."

An odd throb built in my head as I slipped on the glasses. The script on the box started to make sense, but only in small pieces. "It looks like a page from the Egyptian Book of the Dead. Not a personal charm, like most of them are, but a copy of one of the panels from...whoa."

She paled, frantically alternating between scribbling notes on the chalkboard and looking back at the box.

"What is it? What did you find?"

She gave me her frantic wave to give her a minute as opened a nearby book. It always seemed to work that way in the library. Whatever you needed was close at hand, unless you weren't meant to have it.

How much influence did Seshat have on the library? She was a demigod who passed information down to the mortals when it suited her. Josiah had taught us how she'd collected knowledge throughout the ages, and was one of the main sources for the library. Mari finished her process with a somber look. "Let it go. Whatever you're doing, stop. This is very old. Very nasty." Slowly, she pushed away from the table.

Very gently, I touched her hand. "Mari, if she sent this up, we both know what it means."

"I think if you pursue this, it will kill you. And probably a lot of others in the process."

It struck me as funny. I started to laugh, which really seemed to disturb my cousin, which made me laugh harder. "Is that all? Mari, I've been on borrowed time for seven years. I've made more than my share of enemies. All the Trial did was change the who, when, and how. Until then, I have things I need to do. Are you going to help me or not?"

She sniffed and held back tears. "Of course." She slid closer to me and pointed to a couple of glyphs on the box. "This looks like the kind of spell we would see in later copies of the Book of the Dead. But it's not. The glyphs are different. I think this is a spell written from the other side, the Land of the Dead. It is a page from the Book of Ammit, the devourer of souls."

I shook my head, trying to understand what it meant. I held the sides of the box and pulled the top up. Mari placed his hand on the top before I could remove it. She said, "Are you sure you want to open this? What did you promise her?"

"I promised her my story, my memories." Her rare austere look caused me to pause. I was pushing her well beyond her comfortable boundaries. Before I'd left, we had been tighter than siblings, and our bond hadn't weakened. I wouldn't drag her where she wasn't ready to go. "Mari, you can leave if you want. I can work through it with the glasses."

"I'm here for you. If this is what you need to do, I'm along for the ride." Mari grabbed the other side and helped me slide the lid off. A note in delicate calligraphy was on top.

Dearest Greyson,

I was gratified by your journey to see me after so long of a time. I hope this child-book, made from many texts, gives you what you seek. It is made from all information available to me on the subject. In return, I trust you will share the experiences which come from it.

I shall count the days until your next visit.

Mari cocked her head and raised an eyebrow. "You always were one of her favorites."

I placed the note aside. If I opened this book, I'd be beholden to Seshat. There was no way I'd give her unfettered access to my mind and memories, even if it was just limited to anything with the blades. If I didn't get the information, I could lose Drea and Brighid, and maybe everything.

Mari was entranced with the cover of the book. Twelve sigils reminiscent of the zodiac ringed a thirteenth on the cover of a night black, leather-bound book. Each sigil dimly glowed garnet red. "So, open it."

The three simple words reminded me how innocent she was. Too innocent. Seshat's deal with her was different. Mari was being used as the lure. How many had come into the library and entered into a deal without realizing it? I couldn't link her to the obligations which went along with the book. "Mari, take a walk. I need a few."

She exclaimed, "What? Thirty seconds ago, you wouldn't let me go, and now you want to boot me out? What is it?"

"Mari," I said, "I need to remove this from town before I open it up. And I think linking you to the book will make you a target. I'll keep you in the loop, and I do need your help. But not this." I put the letter back on top of the book and replaced the lid. "I want you to be safe."

"What? I...." She looked away when she understood by what I meant. She opened the door and sulked as she returned upstairs.

"REVEAL YOUR SECRETS." I ported into my lab from the library. It took a few minutes to clear a space on the table, and I took a few extra minutes, killing time, by loading supplies into my pack. I was running low on a lot of the basics in my stockpile and would need to resupply soon.

I placed the box on the table and removed the top. I stared at the note from Seshat and tried to ignore the obligations which went with it, before placing it aside. On removing the book from the box, I saw a piece of parchment and seven stone tubes were anchored in the bottom of the box.

I slit open the seal of the parchment note.

Dearest Greyson,

The box contains the means for your sojourn. I trust you will abide by our agreement at journey's end.

Travel   with   Fortuna.

Fantastic. More riddles. I took a deep breath and opened the book. The sigils on the cover flared briefly. The deal was done.

I skimmed through the pages until I found the incantations used with the blades. All of the rituals were advanced, but much of the work could be done beforehand and the energy stored in the blade. I absorbed all I could, which was a fraction of the text. I was tired, but I needed to see Josiah.

I ported back to the library. Walking up the stairs to the main level, Mari stopped me. "You have a visitor." She shifted nervously. "Josiah doesn't think it is a good idea for you two to talk, but he went to meet someone. I don't know who, but he left quickly after he got a call."

So much for a quick meeting with old Granddad and then a nap. "Who is it?"

She looked around, and whispered conspiratorially. "Rhea Sinclair. She seems quite upset."

"Where?"

Mari stammered, "Third floor."

Brighid's mother sat in a rocking chair, staring out of the window at her house. The room was mostly used for storage, like most of the Library, but it had a small widow's walk around the upper floor.

Rhea had obviously been crying, but looked to be out of tears. I wasn't sure she'd noticed me enter when she spoke. "He's going to take her."

"What?" I asked.

She looked at her shaking hands folded in her lap. "Reginald. He's going to take Brighid from the room. I don't know how. I think he's doing it to punish us both."

I knelt in front of her. "When? Do you know when?"

She shook her head. "I don't know exactly. He was going to do it tonight, but he was called away."

I was starting to wonder about the timing. Both him and Josiah. "Let me go take a look."

It was early, but night had already fallen with the aid of heavy clouds. I managed to sneak unseen across the street and opened my Sight to examine the side of the house where Brighid's room was attached. The practitioner's sigil glowed brightly on the outer wall. A ribbon stretched into the ether. The room was built to act like one of the Anima Arca crystals, to house a soul.

Rhea caught up to me.

I said, "We need to see Brighid."

We both walked into her bedroom, and Brighid materialized as Rhea closed the door.

Brighid looked a little less solid than the night before, but smiled. "You came back." The view through my Sight was concerning. Cracks were forming in the bubble which kept her safe and intact. I couldn't tell if it was coming from something from outside, degradation of the energy, or something else.

I said, "Both of you, listen to me. I think there is a way to get you out of here. Brighid, I don't know what it will be like for you, but I have a place we can hold you, until I can restore you. Your body *is* out there alive, and you can help me find it." I wasn't sure if the last part was true, but it was worth a shot.

Rhea nodded.

Brighid smiled. "I know you will protect me."

"I'll be back in a few minutes. Rhea, I need you to work something up while I'm gone."

I ported back to my lab from the library and opened the text. I found reference to the idea of being able to house multiple souls in a sort of energy lattice, and the ability to remove them. It looked pretty similar to what I needed, at least in principle.

I laid out the black dagger on the lab table and removed the crystal. It had held some of my own essence. Had it been damaged when Eric reversed the process? How had he known what to do? Should I try to find him to help?

The clock was ticking.

Through my Sight, the crystal appeared intact and undamaged. I followed the instructions and Pushed a small amount of energy into the crystal with a command. I slipped the crystal back into place in the dagger handle and a small hum of power surged through the blade.

The incantation was complicated, but I understood it to be a way of focusing my intent. I was starting to get the idea that the blades were very complex in design, but elegant in their simplicity to operate. They were basically capacitors, and they just needed to know which way for the energy to flow.

I'd prepared the dagger as best I could. There was no guarantee it would work. It might even kill her.

My heart raced as I tried to center myself. Was I doing the right thing? I had to try, at least for Rhea's sake. I'd be a fugitive again as soon as I did it.

I changed into a Leviskin skinsuit and Pushed it to become tactical wear. I slipped my gear into the usual slots, and holstered the Colt. I created a new padded slot for the black blade and slipped it into place.

I hoped none of it was necessary.

It was nearing midnight when I ported back into the library, stepped into the inky darkness of the alcove, and shadow-walked to the third floor. A light was on in one window of the house across the way. It was the all-ready signal. I shadow-walked to the back door of the Sinclair house and knocked.

Rhea was shaking when she opened the door.

"Is everything set?"

She nodded. We walked into Brighid's room, and I explained what was about to happen. The three of us agreed to proceed.

Rhea took her place outside of Brighid's room, and I walked to the back of the house, standing in front of the sigil outside. I opened my Sight and focused on the glowing mark. I ushered my doubts aside and drew the blade, touching the tip to the sigil and Willing it to draw her spirit into the crystal.

The crystal pulsed until it was a solid, emerald green glow. The mark on the wall dimmed until it faded completely, leaving the barest trace of the original spell. I checked the crystal as best I could, and gave Rhea the signal the transfer was complete.

I'd asked her to charge an object with her own energy which we could use to make it look like Brighid was still here. When I Sensed the energy flowing from inside, I used a bit of my own energy to draw the sigil, and created a beacon which would complete the illusion. Daylight would wash it away, but buy some time.

Rhea looked at me sadly from a nearby window and waved goodbye.

I WAS COMMITTED. I left a note for Josiah asking him to watch the furball for a few days, and a secure way for him to drop me messages. I wasn't about to trust FaeMail.

I ported back into my lab to rest and decide my next steps. It was possible when the illusion at Sinclair's dissolved at sunup, he would believe its energy matrix had collapsed. If I could see it starting to collapse, so could he. Whatever he'd planned may have been what started the collapse. I had to trust in Rhea to maintain the story.

I wanted to fight sleep. I was exhausted, but the odds were Tsauriel would want to chat. I needed to find a way to control her access, but nothing had worked so far. I was really tired of being summoned on demand. An idea crawled forward and I cobbled together the ingredients before I thought about what I was doing.

Two hours later, I was wrapped in a cheese cloth which smelled of ozone-singed lilacs. It was a Shroud of the Dead spell to hide a living soul from all sorts of divination. It also had the ability to entrap some ethereal creatures. I decided to give it a try, and wrapped myself snugly as I curled up on the cot to sleep.

"Cute, Greyson. You cannot hide from yourself." Tsauriel pulled the shroud from my face. "Get up."

Damn. I balled the useless shroud and threw it in a corner of a small room. I was laying on a roughly built but comfortable bed. From the curve of the stone walls, I figured I was in the tower.

Tsauriel sat on the edge of the bed. "I believe we may have started off on the wrong foot, you and I, but time was of the essence. We have prepared you this room, such that these transitions are easier for you, and it gives you a space here."

The room was simple. A bed, a roughhewn standing chest, and a window. I climbed from the bed and looked out of the window. It had a beautiful view of the grounds and the forest beyond.

"You shouldn't have. Really. I'm not really one for roommates, unless you're renting out space in here." I tapped my head.

"Not exactly where we are located, but I get your point."

I paced the room and fired questions at the angel. "Why are you doing this? Why me? What's the end game?"

From behind, I heard a gentle but sad laugh. "You are but one piece on the board. The one to determine if this and all worlds will merge under peace, or shatter into eternal darkness. I am here to make sure you are prepared."

"I thought this story was already written with a happy ending."

Tsauriel stood next to me, staring out of the window. "One must have hope. Just because the plan is written, it must still be executed. And I don't know if you noticed, but there are a lot of different versions of it out there."

We watched Ladon stroll through the grounds. He was touching the ground in places, but I couldn't tell what he was doing. "So, what's Mr. Cheerful's place in all of this?"

She clucked. "Excellent question. I am still unsure how he got here, but it appears for now, he's your trainer. Learn well from him. He's a bit surly, but I've grown accustomed to his company."

"You've said that a couple of times. Big war. Training me for some role in it. What am I training to do? Why me?"

Tsauriel stared past me into the distance.

I glared at the angel for a few moments. Even through the stoic look, I saw her internal conflict. Ladon swung at fireballs with a cricket bat. "He fancies you. Finds you quite a challenge. He also believes you will die quite horribly, and in a way which will take us with you."

I grabbed Tsauriel and turned her to face me. I stared into her eyes. She grabbed my temples. I lost the war of wills.

Terrible visions burst by too quickly to latch on to, but slowly enough to traumatize me. Angels, demons, men, and all manner of beings were locked in battle. Flashes of swords, fire, and gore. I looked through another's eyes. A tall figure stood a distance away. He wore shiny, black armor and carried a shield crackling with death. He carried a whip-like weapon. Violet surges of energy ran its length and streamed from the spikes in all directions each time he cracked it.

Anyone touched by the bolts of energy fell dead where they stood.

The being removed his helmet and threw it to the ground. His skin was so pale as to be translucent. His eyes shined as black as his armor. His expression was as solid as death.

We ran towards each other. I dodged as the whip cracked and flew past me. I reached to thrust my sword into his chest as the tail of the whip burst through my chest from behind and yanked me away.

The sword sliced through the whip with a blinding flash. The tail of the whip flailed from my back like a wounded snake as I completed the turn and plunged my sword through his armor into his chest. We locked eyes and clung to each other as we slumped to the ground. I grew cold as my life slipped away. I was being drawn into the dark whirlpools of his eyes. "Gundaric. Stay with me."

A figure in monk's robes held my head and mumbled something. I wanted to sleep. Another voice grabbed at the edges of my consciousness. "Come on, Ennius. He's gone. We must keep moving. We must move forward."

The visions faded. "What the hell?" My vision cleared. The angel held my head in her lap.

Her voice was monotone and lifeless. "That was a vision from the last time the darkness took form on this plane, in the form of Apollyon. Rome had fallen, and the former empire was in disarray. Somehow, it was raised into form and led an army. In the Dacia Ripensis, a battle was fought and you saw the moment the beast was banished. Someone is trying to raise it again."

I still felt the emptiness of the deathly vision. "To what end?"

"This entity is a blunt instrument. It is capable of crossing between the realms at will, and only has the goal of destruction. And it has the ability to usher other beings into your reality to achieve those goals."

I was really missing the days of being clueless and hunted in only a couple of dimensions. What did I really know? What did she think I could do against something like that? "Who would do this?"

Tsauriel took my hand. "You protect your world from what you see as the Veiled worlds. There are more dimensions beyond, some fantastic, others horrific. Even with your Senses, your knowledge, there are things beyond your comprehension, and even mine."

300

"This isn't going to end well for me, is it?"

She patted the side of my face. "It is not for me to answer. One must play the game to know the outcome. I can only tell you who is on the field." She sniffed and prodded me from her lap. "Enough chatting for one day. Ladon is growing impatient to resume your training. I suspect it will be quite challenging today, since you have kept him waiting."

Damn you, you Divine buzzard.

SORE AND TIRED, I awoke still wrapped in the shroud on the small cot. I wrinkled my nose at the juices I'd marinated in and tossed the used cheesecloth aside.

Ladon must have been tightly wound based on the workout he'd run me through. It wasn't entirely one-sided this time. Now that the bindings were peeling away, I'd come up with a few tricks and a few good hits.

As I stretched, I realized I was still fully dressed in the tactical gear. What was I becoming? I'd gone to Sinclair's fully expecting it to become a shooting war. He wanted a duel and I was ready to give it to him. Wasn't I?

Deep down, I knew it would have to end badly if I couldn't bring Brighid home. Would it be enough? Was there more to his hatred of me?

I doubted the illusion of Brighid's cell collapsing would hold for long. The sun would have been beating down on the house for most of the day.

I randomly opened Seshat's tome and found a story where a soul had been split. One half stayed in the body and the other half was imprisoned. Over time, both halves went insane. Was it happening to Brighid? The emerald crystal glowed silently.

With more questions than answers, I found a way to make a tracking spell which would let me follow the link between the crystal and her body. What would happen when I reintegrated the two halves? I also hoped the reverse would work, for Drea's sake.

I had most of what I needed for the potion, and made a list of the rest. I couldn't risk going back to the Grove. Not yet. My next worst option was LA.

Damn.

I prepared the permanent circle in the floor, and targeted the semi-permanent circle in the resort penthouse of my part-time home. I hadn't been there in months. I hoped Priscilla hadn't changed her mind about me having the place. Or that I had unexpected guests.

"Off to see the stars."

I stood in the closet and listened for a few minutes. I stretched my Senses, but knew I was alone. My bedroom was just the same as when I'd left for Atlanta, except the bed was made.

I grabbed the gear bags and laid them out on the bed. I called down to the desk to have them get a car ready. An hour later, I pulled up in front of the Gin House.

Ichabod gave me a high-five tentacle as I passed through the inner door. Alvin waved. Fifteen minutes later, Obi had acquired the supplies I needed, along with a warning to watch myself. It was becoming a recurring theme.

In under ninety minutes, I was back at the door of my suite. But I wasn't alone any more.

With the Colt 1911 in my right hand, I Willed an energy ball into my left. No point in burning the building down if I didn't have to. I Pushed my Senses, but my own wards minimized what I could detect. I bumped the door open with my shoulder and rammed my way through.

Movement came from my right. I shoved the door back and heard a cry. I dashed left and knelt behind the couch to take advantage of its meager cover.

I pointed the Colt directly at a surprised Onyx on the couch as I rose to my feet. Raines leveled her service weapon at me from behind a door frame.

I said, "Hi. You should have called ahead. I'd have ordered a pizza."

Onyx peered over the top of the book she was reading. "Hello?"

Raines cut me with a sharp look. "Lower your weapon."

"You first." Her stance told me something bad had happened. Or maybe it was the trickle of blood over her eyebrow where I'd slammed the door into her.

Onyx said, "Both of you, calm down."

I calculated the situation. I didn't Sense anyone else in the suite. I holstered the Colt, but held the energy ball in reserve. "Your turn."

Raines stood frozen with ice in her eyes.

Onyx closed the book and placed it on the table. She reminded me more and more of Priscilla. "Beth?"

Finally, Raines lowered the weapon, but kept it in her hand. She also kept her eyes on me as she closed the door.

I took a deep breath. "What's happened?"

Onyx shuddered and buried her head in her knees.

I sat next to her and put my hand on her back. "Is it Drea? Is she...."

Raines pulled a chair around and placed her weapon in her lap.

Raines said, "The Longbow holding facility was raided a few hours ago. They took Dick Gibson, and a couple of other prisoners. Chain of command is gone. After the last couple of months, things are bad. And you've been nowhere to be found."

This was going to be hard to explain.

Onyx said, "I was at the hospital with Drea when it happened."

Raines said, "When did you get back to town?" The implication in her tone was obvious.

"Ninety minutes or so ago." I had to defuse the situation. "I've got something of a back door here."

Raines trembled. Her unsteady hand locked around the weapon. "Like the back door they used to get into the facility. They used the portals you built to get in and out." The accusation was impossible to miss.

I'd taken precautions with the portals. Every one of them could be locked down easily, and was paired with another facility. And if that failed, the whole system could be locked down, and if needed, destroyed with the flip of a switch. "It was not me. I promise you. I didn't know anything about this. Beth, tell me what's going on."

She placed her service weapon on the table. "Onyx said you had been in some sort of trial, and you were released a couple of days ago. No one else in Longbow knows you're back, beyond Wynn and myself. You're wanted for questioning about several incidents in the last couple of weeks, and about your disappearance. I was on the edge of town, on the way back from the Nevada site, when the Longbow facility was hit. My team was waved off, so I haven't been in yet. I don't know how bad it is." She looked exhausted. "A few minutes later, Onyx called me and said the alarm had gone off here. Your turn. Where the hell have you been?"

"You're closer than you know." I huffed at my own inside joke. "The Trial is over, and I was cleared. But there were still repercussions at home."

"You couldn't get us some kind of message? In all that time? Wynn checked in every day with that thing you gave him. I think he was about to give up."

"All I can say is I wasn't exactly on this plane. And no, I had no way to get any sort of message out. I was either getting out or I'd just cease to exist."

"And now? Why are you here now?"

"I needed supplies. I think I found out how the dagger works. I may be able to track down Drea herself. And I might be able to restore her, if I can find her." No way I'd go into details about Brighid. "I made a quick trip to Obi's for a couple of things." I pulled a bag from my pocket.

Raines said, "A lot of maybes."

Onyx lay her head on my shoulder. "It may be too late. Her body is slipping away." The resignation in her voice launched a lump into my throat.

"I need to see her." I had to see her, to see if there was anything I could do or,   worst case, to say goodbye.

Raines said, "Bad idea. You'll be picked up before you can make it to her room. Even if you get there, you'll never make it out."

I had to believe any questions about me could be resolved, but it would take time. Maybe a long time. "I need to try."

Raines nodded. "Good luck. I need to get back to the Nevada site." She was cold, but my answers seemed to have been enough for her. If not, they'd be ready for me at the hospital.

Nevada? Again? "What's happening in Nevada? Where?"

Raines pursed her lips. "Near the Cali border in the Mojave, Homeland drones reported activity they thought might be trafficking. Instead, they encountered something else. We think it's an Erebite hideout or a gateway, but we're monitoring it." Raines pulled out her tablet and starting flipping through surveillance pictures. "I think you know a few of our friends in this shot. We're trying to identify the others."

The picture was of the front of a small cave system in the side of a hill. Several cars and vans were parked around. Raines pointed to Betty Gibson. "She seems to be running things from here, or nearby. A couple of their security detail are missing Longbow personnel. We haven't been able to identify this one, though."

Raines flipped through a couple of pictures and stopped on a particular one. They may not know who it was, but I did. Brighid Sinclair. "She's been coming by sporadically, once a week or so. We think she's a messenger or a courier."

I flipped through more of the images. Brighid showed up a few more times. "What's your plan?"

Raines spoke in a monotone. "I'm not entirely sure. I only have a small team, barely enough to do recon. I was coming in to discuss options and get reinforcements. Now, I don't know. I guess it depends on how badly Longbow has been compromised."

THE CONCOCTION SMOKED as I dropped in a grain of the Sands of Time. Raines had left to check in with Wynn and her team. She'd promised me an update in a couple of hours.

Onyx leaned back from the noxious fumes and wrinkled her nose. "What's this for again?"

I watched intently, waiting for the color change to tell me if I'd done it right. "Tracking spell. It will create a sympathetic connection between Drea and me that I can use to find her, once I'm in the hospital."

"One small problem." She picked up a vial on the counter and looked at the grainy contents. "Getting inside."

"Don't touch that. Not unless you want to do a lot more shaving." I guided her hands down to gently return the vial to its place. "I've got a plan. I think. This needs a little time to steep before I can bottle it up and be ready to travel."

She asked, "What can I do?"

I took the vial Delacroix had given me out of my pocket. "Don't disturb me for the next little while. And don't let anyone else either."

She said unsurely, "OK?"

The instructions on the bottle read "Consume in sunlight." The sun was large and red on the horizon. I hoped the rays would be enough. I needed an idea if I was going to get in and out of the hospital undetected.

The top of the ampule snapped off easily between my fingers. It smelled a little like fresh-cut grass in a spring shower. Vanilla and fresh mint rolled down my throat.

Was that it? I leaned on the rail. Nothing changed. Was the setting sun too weak to break down the...whoa...I felt heavy and light simultaneously. I puddled into a caftan chair.

A warm stream of power coursed through my veins. The orange rays of the setting sun reached out and stroked me. I found myself wrapped in a rainbow of light, but looked deeper to see the incantations and power in each color band.

A filament of light reached down, and intertwined with the red spectrum. A golden script flashed into view and then dissolved, taking the color band with it.

My nails buried themselves into my palms as my body seized with a shock.

The cartoon sun waved a flare for a hand and dipped behind the horizon. I relaxed and closed my eyes.

DELACROIX WAS RIGHT. The stuff gave me a hellacious hangover. I shook my head, and wished I hadn't.

From the looks of it, the experience hadn't lasted long. Or I'd lost a day. By the third bottle of water, I could think.

"Your stuff has turned the color you wanted, I think." Onyx handed me the pills from the counter, which I quickly swallowed. "Now what?"

"We go to the hospital after I get a change of clothes."

She yelled at me through the closed door. "Are you sure this is smart? How are you getting in?"

I adjusted the skinsuit to a casual configuration once I had my weapons in place. The Anima Arca slid in easily on my hip, and melded out of sight. I opened the door. "You're carrying me in."

"Am I dressing you up like a teddy bear? I'm not sure if she's into furries."

I quieted her with a look. I needed to do this while I was still hung over and thought it was a good idea. "A mirror trap."

If you were creative enough and a little skilled, mirrors made handy portals. With a little more work, you could even use them to hide and carry items. I didn't trust anyone enough these days with the power to lock me away and not let me out, so I'd gone to the next level and paired a set to have a gateway within a gateway. If something went bad, I could escape out of the second mirror.

The hospital was warded against what I was trying to do, but ultimately, locks only kept out the honest and the lazy. I put the mirror in the bottom of a small vase and put a small hex on the

310

vase so it would fall apart after a given period of time. As a backup, I did something similar with the other mirror and hid it. "Once I'm inside, all you have to do is carry me in and set me in the room."

"This plan sucks."

"Do you have a better one?" I was focused on the mirror in the vase.

She shook her head.

"Then don't drop me." I gazed into the mirror. "Off to the carnival. "A whooshing sound surrounded me as I was sucked towards my distorted reflection. It felt like being run through a taffy puller while looking at a fun house mirror. It didn't help the hangover, either.

The already-distorted view was obliterated when Onyx filled the vase with water and dropped a few flowers on top as planned, to mask the magic and get it past the wards. I hoped.

I slumped in the corner to wait.

MY BODY TINGLED. I prepared myself, because I had no idea where I'd appear, or who'd be nearby. With any luck, I wouldn't materialize in a cell.

The return trip made me dizzy and a little claustrophobic, but the hangover was mostly gone. I stood and stretched my body and Senses. The regular beeps and sighs from the medical equipment helped me center myself.

I stood alone in Drea's room. Actually, I was leaning in a puddle of water on the small ledge in the window, where Onyx had put the flower vase. Broken glass littered the floor.

It was a little after midnight. The ward was quiet. I should have a little while before the next round came through to check her vitals. I sat in the chair next to the bed and watched her. She could have just been asleep. Her face was a little drawn, and some of the definition had left her muscles. Her face was at peace.

I had a little one-sided conversation with her about what I was going to do, losing my sliver of hope it might wake her up.

I pulled the vial for Drea out of my pocket and lay it on the table. I opened my Sight and focused only on her. The thin tendril of energy running to her was brilliant, but thin. I Sensed it was from someone was slowly choking the connection, rather than her life fading away.

The incantation worked by strengthening the energy connection between body and soul. The potion in the vial would help create the sympathetic relationship, once I added a little more to the mix. I would need to connect her energy to the concoction, and then drink it to create a direct connection to myself. If anyone was watching, it would also light me up like a flare at midnight.

I plucked a loose hair from her head and added it to the vial. I focused, blocking out everything except for Drea, myself, and the connection, and recited the incantation. A thin thread grew from the main branch and energized the contents of the vial.

"Here's to you." I choked the mixture down.

A sharp snap echoed in my head. An odd but pleasant feeling coursed through me.

A long, thin hand materialized and touched mine. "Grey." A couple of intimate images formed in my mind. I felt her coursing into me.

Machines beeping snapped me from my bliss. Drea's body had gone into a seizure. The connection didn't have enough energy to sustain the connection to me and to her body, and she was choosing me. I had to strengthen the connection or she would totally let go of her body.

Hurried calls of "Code Blue!" and slaps of feet rushed my way. I threw a quick energy field which would hold the door shut. Nothing they could do would help her.

I poured all of the Will and energy I could into the stream. I was being split between the material world and wherever she was. I stretched out and found myself inside of a shaft of light.

"Grey, help!" Drea shouted frantically and clawed against a wall closing faster than she could dig with her hands.

I swam against the weakening flow until I reached the wall. The hole had closed to where I could barely see her on the other side. I grabbed a few handfuls, and knew it wouldn't make the difference.

313

In less than a minute, the wall would close and she'd be gone.

A voice whispered in my mind. "Use the blade." A page from the book appeared clearly in my mind.

I drew the Anima Arca from its sheath on my leg and slashed at the opening. I grew frantic as chunks of wall flew into the ether, until the hole widened enough for her to come through. Her hand touched mine.

I was back in the hospital, poised over her body. It was now or never. I touched the blade to her chest and channeled the connection. I seized up as the power flowed through me, into the blade, and into her.

I was back in the tunnel. I grabbed Drea's hand to pull her through.

"Not so fast, coward." Drake's hand shot through the opening and grabbed her leg.

She screamed as we both tugged.

"Take the blade," I said.

Drea grabbed the Anima Arca from my hand and sliced into Drake. He screamed, and we both tumbled down the tunnel.

Back in the hospital room, the etheric blade was buried in her chest. "Restitue Animam."

Her body glowed and a concussive wave blew the blade from her chest. It threw me against the wall. I lost focus and the field holding the door shut collapsed.

Doctors and nurses rushed to her side. One slapped me. "What did you do?"

I couldn't answer. I was focused on the barrels of the weapons the security detail had aimed at my head.

A doctor shouted, "She's waking up."

I butted the nurse aside. "Drea?"

Wynn was behind his service weapon. "Yes, Greyson, what *did* you do?"

A feeble voice from the bed asked, "Who's Drea?"

I STOOD UP. Wynn told his people to evacuate the room into the hall. Deeply confused eyes darted around and focused on me. "Grey...Greyson?"

I grabbed the blade from the floor. The crystal was no longer an emerald green, but now a deep violet.

I was terrified to ask the question. "Brighid?"

Drea's face held Brighid's kind smile. She croaked out, "You did it."

One of the security detail asked Wynn if they should detain me.

Wynn responded, "I don't think which would work out well for you."

"I'm here." I touched the tears streaming down her face.

Wynn placed his hand on my shoulder. "Come with me for a moment."

I nodded. "I'll be back." I kissed her forehead. A doctor gently nudged me aside to do his examination.

"Get rid of all the mirrors," I said. Wynn nodded to the nurse. The security detail looked nervous, but no one moved to stop me as I sheathed the blade.

The security detail followed at a safe distance as we moved to the interview room on the fourth floor secure ward. I knew the move was designed to get me behind a few more barriers, and I was willing to go as a sign of good faith. I was still on his side.

But I flinched inwardly every time another security detail appeared.

Wynn closed and locked the door behind the two of us with the escorts just outside. He studied me carefully as we took seats.

"Hi, Gerry. It's been a while."

The special agent was unreadable as he studied me in his deliberate style. "Yes, it has been a while. Do you want to bring me up to speed?"

"You know about the Trial?"

He nodded. "I was told you were cleared in whatever those proceedings were."

"More or less." I swallowed. "Some people weren't real happy with the outcome."

"I heard. How long have you been back?"

"Since late afternoon. I had a few things I needed to get here. I was trying to wrap up things at home before I came back. I came to LA to get some supplies to try and track Betty and her crew down."

Wynn asked, "Why didn't you come in? Or at least give me a call?"

I paused. I opened my Sight. Wynn was the same soul he'd always been, just a little more broken. "Longbow has been compromised. Dorian told me that, and so did Beth. And I thought you were injured and sidelined."

"Wait." He leaned across the table. "You've seen Raines? When?"

I shrugged. "Early afternoon, a couple of hours after I came through the suite. She and Onyx were waiting for me when I made a stopover. They told me that Drea was slipping, and I was being hunted. I had to see her, even if it was to say goodbye."

Wynn leaned back in the chair and bit his lip.

A commotion rose in the hallway. I Sensed the power before I heard her voice. Priscilla was snapping orders outside of the door.

Anxiety appeared in his face as he placed his hand on the door and let out a nervous laugh. "Maybe I should have let them shoot you, for your sake."

Drea's grandmother stood just outside, her arms crossed and her eyes locked onto me. The security detail had backed further away, their weapons at the ready.

Wynn motioned for them to leave.

The door frame bent slightly when Priscilla slammed the door. She screamed, "What in Hades have you done?"

Maybe Wynn had it right. Would they shoot me for trying to escape? "Priscilla, hold on." I raised my hands and backed up a few steps, not that it would do any good.

The table groaned as she leaned over it. "I'm listening."

He gently placed his hand on her arm to calm her, but quickly removed it when she looked at him.

She eased herself into a chair. "Start from the beginning."

My heart raced. "Someone I'd been close to, and who I thought was killed that night in the Grove, came to me when we were all in Atlanta. She wanted me to leave with her, said we were in danger. I refused, and then the night of the big party, we were attacked by Betty and her group."

"I'm aware of the events."

"What I didn't have time to tell anyone is that the woman who came to me, her name is Brighid, was the one who attacked me the night of the party. She was with the Erebites and stabbed me with one of the blades like the one used on Drea. I was lucky to survive, and was able to capture the blade." I drew the Anima Arca from the sheath and laid it on the table. "I didn't have time to recover or warn anyone when I was taken for the Trial."

Wynn asked, "You were taken directly from Atlanta? We searched for you for most of six weeks. There were rumors of sightings a few times, but nothing we were able to confirm."

Priscilla nodded. "I let you know as soon as I got confirmation of his return. I had little notice myself."

"All I can say is I wasn't anywhere someone might have been able to see me." Even the hint was enough to feel a twinge in my chest. "In the two days after the Trial, I was able to get my hands on some information about the Anima Arca and was working on a plan. Then everything went sideways. I found out Brighid's essence, or at least part of it, was being held in her family home using the same type of magic."

Wynn shook his head and laughed. "That's when things went wrong?"

Priscilla held her hand up to stop the agent. "You're saying Reginald has been using this power to keep her locked away? Then who is in her body?"

"No idea." I shook my head. "The container was breaking down, and I used the Anima Arca to save her essence and hopefully put it back in her body. I don't know if she was split and part of her stayed in her body, or if it's possessed."

Priscilla stared at the table, clenching and unclenching her fists. The power of her rage soaked the room. "Instead, you decided to put her in the body of my granddaughter. A way to get them both back in some twisted fantasy?"

I put my hands in the air and waved. "No. Absolutely not. I came to the hospital to try and trace Drea's location. She wasn't strong enough for it, and her connection was choked off by Drake. I was losing her. I didn't have a choice. I used the blade to open the blockage and pull her back through to this side. I was channeling her back into her body, and I didn't think about Brighid being in there. I just acted on instinct. I think to make room for Drea, it Pushed Brighid into Drea's body." I stroked the blade. "Drea's in here."

For the first time in what seemed like hours, the room was silent. The hall outside was still.

A sense of calm started to overcome Priscilla's rage. "You have her. Here."

I nodded.

"Then put her back in her body." Priscilla looked at the blade. "Now."

I fully expected her to slice me in half when I answered. "I can't. Not yet."

Accusations filled her tone. "Why?"

"I don't know how." I broke down and rambled. "If I had an empty crystal, maybe. Our best bet is to find Brighid's corporeal self."

Priscilla jumped when Wynn placed a hand on her arm. "He was with Raines earlier today. And Onyx."

She gasped. "Where?"

I said, "The suite. They're the ones who told me about Drea. Now, can you two tell me what's happening?"

Wynn opened his tablet. "Kansas City, right after Atlanta. We never made it to Jacksonville. It was supposed to be a simple recon following up on the group coming to Atlanta. We were at a small warehouse district between KC and Leavenworth. I was in OPS, Raines was leading team one, Duarte led team two, Hicks was on team three, and Hall had team four. It was a trap. I was a little bruised up and the OPS van didn't fare well at all when we got hit. Hall and his four-man team were ambushed. We only found one body. Duarte lost two guys. Hicks was pretty badly hurt and lost Carlisle. Raines and her team vanished without a trace. We sent the casualties for help, and I took the rest of the team to ground to look for the missing. We came back in a couple of weeks ago, but have been laying low."

I asked, "What about Vegas? Hayden's team?"

He said, "You know about that." He cut an accusing look at Priscilla. She returned an indifferent shrug. "Hayden runs a team which mostly does archaeology and artifact recovery. They were looking into a site in the desert tied into some artifacts from a ritual in the early forties. They were examining a spot where reputedly some practitioners may have been able to open a portal. We don't have an exact location, and the team is gone."

"Raines isn't running a surveillance team in Nevada?" I was getting a sense as to how bad things really were.

Wynn shook his head. "Not for me. And she's listed as MIA with Longbow and the Bureau."

Priscilla touched my hand. "You have seen Onyx?"

321

"She was with Raines at the suite. She told me Drea was slipping away."

Priscilla and Wynn shared a look making me nervous. "Onyx has been missing since right after things went poorly for Agent Wynn's team. Dorian, Nicomedes, and I were just in Miami, trying to track her down. We think she may be with the gentleman she met in Atlanta." A slight sneer on the word "gentleman."

"Wait." I shook my head. "She was at the party in the Grove a few days ago, with Kizzy, Mel, you, and everyone else. The night I was freed."

"There was no party." She sneered and looked at Wynn. I guessed she was evaluating what she could say. "After the Trial ended, Josiah, Dorian, and I took you to your grandfather's, where you slept for a few hours. Nicomedes went with the Dagda to speak with the Inquisitor, and then with Sinclair."

"But I remember…"

She shook her head. I guessed it was to remind me of Wynn sitting in the room as much as to tell me the memories were false. What was real?

She said, "You awoke and came down and sat with Dorian and myself for a while. The Dagda came in with that concoction of his. We sat around and had a few drinks. You went for a walk. Sinclair came by and he and Josiah had a few unpleasant words. You returned a little while later. We all sat down and discussed a little bit about what had been going on. You agreed to keep a low profile while you recovered, and we left."

I held my head in my hands and fought to remember. I focused on my memories. The ones that were a little more real

322

solidified, while others faded into ideas that had been implanted, and I filled in the rest. "Someone messed with my head." Who?

Priscilla nodded. "Whoever, or whatever, it was is gone now. But it wouldn't have been hard that night while you were recovering from the stresses of the Trial. Your defenses are back to normal now. I would guess they were only able to subtly influence your memories."

Wynn said, "You aren't the only one. Some of my team have been influenced, too."

"What about the attack on the holding facility here? Did they break out Dick Gibson?"

Wynn said, "What attack, and how'd you know they're moving him here? He's set to be delivered in a couple of hours. We've been moving him between facilities every 3 days. We only found out this morning they're bringing him back here for questioning."

"Raines," I said. "She said she was waved off from reporting in for debrief because the holding facility was hit from inside. They used the portals. She said they'd grabbed Gibson and pretty much leveled the facility."

Wynn stood. "I need to go."

"Not without me." I stood.

Wynn said, "You're being detained until you can be debriefed. You're not active. Raines was right about that much."

I said, "Fine, consider it transferring me for debrief, but if something is happening, you'll need all of the help you can get."

Priscilla stood. "Check in with me later. I need to have a word with your friend downstairs. I'll pass on your regards."

WYNN GRUMBLED NERVOUSLY on the drive to the holding facility. They were going to sedate Brighid in Drea's body until she was stable.

Wynn said, "I want to believe you, but it's one hell of a story."

"I wouldn't believe it, either. Parts of it, apparently, I can't believe." And those were just the pieces I was able to tell him.

Everything looked quiet for a few blocks surrounding the facility. Wynn said, "I'm not sure what they'll do when we get to the facility. People are very nervous these days. Are you sure you don't want to take a walk?"

I shook my head. "Something is about to happen. We'll all have to choose sides. I consider us friends, and I'll back you as best I can. If you can't or won't trust me, at least tell me I can do what I need to do alone, if necessary."

Wynn put the truck in park at a stop sign. "One more thing you need to know. Selene LeGasse is here. She's been given operational oversight."

Things were changing rapidly, then. It was an understatement to say LeGasse wasn't a big fan of mine. That, plus the fact she was on the record saying the Veiled peoples should be tagged, tracked, or exterminated, meant her having real power didn't help my case. How did a spin doctor rise so quickly to running operations for Longbow? "How much power does she have?"

Wynn was not a big fan of hers, either, but he followed orders. "She can make recommendations, and be a pain, but Director Norwich is still calling the shots. For now."

"One problem at a time." Most days, I was on Norwich's good side. Security was very tight as we entered the facility situated underneath several acres of warehouses and light industrial neighborhoods which looked mostly vacant. We drove into a small auto garage. After the bay door rolled down, the back end opened into a downward ramp. We finally parked thirty feet underground. Wynn said, "Part of the expansion."

Wynn escorted me to the new offices for his unit. Much of the underground had been built in the sixties as Continuity of Government and fallout shelter facilities, but they'd been renovated, which had increased the space significantly. We stopped in the locker room and Wynn had me check in most of my gear. I took advantage of the Leviskin suit's hidden capabilities to hold onto a few items.

LeGasse greeted us impatiently from the other side of the security entrance. She wore an expensive gray suit and three-inch heels. Her long, blonde hair was pulled back into a tight bun. Her tablet floated in her crossed arms. "Mister Forrester. Another of our prodigal children returns."

Wynn asked, "Another?"

LeGasse ignored me and turned to Wynn. "Fitzhugh showed up about an hour ago." He was Hayden's second-in-command. "They're debriefing him now, but it sounded like his normal babble. I never can tell what the artifact hounds are talking about."

"Can I see him?" I asked.

LeGasse flashed her fake smile. "Mr. Forrester, you are on your way to be debriefed as well. It has been far too long since we had a chat and we really must catch up." She said to Wynn, "Please follow me for a moment." She pointed to two men from

326

the security detail. I knew one of them. "And escort Mr. Forrester to my office."

Wynn cut me a look and followed LeGasse.

The detail escorted me down a hall of working space to a large, glass enclosure. "They gave her a fishbowl?"

The guard I knew warned me that LeGasse had been locking down on people. Hard.

I took a seat in an ergonomic chair next to a glass-topped conference table. The office was sparsely decorated, but it was obvious LeGasse intended to make herself at home. The gorgon was slithering through her new found labyrinth.

After what she felt was an appropriate delay, LeGasse marched in, with Wynn in tow. He looked like he'd been beaten down as he found the seat next to me.

LeGasse played with her tablet for a few minutes of self-importance before acknowledging me. "Mr. Forrester, would you care to share where you have been for nearly two months? I hear you had some issues at home. I trust they are resolved?" The attempt to feign compassion oozed with condescension.

"There were some family issues. Thanks for your concern."

"Excellent. Next time you need some personal time, maybe you can schedule it in advance."

I nodded. "I wasn't controlling the schedule for the family trip. You know how it goes."

LeGasse dropped her smile. "Mr. Forrester, my understanding is that whatever issues you had at home were handled internally. I really don't care about what happened to you in fairyland. I am more concerned with events here. Your actions at the hospital were quite suspicious. It appears you have been consorting with other missing and likely renegade resources from this organization. And you have made mention of this facility being attacked, and you had knowledge of the movement of key detainees not long after I did, indicating I have a breach. I'll find out if there is an immediate threat, and if you are a part of it. Once the investigation is complete, we will determine if you still have any place with this organization or, in fact, if you should be added to our list of permanent guests." From the look on her face, I knew what she preferred.

Before I could respond, LeGasse's tablet beeped and there was a small commotion in the hallway. LeGasse swore and stood. "Pardon me, gentlemen."

A security detail stopped outside of the door and two men walked in. The first was Director Edward Norwich. The second man was middle-aged, but of more genteel roots. He reeked of old money, and wore an expensive and finely tailored suit. He was in shape, but obviously spent most of his time behind a desk.

LeGasse flipped the switch on her television smile as Norwich led the second man into the office.

The director said, "Selene, please let me introduce you to Regent Wallace Kelso." The proper introductions flowed like water. "And please meet Special Agent Wynn and one of our valuable consultants, Mr. Greyson Forrester."

LeGasse grit her teeth over Norwich's thick London accent.

Regent Kelso had a soft but commanding voice. "I recognize these gentlemen from your reports of their many successes. It's always good to put a face with the names."

LeGasse tried to usher Wynn and I out, but Norwich asked us to stay. "Selene, since we are here, what revelations did Mr. Gibson have for us?"

LeGasse let a look of surprise slip. "Director, Richard Gibson only arrived in the last hour. I am unaware if he's said anything as of yet. He's been all but mute since Agent Wynn apprehended him."

I thought, but held my tongue, Thanks for the recognition for bringing him in, you credit hogging hawk.

Norwich scowled. "Miss LeGasse, I received your communication that Mr. Gibson had decided to speak and I needed to be briefed immediately. The regent and I were in a meeting, so he elected to come along and visit the facility. Are you saying you did not send a coded priority message?"

I said to Wynn, "We need to get them out of here. Now."

LeGasse objected. "This is a secure facility." LeGasse typed something into her tablet. "Let me lock it down until we know what's happening. You'll be safer here."

Wynn motioned to the security detail. "Take them out the back emergency exit. I'll have your motorcade pick you up there."

A series of small explosions rocked the far end of the building.

I said, "It's the portal room."

Wynn yelled, "Go!"

The special agent led the regent and his detail away.

LeGasse chased me as I ran through the crowded hall towards the explosion. Lucky me. I ignored her yelling until I hit a sealed door my ID wouldn't open.

LeGasse said, "Your access was suspended and limited after your disappearance. Protocol. We are on lockdown."

"Open the door." Weapons fire cracked and the tingle of magical energy charged the air.

LeGasse said, "No." She opened a camera view from her tablet and swore. "You should be in a holding cell until this is resolved."

From what I could see in the video feed to her tablet, things weren't going well.

"LeGasse!" I was yelling. "Open the damn door! Your people in there are not equipped for this."

I pointed on the tablet to the figure in the middle of the room. The beast that Drake had become was hurling fireballs.

LeGasse grew stone-faced. "I am not opening that door and allowing them into this part of the facility. We have to ensure the regent and the director get out safely."

She was right to not open the blast door. But there was a series of airlocks left from the construction of the wing. I'd been through them when this area was under construction. I said, "The construction doors. We can get in there without risking this part of the facility."

LeGasse said, "I am not going to let you join your compatriots. I knew you were involved when I heard the explosion. As soon as this is over, I will find the deepest hole I can and bury you in it."

I did the only thing I could. I stunned LeGasse with a quick blast of energy and took her access card.

MORE EXPLOSIONS ROCKED the building and rained debris down. Luckily, LeGasse wasn't very observant about her access code. I'd watched her punch it in a couple of times while I was in her office. In lockdown, the scanners would need biometric authentication as well. But the airlock was temporary, and only needed a valid card and code to override the lock.

I closed the first door behind me and punched in the code to open the second door. The sounds of combat were much louder, but the weapons fire was dropping off. I took a nearby dead guard's sidearm and extra magazines.

Drake stood in the center of the large room surrounded by the smaller portal rooms. He was unleashing devastating magic down the main hall at anything that moved. A four-man team of former Longbow personnel was taking cover in the portal rooms and laying down suppressing fire on the remaining faithful Longbow security forces.

The detention cells were down the hall straight across from me. All I had to do was run through the crossfire and past FrankenDrake without being turned into a kebab. Nothing but a thing.

A second four-man team was coming down the row of detention cells. They were leading Betty Gibson and Ailbhe's second-in-command, Sonja. Between them, they half-carried Dick Gibson.

No one had seen me yet, so I opted for the element of surprise. I summoned up something Ladon had used to beat me half-senseless and readied a chain of voltaic plasma balls.

Sonja was yelling for Drake to lay down cover fire for them.

I unleashed the pent-up energy. It looked like a string of giant pearls held together by lightning bolts. A couple of them hit and wrapped around Drake, who jerked and shook like he was being poked with a cattle prod.

The security team shielded Betty and Sonja driving them back and took the brunt of the rest of the jolts, except for a lucky shot catching Dick around his thigh.

The first team, hidden in the portal chambers, turned to unleash hell on my position. Drake unleashed a fireball at me in a fit of fury.

In the confusion, Betty and Sonja dragged Dick into one of the portals. It looked like my attack had all but finished him off. Drake backed up into the portal, flinging spheres of magical napalm as quickly as he could summon them towards the security team and me. He sealed the entrance with a jet of dripping fire.

The concrete walls weren't burning, but were coated with flaming residue. Visibility was nil as greasy black fog filled the chamber. The Longbow security team was trapped and was of no help even if they were still alive. I dashed and ducked, trying to work my way to the portal rooms. I could lock it all down if I could get to the control room. I'd built-in safeguards which could destroy the portal rings and trap anyone trying to use them inside. Where was the operator who was supposed to be running it?

I stunned two more of the attackers in the alcove as the last two retreated through the flames into the portal room. The glow from an energy field being raised carried into the hall, along with the subtle shift corresponding with the use of the portals. I ran into the portal wing and saw they'd left some gifts. Each portal ring had a device sitting on top. I had no idea what they were, but they couldn't be good.

If Raines was right and they planned to destroy the facility and a large portion of Los Angeles, those devices would have to be what did it.

Everything had been destroyed. All of the work I'd done to create failsafe controls had been mangled. The remains of the Longbow security officer who had manned the station were splattered around the room. Drake was the only one with this kind of brute power. The devices started to shimmer and hum with power as the portals energized. I suddenly knew what they were trying to do. The whole room smelled of ozone.

I went with the only idea I had. And it sucked.

All of the portals were powered from a single crystal buried in the floor. No one else knew it was there. I stood over the crystal, channeled every ounce of power I could stand, and raised a shield around the room. I hoped I could contain the blast.

An incantation came to mind. I Pushed a final surge of raw energy into the shield as the room flashed in a blinding light.

THE BUZZING FADED, replaced by an icy tingling through every fiber of my body.

"Forrester." Someone snapped open a pack of smelling salts. "Forrester. Are you in there?"

I opened my eyes. "Hi, Gerry. Are we dead?"

The room was dark and reeked of acrid smoke and ozone. Emergency lights danced in the fumes.

Wynn frowned. "No. How're you feeling?"

The tingling was fading, leaving a sensation like my entire body had been asleep. Pins and needles stabbed every inch of my body as my nervous system came back to life. "Surprised. Shocked maybe."

The fire had been extinguished, and the remaining invading forces had been restrained with riot cuffs and were lined up on the wall.

Wynn pulled me to my feet. "What did you do?"

"Betty left us some surprises. I didn't have time to try and disarm them. I went with the next best option."

Wynn struggled to understand. "So, what'd you do?"

"I raised a shield around the place. I was hoping to block the portals and contain the explosion. At the last second, I sent out the magical equivalent of an EMP and fried the devices. And the portals. It fried everything, but there was still energy needing to be released."

One of the Longbow security detail yelled, "Agent Wynn, sir. You should see this."

The attackers I'd stunned were restrained and stacked against the wall. They all wore identical black tactical suits. A small rune was painted on each of their breast plates. Wynn looked at a soldier on the ground. Wynn knelt down and said, "Hayden."

They removed the balaclavas from the other soldiers.

Wynn said, "These are all Hayden's men."

I opened my Sight. A distinct energy signature resonated from each of them. I removed Hayden's vest. He was still out cold. He was wearing a necklace with a small silver rune. It was just like the one I'd seen around Raines' neck in Atlanta.

LeGasse tripped in her high heels as she stormed through the debris. A full security detail struggled to keep up. "Detain him."

Wynn stood. "Enough. He just saved this whole facility and everyone in it."

LeGasse had a mad grin on her face. "You think you're so smart. Save the day at the last minute, but let them out of here with Gibson. And you set it up so they could take the regent and the director."

Wynn said, "What?"

LeGasse snarled, "You took them out. Are you in it with him? Someone hit the regent's motorcade just outside of the district. They took the regent, the director and his staff, and neutralized their entire escort. Only two survived, both in critical condition."

Wynn pointed at Hayden. "And these are our guys."

I snatched the necklace from around Hayden's neck. "This is how they are doing it. These have an energy signature. If I had to guess, they are mucking with their minds and making them see or think whatever." I Pushed a small surge through the necklace and felt the energy dissipate.

Wynn looked at LeGasse. "And the request to the director came from *you.*"

I'd studied looked at LeGasse earlier. Even now, I didn't see anything out of the ordinary. She was still the same bling covered self-righteous hater of mine she'd always been. "She looks clean, as best I can tell. You could always lock her away just in case. I know I'd feel better."

Wynn scowled. "So who hit us?"

I shook my head. "I saw Betty Gibson with Dick. The other one, I believe, was Sonja. And the big freaky one was the new-and-improved Drake."

LeGasse said, "As in the fairy taken from the hospital? There was nearly nothing left of him."

I was almost impressed. She actually had paid a little bit of attention. Maybe there was something to doing reports.

I nodded. "They seem to have acquired pieces to rebuild him. He's now a chimera of the Divine and the Veiled."

Wynn asked, "Can they build more of those? The only thing that phased him was whatever you threw at him."

"I don't know." I surveyed the damage around us. "At least some of his parts should be hard to come by. I'm more concerned with who managed to create him. I don't think they can build an army like him." We were screwed if they could.

"We need to talk to Hayden's second. I'm betting he's being influenced as well. We might be able to determine how and to what extent they're being controlled."

LeGasse ordered Hayden and his team be taken to holding cells. I was only slightly surprised when she ordered me to be taken to holding, too.

I protested. "You're still wanting to lock me up? Right now, we need to find out why they wanted Director Norwich. And why they wanted Dick back all of a sudden." The security detail stood a respectable distance away.

LeGasse sneered. "You haven't been cleared for duty, and as far as I am concerned, you're completely accountable for this incident. At best, your work was inept and allowed this to happen, and at worst, you engineered it. As acting director, I need to know which is true before I let you go anywhere."

Wynn said, "Every second fleeting by, they're further away. I need my people. And he's the only one who might be able to track them."

I could almost see the wheels turn as LeGasse planned her next move. "We will continue this discussion in my office." It at least meant she was considering Wynn's statement. "And Forrester, please return my access card."

I pulled the ID card from my pocket, now charred and semi-melted. I smiled as I handed it to her. "I made sure it couldn't be used inappropriately by the hostile forces."

338

"HOW LONG, GREY?" The halls were flying with people trying to restore order. Wynn was escorting me back to LeGasse's office. "How long do you need with Fitzhugh?"

"What?"

"Fitzhugh." Wynn turned towards the holding cells. "I can get you about two minutes. Can you do anything in that time?"

I said, "I'll give it a shot."

Wynn waved off the security detail outside of the holding cell. "Two minutes. Then get him down to the office."

Fitzhugh was slumped over in the chair, mostly catatonic. He wore black BDU's and a silver necklace with the now too-familiar rune. I opened my Sight and examined him. The rune on the necklace shone brightly, pulsing gently every few seconds. Every time it pulsed, dozens of thin trails of energy ran into the ether.

The room was giving off a strong residual energy signature. It took me a few seconds to zero in on Fitzhugh with all of the noise. His own aura was very weak. Large holes of black were surrounded by waves of red and yellow, and fading quickly.

"Wynn," I yelled. "Get the medics now!"

Fitzhugh fluttered his eyes. Milky cataracts stared at me. "Hello?" a weak and terrified voice asked.

"I'm here," I said. "I'm Grey. Just hold on."

Fitzhugh stared into space. He took a shallow breath. "Trust...no one. Longbow has been...comp..." I watched the last of his energy fade as his eyes closed.

I passed the medics as I walked into the hall. "He's gone."

Wynn nodded.

LeGasse was sitting behind her desk when we entered. "Keeping me waiting does not help your case for urgency."

Wynn sat down. "Fitzhugh is dead."

LeGasse was unmoved. "I take it you took a detour."

I opened my Sight and looked at LeGasse. I still didn't see signs of her being under any influence other than stress. Something kept drawing me to examine her. Was it just how much I didn't trust her or something else?

I gave Wynn a quick check as well. "I think I know how it was done. How they breached the facility."

LeGasse leaned back in her chair. "Do tell, Mr. Forrester. We wait with bated breath."

She wouldn't even believe me if I confessed to being the ringleader of the plot. She'd like this even less. "You let them in."

She laughed, as much in frustration as disbelief. "So this is our fault? The best you have is to blame us, or is it just to blame me?"

"No." I had to say this quickly, before she tried to put me in a deep hole and I had to make my own way out. "The necklaces are a fetish. I didn't get much time with Fitzhugh to see how they work, but my guess is they carry a compulsion of sorts. He used the same phrase as Raines: 'Longbow has been compromised.' I don't think they're being controlled, not directly. They're being led to believe Longbow had been compromised from within. And if I had to guess, they believe they're on a rescue mission."

The thought seemed to jolt LeGasse. "Not possible. Our people are regularly screened for any kind of irregularity in behavior. Seeing how all of your behavior is irregular, you can understand why you stay under such scrutiny." She seemed to back off slightly. "Let's say I buy this. How did they get past your security measures?"

This was going to be the moment of truth. "The agent in the control room blew them up. It was the first explosion."

LeGasse and Wynn both paled. "How? You said explosives wouldn't work."

I shook my head. "Conventional explosives wouldn't. I didn't expect someone to smuggle in energetic ones. I think you'll find out the operator was under a compulsion. He just didn't know it. I think Fitzhugh was charged up, too, but for some reason, he didn't go off. He just blew himself out."

LeGasse leaned against her desk and wrung her hands. Did she still think I was lying? Insane? "How did they get them in? We scan everyone."

I shook my head. "They didn't bring in devices. They *were* the devices. I'm betting they were primed with telluric energy which they weren't trained to use or release. I'm not entirely sure how it would work, but we learned how to do this sort of thing on a smaller scale. We could build up an extra charge in our bodies for a short time before training. We also could top each other off, by adding more than an individual could do on their own. Normal people can carry the charge, but wouldn't know how to control it. A compulsion could make them hold it and release it in a burst, and I'm betting he took some extra explosives from the armory which would make a big bang and fry everything."

341

Something clicked in Wynn. "OK, so all of your portals were set site-to-site. If there was no control room, how did they use the portals to get in and out? You can't go up in an elevator without a button."

I hadn't thought about that, either. I was still a little fried. "Oh, damn."

LeGasse said, "What?"

I really hadn't figured out what Dick was good for. He seemed a little dense and didn't seem to know much. Because he didn't. "Dick. Dick Gibson. It's the only thing making any sense."

"Would you care to share? I don't know about Miss LeGasse, but I'm not a mind reader."

"Something about Pageland's Ferry bothered me. They had the chance to take Richard Gibson with them, but didn't. The reason was they couldn't. He'd opened the portal for them, but had to keep it open because he couldn't go through himself. He has the ability to control them, and I think he can create them on the move. Some sort of savant."

LeGasse said, "It's a lot of planning, but they walked out with a regent as the reward."

I shook my head. "He was the bonus. They wanted Director Norwich. And if I hadn't stopped it, the ripple effect from the portals would have blown apart not just this facility, but every one they were connected with. The Longbow Initiative would have been crippled severely. But, on the plus side, we wouldn't be having this conversation."

LeGasse narrowed her eyes and leaned in. "What do you mean, blow this and the other facilities apart?"

I should have pressed Raines harder for details on what she thought had happened. "When I talked to Raines, she believed this facility had been destroyed. She also told me the chain of command was gone. That was her phrasing when I talked to her earlier in the day. When Betty and crew ported out, they left devices on each portal. It looked like they were going to open and crash the portals. That much energy would have exploded not only here, but also on the other ends. Pretty much every facility would have been a crater. I did what I could to contain it. It must have disrupted something."

Wynn asked, "What do you mean?"

"The devices went off. The portals were forming." I took a deep breath and tried to visualize the last few seconds before the blast. "I saw the flash. I should have been vaporized."

WYNN STASHED ME in a conference room. While awaiting a decision on my fate, I studied the rune necklace I'd taken from Fitzhugh. It was a piece of very delicate work. I finally figured out how the signal could be blocked, and it looked fairly easy to cancel out the effects. We needed to know how many more within the organization were being influenced.

I worked a little incantation and modified a two-way radio that was sitting in the room to turn it into a rune detector. I was betting anyone being influenced would need to be wearing or in contact with one of the fetishes. I waved the radio over the necklace a couple of times. The two-way emitted a loud squelch. I was also able to tune it to help track down the signal from a short distance.

The door clicked open. Wynn came in and sat down at the table. He put his head in his hands and rubbed his temples before sitting up and sliding an envelope across the table. "New credentials. You're active again. LeGasse is pissed off, and made it clear she still thinks you're a threat. She bounces back and forth between you being incompetent or a willful saboteur. Apparently, you have fans a little higher in the food chain, but she's held onto the acting director chair. Much to her disdain, I'm her acting assistant director."

I nodded. "One of these days, you'll have to tell me how this place operates."

"Not today." Wynn nudged the rune necklace sitting on the table. "So, what can we do about compromised agents?"

I held up the radio and waved it over the necklace. "Use this. Scan everyone coming and going. It's probably good to about ten feet. I think we can break the enchantment fairly easily. Priscilla will have someone who can help. Detain anyone

344

suspicious. I think anyone being influenced will have one of these on them, but I can't be positive."

Wynn picked up the radio and gave it a couple of test waves.

"What's the plan for Norwich and Kelso?" I asked.

Wynn held out a briefing document. "Teams are being transported in from Europe. The search has started, and evidence from the abduction site is being examined. For the most part, we're in lockdown. No one comes in, no one gets out."

I said, "It's likely other teams have been infiltrated or compromised. A lot of people were coming through here as a hub. I want to have Drea, um, Brighid moved to one of Priscilla's safe houses."

He agreed. "It's her call, but I suspect Priscilla would feel better about that as well. You can ask her once you're outside. I need you in the field." He handed me the initial incident report. "Intelligence indicates those are the active sites. Do you think you can make your own silent exit?"

I smiled. "I think I can find a way. What about LeGasse?"

The new assistant director drooped in his chair. The field promotion was visibly weighing on him. I could only imagine the stress of trying to hold his organization together and not knowing who he could trust. "I can handle her. She'll have plenty of other distractions. Can you make a few more of these things?" He waved the radio.

"Sure. It won't take but a few minutes for each one."

Within an hour, I had converted a dozen radios. Wynn brought through twenty of his team and the security detail to be

345

checked out. All of them tested clean, but one of the security detail was acting strangely. Wynn had him sequestered for observation. I trained the rest on using the radios, and how to look for other signs. I slipped the remaining necklace into a shielded pouch.

LeGasse had a shiny new toy to play with and took a team herself to examine her staff. Wynn gave me a pouch of secure communications gear. I grabbed the rest of my essentials from my locker.

Most of the facility was shielded from beings porting in anywhere except for what had been the portal room. Wynn had teams clear out the area and lock it down. He let me through under the guise of making sure it was secure. I checked out the remains of the portals and the devices they'd used. About half of one of them was intact. It had been a ring, a foot in diameter, made of threaded inlays of gold, silver, copper, wood, glass, and every other material you would expect in a permanent portal ring. I found a few other materials I couldn't readily identify. I dropped the remains of the device into my pack.

I looked over every inch of the portal room. All of the portals were fried. Most of the security barriers and wards were weakened, but were miraculously in place. The portal room they'd used to escape was linked to a lab not far from Barstow, California. It was meant to be a quick transport to a safe location for desert training.

Wynn observed me working from the doorway. He must have seen something in my face. "Problem?"

"Has anyone heard from Barstow?"

"I don't think so. But we haven't had any traffic there in a few weeks." Wynn tapped at his tablet. "There is one small project going on out there right now, a dozen people or so. The gateway on that end would have been locked down. I'm not getting a response from them, though."

"I think they might have come in through there, but they definitely used it as an escape route." I cleared a spot over the power crystal buried in the floor. I'd built a small back door for myself. I drew a small circle and a couple of sigils in chalk. "Can you erase any traces after I'm gone?"

"Good luck. Contact me when you have something." Wynn shook my hand. "I'm stretching my neck out for you. Remember that."

"You should be used to it by now." I ported directly into my lab. In the event I ever needed a back door, I couldn't be followed here. It was a quick stopover. I picked up a few items I needed for a tracking spell, and ported to the resort in LA.

I stepped out of the closet in my bedroom to a half dozen various weapons aimed at me.

"IT'S JUST ME." I raised my hands.

The voice of a child came from my left. The head of a small girl peeked from behind the door to the bathroom. "He's clear." She was dressed as one of the Sibylline initiates. A young seer.

Melanippe lowered her bow and her tactical helmet morphed into a balaclava, which she pulled off. "Welcome home." The rest of the people left the room and returned to the common area. "She'll be thrilled to see you."

What had been a spacious den was now an executive war room. Priscilla sat on the couch, typing away on a laptop and firing orders through a headset. She wore a full set of light tactical gear which she made look hot. I couldn't hear who she was speaking with, but from the look on her face, she wasn't happy. The furball was curled up next to her the couch, contentedly asleep.

Priscilla rose and tossed the headset onto the couch with delicate anger. She looked at me with a raised eyebrow. "Greyson." Buried in my name was both a question and a statement, but I didn't know what either was.

Mel and Kizzy remained behind and tried to be inconspicuous as the rest of the room cleared.

I wasn't sure if I should run for cover from the look I was getting. I decided to opt for standing my ground. "I wasn't expecting a welcome home party." She curled her eyebrow.

I took the cue and sat in my favorite overstuffed chair. The furball looked over and went back to sleep. That's loyalty. Man's best friend, my ass.

She said, "I had to bring your 'guest' somewhere safe for as long as she's on a ride along in my granddaughter. And seeing how my house in Long Beach just underwent an unplanned explosive renovation, I brought the family down here and invited a few trusted friends who are concerned about current circumstances to join us. We have the entire building locked down. The tourists are in the other tower to keep up appearances. How are things with our friends at Longbow?"

"They blew up your house?" OK, so subtlety wasn't my strong point. "Who?"

Priscilla rolled her eyes. "It is not the first, and I doubt it shall be the last time someone burns me out of house and home. They only managed to damage the reception area. We raised a glamour to make it look much worse."

This meant they had a larger attack plan in mind than I could figure. "Things are pretty bad, and going downhill rapidly." I gave a quick recap on the events at Longbow. "Had things gone as planned, I think the Longbow Initiative would be non-existent. And most of the greater LA basin."

Priscilla sighed. "I believe you may be underestimating the situation." She turned on the big screen television to the news.

"...we have a live feed coming in from the location now. Initial reports are of a meteor strike in the desert about twenty-five miles from Barstow earlier this afternoon. The dust cloud is still obscuring most of the area, but unconfirmed reports from the ground are that a large crater..."

Priscilla changed the channel.

"...impact is being blamed for the unusual weather patterns forming on the West Coast. The center of the storm is now between the impact site in California and Las Vegas. People are being warned..."

Priscilla said, "Does that look familiar?"

349

"Barstow lab." It confirmed my fear of the portal explosion had channeling there. "How bad is it?"

Priscilla pointed me to the drawn curtains. I opened them to blazing red skies and a roiling Pacific Ocean. The orb of the setting sun was almost completely obscured behind thick clouds of dust whipped around by vicious winds. The few standing trees in sight were tossing in the wind. "It's getting worse by the hour." Priscilla appeared more concerned than I'd ever seen her. "I'm supposing all of this is connected?"

I stared out at the storm. It reminded me of the weather in Purgatory. Were all of the realms destined to go to hell? "It's a good bet." What was Ailbhe trying to do? What could be the benefit in all of this? Maybe this wasn't part of the plan. Possibly the storm was an unintended consequence. Likely, the blast had killed Drake, Sonja, the Gibsons, and anyone else in their proximity. "I need a few minutes."

I dumped supplies on the counter and cleared a space on the table. I took out one of Onyx's hairs I'd kept to help me track her. I'd collected samples from her and a few other people I cared about. Once it dissolved in the solution, I dipped a ball bearing into the mix. I unrolled a map of the Southwest and placed it on the map. Within a few moments, it had rolled to an area in the Mojave Desert. I repeated the process for Raines. It stopped in the same spot.

I dug around and found Brighid's hair, the one she'd wrapped around her necklace. I broke off a piece, dissolved it, and dipped a third ball bearing in the solution. I placed it on the page and uttered the incantation to search. The ball rolled around the map and stopped over the coast outside of LA, near the resort. I'd made it specifically to find her corporeal self. Was it possible she was here? Was she trying to recover the rest of her essence?

I mixed a few more ingredients into the potion containing Brighid's hair. I pulled out a cheap pair of glasses and rubbed some of the solution on the lenses. I slipped the glasses on and uttered the incantation. I looked in Drea's room, where Brighid slept peacefully. She was securely nestled within Drea's body. I began looking around. If Priscilla hadn't known me like she did, she likely would have thought I'd lost my mind.

Maybe I had. This chain of thought certainly wasn't my happy place.

A small, glowing ball appeared in the lens and I tracked its movement. It was a couple of floors down. I kept it in focus as I walked into my bedroom, Pushed the Leviskin to become a tactical suit, and slipped the Colt into its holster.

I waved as I went out the door. "I'll be back in a few minutes."

Priscilla looked concerned as I jogged out the door.

From the stairwell and outside of the wards of my suite, the dot took on a human shape. Three flights of stairs later, the form stood in the stairwell one flight below me. I drew the Colt 1911 and looked over the railing. Brighid leaned against the wall in an innocent yet seductive pose. Her bright sundress billowed in the winds rushing to escape above. She beamed at me and said, "Hello, love."

She didn't flinch as I worked my way around the last flight of stairs, my weapon trained on her. I stopped one step up from the floor, just feet away. "Hello, Brighid."

She gave me a sly smile. "No need for that." She waved her hand and the Colt became very hot, forcing me to drop it. I pulled

351

energy into my hands. "I'm here to take you with me. To safety. We can be together, like we planned."

The silver rune necklace glinted in the artificial light. "Why don't you come upstairs with me? We can discuss it?"

The innocent smile she gave me sent shivers through my entire body. "I wish I could, but we don't have much time. This building won't be here for much longer. Come with me and we can talk. All you want."

Chatter came from above and below. Melanippe yelled, "Stop there, creature!" Her bow was drawn and aimed at Brighid.

I yelled, "Wait Mel—"

Brighid shook her head with a sad smile. "I'm sorry, love. If you make it, you know where I'll be. If not, meet me on the other side." She stepped backwards into a waiting portal in the wall. It closed instantly.

I opened my Sight and scanned the building. Telluric energy was building just down the hall. "We have a problem on this floor. Start evacuating everyone now."

"KEEP THEM BACK." I motioned to Melanippe to keep everyone away from the door. Telluric energy oozed into the hall. It was like swimming in a pool of molasses.

I scanned the door, but I didn't Sense a trap. Melanippe pulled out a master access card which would let us into any room in the resort. I stood to one side as she unlocked it from the other. I pulled energy into my hands and readied myself. Melanippe nodded and flung it open. I rushed through.

A fire elemental floated over a portal ring, which in turn hovered over the bed. She looked terrified. She was in half-humanoid and half-fire form as she floated over the ring. She'd been smart enough to melt the sprinkler head.

Tears of flame rolled down her face, only to be reabsorbed into the plasma of her lower half. "Help me! They stormed in. They said if I touch the ring, we all die. I don't know how much longer I can stay here."

Mel said, "Hold on, Edana." She looked at me pleadingly. "Help her."

I knelt down and studied the portal ring. It was floating a few inches above the bed. Edana was floating just above the horizon of the portal generator. "Hold on." Energetic bindings held the elemental to the ring and stopped her from floating off. She was using her physical form to hold the bindings back. "I'm going to try and break the field holding you in, but I'll need to get the ring out of the hotel quickly." As soon as she was out of the ring, I Sensed it would explode like the ones in the portal room.

I motioned for Melanippe to back up. If this didn't work, a few feet wouldn't matter, but it would protect her from breaking glass. I hurled an energy ball and blew out the window. The storm outside sucked anything loose out of the room.

I focused on the bindings and started to pull. Every tug moved Edana closer to the portal. She weakened rapidly as she poured more of herself into not falling into the ring. "I need more time."

Edana had nearly completely converted to plasma. "I can't hold it any more. Do what you have to."

"Give me just another minute." I probed for a weak spot, enough for her to slip through.

The elemental used the last of her strength to say, "Now."

The ring powered up and the glow intensified. I had no choice. "I'm sorry."

I used all of the energy I had in me to slingshot Edana and the ring through the window over the Pacific. As I ejected her from the room, the top of the field hit the window frame and drops of flaming plasma left a trail like a small rocket. Edana and the ring arced until she exploded in a ball of fire and plasma, fed by the energy from the portal.

Little of the fireball reached the resort, but the shock wave shattered every window overlooking the ocean. The concussion blew me halfway to the hallway.

"GREYSON, DON'T MOVE." Melanippe leaned over me. "Hold still." She shoved me down as I tried to sit up. She leaned down over me and put her arms under my shoulders. "Quit squirming. This is going to hurt."

She stood me up, and one of the Calypso tactical team held me up by one arm and Mel slid under the other. I looked down and saw a long, jagged piece of glass in my thigh. Another was sticking out of my side.

She said, "Let's get him upstairs."

They held me up as we rode in the elevator.

Priscilla propped the suite doors open. "What the hell just happened?"

They laid me out on the couch. Melanippe uttered a few words and my Leviskin armor shifted into thin cloth.

The Woodland Fae healer who had been caring for Drea rushed in, carrying her bag. She began cutting at the cloth around the wounds. Her yellow skin was flushed with red patches.

Melanippe said, "Edana. Someone turned her into a bomb. We tried to help, but it was too late."

Priscilla waved to several people standing around. "Gather up any remaining flames you can, and *do not let them be extinguished.*"

Melanippe gave a quick but detailed review of the events to Priscilla. People streamed in and out with reports on damage and injuries. Someone rolled down the storm doors, mostly closing off the room from the maelstrom outside.

The green goop the healer packed my wounds with smelled like a swamp. She topped them off with a few stitches. She said, "You'll be fine. None of your injuries went too deep, but it will take a week or so to heal." She dashed out of the suite to respond to other casualties.

The activity in the suite had slowed as people cleared out to other urgent tasks. Someone was already cleaning up the glass and other debris.

Priscilla leaned against the bar, a drink in her hand. "We need to get you into hiding." She looked at the room where Brighid lay in Drea's body. "Both of you."

"No." I took a healing potion from my pack and drank it in one shot. "I'm going to give them what they want before this goes any further."

Priscilla said, "What do they want?"

I looked at the map I'd used for scrying earlier. The third ball had moved to join the other two in the Mojave. "Me. They want me."

"Absolutely not." Priscilla's mood was matched by the storm outside, now rattling the storm doors. "Have you looked at yourself? If they want you this badly, it cannot be for a good reason."

"I must go. If they want me, they can have me if it'll stop all of this. I didn't say they would get what they wanted from me." Unless it was a fight. "Onyx is there. So is Raines. And who knows who or what else."

Drea's voice came from the doorway. Brighid said, "Us. We're going."

Priscilla and I both said, "Absolutely not."

Brighid tentatively walked into the room. "I'm just as much a part of this. Some bitch has my body, and I want it back."

Someone must have explained her situation. "You are definitely not in shape for this."

Priscilla said, "You need to rest. The more you acclimate to this body, the more implications there may be."

Brighid sat on the couch. Drea's body was physically weak. It hadn't had any exercise in months. And I had no idea how much damage trapped in her one room prison had done to Brighid's mind over the years. I sat next to her on the couch and took her hand. "Trust me to do what needs to be done. I never meant for this to happen."

I looked at Priscilla. "I have to do this."

The queen of the Amazons searched the room for any other solution, and found none. "What's your plan?"

I showed the map to Priscilla. "All roads lead here. A spot in the Mojave."

Priscilla pulled up a weather map on her tablet. "The eye of the storm. It looks like the storm hasn't moved since it formed, but it's getting larger. And stronger. How will you get there?"

"Where's Ktesippe?"

KTESIPPE GRUMBLED QUIETLY as I rifled through the storage compartment. After her house was bombed, Priscilla had had my possessed and sentient garnet 1955 Indian Warrior brought to the resort. The motorcycle had been overhauled and covered in a Leviskin suit giving me a lot of options.

She let me know how unhappy she was about having been left mostly alone for months. Unfortunately, I wasn't yet looking to take her for a ride. I just needed a few items I kept in her storage. The weather outside only encouraged her to want to go for a spin.

Now came the fun part. "Melvin!" I yelled in the general direction of the sky. Desperation had set in. If anyone knew how the portal ring worked, it would be him. I held the cursed device in the air. "Melvin, is this your doing?" If anyone had walked into the garage, they would have thought I'd lost my mind. It wasn't far from the truth.

"Dude, you don't need to yell." Melvin appeared, sporting a white tie, tails, and top hat.

I asked, "What's with the outfit?"

Melvin smiled. "Nothing like a doomsday to bring out the partiers." He threw his hands in the air and tap-danced in a circle. I knew he thought he was being elegant, but it reminded me of a baboon. "Gotta go out in style. And this is a whole lot better than a toga party in a flood."

I should've known. Doom and destruction meant more to rebuild. And new ways to inspire the poor fools left behind. "Follow me. I've got a couple of things for you to look at." I handed him the remains of the portal ring.

Melvin pulled out his ever-present loop of magnifying glasses and filters and started studying the artifact as we rode up in the elevator.

Priscilla barely covered her surprise. "Melvin, nice to see you as always. Greyson, may we speak for a minute?"

I pointed Melvin to a counter he could use while Priscilla dragged me to the side. "You called him in? Are you so desperate?"

I shrugged. "If he didn't inspire its construction, he'll know who did. Worst case, he may have an idea on how to defend against it."

Priscilla said, "Or it may give the loon a new idea on how to unmake the universe."

"Give him time. He may pull it off yet. Until then, can you get people together? I'm planning on leaving for Vegas in a few hours, and then into the eye of the storm. I should have a plan by nightfall." The thought reminded me how long it had been since I'd slept.

Priscilla nodded. "Just let me know what you need."

Melvin waved me over excitedly. "This thing. Where'd you get it?"

I explained how I'd run into a few of them, and how they were being used.

Melvin was about to explode with excitement. "This doesn't make portals. It makes dimensions. It can use a portal to open a way. That's why it is so energetic, man. They're making miniature openings to the Abyss. The universe outside the universe. Dark matter. Cool."

I was afraid Priscilla had been right. He might get motivated to find a way to end the universe. At least the one we were in. "Who built it?"

"This work, it's impressive." He was manic as he examined the fragment. It sparked when he touched a piece with a small implement. "Iason. He mentored with Hephaestus for maybe a thousand years? But no one has seen him since maybe the Ptolemaic Dynasty. Pieces of his work show up now and then. But I know his mark."

I pulled the rune necklace out of the shielded pouch.

Melvin drew back like he was in pain. "Where'd you find... that? Put it away."

I dropped the necklace back into the pouch. "What can you tell me about it?"

Melvin turned up his nose like he was snorting tear gas. "Evil. Pure evil. That's an anathema to the game. Those things can subvert anyone's free will. You don't even have to accept it. It can be slipped on you. They are really subtle. No warning. The laws prohibit someone from even creating one of those."

"What do you mean? All sorts of things subvert free will. Why is this so much worse?"

Melvin shuddered. "No, man. The rules of the game are, to override someone's free will, they have to accept it. Sometimes it's subtle, but you can't do it to someone who doesn't allow it in some way. Sometimes the rules get fuzzy, but there's always a loophole. That thing. It suppresses, no, it encapsulates free will so you don't have it. It can't be made."

I dangled the package in the air. "I've already dealt with at least twenty of them."

Melvin stared at the necklace. "Hang it on the hook. I'll need to study it." Even he was starting to look nervous. And a little excited.

I gave the necklace to Melvin and called Father Mike. I felt some relief when he answered, even though I could hear the roar of the storm on his end of the line. He said, "Greyson? Grey, is it really you? Where have you been?"

"It's me." Who knew how many others were listening in on the line? "I need to know, is there another gateway nearer to us? Rather than the one in the mountains?"

Fr. Mike breathed heavily on the other end.

"Mike?"

He said, "The eye of the storm. It's not a direct gateway, but there are paths in the area of the eye of the storm. But you can easily be lost in places much worse, from which you will not return. Are you thinking it's connected to the storm?"

I said, "Thanks, Mike. That's what I needed to know."

Fr. Mike said, "Whatever you're thinking, it's a bad idea. Be safe, my son. I'll be praying for you."

I said, "I'll see you soon." Which would be a hard conversation when it happened. I needed to know how much the old priest knew about his mentor, and what was really happening. Pain be damned.

"Wait," Fr. Mike said. I paused before hanging up on the padre and he continued. "Grand Inquisitor Francis Delacroix is looking for you."

I wasn't sure what made me more curious: The factMike knew Delacroix, or that the Inquisitor was looking for me. Either way, it would have to wait. Melvin needed a couple of hours, and I needed sleep. But I needed something else more. I lay down on my bed and closed my eyes.

I awoke in my room in the tower. I must have snuck up on Tsauriel and Ladon for once, as they were startled when I came in.

"Ladon, I need some new tricks, now." I stood at the door and Pushed myself into full combat gear. Tsauriel started to object, but I told her, "You wanted me in the fight. This is how it begins."

Ladon gave me a smile which would have terrified me any other time. Now, it just gave me a small measure of hope. "Well, then. Shall we have a go?"

MELVIN PACED IN the kitchen, brooding. Every few laps, he poked the necklace with the wooden spoon and set it swinging from a hook over the stove. He was working with his never-ending bag of tools. Some of them seemed to exist only partially in our reality.

Other than Melvin and me, the suite was empty. The war room had moved elsewhere, or maybe no one wanted to be too close to Melvin. Based on his scowl, I wasn't sure I wanted to, either.

I stared, lost in thought, for a few minutes as I shook the last of the fog out of my head. Ladon's workout had stretched me in ways that awoke more of the power within me. I'd have never guessed he'd been holding back some of what he threw at me.

Melvin jumped when I said, "Any progress?"

The angel scratched at his mussed hair. "This thing wasn't made in any of our material realms. It does what it does without…Od. It came from…outside. There's no sign of the Od."

"You mean, from the Abyss." I opened my Senses and could feel an unusual energy flowing from it. It still looked like a charged piece of silver. "And what do you mean 'Od'?"

"Yeah. We really need to come up with a better name than the Abyss. You can't pronounce what we call it, but yeah. What you see as the Abyss is the gateway. Just don't go through it." He picked up a house plant. "Open your Sight and see what happens." Melvin waved a blessed silver necklace over the plant. The aura of the plant strengthened with the touch from the charm.

Melvin rifled through his bag and pulled out a set of leather welding gloves, a pair of goggles, and a box. He put on the gloves and goggles, and opened the box. A small ornate dagger lay in the bottom. It emanated waves of dark energy. Carefully,

Melvin waved the dagger over the plant, and the aura of the plant retracted, the edges of the leaves curling and blackening. "This one is cursed. It's the Pugio Narcissus used to assassinate Commodus, and it's seen a lot of action since then." Melvin put the dagger back into the box and closed the lid.

Melvin said, "You saw what happened? Even the plant knows good and evil. Now watch." Melvin held the plant near the rune. The closer he moved the plant to the pendant, the more of the plant's aura was being drawn to it. The fields turned and twisted like they were attracted to it, but couldn't touch it. When the plant was less than an inch away, the aura of the plant was drawn around the charm like a bubble. Melvin touched the plant to the focal piece, exploding the bubble. The aura of the plant spun, twisted, recoiled, and formed the bubble around the rune again. It ran through this cycle over and over as the aura of the plant continued to weaken, until it was nearly gone and plant wilted.

Melvin pulled the plant away and sat it in the sunlight of the window. The rays of the sun washed away some of the effect. "You see, that damnable thing messes with you. Call it aura, Qi, Od. It's the energy flowing through all of our reality, and everything that exists has a little of it in them. Good or bad, everything in the universe is connected. But not this."

"I saw one of these take the last bits of life from one of Longbow's people. He'd been made into a bomb of sorts. They built up something in him. It only partially detonated, but they were successful with another person. They used him to take out the control room for the portals. Could the pendant have been the device?"

He chewed on a feather from his wing while he was thinking. "I doubt it. But it could be the trigger. And how they charged them up."

"How do we stop it from happening again? And what else can they do with people they have under their control?"

He shrugged. "I guess it depends on what the person has the ability to do."

We were losing the first rounds of the war, and badly. "How do we stop it? How can we neutralize the effects of the rune?"

Melvin dug through his bag. "Well, first, if you can get them away from people, the effects will dissipate over time. But you need to shut down however they are getting these across the threshold. Closing it off may unmake them in this reality." Melvin pulled a small pouch out of his bag and tossed it to me. "Take this."

I opened the bag and dumped a river rock into my hand. "It's a rock?"

Melvin said, "Yeah, it should help you get rid of any remaining negative juju after you get the necklace off of them. It's a relic. Just wave it around them, and it will soak up any weird energies. We can cleanse it when you get back. Or leave it somewhere I can get to it, if you don't make it back. It's an heirloom."

STRONG WINDS BUFFETED and whipped past me in the meager cover of the garage. A wide crack ran the length of the stairwell and the warped door had created a wind tunnel. I left a note in the suite, and loaded up Ktesippe with supplies, ammunition, and a few handy toys from the Calliope armory. I tried to leave the furball with Priscilla, but one or both was fed up with the other, and he insisted on going with me.

Now he wanted to be wizard's best friend.

The garage next to the resort was packed with vehicles, but no one was around. The last palm tree in front of the resort had blown over. I took shelter in a storage room to check in with Wynn.

I pulled out the satellite phone and dialed the preset number. A static-filled response came from the other end of the line. "Wynn."

I said, "I'm checking in. I'm in LA right now, but I'm about to head out into the desert. Has LeGasse figured out I'm no longer in the base?"

Wynn chuckled. "Yeah, it took her a while. I told her you were out running down a lead. She threw a fit, but this storm has everyone pretty well tied up. Do I want to guess where you are going?"

"No." I took a deep breath as something crashed outside. "Is there any hope for backup?"

The static decreased as Wynn stepped into a quiet room. "We have a couple of prototype VTOL troop carriers inbound, but they won't be here for at least eight hours. If the storm doesn't get any worse, we might be able to have four teams there in twelve hours or so."

The clock on the phone said it was a few minutes after one p.m. That's when it hit me. It was 1 p.m. on Salween eve. In less than eleven hours, it would be the seven year anniversary of the night my life went to hell. Factor in the time change, it was more like eight. There were no such things as coincidences. "In twelve hours, whatever is going to happen will be in full swing, maybe even all over. If I make it to the target, I'll send a signal."

"Be careful." Wynn paused. "Greyson, we haven't always seen eye-to-eye, but I'll trust you on this, not that I have a choice. Is there anything I should know?"

I swallowed. My heartbeat was drowning out the storm outside. "Gerry, I don't know what's going to happen, but know I'll do everything I can to help your people and mine. If I fail, I think the world will go to Hell pretty quickly in a very literal sense. I don't know exactly what they're doing, or how to stop it, but I'm convinced this storm is just the beginning."

"You're always full of good news. We'll be there as soon as we can."

I hung up, turned the phone off, and pulled the power supply. No need to kill the battery. Or to let them track me.

I climbed onto Ktesippe and slipped on the helmet. She purred in my ears. "We finally get to go for a ride?"

"Are you up for a cruise?"

Ktesippe cooed in my ear. "I'm assuming straight into the storm? I've looked at the radar and satellite feeds and I'm plotting a path with updates in real time."

"We need to get to the eye. Can we make it?"

She said, "Only one way to find out." She raised a sheath around us from her Leviskin coating. I couldn't see much of the outside through the small slit she left open, but it looked like she'd raised small fins to help with the wind.

I tried to raise a portal which would get us closer to the neighborhood, but the storm was creating too much interference. We'd have to get there the hard way. I let her drive. She could adjust the Leviskin coating and steer faster than I could make adjustments in the wind, and within a couple of blocks, she'd the shaken the configuration out. The roads were clear of cars, except for a few roaming National Guard and police vehicles, and even most of them were parked.

I flashed my credentials to get past the checkpoint on I-10, but we were stopped at the edge of civilization on I-15. A young corporal with the National Guard stepped out of an armored transport. He looked at my credentials. The wind howled around us as Ktesippe opened a slot for us to talk. "Sir, I can't let you out there."

I yelled over the wind. "What's your name, Corporal?"

I could see the corporal wanted me to turn around and get out of the storm. "Mills, sir."

"Corporal Mills." I formulated a quick plan. I'd feel bad about it later, if there were a later. "Can we step out of the storm for a minute? I need to check in with my boss."

Mills opened the hatch of the APC. A young sergeant sat at the communications center.

I tried to be friendly. "Any updates on this mess?"

The sergeant spoke sideways at me, as he was locked onto the monitors. "It's getting stronger, sir. The eye is stationary, but the effects are intensifying."

I pulled energy into both of my hands. "I'm sorry about this, guys, but I really need to get moving."

Mills had a half second to slip out, "Sir?" as I hit each of them with a blast. It would only stun them for a few minutes, but I'd be long gone.

Ktesippe closed the shield around us. She asked, "So, we're cleared to go through?"

"More or less. Let's go."

VISIBILITY WAS ZERO. Ktesippe had closed off the useless slit I'd used to look through, and instead, I was relying on the Sense and her navigating by feel. It was after five by the time we reached the Barstow area. The zone was cordoned off and quarantined, so we took to off road.

The bike wasn't built for this, and even with Kizzy's modifications and Ktesippe handling the weather on the fly, it was a rough ride. At this pace, we'd never make it even if we managed to not get lost in the desert in the storm. All communications, GPS, everything, was being blocked by the interference.

And Special K was having the time of her life.

The only way we knew night had fallen was the intense cold. It wasn't the only reason I was shivering under the winter gear. We had barely managed to cross a couple of small mountains in the process. Ktesippe was struggling to hold us upright in the hurricane-force winds, and the sand was grating away at the Leviskin. A lot of sand had seeped into the bike as well.

Ktesippe whispered in my ear. "I'm not sure how much further I can make it. I'm sorry, Greyson."

I opened my Senses and tried to feel in the darkness. The storm was highly charged, but I was able to find a few shadows nearby. "Just a little further."

We had gone about a mile when we found an abandoned, one-room shack which had miraculously survived so far. I pulled Ktesippe and the furball in, and reinforced the walls with a Push of energy. Ktesippe dropped the Leviskin, pouring sand and debris onto the floor.

I checked her out. Sand had permeated every inch of her. I cleaned out as much as I could, but she was going to need a serious overhaul. Kizzy was going to both be furious and thrilled with the challenge.

I topped off the gas tank, but I needed energy for Ktesippe. All of the magical energy in the storm was draining her, and me. We couldn't get much further in this condition. And it was almost nine. Three more hours. Too bad I couldn't pour some of this sand into the hourglass.

I Pushed some energy into Ktesippe, draining myself in the process. The furball was curled up in the sidecar and I was almost ready lie down and wait out the storm, knowing it might never end, at least not in time for us. I had no idea where we were.

The cabin was a leftover from a long-dead prospector. It sheltered us from the worst of the wind, but was rattling and shaking in the gusts. The plat on the wall was crumbling and dry. Fading notes showed all of the places he'd dug, and the meager results. "Ktesippe, do you have any maps of the area?" I slipped the helmet back on.

"Sure." She snapped awake in my ear.

I said, "Take a look at this. Do you think you can use it as a reference to figure out where we are?"

Ktesippe hummed in my ear as she worked. "Well, I have a pretty good guess. If this cabin is roughly in the center of the areas marked, and this isn't just an old souvenir."

"Well?" I braced myself. "Where are we?"

Ktesippe displayed the satellite image of the region she'd used, mapping out the trip on the HUD in the helmet. Then she overlaid the outlines of the plat from the wall. She said, "I think we are in this area." She drew a circle around a hill next to a washout basin. She then overlaid the satellite image of the storm from hours

371

earlier. "If the storm hasn't moved, we are approximately six to eight miles from the outer edge of the eye."

Luck had finally broken our way. We were much closer than I could have ever hoped. But in this storm, it could just as well be a thousand miles. Or she could be wrong. "Can you make it?"

She steeled her voice. "With my wheels, or you can carry me back on them."

We had a little more than two hours before whatever was planned would start.

Ktesippe plotted a route along a narrow crevice running several miles through a dry riverbed. If we could located it, we'd be well protected for most of the trip. Assuming we could find it, and assuming it wasn't full of sand. Or worse. Maybe it ended in the cave system where I believed the portal to the Underworld sat. Such a find would shock an old prospector.

She restored the sheath around us and we dove back into the storm.

FORTUNA FAVORED US. We were closer to the fissure than Ktesippe had thought. I opened my Senses and found it quickly. The sand in the ravine was a few inches deep, but the bottom was solid rock and baked clay.

The storm continued to intensify as we neared the wall of the eye. The ravine provided great protection, until it abruptly ended and dropped us into a wide-open salt flat. The howling winds were deafening and flashes of lightening shone through the Leviskin. The blowing sand was eating huge holes through the shield.

I was almost ready to turn back when Ktesippe yelled, "Hold on!" Straps wrapped around me and she pulled me close to the frame of the bike. She wrapped the Leviskin frame in a protective bubble barely in time for us to be picked up and thrown.

We bounced and rolled for a quarter mile and then the buffeting stopped.

"Are we through?"

"Not yet. Hold on." Sand rained in through a gash in the armor length of the bike as we plowed into a dune for our final landing. The roar of the wind had subsided, but only slightly. The air around us was absolutely still.

Ktesippe released her hold on me and dropped the remnants of the shell around us.

I tried to pry myself out of the dune. "Are you OK?"

"Never better," she gasped in my ear. "But I think I'll be staying here for a while."

"Yeah." I tried to pull her out, but couldn't even start to rock her. "You should take a break. I'll be back for you."

An uncomfortable tingle ran through me. "Remember that little spin next time Kizzy wants to do upgrades."

Someone would find her. I wasn't betting it was me, and hoped her next master would take better care of her.

It was a little shy of eleven. The wall of the storm was a swirling mass of debris, sand, and static lightening. I had no idea how we had made it past the wall of the eye mostly intact, other than sheer luck. An infinite field of stars twinkled overhead. There was no moon to light the way. Looking across to the other side, I estimated the eye of the storm had shrunk to five miles wide.

I checked on my mutt. He was still securely strapped in and wearing his helmet, but didn't have a happy look when I took it off.

"You're the one who insisted on coming. Maybe you'll learn to listen to me yet, o little ball of fluff. "

He shook as much sand out of his fur as could fly while giving me an evil look. Snort.

I pulled out the pack and started hiking. We stopped at the top of a nearby hill. A little over two miles distant, I saw a spot of lights that looked to be fires at the base of a large hill. I opened my Sight and Senses as much as I dared, and edged forward.

THE AIR CRACKLED with the energy from the storm surrounding and pounding us in slow waves. It left my Senses in a fog, and I didn't detect anything until we were less than a half mile out. If I hadn't been looking for it, I'd have missed the strong signatures from the rune necklaces as I neared the lookouts. Pairs of sentries were well hidden in nests ringing the hill at hundred foot intervals surrounding the site. I pulled out a set of the latest in night vision, courtesy of Mel. It looked like missing personnel from Longbow made up the security details.

One of the toys I'd grabbed from the locker at Longbow was a flechette rifle and sleeper darts. I screwed in the long barrel for ranged shots and sifted the skinsuit to make sure all of my weapons were readily available. The furball trotted beside me as I crawled to the edge of the hill and stopped fifty feet from the closest nest. I had no idea how sensitive the people were, or what kind of information would flow back to whoever was on the controlling end of the necklaces, but I needed to clear a path on the hill.

I took aim. The wind carried my first shot wide. My second and third shots were true, and neutralized the nearest nest of guards.

The furball crawled next to me as I snaked across the ground until I was able to roll into the nest with the incapacitated guards. Both of them were breathing regularly and out cold. I took the radio from one of their belts and jacked it into my own comm system.

Using the scope on the rifle, I did a quick survey of the area. I was a three hundred yards from the action. A semi-circle of a dozen large bonfires blazed with life as they lit the cliff face to hellish effect. Sixty or so acolytes shuffled about and seemed to be anxiously awaiting something.

A quick burst came over the appropriated radio. "Two minutes."

They were set to start at midnight. Acolytes in different colored robes formed up into a semi-circle, just inside the ring of bonfires. I pulled out the satellite phone but had minimal signal when I tried to call out. I activated the beacon, plugged in the small camera, and buried both in the sands, leaving the camera with a view of the hillside. With the storm, I doubted anyone was seeing it, but at least there'd be a record when it was over.

"One minute." Not for the first time that day, I had the sense I was being watched.

The lightening inside of the storm wall was becoming an almost solid wall of energy. Flashes sparked and flying debris was vaporized by lightning strikes.

The voice on the radio cried excitedly. "Zero hour."

Streaks of red slashed through the wall of the storm.

I felt more than heard a low rumbling from the hillside like a panicked herd of buffalo. The bonfires danced from the vibration.

The acolytes were chanting, "Aperi Portae! Aperi Portae!" Open the Gateway!

The wall of the cliffside groaned and shuddered. A layer of sand and stone fell away to reveal a shimmering, dark, waterfall-like portal inside a large cave.

The chanting was replaced by rhythmic humming. Two pairs of cyclops, each around eighteen feet tall with rippling olive skin, lumbered out of the portal. Their giant, centered eyes were glazed over, as if they were in a trance. They wore robes similar to the other acolytes and carried large sabers at their sides.

Between them, they carried a large, obsidian-looking dais, which they placed in front of the gathered crowd. They then took stations, two at each end of the platform.

Next appeared an acolyte in red escorting a blond man in his twenties, who wore a simple black robe. Another pair, this time an acolyte and a young woman in the black robe. Seven pairs in all. In the last couple, the one wearing a black robe was Director Norwich.

The humming was disorienting. I was fighting falling into a trance myself. I shook the effects off and Pushed a little energy to protect myself.

Seven more acolytes came through the portal. Two young Fomorians, a Fae, and the rest were human. They took up positions along the back of the stage.

The thick air was palpable with anticipation.

The crescendo hit when Dick and Betty Gibson stalked out in priestly garb. They were followed by Sonja, dressed in all of her high priestess finery. The acolytes collapsed to their knees.

Sonja strode to the center stage and threw her hands in the air. Snippets of an incantation carried to me as an altar rose in the middle of the stone dais. She lowered her hands and the altar stopped at waist level. The humming stopped, and even the storm seemed to lessen in intensity.

Sonja began chanting in a language I didn't recognize or understand. Dick walked forward, escorted by Betty, to stand at the head of the altar. Sonja shifted into Latin and I was able to get some of it between phrases I didn't know and what was lost over the distance.

"My children. We gather at the dawn of the day when the Veil between the worlds is thinnest. The world sees our power, though they do not yet know it is ours. By the time…will rule this world…ready for the return…Erebus."

This couldn't be good. The acolyte escorted the blond man to the altar. He dropped the robe to the floor, and lay down naked on the black obsidian. Dick Gibson leaned over the man, placing one hand on his forehead and the other on his heart. I opened my Sight. A black energy was being drawn from the man on the altar into Dick. The man had been the vessel for a powerful energy.

The second acolyte escorted a woman to the altar. She dropped her robe to the ground and waited for Dick to finish with the first. The blond rose and stood at the edge of the altar.

The acolytes below the altar crowded closer. I took a chance and spotted a nook in the darkness above the cave. Shadow-walking was an iffy prospect on the earthly plane in unfamiliar places on a good day, and I was very much out of practice. With all of the magical energy flying around…

I grabbed and held the furball tightly in my arms. I focused on the dark area at the back of the alcove, and rolled into the darkness next to me.

MY BODY JOLTED like I'd grabbed a 220 line. An edge on the lip stopped us from falling out of the safety of the alcove. The furball whimpered slightly. I knew how he felt. It had been a tough trip through all of the energy, but we'd made it.

I just wish I had a plan.

My vision cleared as I peeked over the edge. Dick was draining the dark energy from a third person. Director Norwich stood naked at the end of the line, awaiting his turn.

The throbbing energy was magnitudes stronger here. Waves hammered over me every twenty seconds. A huge version of the portal ring sat like a crown on the mesa, over thirty feet wide. The jewel in the center was the remains of the floor and portal ring from the room from the Barstow facility. They'd used the explosion to charge up and power the device to control the storm.

I didn't have anything on me which would make a dent in the ring. But I did have a tracker. Flipping the switch to designate it as a heavy target, I set the device in the alcove where I was hidden. I couldn't be sure the signal was getting out, or even if anyone was listening, but I had to try. I'd done what I could.

I verified the Colt was in its place and put a new magazine in the flechette rifle. Norwich was climbing into position on the altar. He closed his eyes, and Dick Gibson started drawing the dark energy flow.

But from here, I could see more. The six who had all been emptied of the dark energy stood with their backs to the crowd. They seemed filled with innocence now, the white light of pure souls growing strong inside them. Norwich looked the same when Dick released him.

Dick, on the other hand, was super charged. A giant, etheric, winged beast as dark as night controlled his body. It leered at me and nearly froze my heart. Dick hadn't moved and stood stone faced looking at the crowd. He was just as much a vessel as the others had been.

Sonja chanted another round of incantations, and Dick walked to the front of the altar. Dick touched each of the emptied vessels and whispered something in their ear. As Sonja's incantation finished, Dick spoke aloud. Or the beast inside of him did.

He placed his hands again on Norwich's head and his heart. "Servant Edward, you have carried my burden for many years. I now free you from this, and give you your reward." Faster than I could react, Dick pulled immense power into his hands and exploded Norwich's head and innards all over the expectant Assembly. "Be anointed in the blood of our brother, the blood of an innocent, to announce our reign!"

SHOCK STOPPED ME for a split second. Then I snapped out of the fugue state and opened fire with the tranquilizer flechettes. I hit Dick a couple of times and turned to the emptied vessels. They dropped like rocks, so I randomly started darting the crowd. The beast inside of Dick turned to grin at me again. The etheric form was several times larger than Dick's physical being and stretching its power.

From what I could see, Dick was trying and failing to figure out what was happening to him. He wouldn't have to wonder long.

I changed the emptied magazine for explosive darts. They wouldn't do much damage, but it might be enough to scatter people. The second dart hit one of the Fomorian acolytes in the head. The explosion knocked him down, but not out. The rest exploded harmlessly off the body formerly inhabited by Dick.

I had to stop the beast within him at all costs.

I swapped weapons and emptied the Colt into Dick. With his newfound power, he barely flinched. I replaced the empty magazine and holstered the Colt.

I drew the pair of blessed silver-plated combat knives and dove.

On the way down, the realization hit me. What was I doing? Would this work? If it didn't, I'd be in trouble. I Pushed energy into the blades anyway.

Through my Sight, I watched as the beast screamed, the blades flying through his etheric form. I crashed into Dick, driving the blades deep into his shoulders. Dick's shocked face was replaced by Drake's angry one as Drake ripped me away and pulled me face-to-face with him.

Where had he come from?

A maelstrom of hate glared at me through his one dark eye before he head-butted me and nearly knocked me out. Acolytes were staring in disbelief at Dick, who had sunk to his knees, screaming as blood spurted around my blades.

Drake tossed me off the stage into the crowd, creating an instant mosh pit.

One acolyte briefly reminded me of a kindly grandmother, except she was about to slam a brass brazier of coals into my chest. I kicked her away with both feet and rolled out of the way of the falling embers.

Hands slick with Norwich's blood and gore grabbed and tore at me as I tried to climb back onto the stage. I was pulled down by the acolytes who were determined to rip me to shreds. I let go of the stage and balled up, trying to block as many of the kicks and punches as I could. I Pushed and reinforced my body armor so it took most of the damage.

Static, then clicking, came in over my comm unit. It was breaking up, but I'd never been so happy to hear Wynn's voice. "Gre...down there...route...light it up."

That was something I could do. I summoned as much energy through my body as I could find, and released it in one burst. It knocked the acolytes back, and seemed to incapacitate the closest of them. The remaining crowd started to close in again until I unleashed a chain of fireballs in every direction. I didn't stop to see if I'd hit anyone, but the screams told me I had.

I scrambled to pull myself on the stage while most of the acolytes had a momentary surge of self-preservation. I summoned as large of a fireball as I dared and shot it into the alcove I'd used for cover. I looked around, but the stage had been cleared, at least of the living.

The shimmering portal at the cave entrance was solidifying again and about to close. Over the cries of wounded acolytes and the storm, a small flash bumped me. With a resounding "Woof," the furball dove through the portal.

Dammit. I really needed to get him a leash.

Wynn came in clearly over the headset. "…about to hit the ground. Status report."

I had enough time for a few words as I ran for the portal. "Hostiles are under influence. Portal closing. Hit the targeting tracer with everything you've got. I'm going in after the Gibson's. Good luck."

Static blasted my earbud as I cleared the edge of the portal. The furball greeted me with a demanding look as to what had taken me so long.

Snort.

WE STOOD ALONE in a cave stretching into an endless tunnel. Oil torches lighted the way. A solid wall was behind us. No going back now.

Looking at the rock, I knew I wasn't in California any more. Or Nevada, for that matter. I was in the Underworld. I wondered which one.

Paths branched off in numerous directions as we followed the tunnel. The opening was large enough to easily accommodate the cyclops from earlier, and even larger beings. Torches flared to life as we approached, and extinguished themselves as we passed. The entire effect was energy efficient and disorienting, and took away any real sense of distance or time. But in the Underworld, those things didn't matter.

I looked at the furball. "You got us into this one. Which way?"

Streaks of blood vanished into the walls and floor rapidly. We wouldn't be able to use its trail for long. I tried to open my Sight and Senses, but was overloaded. I dialed it back to a tolerable point. The furball had a large aura growing around him as he sniffed and trotted along the main chamber, torches lighting his way.

I couldn't be sure if it would do any good here, but it made me feel better to draw the Colt. I also slipped one of the silver throwing knives into my hand and charged it with a little energy, just in case.

The adrenalin faded as we walked for what seemed like hours. Every so often, a smaller tunnel would branch off. I checked a couple of them. One I followed ended in a portal. On the other side, rolling fields climbed into snowbound mountains. It looked like a pretty good option to me. The sensation of being watched, and maybe followed, grew stronger.

I found with a little thought, I could control the torches along the tunnels. I could turn them on and off, and even control the brightness a little. I needed to figure out how to install these at home. What home would that be? Why would I use fire? My thoughts were muddled again.

The furball stopped and altered he sensed something. Faint sounds like footfalls and something heavy being moved came from ahead. A cart maybe? He trotted behind me silently as we extinguished the torches and hid in a side tunnel. The darkness was absolute.

Light crawled towards us in the main tunnel as the scraping and footsteps grew closer. I dared a look while I was still safe in the shadows. A team of four beasts pulled a wagon cage. The closest description I had of the beasts was to call them centaurs. If the horse end were mammoths and the top half were cyclops with tusks.

The stench of brimstone and blood grew overpowering as the train approached. I backed up further in the tunnel for less foul air, but it lingered. I hoped it wouldn't soak into the Leviskin. I'd never be able to get it out.

One cart turned into two, and then three. They were full of wretched creatures, but they were so dirty and matted, I had no idea who, or what, they may have been. The beings trailing the wagon train were even viler in appearance than their prisoners, armed with axes and covered in armor dripping with gore, as if they'd been bathing in it.

The darkness returned and the fetid odor began to disperse. I nudged the furball with my toe to send him down the tunnel. The nagging suspicion someone was on my tail was too much to take. I kept the tunnel dark until the pup had gotten some distance. Torches began to light up behind us.

A voice swore lightly in the darkness and started running. I held the Colt and the knife in front of me, and Willed all of the torches on as I stepped into the tunnel. A figure in black jogged down the tunnel.

"Stop right there." The figure, about my size, stopped in the middle of the tunnel and turned to face me. He aimed a silenced MP5 at my chest and removed his balaclava.

I leveled the Colt at his head. "Hi, Eric."

Onyx's boyfriend stared at me down the sight of his MP5. "Greyson." His eyes were ice cold.

"What brings you to the neighborhood?" We each side-stepped to the edges of the tunnel, where we might be able to take cover.

Eric moved with the grace of a stalking cat, minimizing his silhouette. "I heard about a fantastic new pub. I must have taken a wrong turn."

"Do they have any good stouts?" I, on the other hand, moved with the finesse of a wildebeest on ice. I tripped. I rolled out of the way, expecting a strike.

Eric stood in the same place, training his weapon on me. He did crack a smile. "One or two."

"So, what's your play?" I watched as my loyal companion snuck up on him. I had no idea what the dog thought he was going to do.

"I'm here for Onyx. And maybe to send a message to the ones who took her. You?" The response felt genuine.

"I'm here to get Onyx, Raines, and any other innocents out, and to find a way to stop the storm. I have a message of my own to deliver."

Eric lowered his weapon and offered me a hand to pull me up. "Well, Dorothy, maybe you and Toto can follow me on the way to Oz."

TENSE MINUTES PASSED. The tunnel seemed to stretch to eternity. "How did you get down here?"

Eric answered in a low voice. "I trailed some of the cultists here and got trapped by the storm. Your less-than-subtle entrance made a nice distraction, so I was able to slip through the portal unnoticed."

I felt heat building in my chest. "You were just going to let Dick kill them?"

Eric stopped. "Let's get this straight right now, shall we? I'm here for Onyx. The people being sacrificed out there signed up for the deal. They aren't my concern."

"What about Raines? What if there are others down here?" Was partnering up with Eric the best choice? Would he abandon me and anyone else as soon as he had what he wanted? "And why did you help me out in Atlanta?"

By the look in his eyes, Eric was having a similar internal debate. I suspected he planned to use me as a diversion or a shield if necessary. "Onyx means a great deal to me. You're important to her. As is Beth. I saved you because your death would hurt her, but I see, based on your careless actions, that all I did was delay the inevitable."

"So, what do you know about the runes they're using to control them?"

He cocked his head. "Is that how they did it? They're using a compulsion fetish?"

I nodded. "The silver pendants."

"How do we negate the effects?"

We? Now it was we? I'd have to take what help I could and watch my back. "First, we have to remove the necklaces. Then, I have something which should speed up the process of clearing the influence. But if we can find the master rune…"

His look made me feel as if I were a trained monkey who had just proven I could learn a new trick. "The redhead. Your girlfriend from Atlanta. I Sensed something from her. She may have the master."

"One more thing to be clear about." I thought maybe I'd just given Eric a new mission in life, one which would not end well for Brighid. "You are not to harm her. She's being influenced as well. I need to get her back."

Eric gave me a sardonic grin. "Won't Drea have something to say about her?"

"I need Brighid back because her soul, or at least part of it, is in Drea's body right now. I need to return it to its rightful body so I can make Drea whole again. So I can make them both whole again." For the second time in this conversation, I seemed to throw Eric.

"Well, then." Eric was weighing his options. "You had best figure out how to handle her."

The implied threat made his position clear. If I handled her, fine. Otherwise, she had best not cross his path. Yeah, this was going to be fun. We resumed moving down the tunnel.

He made a motion to stop. "Quiet from here on. Something is happening in one of the workshops ahead."

I whispered, "You've been here before then."

Eric stopped. He pursed his lips as his mind worked out what he was going to tell me. "Yes. This tunnel system is used for building and maintaining different domains of the Underworld. Some other realms as well. There are entrance points all over the world, if you know where there are. But there are repercussions for using them."

I sensed he was reflecting on personal experience.

"So, who are you?" I'd known since he'd pulled me out of the time warp in Atlanta that he was a supernatural creature. I just didn't know if he was Fae or Divine. I'd made a snap judgment and underestimated him at the gathering in Pageland's Ferry. I'd been wrong. "Who, or what, are you?"

Eric was crouching and staring straight ahead. "I'm the one who is about to intercede with you to help people we both care about." The torches in the tunnel went dark. I guessed he knew that trick as well. "I believe we'll find them in there."

I CENTERED MYSELF. My eyes quickly adjusted to the dark. The surging energy overwhelmed me, and I had to close myself off.

Dim light came from the branch of a tunnel to the left. Fragments of a conversation, too muted to make out anything, came from just ahead. We approached silently, each of us taking a side. The furball was on my heels.

This channel was different. It had several smaller paths splitting off about a third of the way down the visible arc. Eric had referred to it as a workshop. I continued following along the wall in the main shaft until I got to a branch sloping upward. Eric stopped and knelt in the main pathway, just inside of a downward burrow across from me.

Shadows moved back and forth in a slice of light coming from underneath a copper door. Eric whispered, "Go up that way, and I'll check this one."

The crosscut had a gradual, upwards-sloping ramp. It ended in a room with four railcar-sized boxes of ore feeding into a downward channel full of wavy washboard sluices. It reminded me of something I'd seen used to pan for gold on one of the science channels. The ore on the tables resembled obsidian glass. The water from the sluices emptied into a pool on the floor below. An unmoving conveyor belt was loaded with ore and ran through an opening in the wall.

Dick Gibson was laid out on a table below. My knives were still embedded in him, one in his shoulder and the other his upper chest. He appeared to be conscious and in pain, and more than a little angry. The beast howled its desire for a new host.

Betty was yelling at Drake. "He can't cross the threshold in this condition. And the ritual was not completed."

Drake appeared unmoved. "Leave him. We can try again later. This means we won't need these." Drake pointed to an area I couldn't see.

Betty pounded on the mutilated Fae's chest. "I will not leave my husband again. And I do not think your masters or mine will be patient with our failure, or ready to wait another seven years or more. We *must* complete the ritual."

Drake pointed at Dick on the table. "It is no longer your husband in that body, and it's too weak to complete the ritual, even if we had suitable candidates. I doubt it had the strength to start with. This is your failure, not mine. You should have chosen a better consort."

I crawled forward under the equipment. Onyx, Raines, and three others sat, bound hand and foot, on the floor. They appeared to be asleep. Regent Kelso was chained to a bench with one of his Longbow security detail. Three of the original would-be sacrifices stood smiling patiently, as if they were oblivious to their fates. Two acolytes in black robes cowered while they attended to Dick.

A large portal door shimmered a deep red from the back of the room. Glowing runes circled the portal ring.

Betty glared at Drake. "Just convey my message and be a good errand boy."

I recognized the grin Drake gave to Betty. "As you wish." The ground quaked with every step Drake took to the portal. He stopped in front of Regent Kelso. "Your Excellency, I trust you are enjoying our hospitality."

Before Kelso could respond, Drake flicked his long tail at the chest of Kelso's escort. The barb went through the man and hit Kelso, drawing a small spot of blood from the regent's shoulder.

Drake turned to Betty and said, "I'll convey your message." He touched three runes around the ring and the portal changed to a blazing red hue. After stepping through, the portal reverted to the same shimmering red.

Betty leaned over what remained of her husband and stroked his hair. "I'll be back in a few minutes with the healer."

I snuck back down the ramp to the main tunnel. Eric was waiting. I gave him a quick description and said, "It looks about as clear as it is going to get."

Eric nodded. "You get to Onyx and the others. Get them ready to travel. I will attend to the beast."

The door moved stiffly, creaking as we cracked it open just enough to slip by. The startled acolytes only had time to look shocked before I stunned them both with blasts of energy.

I cut Kelso loose and checked on his guardian, who was very dead. Kelso was covered in his blood. "Regent, are you hurt?"

Kelso smiled. "I believe, under the circumstances, you can call me Wallace. I'm fine. This is but a scratch. Poor Trevor. He's been at my side since we were in the service. He deserved better."

I attended to Onyx, Raines, and the others. Each stirred slightly as I removed their necklaces and dropped them into a shielded pouch. I pulled out the rock Melvin had given me and waved it around Onyx. Nothing. I opened my Sight. The rock was having no effect. What was this useless thing?

The energy around them was dissipating very slowly. I had an idea about modifying an incantation used for cleansing spaces. I chanted and built up a wave of energy, and did a slow Push through them all. It seemed to work. The heaviness around them was fading faster. Raines was the first one to start coming out of the fugue.

I hadn't noticed her return until Betty shrieked, "What are you doing!"

Eric had one hand on Dick's chest and the other on his forehead. Through the little Sight I was able to muster, I saw the transfer of whatever beast had been in Dick moving into Eric. Betty was drawing in energy, but I couldn't tell for what. She was sucking so much into her, I couldn't summon anything from the environment around us.

I still had Melvin's rock in my hand. I threw it at her like I was skipping a stone across a pond and struck her in the side of her head, stunning her. Whatever she'd been trying to do backfired on her and she screamed in pain, shaking like she was being electrocuted.

She released an electrifying blast trailing off in all directions. I managed to block most of it, but enough got through to make my hair stand on end and my skin burn. I watched in sick fascination as the last wisps of the dark energy flowed into Eric. But the beast didn't stare back at me from him. Somehow, he'd taken it into himself with no visible effect.

Dick was moaning and looked to be in shock. He was fading quickly without the beast in him to keep him alive.

Eric propped Betty against the wall and crouched down in front of her. She was sobbing. "What are you doing here? You're nothing."

He said, "Gertrude, I tried to warn you as to what would happen. And now I must finish the ritual, before it rips everything apart."

Betty tried to grab Eric as he stood, but was only barely able to move and fell over. She sobbed louder. "No. Please. No."

Eric pulled my knives from his torso and handed them to me.

"What are you doing?"

He sighed. "What I have to. Please attend to the others."

I stood transfixed as he lifted Dick into a sitting position and held him there by his hair. Whatever sad mind was left in Betty's husband could see what was coming, and his eyes went wide with terror. Eric placed his other hand over Dick's slowing heart.

He muttered an incantation in the same unknown language Sonja had used earlier. Dick disappeared in a red mist. All that remained were his legs twitching on the bench, and his unattached arms, which fell to the floor.

Betty curled up in a fetal position and wailed.

Onyx had come around, as had the others. I cut their bonds. Onyx and Raines both hugged me. Onyx then ran to Eric.

I said to him, "Get them out of here. All of them."

I tied Betty's hands and feet and muttered an incantation which would bind her abilities.

My temporary partner asked, "Even Gertrude? You should put her down now. Or allow me to do so."

"Who's Gertrude?" I pulled Betty to her feet.

Eric gently shook his head. "Your people should do better research. Bethany Gertrude Gibson. Or her maiden name, Bethany Gertrude Norwich. Edward's niece and one-time protégée."

I shook my head. He'd thrown me. "She goes. Deliver her to Raines' people. And the regent's bodyguard, too."

"As you wish. What are you planning to do?"

I pocketed the rock. I intended to pelt Melvin with it, even though it ultimately had come in handy. "I'm not done yet." I cleaned Dick's blood from my blades.

He said, "Don't be a fool. You cannot win against Drake, especially alone."

Raines was pale and shaking. "I'm coming with you."

I laughed. "No, you're not. You are going to escort the regent to safety, and then get checked out in the hospital." She could barely stand, and I wasn't sure she could return if the portal went where I suspected.

I even doubted my own ability to get back through, if I survived.

Raines nodded, and hugged me again. She knew in her present condition, she'd be more of a hindrance than a help. But I appreciated the offer. "Be careful."

That made me laugh louder. "Take care of them."

Eric was preparing a circle in the floor.

"Can you get them out?"

"Yes, I've done this a few times from down here. I will be able to get them somewhere safe. You should come with us."

396

If only it were an option. If I had any chance to make things right, I needed to find Brighid, but I was lying to myself if I thought it was the only reason. Part of me was screaming to listen to Eric and get out now. There'd be another chance. But that too was a lie. It was now or never.

"Thanks for the help, Eric. But know we aren't done. We will be having a discussion when I get back topside."

The smile on Eric's face silently screamed he doubted I'd live up to my promise. "I look forward to it."

ERIC GATHERED EVERYONE into the circle, including the body of the regent's escort and friend.

He said, "This may be of some use to you." He handed me the MP5 and pouch of spare magazines.

Raines and Onyx held onto each other and waved as they were ported away. Betty's glazed eyes looked at me with venom.

Eric gave a little nod, and in a flash, the furball and I were alone.

I slipped the sling of the MP5 around my shoulder and dropped the extra magazines into a side pocket. It wouldn't be much help against Drake, but it was in easy reach. I drew the Colt 1911 and slapped in a magazine of explosive rounds. It had a better chance of at least slowing him down.

A deafening echo from what sounded like a pile driver came from behind a side door. It was safe to assume if anyone was within earshot, they would have already rushed in. The door opened onto a maintenance hallway. The conveyor belt ran a hundred yards to an arched opening lit by an ominous red glow.

The hallway ended in an enormous cavern housing a device which would have made Rube Goldberg cry with envy. And likely scared him to death.

Dozens of conveyor belts channeled the ore into a hopper the size of an apartment building. The hopper fed a pair of giant lifts which poured the ore into a crusher that then rained a fine mist of shimmering dust onto a large black wall.

At the same time, red pulses ran down a clear tube the size of a bus and split into a dozen channels feeding into long, black pikes made of the same material as the blade. Every few minutes, the pikes glowed and released a giant burst of energy fusing the falling dust into the back wall of... the Abyss. They were building it. And those pulses triggered the lightening in Purgatory.

The thunder had come from this machine. And then I saw what announced the Call.

Red pulses were also feeding a gigantic bar of the cursed metal the size of a freight train. And this one was on tracks. Each pulse drew the bar back a small distance as it charged it with whatever energy it used. If the smaller pulses added mass, then the big one rammed it out in a giant piston. It was building up the charge to fire again.

Since the shock waves off the small blasts were almost enough to knock me down, the big one was pretty certain to vaporize me. It explained why no one else was around. And I needed to be somewhere else myself before this thing went off.

And then my destructive nature kicked in. The thing about Rube Goldberg devices was when all of the parts worked, it was a beautifully complicated ballet. And when they failed...

The tracks on which the giant rode sat on didn't look well maintained. Somehow, I doubted the demons or whatever had built this were concerned with safety. With a few minutes of effort, I managed to redirect a pair of the pikes into the main rail. Ten minutes later, the blasts had bent them enough to aim the ram into the main hopper and away from the Abyss. I couldn't be sure exactly what this would do, but it would definitely slow down the progress.

TIME WAS UP. I decided I'd waited long enough waiting for Drake to return. Besides, the main rail would soon be ready to fire, and I didn't really want to be there to find out what would happen with my adjustments.

It was good odds there was an ambush waiting for me if I went through the portal. Since no one had come back through, it was also good odds they knew we had captured Betty and Dick was dead. I touched the same runes Drake had used. The portal opened and shimmered.

I grabbed the furball and stepped through the portal into a scene much like what I'd seen on my virtual tour with Seshat. It looked to be part of the forge in Tartarus. Giant cyclops, wearing only loincloths, worked at three large furnaces in the sweltering room.

They paid no attention to us as we came through.

The furball trotted up the tunnel to the right, so I followed him. Each room we passed was a workroom of some sort, and all were operating at capacity. We stopped when the tunnel took a hard turn. A large room was around the corner.

The room looked like a staging area. Digging equipment had been set aside after they'd hit a pocket of what appeared to be more of the obsidian. Closer examination showed microwaves breaking on the glassy surface. It was a patch of the Abyss. The rock face had crumbled, or been consumed, to the point the Abyss made up most of one wall. They were mining it.

Two steel cases sat on a bench carved out of the stone. No one seemed to be close by, so curiosity led me to look in the cases. The first case held a silver necklace with gold and copper threads. The focal on the end was round, and had a space as if something was meant to fit in it. The case also carried a black stiletto knife with runic script running its length. It looked to be made of the same material as Drake's armor.

The second case held rows of cylinders, each of which contained a glowing crystal. They gleamed in several different colors, and I instantly recognized them as crystals for the Anima Arca. And they were all occupied. Unfortunately, the only label was in code.

I closed and locked the cases. I was willing to bet these were important enough to delay my pursuit of Brighid. I drafted a note which would motivate them to come find me, saving me the trouble of wandering around the Underworld. I needed to find a way out.

The furball let out a growl in time for me to see Drake, but not enough time to stop him from grabbing me by the throat. The furball dove to take a bite out of him, but fourteen pounds of fury didn't do much. My heart broke when Drake kicked him. He thudded into the wall and lay still. I managed to whip the MP5 around and empty the magazine into Drake's chest. Several rounds ricocheted back into me, but my body armor took most of the energy left in the rounds.

Drake head-butted me with a shiny new set of horns and threw me into the wall like a rag doll. I made a useless attempt to brace for the impact and hit with a loud crack.

Something sticky and warm coated my left side. An invisible elephant was laying on my chest. I was pretty sure my arm and shoulder were broken, as well as several ribs. I tried to turn and cradle it away from another attack.

Drake knelt down over me and gloated. "You should not have come here. Maybe it is time I end your misery, so I can reclaim my place at her side, instead of at her feet. I am going to enjoy this."

I struggled to get the 1911 out of the holster. I got two of the explosive rounds into Drake before he knocked the gun away and picked me up by my armor. Drake had procured a few upgrades since our meeting in Purgatory. The limbs they'd given him had melded well with his body, and were more muscled. The angelic arm shone with the dark brightness of a fallen angel.

He grasped the neck of my breastplate pulled. The armor protested loudly as I Pushed in Will to strengthen it, but finally the Leviskin and my resolve broke simultaneously. He dropped the fractured remains to the ground.

I was exposed and exhausted. "Do...it," I gasped.

Drake held me by the throat with his angelic arm and drew his black arm back. He focused intently on his killing blow. "Good riddance, coward."

I steeled myself for the blow. Instead, I was as startled as Drake when a shadow crashed into his chest and threw us both to the ground, causing him to lose his grip. The visible world was tinged in red when I landed several feet away.

It was the furball, all five hundred pounds or so of him, still in the tiny package. Drake screamed as the etheric hound bit into Drake's throat. Enraged, Drake grabbed him by the scruff of his neck and punched him in the head before throwing him into the passageway.

Blue blood spurted from Drake's neck as he kicked me in the ribs on my right side with a loud crack. Unprotected, they shattered easily. I was pretty sure the blow had just given me a matching set of punctured lungs.

He said, "I'm going to use your pet to feed the hellhounds. But first…" A fireball materialized in his hand.

I was ready for the inevitable.

Brighid yelled, "No! Stop now."

The monstrosity reeled back. The flaming orb vanished as if he had been hit by an invisible train. He roared and drew a long, black blade.

Out of the corner of my eye, Brighid made a throwing motion with her hand and sent Drake flying into the wall. The crash sent ripples through the obsidian. He was solidly stuck to the obsidian wall of the Abyss, hanging about a foot off the floor.

Brighid knelt by me and took my head into her lap. "Drink this." She held a vial to my lips. Warm water washed over my body. The pain became distant. It became a little easier to breathe as my punctured lungs sealed, but the broken ribs meant every deep breath bought the pain home.

"You saved me." I was both annoyed and relieved.

Brighid stroked my hair. "Of course, my love."

Power poured from a rune pendant dangling around Brighid's neck.

She saw me looking. "Oh, this. Is it bothering you?"

I nodded and swallowed.

"Just as well. It's served its purpose." She propped me against the wall, removed it, and whispered an incantation. It dissolved in her hands. "I'll be back in a moment."

Drake struggled and flailed against the Abyss like an animal in a tar pit. The more he struggled, the more entangled he became and the further he was drawn into the tarlike blackness. "What have you done to me, witch? Get me down."

Brighid stood in front of Drake, her arms crossed. She said gently, "Drake, I've been patient, but this is just not working out for us. I think it's time this collaboration ends. Look at it this way: you had a lot of fun with the new parts, while it lasted."

Drake whipped his tail at Brighid.

She stood just out of range, but caught it between her hands as the tip missed her face by less than an inch. "Drake, I'm sorry we must part this way." She ripped the tail off and threw it into the Abyss. It flailed on its own until it was fully absorbed. Only the angelic arm appeared impervious to the Abyss as it swung at air. "Have a nice trip."

Brighid returned to me, seemingly oblivious to Drake's swearing and yelling. She knelt next to me and Pushed some healing energy into me. It eased more of the pain. "I'm happy you have finally come around, my love. To join us. To join me, at my side."

"Brighid, I..."

Brighid jumped back, dropping me to the ground. "Brighid?" She paced and shouted at me. "Brighid. When will you let this go? I took this body to prove something to you. I can give you anything you want. Any *one* you want."

Realization set in. I should have known. Somewhere deep, I supposed I always did. I slumped against the wall. "Ailbhe."

A thin scowl set in on her face. "Yes. Now you get it."

Drake cackled.

"Don't you have nowhere to be?" She hit him with a burst of energy. His chest collapsed and he coughed up a spray of blood.

Ailbhe spun on her heel and unleashed her fury at me. "Everything I've gone through. For you. This body. The work to get the necklaces onto the Fae actresses so you could get used to attention and adoration in public. Do you know what it took to get an entire vial of the Essence of Aphrodite? What I had to promise that shill of a priestess to enchant you with it? I've given you gifts other fools could only imagine." She lashed out at Drake with another bolt of energy to stifle his coughing laughter. "When you stand by my side, we will be complete, as one. I'll give you anything you want. Any one you want."

"You took their free will and forced them to like me?"

She jeered. "Free will, what a farce! Most fail to use their will at all. They float through life, choosing to do nothing. But no, I did not take their will. I just gave them the nudge to do something they already wanted to do. Your other friends, Onyx and Raines, they were much more difficult to influence. Their wills were strong, but I could give them just enough of the right ideas. The rest were easy. All I had to do was to give a little more energy to the fears and doubts they already had."

In a way, I felt better, but was there anything she wasn't willing to do to get to me?

"Why me? What is it you want so badly?"

She crouched next to me and stroked my hair. "Because you are my consort, my general, and my king. This is your destiny, and mine. Our time is now, and the war for the future has started.

For years, I've waited and steered events to get us here. And now, it is time you take your place and live up to your vow."

What? What vow? I didn't understand what was going on, or what she meant. But I knew what she wanted. Something about what she said rang true. Maybe it was my destiny. Our destiny.

"Yes, you're right. But there is something I want first."

AILBHE SMILED WARMLY. On anyone else, it would have endearing. But with her projecting through Brighid, the smile was chilling. She had her victory. "Anything, my love. Anything you want."

I summoned every bit of energy I had left. "Get the hell out of her body." I released it all in one of the silver balls which instantly flew through her chest. Brighid's newly vacated body collapsed to the ground.

I fought to keep conscious as tunnel vision closed in. I was spent. I managed to drag a vial of healing potion out of my vest and sip it down. The blood running from the gashes covering my body slowed.

I rolled over to check on Brighid. Her breathing was raspy, shallow, and fading fast. I'd been wrong about some part of Brighid being inside, or if she was, it was not enough to keep her body alive in the Underworld.

She was slipping rapidly, and I didn't have much left in me, either. I was going to lose her.

Drake was still laughing, hanging from the wall. I needed energy. I struggled to my feet and leaned against the wall to drag myself to Drake.

He coughed up a spray of a black, oily substance which must have passed for blood in his monstrously fabricated body. His armor was caved in at the two places Ailbhe had slammed him. He was still arrogant and defiant even as he was slowly being drawn to his death. More than half of his body had sunk into the Abyss. "Coward. You're pathetic. When she admits that to herself, you'll just be another vermin to squash underfoot."

"Drake." I tried to feel something for the creature hanging before me, but the only thing I could dredge up was contempt. "Maybe so, but you won't be around to see it." I grabbed onto the angelic arm hanging free. I drew all of the power I could tap from it, and latched onto the power running through Drake. Something else was coming through, too. Something from beyond the Abyss. It tried to take hold of me from the other side. My reflexes kicked in, and I was able to break the link.

The jolt of power renewed my strength. When the high faded, I realized Drake had been screaming. Whether in pain, rage, or both, I couldn't be sure.

"Go ahead and kill me. If you can. If you don't, I *will* kill you."

The fire of life returning surged through my body after tapping off of Drake, but I also felt a vile sensation creeping through me. It would take some serious work to purge his energy, but I had to live so long first.

Brighid's body convulsed. I held her hand and knelt next to her. What could I do?

The miracle of Leviskin was its ability to shift based on the most subtle thoughts. The more you used it, the more you developed a relationship with it, to the point of truly wearing a second skin. Sometimes, it felt like it had a mind of its own, or at least became an extension of yours.

The sheath holding the Anima Arca formed on my hip. It still held the crystal. It held Drea.

I didn't think. I couldn't think.

I grabbed the hilt and drew the blade.

This was wrong.

It was the only way I could save them both.

I plunged the etheric blade into her body, emptying the crystal.

She stopped convulsing.

Then she stopped breathing.

My heart pounded.

Pain shot through my chest and through my battered body as I started CPR.

Drake continued his maddening cackles of laughter.

Nothing.

She wasn't breathing.

I couldn't get a pulse.

She was gone.

UNABATED RAGE SURGED through me and took over. If Drake wanted to die, I was ready to help him on his journey. I flew to my feet. I had no idea what the emptied blade would do with such a tortured soul, but I figured I could find out. Maybe I could build him his own room, somewhere I could torment him for eternity. Somewhere I could leave him in silence.

I drew the blade.

Drake chided me. "Do it! Do it, you coward!"

I drew the blade back. I'd have this wretched creature's soul powering a lava lamp.

Deep, raspy breaths came from behind me. Brighid's body. She was breathing and coughing. I ran to her side.

She opened her eyes. "Greyson?"

"Drea?"

She gave me a pained smile. "I feel…strange. Weak."

I Pushed as much of the meager energy I had left in me into her. "We have a lot to talk about, but we need to get out of here first."

I leaned Drea against the wall. Confusion set in as she tried out the unfamiliar body.

"Don't think about it. Can you move?" I asked.

She shifted. "Give me a minute." Ever the warrior, she would trust me for now, but there'd be questions later. And hell to pay.

Drake was screaming and ranting. "Do it! Don't leave me here. Don't leave me to…this.   Do it, you coward!" The oily

410

substance coated the floor around him. Very little of him was material on this side of the Abyss. His face and part of his upper torso were barely still on our plane. Apparently, the angelic arm couldn't cross over and lay on the floor, the end of his stump barely visible.

I had no idea what has happening to him, but his eyes were saucers. For the first time, I saw real fear in the corrupted Fae. And I felt some pity.

But not enough. "Drake, according to our queen, you have a deal to live up to. Who am I to interfere? Or are you a coward?"

Drake screamed in a blinding rage and spit blood at me.

I was willing to help him on his way. I summoned the energy I could. "Don't worry about sending any post cards." I hit Drake in the forehead with a blast and watched him vanish into the Abyss. A few ripples ran out where he'd been, then smoothed over again to black glass.

I picked up the two steel cases and checked on Drea.

She said, "I'm as ready as I'm going to be."

I didn't know how to create an exit in the chamber. I took a strap and hooked the two cases together, then looped them over my shoulder. Drea and I propped each other up as I led her into the tunnel. The furball limped behind without a whimper.

It was a long, quiet walk back to the portal.

I set the cases down and studied the runes around the gateway. Now what? I'd copied Drake to get here. Another brilliant plan I hadn't quite thought through. I randomly tried a few combinations without result.

Drea was propped up by the wall. She was pale and sweating, but putting on a strong front. "You always take me to the nicest places."

I was going to have to try to port us out. The only place I had a shot at was the lab. I could leave a small grenade to wipe the address after we left. It was very unlikely someone would be able to access the lab even with the right combination, but I wasn't ready to risk it.

I drew a circle and began the ritual to create the link. Within a few minutes I was ready, and set the cases in place. I pulled Drea against me inside the circle, and tried to connect. Nothing. I couldn't feel the other end. Either it wasn't accessible from here, I didn't have the energy, or something was blocking it.

Ultimately, the why didn't matter. The only way out I saw was the portal.

I erased the marks on the ground and dug into the recesses of my mind for something. Anything. There had to be another trick in there. It couldn't end here.

But nothing was coming forward. I couldn't even think of what deity to try and bargain with. Without food and water, Drea and I would soon be finished. If we looked long enough, maybe we could find some supplies Ailbhe or someone had stashed down here, but neither of us were in any shape to explore.

Drea was half-sleeping on the ground, leaning against me and the wall while I studied the runes and tried to stay awake. I hoped for some great revelation. A working combination.

The furball was curled up at her side, whimpering in pain.

The ground shook and a low rumble echoed through the chamber. I couldn't be sure how far away it was, but I had to assume it was the Abyss engine self-destructing.

I was still laughing to myself when the portal let out a popping sound. The shimmering image of an open portal seemed like a dream.

I struggled to draw the 1911 as a last stand. It cleared the holster and clattered into my lap, clutched in my hand. There was no real need to wake Drea if we needed to defend ourselves. The portals were one way, so there was no hope of jumping through while it was open. Would it be a better alternative even if we could?

No. I'd get a destination from whoever comes through. Or at least try.

Who was I trying to convince? We'd either be captured or killed. I was spent and any battle was already lost.

Sonja stepped through the portal in a black skinsuit with a shield raised around her and a knife in her hand. She was seemingly alone, and the portal closed behind her.

I shook as I lifted the 1911, knowing it wouldn't mean much. "Hi, Sonja."

"Hello, Greyson. You can put that away."

On a good day, I would've been outmatched in a head-to-head fight. We'd both leave bloody, but four times out of five, I was convinced she could take me. My newly freed abilities might have closed the gap some, but in my current shape, there was nothing I could do. I shook as I holstered the 1911.

Sonja knelt down and checked on Drea, who tried feebly to fight back, through only semi-conscious. Sonja shushed her, and then knelt next to me. Her face and neck bore light scarring from the fireball I'd reflected back at her when we'd fought at the Underhill estate in LA. Magical healing really does miracles.

"I see you're in a bit of a quandary."

"Did you come to gloat?"

She shook her head. "No. We need to talk, and this is about as private a time as we'll ever have. Ailbhe is quite cross with you, and still recovering from whatever you hit her with." She gave me an amused smile. "And your little distraction just pulled any other attention elsewhere."

I shrugged.

"There's something you should know." Her appearance shifted. What I saw nearly threw me over the edge of sanity.

"Mom?"

MY MOTHER'S EYES stared back at me from her strong face.

"No, but close. Your mother was my twin. I am...was...Calie, and until a few months ago, I hadn't seen you since you were a child. I held you as an infant and even babysat you a lot until your parents returned to the Grove."

"If that's true, why didn't you go with them? And why don't I know about you?" It had to be a trick. It couldn't be real. Could it?

Deep in my soul, I knew it was true.

She said, "We don't have much time, and it's not important now. What you need to know is this: not everything you have been told is true, not everyone is what they seem, and there is more at stake than you even know. Had you passed the Trial, so much could have been avoided."

I started shaking. "What...What do you mean? I survived the Trial."

"No." She shook her head. "You endured an ordeal, it's true. It acquitted you before your people. But you did not face the Trial which had been intended. Had you done so, and been victorious, all of this could have been avoided. The events tonight. The storm. And the challenges which shall now face us all."

"I don't understand."

"Nor would I expect you to. Others saw to it you wouldn't be properly prepared. It matters little now. Events are in motion. Soon, you will need to choose your side. My decision was made long ago, and I'll have to live with it. Queen Ailbhe, her patience is growing thin, and time is running short."

I asked, "Why me? What's it about me she wants so badly?"

She opened one of the steel cases and placed something inside before closing it again. "You'll need this to find what you seek. But you may not like the answers if you continue on this path." She placed the cases in front of the portal. "Have you not wondered why you are surrounded by the beings you are? Not everyone has happy hour with deities and demigods."

I shrugged. It was a question which occasionally came to mind, but it had been this way my whole life. I didn't know any other way.

She cupped my face in her hands. "We didn't want this for you. It wasn't supposed to happen this way. But now that it is, you have to step up your game. Everyone around you are grand masters in chess, and you are still learning the fine art of tic-tac-toe."

"What?"

"You are hoping to tie and survive these little skirmishes. You're behaving like a pawn to be sacrificed. You're much more than a piece to be sacrificed, and it's time you started acting like it." She closed her eyes. "No matter what, you're family."

"What is it you expect me to do?"

"First, get out of here. Then you need to find your calling, and your power." She pulled me to my feet. "Where do you want to go?"

"We need to get to LA. I need to go there first."

She nodded. "Interesting choice. The storm damage there was extensive. But it is worse in other places. I can port you into a safe house there, but I wouldn't plan on staying there long, if I were you."

"Thank you." We pulled a semi-conscious Drea to her feet.

Calie said, "Consider what I've told you carefully. This is the only time I'll be able to help you. I reveal myself to you only because I have no other alternative, and because you need to live to fulfill your destiny. From here on out, you're on your own. And if we wind up on opposite sides, I will do what I must. As shall you." She touched six sigils. "Are you ready?"

I nodded, and she touched a seventh. The portal opened into a small dark room. "Travel safely. We'll see each other soon enough."

"Where is my mother?"

Calie shifted back into Sonja. She smirked. "The portal is closing. You had best hurry."

I threw the cases over my shoulder, and dragged Drea through to the other side.

The portal closed behind us. I wondered how true Calie's statements had been, or if she even was who she claimed.

The dark room opened into a closet off of a small den. I lay Drea on a couch and found a land line. Within minutes after a quick call to one of Priscilla's emergency numbers, a van pulled up with medical techs, and we were both rolled out on stretchers.

BEEPING NOISES WOKE me in what looked like a makeshift hospital room. Drea, in Brighid's body, lay in a bed next to me, asleep. I was pretty well bandaged up. A cast sealed my left arm and carried around my shoulder and torso. I had a vague memory after I was loaded into the van of being hit with a tranquilizer, and being out of it through most of the ride. I was pretty certain I was happy to have been drugged because of the convoy of tanks that had used me as a roadway.

The furball was curled up next to me. He, too, was wrapped in gauze, and seemed to be just a little bigger. His once jet black fur now had a single lightning bolt of pure white running down his side.

Priscilla floated into the room, pulling a chair next to my bed. "How are you?"

"I think you might know better than I do."

She laughed nervously. "Well, it looks like you drank a couple of those noxious connections of yours, and it was enough to keep you from dying. Your eight cracked ribs and your punctured lungs are healing. You also had two breaks in your left arm and a fracture in your left leg, along with various gashes, bumps, and contusions. You'll live."

"How's Drea?" I looked at the bed beside me.

Priscilla said, "This body appears in good shape, but we need to get her back in her own. She's having issues staying stable in her borrowed shell. And I believe your friend would like to be back in her own as well."

I nodded. "Give me a day or two to recharge."

She clucked. "I believe you may need a little more than that."

"Where are we?" I didn't recognize any of the surroundings.

Priscilla said, "Safe. The storm did a lot of damage. The resort is currently uninhabitable. Our care facility was taken out of service as well. Some of the less savory beings in LA took the opportunity to raid the secure floors and release some of their own. In fact, much of the region will be in a state of recovery for some time."

"Onyx? Raines?"

"Eric delivered Onyx and the rest to me. They are all shaken, but otherwise appear fine. Except for the regent. He was moved to a Longbow medical facility. He may have been poisoned somehow."

"What about Wynn? I heard from him just as I was entering the portal."

Priscilla said, "He's fine. From what I hear, he led a couple of teams on a HALO jump into the eye of the storm. They were able to clear the cliff and secure the survivors. Two of his men were lost in the raid, but the rest are fine except for minor injuries. He recovered Ktesippe and Kizzy is working on her."

I sensed Priscilla had come in to give me more than a health update. "Spit it out."

Priscilla nodded. "With recent events, we are making preparations to move people to safety. Many are fleeing to Phoenix Grove and the other sanctuaries. We will be moving out in a week or so, once preparations are complete."

"OK."

She said, "A lot of the Veiled peoples are scared of you, or who they think you are. Stories are spreading, and not all of them are favorable. Some think you have brought misfortune to our steps. I am not one of those, and neither are the people who know you. However, in a couple of hours, we will move to a temporary location while one of the old Sanctuary villages is brought out of the mothballs, as it were. You are welcome to join, but I believe it best if you are kept isolated. For now. Calypso will continue operations in the mortal world for as long as we can."

"So, is there any other good news?"

She sighed and looked down. "Inquisitor Delacroix is en route to speak with you about the events of the past few days. I believe it is the precursor to another inquest."

Let no good deed... I rolled over, and she left me to my thoughts. I tried to watch news coverage of the storm and cleanup. It had done a lot of damage across half of the country and into northern Mexico. So far, the cover story of a meteor strike was holding up. In the hours I'd spent underground, eight days had passed.

I closed my eyes.

"Greyson." Tsauriel sat at my bedside. I lay in the bed inside of the keep. "Greyson, let me look you over."

Ladon's voice came from the doorway. "No time for delays. He needs to prepare."

Epilogue

Nora was shaking. Tears welled in her eyes as she closed the book.

It was one thing to read about the events through someone else's eyes in order to try to understand the what had led up to... now, but everything she'd been taught about the catastrophe which had fallen on them was looking like lies. Her mother's lies.

She carried the volume in her crossed arms until she reached Miss Tee's empty desk. With no outlet for the tempest she'd built up in herself, she trembled as she lay the book on the desk. No need for a tantrum if no one was watching, right?

Gentle clinking sounds came from the hallway. She followed them until she found Miss Tee waiting in the small study, sipping on hot tea. A project lay in a basket, waiting for her to resume knitting.

Miss Tee said, "Would you care to join me?" She stopped stirring the cup of tea. It was clear she'd made the noise to draw Nora down the hall.

Nora plopped herself into a nearby chair and waited for her cup to be poured. Her mother wouldn't forgive bad manners at tea time. Once the cup was in her hand, she asked, "Why are you showing me these things? I thought I wanted to know...I can't believe..."

The old woman cocked her head. "Do you wish to stop your education?"

Nora hadn't considered it as an option. "Please, just tell me why?"

"Greyson asked the same thing, many times. I am getting quite old, something I never thought would happen. Someone else needs to know what happened and why. And maybe, just maybe, someone can become the caretaker of this place. But not you. You have a destiny to fulfill. You should understand what, and why." Miss Tee looked down at her cup. "It is your choice, of course."

"So, what is this destiny? Mother refuses to speak of it, and insists I be... normal."

"Time will tell, Nora. Time will tell. I don't know what your future holds, only that you have a key role in what's coming. And if you learn from Greyson, maybe you shall not repeat his mistakes. But it is up to you. If you wish to continue your studies."

She sniffed. Quitting wasn't an option, but this old wretch didn't need to know that. "How much of what I've been taught is true? Nothing I've read in the chronicles so far ties to history."

"History is written by the victors, and through people's own motives. You are reading Greyson's story through his own eyes. And his biases. People rarely see themselves as the villain. You would do well to remember this."

Nora was cornered. There was no way she was letting go of this. But it had to be on her terms. As soon as she figured them out. "Fine. When do I get the next one?"

The look on Miss Tee's face nearly sent Nora into a rage. Her self-satisfied look told Nora she was just a pawn herself in another game. But she wanted to play. She had to play. *Suck it up, buttercup*, she told herself. *The pawn will become the queen. The most powerful piece on the table.*

Miss Tee said, "Soon. The restoration is well underway. Until then, I suggest you contact this... person." She handed Nora a small envelope.

A short instruction and incantation were inside on a delicately handwritten card. "Who, what?"

Miss Tee said, "And if you proceed, your mother must know absolutely nothing of this. Do you understand?"

Nora was beginning to understand all too well. "Yes." The toughest part was not being able to talk about this with her mother. With anyone.

Acknowledgements

I have a lot of people to thank to pull this one together. Ruth, Babe, and Julie for doing test reads and pointing out sometimes I'm a maroon.

I could write another three pages on all of the people who have (mostly) encouraged and supported these little tales, and getting them out to you, but you know who you are.

I use one of my favorite conventions in the story for a setting, the annual circus which is Dragon*Con in Atlanta ever Labor Day weekend. If you haven't been, it's definitely an experience worth having.

Huge thanks to my friend and fellow author Calandra Usher, who put in a lot of time with feedback and putting finishing touches on the manuscript. She's also bugging me to give the furball a name. It's coming, I promise. Check her out! Her fourth book on the four horsemen of the apocalypse just came out. What could go wrong? Swing by http://homeoftheriders.com/.

About the Author

Jim has a long-standing love for and interest in history, anthropology, the sciences, and literature, which have been run through the blender of his twisted mind to produce this work. When not trying to get the strange ideas floating around in his head out in text, Jim lives in the central Carolinas with his wife, three dogs, and the occasional fish. When not clicking away on a laptop pretending to be the monkey writing Shakespeare, he is usually behind a different laptop adding to twenty-plus years on technology projects or playing with glass in fire.

To contact me with snarky comments, please visit

http://jim-mcdonald.net/ and sign up for the mailing list.

Or follow me on Facebook:
https://www.facebook.com/jimmacauth

Goodreads:
https://www.goodreads.com/author/show/8119076.James_McDonald

Twitter: @JimMacAuth

And eMail: jim@jim-mcdonald.net

Thank you for reading, and please watch for the next installment, *Unbound and Determined*, and several novellas are forthcoming. And reviews are always appreciated —they let authors know what you think and what you loved so we can give you more of it.

Happy reading!

www.ingramcontent.com/pod-product-compliance
Lightning Source LLC
Chambersburg PA
CBHW030618250626
47154CB00006B/1831